A DOOR

IN THE

EARTH

ALSO BY AMY WALDMAN

The Submission

A DOOR

IN THE

EARTH

AMY WALDMAN

Little, Brown and Company

New York Boston London

Little, Brown and Company
Hachette Book Group
1290 Avenue of the Americas, New York, NY 10104
littlebrown.com

First Edition: August 2019

Little, Brown and Company is a division of Hachette Book Group, Inc. The Little, Brown name and logo are trademarks of Hachette Book Group, Inc.

The publisher is not responsible for websites (or their content) that are not owned by the publisher.

The Hachette Speakers Bureau provides a wide range of authors for speaking events. To find out more, go to hachettespeakersbureau.com or call (866) 376-6591.

ISBN 978-0-316-45157-4
LCCN 2019933751

10 9 8 7 6 5 4 3 2

LSC-C

Printed in the United States of America

To Alex, Ollie, and Theo

Antimachus was a friend of Paris
Who put the case for war
He opened a door in the earth
And a whole generation entered

—Alice Oswald, *Memorial*

PART ONE

Chapter One

Arrival

As soon as she saw the road, she understood how it had seduced him. Unmarked and unpaved, it rose up between mauve foothills, then slipped through them. If you were bored, as Gideon Crane had been—by your traveling companion, by the very journey (to where, exactly?) that you'd insisted on undertaking—the mouth of the road would have leaped at you like a spark. You would've ordered the driver, as Crane did, to leave the highway, and when he refused to risk either his truck or his payload of melons to satisfy a foreigner's curiosity about a shit road to nowhere, you too would have climbed from the truck and taken the road by donkey.

Parveen Shams was being carried onto the same turnoff in a white Land Cruiser, which made her admire Crane's grit all the more. She was giddy at retracing his steps, six years after he'd first made this journey. In his memoir—the book that had propelled her here—Crane had written of the "hunger for adventure" that had thrust him onto this road and of his conviction that going deeper into Afghanistan would take him deeper into himself: *What we think of as comforts are buffers, ways of not knowing ourselves, not becoming ourselves. I wanted to turn myself inside out, to empty my pockets and so to learn what I contained.* At twenty-one—roughly half Crane's age then—Parveen believed herself similarly fashioned. She was traveling to a remote village to join Crane's crusade to save Afghan women from dying in childbirth; she would live with a family there and share its privations. Clearly she was hungry too.

But that self-conception soon jolted against the rocks littering the way. Crane had described the road as a "wretched rutted hell," a condition that felt less romantic beneath the axle than it had sounded on the page. The surface was an obstacle course of pebbles to jog over, boulders to ease around, craters to gingerly traverse. Mud bogs sucked at the wheels as if trying to draw marrow from bone. All of this slowed the car to a walking, lurching pace, and time seemed to slow too. As the minutes crept by, as her apprehension mounted, Parveen began to question her own fortitude. She'd been born in Afghanistan but left at the age of one and hadn't returned until now. She'd lived a sheltered American life—just how sheltered she saw only as its comforts receded. She'd consciously tried not to drink too much tea before they'd set out four hours earlier, but the Land Cruiser's jerks still sent unwelcome tremors through her bladder.

They left the foothills behind. Taking hairpin turns, they wound along a canyon lined with towering cliffs of schist, and amidst the powerful sensation of being constricted by these mountains, Parveen briefly forgot her physical torments But then she noticed that the so-called road had dwindled to nothing more than a one-car-wide dirt lane hewn from the rock face. When she dared to look out the left window, she saw nothing; it was as if they were aloft. In fact, they were inching above a crag that fell steeply to a river below. She gripped the armrest, envisioning the car plummeting off the edge and tumbling down to the water. It was a sullen green, the canyon in gloom even though the day was sunny. Only over the opposite cliff face was there a startling strip of blue sky. She was chilled, hungry, and stiff. Knots ridged her back. As the road twisted, she scanned for signs of the village, but the only evidence of habitation she saw was, high on a pinnacle of rock, a nest.

"How much longer?" she shouted to the driver, Issa.

He didn't respond, nor, by now, did she expect him to. From the time he'd collected her in Kabul, he'd kept music blaring—mostly Bollywood soundtracks to which he sang along in a surprisingly pleasing falsetto—which made him deaf to Parveen's queries. His conversation was saved for her cousin Fawad, a college student who was acting as her chaperone and to whom Issa had offered the front seat. Parveen he treated as a package he was tasked to deliver.

He wasn't what she had expected. Issa was Crane's right hand in Afghanistan. The memoir described him as an impish do-gooder who'd abandoned a career as an antiquities smuggler to help save Afghan mothers. When Crane had sought to build a clinic in the village to which Parveen was now headed, Issa was relentless in his efforts to help, dogged in his negotiations with bureaucrats, bandits, and the Taliban, saying and doing whatever it took to save more women's lives, in part because his own mother had died giving birth to him. As a boy, Crane wrote, Issa had slept with her shawl; as a man, he still dreamed of her touch. Long before Parveen met him, she'd pitied the motherless boy within, though this was too personal a topic to broach. It was odd to know more about someone from a book than from what he chose to share, which was almost nothing.

Instead of puckishness, Issa had inert eyes and a dour mouth; his fertile mustache, black and thick, was by far the liveliest thing on his face. When they met, he'd grunted a greeting, then scanned her clothing—a red tunic as long and loose as a dress, a pair of jeans, and a navy-blue head scarf—as if it were a puzzle he couldn't solve. Eyeing her three suitcases, he'd said, "Village women dress very simply." Men usually responded to, if not her beauty, a sensuality she'd been told she possessed—abundant dark hair, lively dark eyes, a lush mouth. From Issa there wasn't a flicker.

She tried to see if Fawad was as nervous as she was, but she was directly behind him. This was his first trip of any distance from Kabul, and he'd come along reluctantly, at the insistence of his father, Parveen's uncle, having been told that upon depositing Parveen with her village hosts, he could return home right away. He wore a leather jacket, fake designer jeans, and fancy loafers, a getup she found faintly amusing for a trip to rural Afghanistan. He'd texted compulsively for a time after they left Kabul but had now given up. The mountains had swallowed the signal.

Just then, as if the sun had breached a dam, light flooded the canyon, painting the river emerald and turning the strip of sky fiery orange and violent pink. A pair of birds crossed their path and flew along the canyon, their shadows trailing in the warm yellow light on the opposing cliff wall. Parveen, her vision aflame, was alarmed, for the lowering sun meant they might not reach the village before dark.

As quickly as it had come, the color was gone. Twilight seeped in, its violet-blue ethereal, elusive, and soon snuffed by night. She'd never seen darkness so thick or a driver so tense. The Land Cruiser's headlights barely pierced the night. Issa switched off the music, although her ears continued ringing with it. He was gripping the steering wheel, and in the dim glow of the dials, his knuckles looked slug-white. He and Fawad weren't talking, and the silence scared her.

The river, the whole world outside the car, had vanished. The road, what she could glean of it in the headlights, narrowed further. Their pace slowed. She felt both terrified and stupid to have taken such a risk with her life, and yet contemplating the possibility of her death made her feel thrillingly alive. She checked her watch, its light flashing in the blackness. It was twenty-five kilometers from the highway to the village, according to Issa, but they'd been traveling for more than two hours with no markers of distance, no road signs of any kind. She'd begun to doubt the very existence of the village when a white building flared in the headlights and disappeared.

"Dr. Gideon's clinic," Issa barked.

"Fereshta's clinic," she reminded him with some force, twisting back to look for what she could no longer see. Gideon Crane was adamant in his memoir that the clinic he built be named for Fereshta, the woman whose death had inspired its creation. Issa was one of Crane's top lieutenants—he had to know that. "It didn't look open," she said. In her imagination, the clinic had been brightly lit and bustling twenty-four hours a day. A beacon. Not that still, sealed building with the darkness closing in.

Before Issa could answer, they were in the village bazaar, the headlights' beams poking at empty stalls. He yanked the gearshift into park, gave thanks to Allah, high-fived Fawad, and said they would walk from there. But first he disappeared into the darkness and left her and Fawad to listen to the sound of him urinating.

Upon his return, he handed Parveen a flashlight and her small suitcase, gave a heavy one to her cousin, took the other himself, then motioned for them to follow him. She shivered a bit. It was the end of spring—a week into June—but the temperature had dropped as the Land Cruiser had climbed.

After some time Parveen stopped and switched off the flashlight to freeze this moment in her memory. She could hear her watch ticking. Sharp, clean air filled her lungs. Charcoal-dark mountains loomed all around. The three of them seemed to be standing on the lip of a plateau. On the plain below, moonlight skimmed the black surface of the water. Overhead, the sky was webby with stars, arrayed in constellations that hadn't been visible back home. This night world might have been created moments before for all the relation it bore to any version of night she'd ever seen.

Issa and Fawad were waiting. She returned slowly to self-consciousness, to the capacity to be embarrassed, and switched the flashlight back on. They angled up through a maze of lanes flanked by earthen walls, which hid the homes behind them. The flashlight did little more than illuminate Issa's back, the moonlight scarcely brushed their labyrinth, and in the dark every noise resounded: the scrape of dirt beneath feet, the roll of suitcase wheels, the unseen animals rustling in sleep, Parveen's breath. All of the walls looked alike, as did all of the wooden doors in them, including the one at which Issa stopped and pounded.

"Fereshta's house?" she asked.

"Her husband's."

A lantern with legs opened the door, or so it first appeared. Then, to Parveen's growing excitement, the man behind the light took form. This had to be Waheed, the husband Fereshta had left behind. He was so central to *Mother Afghanistan*, Gideon Crane's memoir, that Parveen felt as if she had summoned a storybook character from word to flesh.

Those words weren't flattering. Crane had called Waheed "a bearded nebbish," depicting him as a nervous, garrulous man bullied by life and unable to step up and save the mother of his children as she lay dying in childbirth. Whether his wife lived or died would be God's will, he'd pronounced. The photograph of Waheed that Parveen had seen most often—the one that seemed to accompany every newspaper story about the clinic Crane had built and was in the memoir too—didn't dispel the impression of weakness. In it the much taller Crane had his arm roped around Waheed, whose eyes were nearly closed.

Waheed greeted Parveen and Fawad as well as Issa, then ushered them in from the path. She couldn't see much of the space inside the wall and perhaps because of that could smell it all the more: the earthy odors of animals and manure, grassy hay, woodsmoke. From behind her came lowing and a sudden hot blast of animal breath. She shrieked, then regretted it, not wanting to remind everyone so quickly that she was an outsider. She sneaked a look behind her. It was a cow. And Issa was laughing.

The small room Waheed led them into once they'd removed their shoes was lit only by a couple of lanterns. Its walls appeared to be adobe, hairy with bits of straw. Its furnishings were negligible—a rug cool underfoot, cushions lining the walls.

Male visitors were received in this room in order to safeguard the purdah of the women in the house. Issa and Fawad sat on the floor and leaned back against the cushions, and Parveen did the same. Waheed unrolled a vinyl tablecloth, and two sons, the younger of whom was missing a hand, brought the food in and set it down before them. Parveen was the only female, although the voices of others drifted in from above. In this borderland between men and women she would live.

Dinner's main course was a platter of rice topped with raisins and carrots. Parveen knew there had to be meat buried inside because she'd grown up in Northern California eating the same dish. *Qabuli pilau* was a staple of all family gatherings, celebrations and burials alike, the lamb pressure-cooked, the carrots chopped to matchsticks, the raisins sautéed until they plumped, the rice boiled, the sugar, salt, cumin, and broth added . . . She'd sometimes found the number of steps tedious, but now it was a comfort to recite them in her head. The admixture of past and present was powerful, as if her family there and this family here were part of one clan, sharing an unseen network of roots. Nonetheless, in the interest of protecting her stomach, she steered clear of the hunk of meat once it was unearthed and hoped no one would notice.

During the meal Issa ignored Parveen as he talked to Waheed without cease. She resented his volubility all the more because she couldn't fully understand it. She spoke quite a bit of Dari, and she'd spent two weeks with her relatives in Kabul working to improve it, but she was catching only words and phrases, just as she'd caught intermittent glimpses of vistas on the switchback mountain road. It was because she kept dozing off, she realized with embarrassment, and she was thankful when at last Issa stood, yawned, and petted his mustache, preparing to decamp for the mosque, where he and her cousin would sleep.

"You should put a light bulb in here," Issa instructed Waheed, gesturing around the room where they'd eaten.

"Why, so I can see your ugly face more clearly?"

The quickness of the joke, if it was a joke, raised Waheed in her estimation.

As she bade her cousin farewell—he was driving out with Issa in the morning—tears started to come to her eyes. They hadn't exactly bonded during the trip, and they'd met only two weeks before. But he was her last connection, however attenuated, to her family.

Waheed led her outside, up a set of stairs, and into a room so bright it blinded her. The source, she saw once her eyes adjusted, was a single light bulb hanging from the ceiling. It was the contrast—to lantern light, to moonlight—that made it so strident. Before Parveen could get her bearings, women and girls surrounded her, crowding in to plant perfunctory kisses on her cheeks and clasp her hands in theirs, which were callused and bark-dry. She stood back to study them but they closed in again, brushing her with their long dresses.

Was she well? they asked. Was her family well? How was her health? How was her trip? The greetings continued for quite a while, in the customary Afghan fashion. Their names came and went. Their odors—smoke, sweat, meat, oil, breast milk, the smells of cooking and mothering—stayed with her. At five feet five inches, she wasn't tall, but she towered over the group. If she'd grown up on a village diet, she thought, she likely would have been as small.

"We kept the generator running late for you," Waheed broke in, and the women fell silent.

His bluntness wasn't endearing. In contrast to Crane's description of him as overly verbose, Waheed seemed to feel no obligation to say other than what he thought. Under the stark light, she had her first good look at him. Like that of most rural Afghans, his skin was sun-cured and lined. Funny that in the picture with Crane, his eyes were closed, because they were his most striking feature, nearly beautiful, the color of dark amber.

Parveen didn't know if he was intimating that she should offer to pay for the extra fuel. When it came to money, she didn't know what was expected of her beyond the seventy-five-dollar-a-month "contribution" to the family's expenses that Crane's foundation had suggested she make. She didn't want to take advantage of Fereshta's family. Yet she also didn't want the family taking advantage of her.

The children began making long-practiced rearrangements, spreading bedrolls and blankets on the floor, then draping themselves atop them. As composed as artists' models, they waited for sleep.

Parveen asked Waheed if she could see her room.

This was her room, he said. This was everybody's room.

Not hers, she vowed, imagining waking to pungent breath and entangled limbs, and she told Waheed that she'd assumed she would have her own room. "I'd be happier that way," she said, not troubling herself with why he should care for her happiness.

"No one in the village has their own room. We spend our whole lives sharing," he answered.

Later she would learn that they found it strange, sad even, that Westerners chose to sleep alone, even stranger and sadder that they forced their children, from very young ages, to do so. Over Parveen's time in the village, she would come to question this solitary confinement too.

But not yet. "I'll contribute more if I can have my own room," she said just as the generator moaned into silence, cutting the light. "Perhaps the guest room, where we ate?"

Whispers scurried through the dark. Then lanterns were lit and Waheed picked up a bedroll and motioned for her to follow him out the door and down the stairs. She was pleased at her own assertiveness, at its evident success. But instead of taking her back to the guest room, Waheed led her to another chamber, small and stinky. With shouts and kicks, he displaced a goat and some chickens but not their manure, laid the bedroll on the straw, and said that he would see about finding a door in the morning. He left a single lantern behind, and in its glow Parveen shook with anger, convinced that coming here had been a grave mistake. Gideon Crane also had stayed with this family, but he had described them as the most gracious hosts. Maybe he was a better guest. Maybe he'd slept where he was told without complaint.

Someone thumped a pitcher of water down nearby, then all went quiet. She blew out the lantern, and the night pulled tighter. *It is not just the inability to breathe that you must fight but the fear of the inability to breathe*, Crane had written of his kidnapping from the village, during which a black bag had been pulled over his head. *For the panic is as much a threat to you as the bag itself. It was the panic that drew the bag to my nostrils, making me suffocate, making me panic more, until I forced myself to calm down and could breathe again.*

She couldn't bear to remove her clothes, grimy as they were from the drive. She crawled onto the bedroll. It still carried the impress of other bodies, and their warmth.

CHAPTER TWO

SPILLING TIME

In the morning, Parveen dreamed that a child was tugging, almost lovingly, on her hair. She awoke to find a goat gnawing on it. The animal seemed nearly as surprised to find a live being at the end of its snack as Parveen was to be snacked on. With a cry she pushed the goat off and chased it out, then crouched against the back wall. Dawn came through the door frame, the light mixing into the darkness like milk into coffee. *Coffee.* Its absence was the first small sadness of the day.

The goat hovered in the doorway, letting Parveen get a good look at its yellow eyes, large ears, and unsightly teeth. Parveen reached for her phone, already writing the caption— *My new roommate*—for a Facebook post. Then she remembered that she had no way to post anything. The village had no internet, no computers, no television, no cell service. *It is not an easy place for someone used to the comforts of America,* Crane had warned in one of his talks. This had only made her want to come more. But now, lacking an audience for her experiences, she felt lost. Unwitnessed. She tapped the screen randomly, then scrolled through photos of her college graduation, which had happened only a few weeks ago, though it already seemed like much longer. But seeing how happy she'd been then just made her more miserable now, and she tossed the phone onto the bedroll.

When the morning light grew strong, she stepped into the compound yard and inventoried its contents: three goats, a few chickens, four cows, a donkey; piles of hay; a vegetable garden; a grapevine; a pomegranate tree; an outhouse; and stacks of dried dung that had been formed into what looked like brown puffy pancakes to be used later as fuel. Between the house and the outhouse hung a line of laundry. The men's pants on it ballooned in the breeze as if they yearned to walk off.

She looked up and nearly fell back, so vertiginous was the shift in scale. The mountains were sharp and precise nearby but softened with distance. They changed colors too, from brown, red, and green to gray and lavender. The farthest were smoky blue and skullcapped with snow. Parveen had flown over these mountains, or maybe others like them, traveling to Kabul from Dubai. Seen from the air they'd been majestic, but viewed from the ground, they unnerved her, and she was thankful when a child descending the stairs broke into her reverie. They stared at each other for a moment, Parveen taking in the girl's scabby face, unbrushed hair, and bright, mildly crossed eyes. Then Parveen smiled, and the girl tore back up the stairs. As her own smile faltered, Parveen resolved to toughen up. She couldn't be wounded by every small slight.

After a few deep breaths, she climbed the wooden steps from the yard to enter the main room. All faces turned to her, and in her anxiety they blurred together. Only the anomalies stood out. The girl she'd just seen at the outhouse appeared to have doubled; she had an identical twin. There was the boy with one hand.

A murmuration of simultaneous questions rose from a half dozen mouths: How did you sleep? What news came in your dreams? Did the goats keep you warm? Did the sun wake you up? Would you like an egg? Do you know how to make bread? Will you bathe? Can you cook?

Tracking who was saying what felt like trying to untangle the string of a kite in motion. Parveen wasn't sure whether she was even meant to answer. She'd forgotten most of the names provided to her the previous night, except for one, maybe because the face it was coupled with was hard to forget.

Bina was the wife Waheed had taken a year after Fereshta's death. She was also Fereshta's younger sister and therefore both aunt and stepmother to the six children Fereshta had left behind. Issa, who'd told Parveen about this development, argued that this was a good thing, to have the children raised by Fereshta's sister. Bina's sallow skin and hooded eyes, however, suggested that it might not be good for her. Her mouth rested in a perpetual quarter-snarl, as if she wanted to bite the world before it bit her. Even if involuntary, this defiant expression saved her from looking completely defeated. Her age was indeterminate, though Parveen guessed her to be in her early twenties, about Parveen's own age, which was likely the only thing they had in common. A baby nestled in a shawl wrapped around Bina; to her skirt clung a toddler and a little boy perhaps four years old.

Seeing these children, Parveen felt a sharp longing for her nephew, who was a year old. Ansar had been the hardest family member for her to leave. There was nothing complicated in her relationship with him; it was a pure love, a very physical love. She never tired of his fat rolls or long eyelashes or baby teeth, of cuddling him and making him laugh.

These babies, scrawnier and dustier, didn't have the same effect on her. Bina confirmed they were hers. Adding them to Fereshta's, she was now mother to nine. She seemed to be breastfeeding and hand-feeding and wiping all at once. She made a point of saying she'd been up for hours; she'd risen before dawn to light the fire for tea, knead the dough for bread, and do a half a dozen other tasks before anyone else woke.

God, you must be tired, Parveen wanted to say. Instead she said: "You must miss Fereshta so much."

The words were met with silence, as if Parveen had tossed a ball that neither Bina nor anyone else reached out to catch. It was a presumptuous way to begin their acquaintance, and Parveen regretted it immediately, but for her, and for the millions of others who had read about Bina's sister in Crane's book, Fereshta's passing was fresh, her memory vivid. Parveen felt as if she'd personally *lived* the death of a woman she hadn't even known.

The main room was a rectangle, perhaps fifteen by thirty feet, with small high windows. This was the stage for the life of the family, the place where they gathered, ate, slept. By day the bedrolls were stacked in the corner, the only other furnishings being an aluminum trunk, a woodstove, and a cradle suspended from a beam by a rope. Aluminum pots hung on the walls, which were patched in places with a darker shade of mud. The carpet on which Parveen sat was threadbare. A narrow wooden shelf held a small battery-operated radio.

She leaned against the cushions along the wall and tucked her legs beneath her. The women served Waheed, Waheed's older son, and Parveen before they served themselves. As she ate—bread, tea, yogurt—the eyes on her face made it hard to chew. No better was the scrutiny of her jeans or her toenails, whose blue-green polish the small girls crawled over to touch.

Between mouthfuls of bread, Waheed issued questions as if it were a physical task to dispatch, like chopping wood. "Who are your parents?"

Parveen gave their names and said that her father had once been a professor at Kabul University. About her mother they asked no questions, and while Parveen could've found this insulting, she was instead relieved. Her mother had died three years earlier, long enough for Parveen to become comfortable talking about it. But the prospect of discussing her mother with this family left Parveen unexpectedly raw. If they were uninterested or said the wrong thing, she wouldn't be able to bear it. Her mother could live for a little while longer here.

"What will you do during your stay?" Waheed asked.

Parveen had assumed that Crane's staff would've explained that. "I want to help at the clinic," she began.

"You're a doctor?"

"No, no, I'm not a doctor, I just finished college."

"So you'll become a doctor?"

"No. I hope, I plan, to be an—academic. To teach at a university. And do research—"

"Then you must've gotten lost, because there is no university here."

The whole family, down to the children, laughed. As amusement ricocheted around her, Parveen put her hands on her knees, as if to hold herself in place. The only consolation was that she understood more of what was being said than she had the previous night.

"We don't even have a school building," said Waheed's oldest child. Jamshid, that was his name. He was around fifteen, with his father's distinctive eyes. Young children learned in the mosque, he explained. Older children, like him, didn't learn at all.

Parveen hastened to explain that she didn't want to be at a university now, that she'd come here to study how the clinic that Gideon Crane had built had changed health and childbirth for women in the village and to understand the risks they still faced. She was blathering, stretching her Dari far beyond its capacities and comprehensibility. She could see this in the expressions of those around her, yet she seemed unable to stop. She kept succumbing to English to fill in the gaps: "I studied medical anthropology, which looks at how people in other cultures live and how the structure of culture determines how medical problems are treated, what the outcomes are—"

"You're married?" Waheed interjected.

"Engaged," Parveen lied.

"And the man you'll marry allowed you to come here?" Waheed asked.

She sensed Jamshid watching her. They all were watching her. "In America, women don't need a man's permission to travel," she said, smiling at the girls. She hoped to be a positive, even motivating, influence on them. Only one, the oldest, a teenager of striking prettiness with glossy hair, gleaming eyes, and a mouth like a pale pink lily, smiled back.

"Your father—he gave permission?" Waheed said.

"In America, women can do anything they dream of," Parveen said, truly irked now. Everything he said fit with a man who'd treated his wife's life as something not worth fighting for. "Women can even run for president. Or go into space. Anything. We don't need permission to do it."

"And with anything possible, you dreamed of coming here?" Waheed said, to more laughter.

WAHEED FARMED WHEAT AND alfalfa; he also grew mulberries. After breakfast, he planned to leave for the fields with Jamshid as usual, but first he asked Parveen for the money she owed him for her room and board. The request flustered her because it suggested he didn't trust her; it wasn't as if she had any way to leave without paying. She hurried down to her room to get the funds. The children started to follow her, but Waheed ordered them to stay put.

Through Crane's foundation, she'd arranged to pay Waheed seventy-five dollars a month for rent and food. Now she and Waheed agreed that an extra twenty-five dollars a month would be added for the luxury of a private room, for, as she thought to herself, a stench so strong she'd barely been able to breathe during the night. She knelt down on the floor and began to count out a huge stack of afghanis. She wanted to pay for three months, both to preempt further requests from Waheed and to bind herself to life here. The discomfort she'd felt during breakfast would lift, she told herself, not fully believing it. She kept replaying the conversation with the family in her mind, trying to figure out what had jarred her, then losing track of her counting—she hadn't brought enough large bills—and having to start over. Her frustration built, and when a chicken wandered in, she kicked at it and yelled, "Are you coming to eat my hair too?" To her embarrassment Waheed and Jamshid were standing in the yard not far from her room, waiting for her. She grabbed the money, marched out, and said to Waheed, "Here, three months."

He nodded then squatted to count it himself. She prayed that she hadn't handed over less than the required amount—he'd think she was trying to cheat him. "I lost track," she warned him. Concentrating, he didn't respond.

"Extra," he said at last, handing her a single hundred-afghani banknote.

At least he was honest. She stopped herself from saying that he could keep it. Even with her lack of experience abroad, she knew better than to act like money was of no consequence.

Once Waheed left for the fields, Parveen's sense of oppression lifted slightly, as if she, like the rest of the family, had been under his thumb. The others seemed to feel freer as well, because as soon as the compound door shut behind him, the children stampeded down the stairs and into Parveen's room.

"I guess I'll unpack," she said cheerfully and crouched to open her suitcases. The children pressed in, gaping at the carefully packed contents: stacks of tunics, jeans, and long skirts; a bazaar's worth of toilet paper, Tylenol, and tampons; sunscreen, underwear, moisturizer, mosquito repellent, mascara, and wipes; PowerBars, notebooks, and books, more than a dozen, including *Mother Afghanistan*. A hair dryer. A jump rope. A yoga mat. An inflatable blue exercise ball, which seemed especially absurd.

The children's gazes landed like flies on each item. "She's very rich!" a small voice called out.

No, no, no, she wanted to rebut, but the fact that the contents of her suitcase were unremarkable for an American was exactly the point. Whatever her strained personal circumstances, her country was rich. She couldn't help but compare herself unfavorably to Crane, who'd come here, from what she could tell from his book, with little more than a medical bag. Through the children's legs she scanned the room, but there was nowhere to put anything. She packed it all back up as though preparing to grab the first ride out of here. Which, given her low spirits, was tempting.

"Out! Out!" Bina chased the children off, then came in herself and bestowed her quarter-snarl on Parveen.

Until now Parveen hadn't grasped how physically small Bina was in both height and weight. It seemed impossible—terrifying, really—that three children had come out of her.

"Is any of that for us?" Bina gestured at the suitcase.

It was—Parveen had brought a host of gifts, from books to candy, for the family. But Bina's tone, which married antagonism and entitlement, made Parveen want to withhold them—to regain control. She did have gifts, she said, but she'd wait to give them until the whole family was together.

Bina asked Parveen why she'd come, and Parveen repeated what she'd said earlier, adding that it had made her sad to read about Bina's sister. She wanted to help, she said.

"Do all Americans love to help?"

"Not all, but many. We've been—fortunate." Parveen said that she also wanted to learn more about the lives of women here. Women like Bina.

"And then, once you have learned, you will go."

It was more command than question. Parveen nodded, trying not to show she'd been pierced. She cried, quietly, but only after Bina had left. This wasn't the reception she'd expected. She knew that she was lucky to have been raised as an American and spared a lifetime of war. But in return, she had chosen—chosen!—to come back, to give back. She had assumed that this generosity— her sacrifice—would be, if not celebrated, at least welcomed. Surely it deserved better than the indifference and even hostility she had encountered so far. Gideon Crane, by his account, had been embraced by this family. Perhaps the distinction lay in the character of Waheed's wives; where Bina was pinched and suspicious, Fereshta had been gracious and warm.

As if to confirm this theory, Fereshta's oldest daughter, the pretty one, appeared smiling outside Parveen's room. Like Bina, she wore a loose-fitting dress of a light, linen-like material, but while Bina's dress had been a drab brown, hers was a pearly blue and better cut. The girl was on her way to milk. By the time Parveen joined her outside, she was crouched next to a cow with a tin pail. Her name was Shokoh, the girl said, a word that translated roughly as "splendor."

Parveen asked her age. Shokoh guessed that she was sixteen. Pouting, she began to complain that Bina made her do the milking each day, then scolded her for taking too long. That Shokoh wasn't much of a milker, even Parveen could see. When she talked, she paused in her milking and then, on resuming, managed only a few jerky tugs before stopping again to massage one hand with the other. In the meantime the cow did a slow tap dance of impatience, and occasionally, swatting away flies, she struck Shokoh with her tail. "That's nothing," Shokoh said when Parveen commented on it. She'd been kicked more than once. The cows, she'd concluded, did not like her.

"Because you don't like them," Bina said from behind them. Shokoh started at her voice. "The cows aren't interested in your talk; they only want to be free of their milk."

Poor Shokoh, Parveen thought; she'd lost her mother and gained an unkind stepmother.

The girl retreated to the house. Bina took over the milking, using motions that were at once rapid, graceful, and economic. She had her own complaints. Every time Shokoh milked, Bina had to come after her to make sure the cows had been emptied lest they get blockages. And only a woman who'd nursed knew how painful such blockages were, she murmured. A child like Shokoh couldn't know that. Shokoh often forgot to wipe off the udder before she started, so bits of straw and dirt and manure made their way into the milk. She couldn't remember that this cow liked to have her two front teats emptied first, and that cow liked the right front and right back done first, then the left side, and that cow never kicked, but this cow did, and when Shokoh got nervous, she let the milk spill onto the ground...on and on Bina went, milking and murmuring to the cows, stroking and scratching their backs, their bellies, and their udders with ease.

Cows were as different from one another as people were, Bina said as she stroked another's white forelock. "A few years ago this cow had a calf, darker, also with white here"—she ran a finger down her nose. "A male. One day, a few months after he was born, he wandered off during grazing and broke a leg, and when Waheed found him, we had to butcher him. Even today, we still talk about this calf—how he looked when he slept, how sloppily and happily he nursed, whether he was afraid in the mountains. If we can't forget it when a calf dies, how could I forget my sister? How could those children forget their mother?"

This swerve caught Parveen off guard. She let out a small gasp in apology.

Bina went on: When Fereshta died, she'd already been gone from her family for a decade. Bina, much younger, had been a girl of only seven when her sister left. She'd never seen her again.

How was that possible? Parveen asked, taken aback.

The village here was two days' walk from their parents' home, Bina explained. Once rural women married, they usually left their families forever. There wasn't time or money for travel, and who would watch the children? Men weren't overly concerned with their wives' family ties.

Four years earlier Parveen's own older sister, Taara, had married and moved to San Jose, twenty-five miles from the family apartment in Union City, California. When their mother was dying, Taara had returned home to live for a few months, and even after that, Parveen and her father had seen Taara just about every weekend, especially once her son was born. And the sisters talked and texted all the time—almost too often for Parveen, who, busy with college, privately thought Taara to be lonely or bored and sometimes let her calls go to voicemail. Her sister had done what was expected in their community: gotten married young to an Afghan-American and had a child within a year. She had taken the paved route, Parveen thought, whereas Parveen saw herself as traveling down an unpaved road much like the one that had brought her to the village. Parveen hadn't hidden her feminist disdain for Taara's choices, just as Taara, four years older, hadn't hidden her disapproval of Parveen's. They often clashed. But now Parveen had a sudden urge to reach out to Taara. She couldn't, and this was the state in which Bina and women like her lived permanently.

"Did you write each other?" Parveen asked.

How could they? Bina answered. Both of them were illiterate. Like most village girls, they had stopped going to school at the age of nine. Word would reach home, after considerable delay, of Fereshta's children. Yet Bina said she'd often thought about her sister over the years—not seeing her hadn't made her any less alive. "Then a message was brought to our family village. That whole time it took to travel to us from here, I was believing Fereshta still lived."

"I'm so sorry," Parveen whispered. As agonizing as it had been for Parveen to watch her mother die, receiving the news unexpectedly would have been so much worse.

Bina picked up the milk pail, full now, and carried it to the kitchen at the back of the house. Beneath her thin dress, her back muscles bulged from her tiny frame. She was strong, as she had to be.

"I thought the message only carried news of my sister's fate," she threw over her shoulder. "But it also carried news of mine."

The news that she would become Waheed's wife and also mother to his and Fereshta's children. Parveen shuddered at the idea of being handed over to her brother-in-law. They got along only because they weren't married.

"Did Shokoh tell you she can read and write?" Bina asked suddenly.

No, Parveen said. She'd assumed Waheed's whole family were illiterate.

"She can," Bina said bitterly. It was clear that she felt inferior to her stepdaughter, who possessed more learning or more intelligence or both. In Parveen's mind, this jealousy helped to explain, if not justify, Bina's cruelty.

"Perhaps Shokoh could teach you," Parveen suggested. They were in the kitchen now, at the back of the house. Bina, straining the milk into a large pot, snorted. She was the one who had to teach Shokoh! Teach her everything! Waheed had told her he was taking another wife because Bina's cooking wasn't good enough. "But Shokoh can't cook at all!" Bina said. "And she spills time."

Parveen thought she'd misheard. "Another wife? Who? I thought Shokoh was Fereshta's daughter. She's so young."

Bina's laugh was mordant. Shokoh was Waheed's wife, she said, placing the pot of milk on a low fire. "I wasn't much older when I came here. It's the same for most of us."

"But—" Parveen stopped. She didn't know what to say—that in America such a marriage wouldn't even be legal? What was the point? Child marriage still took place in Afghanistan. She didn't know what to ask other than when the marriage had occurred.

Last year, before the first snow, Bina said. Waheed, after telling her that he was taking a new wife, had gone to marry. When he returned with his young bride, Bina was expected to incorporate her into the household. "She still needed a mother," Bina said with distaste, as if this vulnerability were a character flaw. Her expression said that Waheed's choice was still a wound, perhaps always would be.

Light-headed, Parveen sat down on the dirt floor. Her mind paired Shokoh's fresh, dewy face with Waheed's leathery one, and revulsion was the natural result. She was wary of being the judgmental outsider; it seemed too easy, too predictable, to be horrified by the backward ways of rural Afghan folk. But Shokoh couldn't have been more than sixteen.

Why was she so surprised to find that Waheed hadn't stayed frozen in a posture of grief? She'd expected this family to exist as Crane had left it, as if his memoir had arrested time. Perhaps this was the problem of first encountering someone through a book— she barely knew Waheed, and already he'd disappointed her.

CHAPTER THREE

AN EXISTENTIAL WAGER

BY THE TIME *MOTHER AFGHANISTAN* CAUGHT PARVEEN'S attention, she was a senior at UC Berkeley, and the book had been on the paperback bestseller list for three years. She'd seen many references to it, of course—it would've been almost impossible not to—but she assumed it was yet another attempt to capitalize on Americans' hunger for information about a country that was newly, dangerously relevant to them. In the more than seven years since the September 11 attacks, the academic tomes about Afghanistan had been supplemented with a host of memoirs about the country—Westerners who'd founded women's secret sewing circles or started beauty schools or served as soldiers or CIA officers or reporters, many of them acting as if they'd discovered Afghanistan the way Columbus had discovered America. She'd read none of these books and dismissed them all.

When she found a paperback copy of *Mother Afghanistan* on a table at the café where she'd gone to study, Parveen picked it up, anticipating that she'd loathe it. The cover showed a photograph of a woman with dewy dark eyes, most of her hair hidden under a black head scarf, this image superimposed over the country's leaflike shape. But the description on the back gave Parveen an unexpected twinge. Gideon Crane, it said, "had fallen in love with Afghanistan."

The possibility that Afghanistan, in its present, battered form, was a country you could fall in love with was news to her. Her parents loved Afghanistan, longed for it, but it was their homeland, one they'd never reconciled themselves to losing. They remembered, perhaps idealized, a different place: the peaceful country, the urbane Kabul, that preceded the Soviet invasion. Their Afghanistan had been a place of Friday picnics amid almond blossoms; of salons at which musicians played and poets declaimed; of thousands of years of history in which many of the world's great civilizations had played a part. Now, though, Afghanistan was regularly described in news accounts as existing in the Stone Age, which was hard for Parveen, American almost from birth, to square with her parents' elegiac memories.

If anything, since al-Qaeda brought down the Twin Towers, Afghanistan had been the stuff of Parveen's nightmares. When the attacks were launched, she'd been fourteen, just a few weeks into high school, her adolescent insecurity at its peak. The new animus toward Muslims felt personal, and the recycled images from Afghanistan of women in head-to-toe burkas and bearded, gun-toting men had posed an almost existential threat. Wanting no connection with those images, for the next several years she took to lying to new acquaintances about where her family was from (Italy, India; dark eyes and dark hair gave her a wide range). By the time she started at Berkeley, in 2005, she'd relaxed a bit; she even, briefly, joined the Afghan-American Society, helping to put on feasts and dance performances to educate her fellow students about her culture. But the country itself she kept at a distance. When she began to imagine a global career doing anthropology or development work, she pictured herself in Africa, Appalachia, or Brazil—anywhere but Afghanistan. Yet here was this American man with no ties to the country finding his life's purpose there. This discrepancy—this inversion, even—

unsettled her. Crane had embraced Afghanistan. Why had she felt compelled by shame to shrink from it?

On her BART ride home to Union City, she opened the book and devoured the early, vivid chapters about Crane's childhood in Africa, where his parents were missionaries. When he described his return to America as a "missionary kid" at the age of thirteen, he won Parveen's sympathy. His alienation—his sense that he would always be an outsider—was familiar to her, although she'd immigrated at a much younger age.

Over dinner with her father, Ashraf, with whom she lived, she kept the book open at her elbow. Since her mother's death, they'd both lapsed into reading at the table often, just as they often ate reheated food that Taara had cooked for them. Ashraf didn't cook, and Parveen, with her school schedule, didn't have time.

She tried to explain what had drawn her into Crane's book and how she identified with his feelings of foreignness. Not wanting to hurt her father by saying that her parents' lack of ease in America had rubbed off on her, she talked instead about feeling foreign among Afghan-Americans, who seemed to value her high GPA less than her honor, her sexual purity, and her marriageability. This she could say without guilt; her father had always encouraged her academic ambitions.

"You'd think it was a bad thing that I'm going to have a graduation instead of a wedding!" she said.

This wasn't a new subject for Parveen, and her father merely nodded in agreement. He seemed only vaguely interested in Crane's story, maybe because in her recounting, Crane hadn't yet reached Afghanistan. Then again, Parveen thought, maybe Crane's connection to Afghanistan was the problem. Even after September 11, her parents didn't speak of returning, although others in their community were doing so. Had all of their longing been a performance? The real reason, she knew, was her father's lack of moxie, which was the flip side of his gentleness. He had no entrepreneurial hustle, as many returning exiles did, no ambition for a government post. Then her mother got sick, which obviated the question of return entirely.

The conversation with her father having stalled, she turned back to *Mother Afghanistan*. Crane was, by his own admission, a cheater, which made it even more surprising to Parveen that so many people wanted to read his book. He'd gone to medical school and become an ophthalmologist, then developed a sideline in fraud, participating in a scheme to bilk the government of hundreds of thousands of dollars by filing phony Medicare claims. Then, although married, he used some of his ill-gotten gains to seduce not one but two nurses at the hospital where he operated. After one of them blew the whistle on him and his co-conspirators, he found, or re-found, religion. He joined the megachurch of an influential pastor, whose congregants advocated on Crane's behalf. Parveen rolled her eyes at this predictable arc—the man who is brought low and then finds God. And when Crane cooperated with prosecutors and reached a plea deal that allowed him to do community service abroad, Parveen prickled in outrage at the leniency shown white-collar criminals who happened to be white when millions of young black men were sent to prison for far less. Only Crane's self-awareness kept her reading. *I'd behaved badly and gotten off easy*, he wrote.

Crane picked Kabul as his destination abroad. It was 2003, and Afghanistan's future seemed promising. There was no sense that the Taliban, so thoroughly vanquished two years earlier, would return, and an influx of foreigners and international aid was transforming the capital. Crane took up residence in the comfort of a guesthouse and spent weeks operating on the eyes of poor Afghans, on their cataracts and melanomas of the iris.

Because of his hunger to plumb his depths, he'd set out from Kabul, accompanied by an interpreter he identified only as "A." At this point, Parveen was reading the book in her room, the same room she'd occupied in the same five-room apartment over a dollar store that her family had lived in since their arrival in Union City twenty years earlier. Her room was still furnished with the donated twin beds that the refugee-resettlement agency had provided for them, and the common space still contained the original furniture package: a sturdy secondhand dining table and one of those clunky generic living-room sets you can buy on installment at those stores that display half their wares on sidewalks. The only thing that had changed in the apartment, other than the upholstery fading from burgundy to pink, was its inhabitants. Her sister, with whom she'd always shared this room, was in San Jose, and her mother had died, leaving Parveen and her father to rattle around a space that overnight became unbearably cavernous. Looking around with the book in her hand, Parveen identified with Crane's restlessness. She'd long wanted a life where she wouldn't know what was coming next.

The valley Crane reached at the end of the road was a kind of paradise, a bucolic pocket untouched by foreigners, unvisited by—unknown to—even most Afghans. Parveen tried to imagine how she would behave if she was the first outsider to walk into a village, as Crane had been. She thought he'd handled it exactly right:

I've been asked often since if I was afraid, and I can say honestly not in the least. What was there to fear? These were no extremists, only ordinary Afghans, living peacefully. The friendliness on the faces that greeted us as we walked into the village was unmistakable. They bore no animus to Americans. I was the first one they'd ever met. Seeing myself as an ambassador for all of my countrymen, I tried to make neither assumptions nor demands. I said I wanted to be at the service of the villagers, to learn their customs, so that I could give Americans a true picture of them.

Waheed and Fereshta, poor but generous, had been his hosts. Fereshta was a "luminous Afghan rose" who tended to him with grace and generosity, cooking savory meals and supplying him with tea and blankets even as she mothered six children and carried her seventh.

But then she went into labor, and in labor she began to struggle, as do so many Afghan women, especially rural ones. Most Afghan women, however, do not have an American doctor at hand. True, Crane was an ophthalmologist, not an obstetrician, but he knew far more than the "ignorant crone" who served as the village's traditional birth attendant. So there was hope, or there should have been. But Waheed said he needed the mullah's permission for Crane, as a foreign man, to help his wife, and the mullah refused. Crane pressed Waheed to let him help anyway, but Waheed wouldn't allow him to. Whatever happened, he said, would be God's will. All Crane could do was try to get Fereshta to a hospital with a female doctor, but there was no car or truck to carry her there. Desperate, Crane put her atop the donkey he had ridden into the village. A donkey!

Parveen read on. Her spirits lifted when Fereshta arrived with Crane and Waheed at the district hospital, then sank when Crane discovered no female doctor there either. But the male doctor at least was not a foreigner, and Waheed agreed to let him help.

I paced around the outside of the small hospital, Crane wrote, *as goats nibbled from trash heaps threaded with medical waste. Her screams came out the windows, tore me apart. I stretched myself on the ground, spread my arms wide, and asked God to take me instead. As I prayed, the screams ceased abruptly. I thanked God; the baby had been safely born. Then a bay, a single extended unearthly note that still echoes in my ears, broke the silence.*

Parveen's stomach dropped. Perhaps she'd already known Fereshta would die, since talk of the book had been everywhere. But Crane's skill as a storyteller was to make Parveen believe Fereshta would pull through. Besides, didn't these types of stories always end happily? Parveen's fear was the kind you ride during a horror movie or on a roller coaster, where there is a pleasure in the terror, which is inextricable from the subconscious awareness of your own safety. Surely Fereshta would live, and Crane, having gotten her to the hospital, would end his own narrative as its hero. That was how these books worked.

I rushed into the hospital, Crane wrote, *and raced down the hall until I saw, through an open door, Waheed bent over his wife's lifeless body.*

Fereshta died, as did her unborn child. Six children were left motherless, and Parveen, reading years later, was devastated. It wasn't a shock to her intellectually. As an anthropology student, she'd learned all the ways—structural inequality, food deficits, austerity regimes, neoliberal policies, inherited wealth, gendered oppression, and more—that progress left people, most of them female, behind. She'd read countless academic studies and texts to that effect. But she'd never read anything that made her *feel* the outrage of this so strongly. Fereshta was singular in her beauty and charm, perhaps, yet her death wasn't. Her life's abridgment had been almost ordained by her birth. Millions of women like her gambled every time they gave birth, and many lost.

Parveen kept reading, faintly hoping for a miracle, as if this might be a fairy tale in which a grandmother is removed intact from a wolf or a princess is restored to life by a kiss. No such resurrection was in store. Crane, bereft, vowed to wrench something good out of Fereshta's death by saving others like her. With heroic effort, he built a clinic in her village and named it for her.

There was no bringing Fereshta back, no restoring her to her children. I grieve for this, ache for this, still. But we can—we must— keep other mothers alive, prevent their needless and agonizing deaths. Imagination is the highest capacity we human beings have. It allows us to grasp suffering we don't experience ourselves, and it allows us to see remedies for that suffering that don't yet exist. I imagined a clinic that could have saved Fereshta, and then I built it. The terror, the long odds, that these mothers face demanded no less.

Parveen closed the book in tears, aware of its sentimentality and yet helpless before it. There was something pleasurable in cynicism yielding to emotion. And within her grief was something grubbier: the sense that Crane's journey was one she should be making herself. Among the feelings that surged through her as she read was envy. Or maybe *possessiveness* was a better word, the petty, proprietary thought that Afghanistan was *hers* to care for, and yet here was Crane, a stranger, adopting it.

IN HER GRIEF OVER Fereshta's fate, Parveen wasn't alone. The book had sparked an unusual outpouring of idealism among Americans, so much so that Crane in one interview compared it to *Uncle Tom's Cabin*, known vaguely to Parveen as the novel that, in vividly depicting the cruelties of slavery, had helped bring about its end.

Church groups, book groups, moms' groups, youth groups— all had been moved to raise money to support the clinic Crane had built in Fereshta's village. A fourteen-year-old girl in New Jersey started a fund-raising initiative called Money for Mothers that spread first to other schools and then, via social media, to other states. Kids across the country held bake sales and dance-offs; they mowed lawns and tithed from their allowances to help women in Afghanistan. Gideon Crane's book signings drew long lines; his lectures, crowds. For the American people, so many emotions had been pent up since 2001: anger at the attacks, concern for the fate of women in Afghanistan, guilt about the volunteer soldiers deployed and killed, confusion about why they were still in the country at all. Crane seemed to provide answers that were a kind of salve.

When Parveen chanced on the memoir, America's war in Afghanistan was already more than seven years old. It had spanned all of her time in high school and now her nearly four years in college too. America had disrupted al-Qaeda and driven the Taliban from power, but the nation's intervention had dragged on long enough, with vague enough aims, to see the Taliban return as insurgents, thereby necessitating the war's continuance. The previous year, 2008, had been the most violent since 2001. There were close to fifty thousand American soldiers in Afghanistan— as many as the Soviets had brought to their initial invasion—and seventeen thousand more on their way. The war effort was ramping up even as public support for it fell. Crane's book seemed to bridge this disjunction by reminding Americans why their intervention in Afghanistan was still needed. And he suggested that the war, if fought differently, more humanely, could be won.

His TED Talk had drawn millions of viewers, and now Parveen joined them, watching on her laptop in her room. Never having seen one, she found the format of the talk odd, like a one-sided conversation, and she was preoccupied at first by Crane's puffy eyes and the way his long arms sailed out to punctuate his points. On the screen behind him flashed images, mostly from the book. One showed Fereshta's clinic, sparkling white in the sun. The clinic already had saved so many lives, Crane explained, through emergency cesarean sections and blood transfusions and intravenous medications. It was taking on the most common causes of maternal death: obstructed labor, postpartum bleeding, fistulas, infection, eclampsia. He had moved on to building clinics in other villages only because dozens of elders had trekked over mountains to beg him to do so. Their women, too, were dying in childbirth. It seemed there was a Fereshta in every house.

Maternal mortality killed more women than war did, he pointed out, yet these deaths garnered no attention. Childbirth remained an existential wager. The screen behind him filled with the startling image of a woman covered by a bloody sheet. If Americans used their power and know-how to address this threat, he argued, the hearts and minds of the majority of the Afghan people would be theirs. Compassion was a tool of war, one the nation was failing to deploy. He had briefed the Joint Chiefs of Staff to this effect; during his TED Talk, he showed pictures of generals holding *Mother Afghanistan* or gripping his hand. But he was even prouder that ordinary soldiers were being told to read *Mother Afghanistan* before they deployed to the actual Afghanistan and that the book was being assigned to every student at West Point.

Parveen wasn't sure how to feel about the war. In October of 2001, as scenes of the Taliban fleeing Kabul were broadcast, her parents had wept with relief in front of the television. They were grateful to the Americans for ending five years of barbaric Taliban rule and hopeful that the Americans would prevent a return to civil war and help rebuild their battered country. But as civilian deaths at American hands mounted, many Afghan-Americans started to question the war (her parents, fighting her mother's cancer, barely talked about it anymore). She couldn't say whether her country was helping Afghanistan or damaging it, and she didn't like not knowing where to stand. She was still young enough to consider ambivalence a cop-out.

Not long after Parveen read *Mother Afghanistan*, Gideon Crane scheduled an appearance at a private university near San Francisco. She bought a ticket and on a rainy Tuesday found herself in an amphitheater with three thousand seats, all of them occupied.

Crane arrived more than an hour after his talk was scheduled to start. For most of that stretch, as pump-up-the-volume music was blasted to fill the empty time, the stage was occupied only by a podium whose protruding microphone began, as the minutes passed, to look as if it were going to begin speaking itself. Yet Parveen did not sense impatience or hear complaints around her; uncharacteristically, she felt little impatience herself. What was the value of their time compared to Crane's? He had earned the benefit of all doubts.

The crowd was mostly around her age, students like her, she

guessed, but different than her Berkeley peers. Less diverse, for one: she couldn't remember when she'd last been in such a sea of whiteness. But also less ironic, more earnest, and she let herself enjoy the enthusiasm bubbling around her. She was enjoying her anonymity, too, the unlikelihood of anyone she knew being in the audience. She didn't have to affect an attitude or have an explanation ready for why she was there, and tonight at least she wouldn't have to talk about the future, which was pretty much all she and her friends did nowadays. The future was mostly what she thought about, too, although neither talking nor thinking was bringing her closer to solving the problem it presented.

She was four months from graduation with no firm idea as to what to do next. Her original plan, to apply to graduate programs in anthropology, had been abandoned the previous September, after Lehman Brothers collapsed. At first its demise had seemed irrelevant to her, but as the repercussions spread, joining with other signs of economic woe, she concluded that it was no time to take on more debt. In the succeeding months, she and her friends, most of them idealistic liberal arts majors like her, fought genteelly and mostly unsuccessfully for scraps: scarce fellowships, meager stipends, nonprofit work that barely paid. The job market was the worst it had been in two decades. Returning home after graduation to wait out the downturn, as many of her friends planned to do, wasn't an option for Parveen, even though home was where she'd lived all through college. Her father had decided that upon her graduation, he would give up the apartment they'd had for two decades and move to San Jose to live with Taara and her husband and son. Taara assumed that Parveen would join them and share a room with her baby nephew until she married herself. Just the idea of this made Parveen sweat; it sounded like a second childhood lived under her sister's judging eye.

Through the fall and into the winter, panic had built in her, anxiety keeping her up at night, nerves knotting her stomach at dawn. Even Barack Obama's election and inauguration, as electrifying as they were to her, didn't dispel the underlying dread. She felt fragile, prone to tears, and alone. Her mother, had she still been alive, would have provided comfort but not necessarily guidance, since she had never tried to find work in America. Her father didn't know how to keep from sinking himself. He was a journeyman professor teaching poetry and Persian at Bay Area community colleges, but now his classes and so his income were being reduced, which was why he was moving in with Taara. The life of Parveen's secure teenage years was being dismantled piece by piece, and walking Berkeley's streets, she sometimes had the dreamlike sensation that she was falling.

When Gideon Crane finally took the stage, to a protracted ovation, Parveen thrilled to his charisma, even though logic suggested that this charisma, rather than inherent to him, was born of his fame. She was struck first by his height—he towered over the university president who introduced him. His hair looked yellow under the bright lights. His face was rumpled with exhaustion, which made her tender toward him. No doubt he was fatigued by his relentless efforts. His suit was rumpled too, and Parveen found this lack of attention to his own person moving. It reminded her of the photo revealing a hole in Adlai Stevenson's shoe that her History of American Politics professor had shown the class.

Much of Crane's talk simply recapped the book. As he told the story of Fereshta, of not being allowed to help her, of the donkey ride, of her death, there was total silence. Then a cell phone rang, audible to all even in the giant space, and everyone looked around in a limb-tearing rage until it was shut off. Crane, unbothered, carried on. His anger at Fereshta's death seemed so genuine, as if drawn from a constantly replenishing reservoir, and his reading of his listeners was so perceptive that they were rapt. He knew that young women especially were preoccupied with preserving the right to choose what they did with their bodies, he said, but he wanted them to remember women in places like Afghanistan who had no choices at all and fight for the rights of those women as hard as they fought for their own. He wanted young Americans to take their heads and hearts out into the world to do good. "But don't forget, while you're young, to have fun," he added. "You don't have to be perfect to change the world." He was talking about himself, Parveen guessed, but his words resonated with her own feelings of being as yet unformed. You don't have to wait until you *become* something or someone to help, he seemed to suggest. Maybe action was how you became who you were meant to be.

When they gathered that he was done speaking, they all rose to their feet to applaud. Even as the university president was walking to the podium, still clapping, Crane was waving a long arm and loping off the stage. He took no questions. He signed no books. They were told that a car was waiting to drive him to the airport for a flight to Oregon, where his next event would take place. Parveen hurried to talk to him, but she was caught in the crush of those exiting, and by the time she'd made her way out of the amphitheater, anyone connected to Crane's organization was gone. She'd hoped to find someone who worked for him because, as he finished his talk, inspiration had struck her. "Go out into the world and be the best of America," Crane had said. "Give the best of yourself." Suddenly Parveen could think of nothing she wanted more and nowhere she wanted to do it more than Afghanistan—in Fereshta's village, to be precise. It made so much sense; she, probably alone in that auditorium, had the language, knew the culture. The ongoing war didn't deter her. By seeing it up close, she hoped, she could decide for herself what it was.

She wrote to Crane through his foundation website. He didn't reply, not to that letter or the next three she sent. This wasn't surprising, given the volume of correspondence Crane surely received; what was surprising to Parveen was that she persisted. She called the foundation, then pestered his executive assistant and chief of staff. The passion Crane had stirred in her was real and so was the ambition. Her identity had begun to form around this idea of going to the village. The awe in acquaintances' faces when she told them her inchoate plan was gratifying, even addictive. To revert to her ordinary self would disappoint. It must serve some human need, she thought, to believe there are individuals willing to do more, sacrifice more, than most people are capable of. Wasn't this what had attracted her to Crane?

When Crane at last responded, he told Parveen to get in touch with someone on his staff about her donation. She wrote back to clarify and received a vague but encouraging response, then a more detailed e-mail from a staff person who had been directed by Crane to help with arrangements. After another long delay, Parveen was told she would live with Fereshta's family. The news thrilled her; she boasted about it. Fereshta's fame, even though it was posthumous, was a magnet.

Later, on that first morning in the village, she would wonder superstitiously if this boasting had landed her in misery. Where was everyone else? The true believers? How was it that of all the legions of fans of *Mother Afghanistan*, only she had been foolish enough to transplant herself to the village? She remembered, a bit sourly, the people who'd cheered her on. Maybe it wasn't nobility she had offered them but drama. There were times she herself had cavalierly exhorted wavering friends to take a risk or do a rash thing—dump a decent but uninspiring boyfriend; change majors midway through junior year—that she never would've done herself. It was a guilty and vicarious pleasure to watch other people leap off a cliff and see how they landed. Still, she did not want to admit that those who'd warned her against coming were right.

THE AGENDAS BEHIND, or the emotions beneath, these warnings had been almost as interesting to Parveen as the words themselves. Her father's chief worry had been the danger the war might place her in. Parveen had assured him that the far northern province to which she was going was safe, but he hadn't been convinced. There ensued a flurry of phone calls to relatives in Kabul, who agreed with Parveen. The fighting was worsening across the country, but it was concentrated in the Pashtun heartland in the south, far from Fereshta's village. The peaceful province was of interest to neither the insurgents nor the Americans. Still, they expressed surprise that Ashraf would allow his unmarried daughter to go on her own to a village, and this got to the heart of Taara's objection: that by venturing off alone, far from her elders' watchful eyes, Parveen would compromise her honor and thus her chances of marriage.

After their mother's death Taara had appointed herself, without asking permission, as a maternal substitute, which Parveen resented, particularly because Taara proved more stifling than their mother had ever been. She acted as if everything Parveen did reflected on her, which became a problem when rumors that Parveen was hooking up with a boy on campus reached Taara. They'd had a screaming fight and hadn't spoken for a week.

For Parveen, her sister's raising of her marriage prospects as a reason not to go to Afghanistan was reason enough to go, and so the battle began. Parveen announced that she didn't care if any Afghan-American boy wanted to marry her; indeed, she didn't care if she married at all, and besides, she was going to the village to be with the women, not the men, so where was the dishonor in that? She accused her sister of not being concerned for the women of Afghanistan, to which Taara replied that Parveen didn't care about the feelings of her own family, which was worse.

It fell to their father to broker a compromise. His strong preference was that she not go, but he wasn't the kind of parent who would forbid it, and for this Parveen was grateful. Her cousin Fawad would escort her to the village, where she'd be safely settled with its women. That her father would make this arrangement despite his opposition moved Parveen. He also agreed to let her put the money she would get for graduation toward her ticket.

She bought the ticket, then made an appointment with her favorite professor to tell her about her plan. Parveen had taken three anthropology courses with Nandita Banerjee, whose groundbreaking work on how cultural attitudes around disease, death, and medical care migrated across borders had earned her a named chair by the age of forty. Parveen, like many students, coveted Professor Banerjee's brains, her confidence, and her style. She had a diamond nose piercing, kept her dark hair short and spiky, and often wore a black leather jacket that, when she grew exercised by her subject, as she frequently did, she took off, revealing arms exquisitely toned by her capoeira workouts. (Students traded tidbits about these workouts, about her yellow Vespa, about her romantic life—her partner was a Senegalese-French philosopher who commuted between Berkeley and Paris.) That she was brown-skinned and India-born only enhanced her credibility. Uncompromised by any American history of her own, she was free to speak the truth, and the lilting Bengali accent in which she spoke it didn't hurt.

Early on in Parveen's tutelage, Professor Banerjee had quoted someone saying that anthropology, while purportedly allowing one to understand other cultures, was really a tool to understand one's own. This idea seized hold of Parveen. She wanted to get far enough outside the forces, historical and cultural, that had made her examine them. During her first class with Professor Banerjee, an introduction to fieldwork, Parveen turned her lens on her peers, examining the cultural suppression of Afghan-American girls' sexuality and the clandestine outlets it found, comparing the dutiful public faces of her friends and acquaintances with their wilder private selves. With the promise that their identities would be completely disguised, per the protocols of anthropology, she cajoled them past their nervousness and into revelations of their intimate secrets. They might as well have been confessing to crimes, they were so skittish. Parveen would conduct peculiar interviews where girls would talk about themselves in the third person, describing, for instance, extra phones they used, as if they were drug dealers on *The Wire*, to deceive parents who might check their photos and texts.

In those girls' bind, she saw her own: any action she took was either conforming to or rebelling against communal expectations about the proper way to behave. She was paranoid about keeping her own sexual history secret because she worried that her parents would be judged for her actions. When the first boy she slept with, a Nebraska biology major named Jim, called out at climax, "Par—uh, Par," she was actually relieved that he'd forgotten her name. (The second boy, unfortunately, remembered it, which was how the news, in a very long game of Telephone, reached Parveen's sister.) Professor Banerjee suggested that her community's conservative attitudes toward female sexuality were not as anomalous as they appeared but of a piece with Americans' gendered notions about how their teenagers should behave. Parveen loved her for this: It helped place Parveen's culture in context, and so it made her feel less strange. Less foreign.

This was during her first year at Berkeley, a time when her mother was weakening. Was it surprising that Parveen attached herself to her professor's strength? When she went back to school in the fall of her sophomore year, her mother had passed away. Before long, she developed a fantasy of following in Professor Banerjee's footsteps and becoming a medical anthropologist. As she would later try to explain to Waheed, she wanted to study health and illness—who gets sick and why, who gets care and why, and the ways in which culture affects these distributions. Parveen was convinced that the lack of gynecological screening among Afghan-American women was why her mother's cervical cancer had not been diagnosed in time, a theory she confided only to Professor Banerjee.

Now Parveen sat in a chair next to her professor's desk, catching faint whiffs of her sandalwood perfume. On the computer monitor, new message notifications materialized and faded in silence; unlike Parveen, Professor Banerjee had the self-control not to look. Her research was stacked neatly on long metal shelves with labels that Parveen, during a work-study stint, had helped to affix. Posters of Franz Boas, Frantz Fanon, and Zora Neale Hurston were framed on the wall.

In a rush of words, Parveen recounted finding Crane's book, hearing his talk, and deciding to go help in his clinic. Her professor paid close attention, nodding occasionally, which gave Parveen the impression that she approved. But when Parveen finished, the first thing Professor Banerjee said was that she didn't need to read *Mother Afghanistan* to know it was meretricious.

Parveen's mouth fell open a bit in surprise. The book had been subjected to "withering postcolonial critique" in the anthropology community and beyond, her professor said. Parveen's own Google searches about Crane had turned up mostly encomiums to his achievement and reports on the sort of appearances that had become the stations of fame. Along with his TED Talk, he'd been to Davos and had been championed by the usual prominent white men (Charlie Rose, Tom Friedman, Tom Brokaw, David Brooks). The more sophisticated debates took place on academic listservs, like mushrooms hidden in the shade for only the knowing to find.

Professor Banerjee objected to a white male American, however well intentioned, ventriloquizing for that most powerless of females, an Afghan village woman, thus reinforcing the very power relations he claimed to challenge. Memoirs by oppressed subjects, native people, or voiceless women were righteous, legitimate, and worthy of both pedagogy and embrace. Those by privileged Westerners—especially if they were about the oppressed, native, or voiceless—were problematic at best.

"I would read Fereshta's story told by Fereshta," Professor Banerjee said, her tongue tap-dancing off that last *ah*.

Parveen found enough gumption to remind her professor that Fereshta was dead, but she knew that wasn't the point. It was as if her professor had caught her reading *Us Weekly* in the supermarket checkout line. When Parveen argued, politely, that Crane was critical of the way America was waging war in Afghanistan— he bluntly condemned the U.S. military's night raids on villages, its drone strikes, its accidental bombings of wedding parties, its backing of warlords with egregious human-rights records— Professor Banerjee smiled.

"Isn't it interesting, then, that the military has so fervently embraced the book?" she said. "Are they in the midst of a sudden and unexpected paroxysm of self-criticism?" She paused for a beat, as if expecting Parveen to answer, then said: "I think not." They celebrated the book, she said, because it offered a path to victory, to "winning hearts and minds," that beloved catchphrase of theirs. The book was not against the war itself, not at all. It was simply arguing for a kinder version of it.

She was referencing Crane's signature coinage, *"kind power."* *If the Afghans think we're here only to drop bombs and raid their homes,* he wrote, *we can't blame them for wanting us out. We need to practice kind power. Rather than continuing as the hectoring yet distant father, America should act more like a loving mother.* The book's title evoked both Fereshta herself and this new role. Love came up a lot in *Mother Afghanistan*: the love of Afghan men for their wives, the love Americans needed to show the Afghans. Sentiment, Crane was suggesting, had a place in war and politics. That, Professor Banerjee grimly noted, was an argument a woman could never get away with making.

"Why *kind power*?" she said. "Why not just *kindness*?" Because power, she insisted, was what it was truly all about. Power meant continued military intervention. Power meant you could revert to weapons and bombs when your kindness failed to persuade. Surely it wasn't a coincidence that just as public support for the war was dropping, Gideon Crane came along to remind Americans why they needed to be in Afghanistan—to save the women, of course. "Parveen, beware feminism that serves imperial or colonial interests or that, in my friend Gayatri's perfect phrase, involves 'white men saving brown women from brown men.' We tell stories in order to occupy."

From the hallway came muffled laughter and the sound of steps dying away. It was gray and drizzling outside the office windows. Back then, it always seemed to be drizzling. Even with the lecture she was enduring, Parveen dreaded having to leave this bright cozy space. Within it, she could believe that someday she would be as successful and secure as her professor. Outside, it was harder to pretend.

Professor Banerjee continued. Surely Parveen understood—didn't she?—that the military's humanitarianism was nothing more than contemporary imperialism. Worse, because Crane claimed to have been "saved" after his fraud was exposed, evangelicals believed that when he spoke of love, he was talking about Christian love for the Afghans. "You are, forgive me, naive. But all young people are, especially idealistic ones," she consoled Parveen, who was listening while also trying to determine whether her professor threaded or sugared her brows.

The subtexts might elude Parveen, Professor Banerjee was saying, but she hoped that her student would consider the class discussions about the historical relationships between conquistadores and missionaries or priests. Remember the East India Company and British evangelicals? "Might opens the door for mission, which in turn justifies might. Controlling land and bodies paves the way for saving souls, and saving souls solidifies control over land," Professor Banerjee had said in her class lecture. She repeated it now.

Crane didn't strike Parveen as much of a missionary, although she wasn't brave enough to say so. She wondered if her professor—and she felt disloyal even thinking this—was jealous of the four million books Crane had sold. His work had entered the national conversation in a way that Nandita Banerjee's erudite, provocative writing had not. Academics, Parveen had observed, often mistrusted mainstream popularity, seeing in it a lack of seriousness or intellectual discernment. But was there envy beneath that contempt?

The question felt especially uncharitable when her professor ducked out to the department refrigerator and returned with two plates of curried potatoes, bitter gourd, and rice that she'd cooked herself. Yet Parveen was unwilling to relinquish her admiration for Crane, and between mouthfuls of the food, which was delicious, she defended his work. "But women are dying in Afghanistan," she said. "I mean, the numbers on maternal mortality, in the rural areas especially, it's like four out of every ten women dying. They do need help, and if men are keeping them from getting it…" Her eyes watered as the memory of her parents weeping in front of the television returned. Had it been wrong for America to depose the Taliban? Wasn't that military intervention justified, even righteous? Many of her non-Afghan friends were reflexively anti-war and anti-military, and they believed America had done far more harm than good abroad. But wasn't that attitude just an excuse for staying home and doing nothing? America had provided her family with refuge and her with opportunity; she wanted to offer something to Afghans who hadn't been fortunate. This wasn't an abstract issue for her, but nor did these feel like intellectual arguments, and she didn't want to get emotional with her professor. She despaired at this sliver of daylight between them, and it was even worse when Professor Banerjee seemed to read her mind.

"I understand this is a sensitive question for you, Parveen," she said. Of course the conditions for women in Afghanistan were abysmal, she went on. But she cautioned against those conditions being used as a pretext for more years of intervention, however "kind"—and here she made air quotes, in case Parveen missed her sarcasm—its nature might be. Then their conversation was interrupted by a package delivery, and when Professor Banerjee resumed talking, she seemed distracted or maybe worn out by demolishing Parveen's naïveté. She turned to her other concern about Parveen's plan: What sort of help was Parveen going to provide? Did she imagine herself as a community health worker? If so, what were her qualifications? How would she turn this experience to good account and convince master's programs that she was serious?

Parveen summoned up the courage to remind Professor Banerjee of her own history. As an undergraduate at Cambridge, she had taken a leave of absence to return to India and support tribal people resisting a dam there. Parveen pointed to a picture on the office wall, a black-and-white photograph, almost like a movie still, that showed a young Professor Banerjee with her black hair down to her butt standing hip-deep in water.

Ah, Professor Banerjee said, but that was before she had decided on a career in academia. In fact, the experience itself had decided it for her. She'd realized that, given her education, offering physical solidarity was an empty act, whereas anthropology—done not as extraction, in which knowledge was hoarded in university halls, but in concert with native participants—could be an effective form of resistance. It could help communities see the structural forces that kept them oppressed.

Then the professor turned unexpectedly motherly—Parveen was having trouble keeping up with her moods—and encouraged Parveen to apply for an exploratory grant from the department with the idea of doing future fieldwork in the village. It would help cover her travel expenses. And, she added, Parveen should get an IUD or bring the morning-after pill with her in case she had intercourse, "desired or, God forfend, not," and while they were on the subject, Parveen should concoct a fiancé to deter unwanted suitors. Her professor also recommended that for the duration of her stay in the village, Parveen ought to consider becoming vegan if she wasn't already. It was an ethical practice, of course, but the vegan diet was also less likely to result in intestinal distress.

Professor Banerjee walked Parveen the few steps to her office door, then paused before the photo of her younger, glorious self. "Look at that girl," she said, without a trace of wistfulness. "So jejune."

The word, Parveen learned when she consulted a dictionary that afternoon, was commonly used to mean "immature." But it came from the Latin *jejunus*, for "hungry."

Chapter Four

The Distant Fire

Parveen spent that whole first afternoon in her stall, as she'd taken to thinking of her room. She swept the straw out with a handmade twig broom, then scrubbed the walls and the floor. The children watched until they lost interest. She napped a bit, wrote in her journal, and compulsively picked up her use-less phone. When, toward evening, her stomach grumbled, she wandered outside. No one was in the yard. She went upstairs and found the whole family assembled for dinner, with Bina and the girls setting food out. They all looked slightly surprised to see her, as if they hadn't counted on her joining them for meals. The boy with one hand shifted over to make room, and Waheed motioned that she should serve herself. She felt too ill at ease to eat much.

Except for the food being served—stew, rice, spinach, beans— the scene wasn't much different from breakfast. But for Parveen, everything had changed. Now that she knew that Shokoh was not Waheed's daughter but his wife, all kinds of submerged currents were visible. When Waheed looked at Shokoh, Parveen saw lasciviousness in his face. Even the way he shoved rice into his mouth seemed obscene. There was a pattern in his dealings with women, she thought, a depravity even. Had he wanted Fereshta to die so he could replace her with someone younger and prettier? This made no sense, she knew, since it was Bina he'd married first. She pondered the question anyway.

Shokoh appeared newly powerful, although she had changed only in Parveen's eyes. There was a lushness to her that made the rest of the family look arid. Her sexual energy seemed only partly in her control, as she shifted between petulance and charm. In what was apparently a running joke, she told Waheed in a bantering tone that he should leave more food for his children. He smiled and Bina scowled. The teenager Jamshid, meanwhile, seemed unsettled by Shokoh's proximity. She appeared to enjoy unsettling him. Seeing him looking at her, she gave a demure smile, as if to say, *Caught you again.* She was barely older than he was.

Shokoh reserved most of her attention for Parveen, plying her with questions that, while routine, seemed designed to show that she knew more about the world than the rest of the family. Had Parveen brought a computer? Did she like to read? How many books had she read? Parveen tried to address the whole family as she answered, not wanting to ally with Shokoh over the others. But she suspected that in Bina's eyes, she already had.

"Are you from New York?" Shokoh asked.

"I'm embarrassed to say I've never been there," Parveen said, then explained that she'd grown up on the other side of the country.

Waheed's oldest daughter, Hamdiya, who appeared to be a couple of years younger than Shokoh, laughed at this. Shokoh gave her a cool stare, as if to say she couldn't possibly have gotten what was funny about it. Hamdiya looked down at her lap and didn't speak for the rest of the meal.

When dinner was over, Parveen hesitated, unsure whether to go help the women or stay with the men. If she went with the women, she might be expected *always* to be with the women, which she didn't want, because their world was so confined. If she stayed with the men, she was implying that she was better than the women. She was overthinking it, but she had no instinct to guide her. She chose the women and for a few glorious minutes felt her choice to be correct. She could've been back home with her sister and her aunts cleaning up after an engagement party, laughing and chattering in the kitchen, although the kitchen here had no sink, stove, or refrigerator. It was merely a raised platform that contained a cooking fire big enough for a huge pot, a small propane tank onto which another pot could be placed, an oven dug into the ground for baking bread, and space for food preparation and washing. Any leftover food was fed to the animals, and the water with which the dishes were washed was poured into the garden. Nothing went to waste.

But when she told them that her aunts cooked *qabuli pilau* the same way Bina did (this was a lie, since her aunts used much less oil), Bina asked her why she hadn't eaten hers.

"I'm not feeling well," Parveen lied.

"My food made you sick?"

"No, no—just all the travel, I think." She hoped the tremble in her voice wasn't audible.

"Bina can make you a remedy for your stomach," Zahab offered shyly but also proudly. "She can cure anything."

That would be great, Parveen replied, although it was her mood, not her stomach, that needed remedying.

"You're an Afghan with an American stomach," Bina joked. "Like a camel with a mouse's bladder."

Parveen laughed along with everyone else, but she saw coldness in Bina's eyes. *You don't make sense; you don't belong here*, Bina was saying. Parveen couldn't even rustle up a comeback; her Dari wasn't limber enough. She despaired of ever being truly known here, where everything that had defined her—her friendships, her politics, her taste in men, music, and books, the campus groups she'd belonged to and the ones she'd shunned—was irrelevant or insignificant. Bina had yet to ask her a single question. She acted as if Americans landed in her house all the time, yet as far as Parveen knew, none had stayed here since Crane, and that had been before Bina's arrival. Parveen had the eagerness to stand out common to those who feel they never quite fit in. She didn't like being treated as a nonentity.

BINA DID TAKE TIME, the next day, to show Parveen her vegetable plot, which was in a sunny corner of the yard. The plot had been laid by Waheed's mother or perhaps his grandmother or great-grandmother and would once have been tended by Fereshta, although this Bina did not mention. She made a point of saying she'd expanded the garden, and she named, with awkward pride, each plant: celery, caraway, chicory, coriander, dill, carrot, fennel, parsley, spinach, and cress. Like many Afghans, Bina had a talent for growing flowers, some of which had curative properties, she said. For example, gul-e-jaafari, gorgeous orange flowers in pots, were conscripted to fight against stomachache, parasites, and diarrhea. Variants—cousins—of the herbs Bina grew could be found in the wild, she said, but those were often poisonous.

"Like me!" Shokoh, who'd trailed them, said wickedly, and Bina nodded as if this were wisdom. Then she was done playing tour guide. It was time to work. For the rest of the day, she gave exasperated sighs whenever Parveen approached and batted away her queries as the cows did the flies. Trying to keep out of the way, Parveen seemed constantly to be in it.

She had grand plans to interview all the village women about their reproductive histories, and she'd thought she'd start with Bina. She wanted to learn about the experiences the women here had in childbirth, she explained to Bina, and asked if they could make a time to discuss Bina's pregnancies and deliveries.

Bina looked at her incredulously, then laughed harshly. "The babies were in me, then they came out. There, we have discussed."

When Parveen tried to help with household chores—rinsing dirt from spinach, straining yogurt, chopping meat—Bina shooed her away, saying, "Better to keep your pants clean and your hands soft." Parveen protested, but Bina said, with feigned lightness, "You're as useless as Shokoh in the house!"

The words stung, especially because Parveen disagreed with them. She'd grown up doing very similar tasks in her mother's kitchen; she was skilled enough at shredding carrots. But she put down her knife and walked away. There was nothing to gain from a fight. She sulked in her room, wondering if she was being punished for the previous night's conversation with Shokoh.

Underemployed, she told herself that this was a well-earned vacation after the frenetic schedule of her senior year. Yet the sense of being unwelcome made it hard to relax, as did her lack of purpose. The women of the house didn't have freedom, but they did have work, an abundance of it. As she sat foolishly in corners or under the grapevine in the yard, the small children staring at her, even her hands came to feel superfluous. Her only previous experience of such female idleness had been in literature—the women of *Palace Walk*, so desperate for glimpses of the world outside, or Rosamond, the destructive, fantasy-prone young bride in *Middlemarch*—and it was easy to see how the condition, the gaseous swamp of boredom, gave rise to ill-considered love affairs and poisonous intrigues. Would men, confined and slack, be any different?

Every time she asked Waheed to take her to the clinic, he replied, "Not now," and she lacked the nerve to venture out on her own, not least because she wasn't sure, given the maze of lanes and the identical doors, that she could find her way home. "*Home.*" Inwardly, she placed the word in quotes. *Not home* was more accurate. Parveen had never lived on her own before and so hadn't known until now that homesickness had physical symptoms: sleeplessness, loss of appetite, nausea.

These were also symptoms of grief, which was perhaps why she missed her mother with renewed acuteness. Parveen scrolled through the photos of her mother she kept on her phone, deliberately making herself despondent, until the ache in her grew so strong she wanted to gouge it out. The image of her father bidding her farewell at the airport kept returning. She couldn't stop seeing his graying hair, dutifully combed, or his frame, which had so doggedly thinned in the years since her mother's death. Or his eyes, expressive and concerned. By now he would have relocated to Taara's place in San Jose, and it occurred to Parveen that there was a hole in Union City where the Shams family had been, a hole that was rapidly closing. It was as if her entire childhood had vanished. Even if she could somehow see back home, the view would be blank.

And would her family, in trying to imagine her situation, picture her balled up on her bedroll in a room littered with straw? Would her friends guess that the first woman she'd tried to interview had shut her down? No one back home would ever know if this was how she spent her time in the village, but *she'd* know, and it was that determination to give her story a different ending that kept her in place. She'd promised her father she would return before Thanksgiving. With June having only just arrived, that seemed impossibly far off. But she wouldn't quit, not yet. She'd invested too much to leave.

She went to her room to read; in light of Bina's sensitivities, it seemed like showing off to do so in front of the family. She turned and re-turned the pages of *Mother Afghanistan*, as if the book might provide the key to this household. But Crane, now that she looked closely, hadn't provided many details about life with the family, and of those he had, some didn't match what she'd found. He'd written, for example, that Fereshta had three sons and three daughters. According to Parveen's tally, the boys numbered only two. Perhaps one had died; she'd have to inquire delicately about this. He hadn't mentioned the identical twins.

He'd said that Waheed farmed rice when in fact he farmed wheat. But then Crane had written his memoir at least a year after leaving the village, and he probably hadn't taken notes. Of course he wouldn't remember petty facts. He'd trained his vision higher.

But for her own accounting, perhaps to avoid similar mistakes, she set down in a notebook the names of the children and their approximate ages, along with brief descriptions: *Jamshid, about fifteen. Hard to see where his father leaves off and he begins.* She was still fresh from her student life, and research was a familiar hand to hold.

Hamdiya, fourteen. Will she be married off soon? Need to learn her knowledge of sex, contraception, etc.

Zahab, twelve, I think. Dutiful. Seems most attached to Bina, maybe because there's a resemblance.

Bilal, about ten. Only one hand—want story but afraid to ask. Sweetheart.

Adeila and Aakila, about eight or nine, twins. Both need glasses. Two or three when their mother died. After she wrote this, Parveen paused. At least she'd known her own mother.

She made notes about the village too—roughly ninety families, Waheed had said, most of them large, totaling about a thousand people. Along the valley spread a dozen or more similar villages, none within sight of the others. But without a professor to test her grasp of this information, it felt inert on the page. It bored her.

On her third night, Parveen stayed in the main room with Waheed and Jamshid after dinner while the women and girls went to clean up. The radio was on, tuned to the BBC Persian service, as it was each evening, radio being the sole medium by which news of the outside world regularly came to the village. An Air France flight with two hundred and twenty-eight people aboard had vanished; a South African woman claiming to be one hundred and thirty-four, and thus the world's oldest person, had died; General Motors had filed for bankruptcy—the family solemnly took it all in.

"It's the worst air crash since 2001," Jamshid told his father. Parveen looked at him with surprise. "I know what happened in New York was much worse," he mumbled almost apologetically. "But there hasn't been this big a crash since."

"You heard about that? About 9/11? I mean, of course you did," Parveen said, feeling silly. "I guess I mean, did you hear it through the radio?"

They had, Jamshid said. He had been seven then. He'd dreamed about buildings as tall as the mountains collapsing down on him. So many innocent Afghans had died in decades of war, far, far more than the number who'd died in New York. This had made the villagers more sympathetic.

"We couldn't believe this had been done to a superpower," Waheed said. "The same one that had brought about the end of the Soviet Union. And we knew it would bring the Americans to Afghanistan." But Waheed was more interested in discussing Iran's elections, which would be held soon. Did Parveen think they would be honest? Was Iran more or less of a democracy than Afghanistan?

She didn't have good answers. In fact, she knew far less about the subject than Waheed.

Had she at least seen pictures of Ahmadinejad? Was the man as short as they said he was? he wondered, and he guffawed when Parveen estimated where on her chest he came up to.

Most of the news they received, however, was about Afghanistan, its politics and its war, reports of which drifted in through the radio like ash from a distant fire. In every other way the war felt remote, as if it were happening in another country. This was a relief to Parveen, for in Kabul it had seemed uncomfortably close, like metal woven through the fabric of the city—a hard, cold presence you kept butting up against in the course of normal life. Her relatives, as they took her to museums and palaces, a Mughal garden, the British cemetery, and the zoo, not to mention internet cafés, kebab joints, and the homes of many distant relatives, often had to pull over for the military convoys that bulled their way through the streets. They pointed out the blast craters left by insurgents' bombs, and navigated around the barricades and walls meant to guard against them. Western embassies and Afghan government offices had all clawed out so much territory for their own self-protection that to Parveen, the city read like an aggregation of security fiefdoms. A reprieve her cousins had planned—a picnic in Istalif, a famously beautiful spot north of Kabul—was canceled after a suicide bomber attacked a NATO convoy on the road they would have taken. Such disruptions were not routine, for they could not be predicted, but neither were they surprising. To Kabul's residents, the war was like a giant pothole that you kept swerving around until you fell into it.

Each night she and her relatives gathered in the living room to watch television, where a more disturbing face of the war was playing out. A few weeks before Parveen arrived in Afghanistan, an air strike in the western province of Farah, some five hundred and fifty miles away from Kabul, had killed more civilians, it was said, than any similar incident since 2001. It made the news in America, but Parveen, preoccupied by preparing for graduation and her journey, had barely noted it at the time. Now she couldn't escape it. It was believed that a hundred or more people had been killed, and most of them were children, mainly girls. Their bodies had been so badly shredded that not all of the pieces could be recovered, leaving Parveen with a new and chilling understanding of the word *remains*. Then there were the wounded children in their hospital beds, including three sisters she couldn't forget. They had singed hair and charred skin that had been smeared with yellow ointment. The youngest, just five, clutched a glass of milk.

"Why is your new president escalating the war?" her aunt asked. "We hoped he would find a way to end it."

The politeness of her voice hid her emotions. Pessimism? Resignation? Suppressed rage? As the sole American in her relatives' house, Parveen felt culpable. She remembered her Berkeley friends savaging the military. How could she argue with them now? She'd expected to find clarity about the war by coming to Afghanistan. Instead, the blur had worsened.

Now, on the radio that Waheed had taken off the shelf and set, like a small pet, to his right, came a discussion of the Farah air strike, in which the U.S. government had at last conceded significant errors. Unable to help herself, Parveen began to speak about it, to describe, as best she could in Dari, the images she had seen on television in Kabul. The girls in the hospital. The men pawing through rubble looking for family members. A mass grave.

The females had rejoined the men and Parveen saw the twins, Adeila and Aakila, staring at her in shock and clutching each other's hands. She could have been describing them, she realized with horror, when she talked about the sisters. She'd given the twins, perhaps the whole family, a new sense of their fragility, their vulnerability, and she wished she could undo that. Although, unlike the radio reporters, she'd witnessed nothing other than what she'd seen on television and the internet, the family reacted as if she were the one offering a firsthand account of the air strike, maybe because this was a place with no screens, to where images didn't travel. Or maybe the family was rapt because of the guilt she confessed to—an admission that embarrassed her. It seemed so American, to act as if everything was about her own emotions and be so shocked by the barbarism of war in a country whose past three decades had been consumed by it. And yet she wanted to insist, but didn't for fear of sounding condescending, that it wasn't silly to expect that your government would act decently and to be crushed when it didn't.

The family looked to Waheed, the patriarch, to say something. He turned down the radio and began to speak, occasionally stroking his beard as a much older man might. The village had a great commander, he said, who'd fought with the mujahideen against the Soviets. This man, Amanullah, had gone into the mountains for years, eluding the Russians who were hunting him, surviving on roots, nuts, mulberries. He'd lost a hand in battle and he'd gained great fame. Because of his valor, Waheed added, almost as an aside, the village forgave him his sins.

Parveen knew about the commander, for he'd figured prominently in Crane's book. She also knew his sins. In the late 1990s, he'd lent his courage to the Taliban, becoming a commander for them and terrifying the region for a time. The commander had whipped women, beheaded men, and run a private dungeon. And he'd kidnapped Crane during his stay in the village.

Waheed didn't speak of any of this. How painful it must have been for the villagers when their hero joined the Taliban, Parveen thought; too painful to be spoken of. No, Waheed talked only of Commander Amanullah's exploits against the Russians until he reached his point, which was that if Amanullah decided the Americans were an enemy, he'd take up arms to fight them, and many villagers would follow him. Not that anyone wanted that, he added. They wanted to stay here and farm. For the villagers, too, this war felt like another country. No one here had even gone to fight for the government, although that was mostly because they couldn't meet the literacy requirement for soldiers.

"But the Americans should be aware," Waheed said, "that this soil has never been hospitable to foreigners."

It was all Parveen could do not to roll her eyes. This was the one cliché about Afghanistan that every American seemed to know.

*   *   *

THE NEXT AFTERNOON WAHEED came back from the fields and
announced, without explanation, that they were going to the
clinic. Parveen wondered if she'd passed some test. From a hook
near the door, he lifted a ring with a pair of heavy, ornate keys.
Nearby hung a row of emerald-green chadris, what Americans
called burqas: the head-to-toe coverings, with netting over the
eyes, that the women wore when they left the house. Parveen
did not take one—her Kabul relatives had told her that, not
being from the village, she should feel no obligation to wear
one—yet their mere presence shadowed her into the yard. She
chafed at the cloister she'd been living in. The women and girls
watched her go.

When she stepped out of the compound she felt free. This
was her first clear view of her surroundings, unobscured by
walls. The village lay in a long, verdant valley that spilled out
from between the feet of the mountains. The valley floor, flat
and rich in river silt, had been given over to fields shaped into
neat squares or sweeping crescents. Wheat and corn, rye and
barley, rice—each claimed its own shade of green. The land
had been terraced, and on higher levels there were orchards:
almond, apricot, mulberry, peach, many trees enveloped in
clouds of pale pink blossoms. The houses, built from tawny
mud bricks, stepped up a low stony ridge, their intricate
patterning guarding the privacy of each family. And ringing it
all, the mountains.

As Parveen was getting her first view of the valley, the villagers
were getting their first view of her. When she was just steps from
the compound, a passel of boys and a few men gathered around,
as if they'd been waiting these past days for her to emerge. Her
hair was covered but not her face, and it was her face they stared
at, their gazes pinning her in place. Her seconds of freedom
vanished.

"Have you never seen a woman's face?" Waheed shouted. "Don't you have mothers?"

His assertiveness on her behalf surprised her, although she sensed that some of his irritation was directed at her for putting him in this situation. The boys didn't move until Waheed took a step toward them and clinked the large keys. Then they scattered, continuing to spy on Parveen from behind walls and around corners. Once she and Waheed reached the bazaar, the boys didn't bother to hide. They stood a few feet away and gawked.

The bazaar was a simple place: two rows of facing stalls, about fifteen all told, propped up by stripped tree limbs, with corrugated tin roofs overhead. The main path was mucky from the buckets of water merchants tossed on it to keep down the dust. Waheed gave one-word self-evident descriptions for each stall they passed: butcher (a skinned sheep hung on a hook, its bare pink flesh flecked with black flies), baker (loaves were stacked for those too poor to buy ovens), and tinsmith, a maker of pots and pans. There was a shop with a desultory hodgepodge of stale biscuits, cigarettes, expired medicines, and pirated DVDs (although no one in the village had a DVD player) of *2 Fast 2 Furious* and Bollywood films, merchandise that had probably been bought and sold a hundred times between Kabul and here, where it had washed up, as an ocean deposits plastic far from its source, to gather dust.

"Some of those things have been here since I was a child," Waheed joked.

The shopkeeper laughed a little too hard. People greeted Waheed deferentially, as if he were someone important, and Parveen wondered if this was because she was with him. He bantered with them but did not introduce her.

The blacksmith worked outdoors, next to his forge, which was made from mud. The coals within it glowed orange, and a large kettle sat atop it. The blacksmith was an inquisitive graybeard with sweat trickling down his face, but it was the man next to him who caught Parveen's attention. He was as big in the belly as he was in the shoulders and had a hennaed beard, a gray turban wrapped expertly around his head, and in place of one hand a metal hook. With his intact hand he was popping pistachios into his mouth, then loudly biting them with a sound like knuckles being cracked. The shells he ejected with a buffoonish *pfft*. This was Commander Amanullah.

She looked in vain for signs of the terror he had inflicted on so many or of his famed courage. What she saw was a grizzled aging man, hardly in fighting shape. Waheed's suggestion that he could lead an army against the Americans seemed comical, a pantomime of threat. But when someone changes slowly before your eyes, Parveen thought, the change can be hard to see.

"You are the American doctor," the commander said after Waheed had introduced Parveen.

She was not a doctor, she clarified.

"Then who are you? We need a doctor here."

"The clinic doesn't have one?"

"The lady doctor comes once a week. We've instructed our wives to get sick or give birth only on Wednesday, but they don't always listen."

The small crowd of men who had gathered laughed; Parveen didn't find it funny. She was about to tell the commander so but Waheed had disappeared, so she held her tongue and instead asked, "Didn't Gideon Crane hire a full-time doctor?"

"I don't know what Dr. Gideon has done." Like Issa, the villagers called Crane Dr. Gideon, she noticed.

Parveen said that she would report the situation with the doctor to Crane's foundation.

"You work for Dr. Gideon?"

"I've come to be helpful to him," she said, uncomfortable with this elision but uncertain what to say instead.

The commander asked if Parveen spoke English. The question

struck her as hilarious until she remembered that of course they had no way to know what language, other than Dari, she spoke. Yes, she said and smiled.

"Let's hear some," the commander said in Dari.

She stuttered, "H-hello, how are you?" and was surprised to hear how strange English sounded to her.

"Yes, she speaks English," he confirmed in Dari to his minions, who laughed because the commander himself didn't speak the language and had no idea what Parveen had said. He asked her if she'd learned Dari in school.

No, she told him. Her family was from Afghanistan, from Kabul, where she'd been born. Her parents had left in 1988.

"So they left with the Russians. Were they Communists, your parents?"

"No! That's just when their visa came through. They were trying to escape the Soviets. No one knew they would with-draw—"

"The little bird has quite a sharp beak," he said, amused by Parveen's outrage.

They'd left everything behind, she went on. They'd started over in America with nothing. Her father, for several years, had driven an ice-cream truck. That this was humiliating for Ashraf didn't register on the villagers' faces. An ice-cream truck was as mythical here as a unicorn. Truck drivers earned good money.

"The suffering of those who left can't compare with that of those who stayed," Amanullah said, and Parveen fell silent. "I've lost two sons to war. And this." He waved his hook.

"I'm sorry about your sons," she said, unsure whether to offer condolences for his hand.

"It's a blessing to lose sons fighting for God," he said.

"Of course." She rebuked herself. She should have known that was how he would see it.

There was an awkward silence. The blacksmith picked up his

hammer and began to bang on his anvil. Commander Amanullah looked away, as if to say he was done with Parveen.

SHE COULD SEE THE clinic from the bazaar. She couldn't *not* see it, since it was two stories high and painted a white so bright that it looked primed for sunburn. It was completely out of scale and character to the rest of the village. If she hadn't known better, Parveen would have figured the building for a wedding hall planted by some entrepreneurial provincial. It looked like the photo in Crane's TED Talk, but it was much grander than the photo in the book, which she had recently perused.

She mentioned this to Waheed, who laughed; the clinic looked smaller in the book because it *had* been smaller. Originally the structure had been just one story with a few rooms, he said. But after the book was published and donations poured in, that clinic was torn down and a new one built at three or four times the original size.

From what Issa had told him, there were three warehouses in Dubai full of unused equipment, Waheed said. "The donations kept coming; the clinic had to keep growing." He sounded almost sad, but his eyes were creased with amusement, as if he understood his own illogic. Supplies were brought in, sometimes by helicopters, he continued. A high wall, also white, surrounded the clinic. Both wall and clinic were repainted at least twice a year, because of the dust, Waheed said, then added: "It can never be defeated."

"Dr. Gideon wants the clinic to look sanitary," Parveen said, feeling obliged to explain for him.

With one of the large keys Waheed unlocked the metal door that led into the clinic's courtyard. Among the children who had tailed Parveen and him, only Waheed's were permitted inside. The rest were harried off. The courtyard was large and dusty, unadorned except for a single shade tree that stood slightly off-center. In the late-afternoon light, its shadow stretched diagonally across the empty space.

"So the doctor comes once a week? Isn't the clinic open any other time?"

Waheed was using the other large key to unlock the building door. "If there's no doctor, it stays locked," he said. "The equipment here is more valuable than all the fields in this village. And what good's a clinic without a doctor?"

His question struck Parveen as unintentionally profound, more profound than anything in Foucault's *The Birth of the Clinic*, which they'd read in Professor Banerjee's class. Parveen had been taken with the idea of the "medical gaze," which was how Foucault described the way doctors, even as they were elevated to sages, reduced patients to bodies alone. She'd been curious to see how that would play out here, in the developing world. That there might not be a doctor to bestow a medical gaze had never occurred to her.

The clinic facility itself was good, staggeringly so, Parveen thought. The interior walls were a soothing white and there was a reception desk and several rows of sturdy metal chairs screwed to the floor in a waiting area. The chemical smells— ammonia, bleach, paint—were acute, almost painful. She hadn't smelled chemicals anywhere else in the village except for the diesel that fed Waheed's generator. There were skylights and— this seemed almost miraculous—a light switch, which Parveen flipped. Nothing happened.

The fuel was saved for when the doctor came, Waheed explained. They couldn't run the generator all the time. After sparking a lantern, he walked Parveen from room to room, beginning upstairs with the ten-bed maternity ward and the adjacent nursery, which held three empty incubators. Downstairs he slung the beam of the lantern into windowless rooms labeled, in both English and Dari, EXAMINATION, LABOR, DELIVERY, SURGERY, and RECOVERY. The equipment looked state-of-the-art. That this pristinely kept temple to health—to modernity—should be in this village, of all places, moved Parveen. If, approaching the clinic, she'd questioned the abandon with which Crane flouted the village context, now she celebrated his refusal to let the village's history or isolation limit its possibilities. The clinic's seeming excess proclaimed these humble villagers to be worthy of the same medical care that Americans were, a message almost as meaningful as the treatment itself.

CHAPTER FIVE

SHAKE THE WORLD

THE NEXT MORNING, WHICH WAS WEDNESDAY, DAWNED CLEAR and warm. After breakfast Parveen practically bounded to the clinic, eager to meet the doctor. She was greedy for another liberation from the house yet uneasy at her own desire. Wasn't the right to flit in and out of a prison that others couldn't leave the very definition of privilege? Neither Shokoh nor Bina had ever been to the clinic to see the doctor. Bina claimed to have never been sick.

"You didn't see the doctor even during your pregnancies?" Parveen asked.

"Why would you need a doctor to be pregnant?" she answered.

This stoicism, if that's what it was, struck Parveen as worthy of exploration. Was Bina remarkably healthy, or did she never allow herself to be called sick, since there was no one to do her work in her place? She wrote this question in her field notebook, which was still mostly empty.

Aakila and Adeila insisted on accompanying Parveen to make sure she didn't get lost. They chattered like baby wrens the whole way. When they arrived, the metal door to the courtyard was unlocked, and women were already gathering inside, giddy at the brief furlough from their homes and duties. They had pulled their chadris off their faces and piled them atop their heads, and they kissed and caught up with one another until around ten o'clock, when they heard a car parking outside the wall. The chadris were down before the car doors slammed shut.

The doctor entered the courtyard calling out ebullient greetings. Her name was Yasmeen Wafa, but the villagers mostly called her "the lady doctor" or Dr. Yasmeen. Behind her came a young man, which explained the rush to cover faces. He was Naseer—her assistant, her driver, her son. Dr. Yasmeen had an open, full face that shone out from her fawn-colored head scarf. Parveen liked her instantly. She was plump beneath her salwar in a way that exuded vigor and health. She had an ample mouth and a wide smile with good teeth (it was hard not to notice good teeth in the village, where they were rare). Naseer was her solemn counterpoint; he had the same full mouth—adorned, in his case, with a trace of mustache—but he was less prone to smiling. His skin was darker, his hair wavy and black, and his thick brows nearly grew together in the center. Parveen guessed him to be about twenty.

The women rushed to surround Dr. Yasmeen, their voices overlapping at a high pitch of excitement. Naseer tried to herd them, verbally, to the clinic entrance. He was ignored. Only when the doctor herself moved across the courtyard toward the door did they budge, although they continued to surround her like ectoplasm. At the entrance all of the women, unwilling to give up their proximity to the doctor, attempted to squeeze through the doorway at once.

Because Naseer stayed outside in the courtyard, once the women were inside the clinic they removed their chadris, laid them on the rows of chairs, and sat on the floor. The lights were on.

Parveen followed the doctor to the examination room and, after hovering in the door for a moment, marched in to introduce herself as a recent college graduate who had come to help the village women. Dr. Yasmeen looked at her with great warmth. It was the kind of reception Parveen had hoped for, and failed to receive, from Waheed's family.

"I guessed you weren't from here," the doctor said. "But America! Naseer will be so excited."

Speaking Dari because she insisted that her English was poor, Dr. Yasmeen asked how long Parveen had been studying medicine.

Parveen confessed that she hadn't studied medicine at all, and she watched the doctor's face fall ever so slightly.

"So how is it you plan to help us?" This was asked pragmatically, without judgment, yet the question embarrassed Parveen, as did the fact that while they were talking, Dr. Yasmeen was doing half a dozen preparatory tasks—putting on her white coat, washing her hands, setting out her examining tools, laying paper on the examining bed, and so on.

Parveen explained that she wanted to document how the clinic was being used as well as the women's reproductive histories and their continuing health problems.

"And this report," Dr. Yasmeen said, "who will read it and what will happen afterward?"

Still there was no needling in the doctor's tone but Parveen grew defensive. "Without information, Dr. Gideon's foundation or others that want to help won't be able to make improvements," she said.

"I'm not sure a lack of information is the reason this clinic has, most days, no doctor." So what was the reason? Parveen asked, but Dr. Yasmeen had no more time. She handed Parveen the soap and told her to wash her hands. "No, not like that. More thoroughly, in between the fingers."

"But I'm not going to—"

"Always be prepared." The doctor smiled. "We'll talk later. They're waiting."

*   *   *

EVEN THOUGH IT WAS the younger women, Parveen would learn, who often had the graver needs, physical and otherwise, the doctor saw the elder women first. Their ravaged bodies shocked Parveen—skin parched, mottled, and bruised; shoulder blades protruding like sharp breasts; breasts hanging like empty stockings. And the majority of these women were under sixty, an age beyond which most didn't live.

A woman, her black hair streaked throughout with gray, entered weeping. To Parveen's surprise, Dr. Yasmeen assumed a posture of skepticism—arms folded, eyebrows raised—and asked, in the weary voice of an actor who has run her lines one too many times, "Saba, are you well?"

"How could I be well?" Saba blubbered. "You know better."

Saba had given birth to eleven children, the doctor told Parveen in Dari as Saba nodded along. Seven of them were living, the oldest ones with children of their own, but Saba wanted more offspring. Her aging ovaries had other ideas.

Saba said, through her tears, that she had taken the pills the doctor had given her, but they hadn't helped.

"They were *vitamins*," Dr. Yasmeen said. "The end of menstruation is not something to be cured. You've watched your mother and grandmother and every woman older than you in this village age. Do they ever grow young again? In a few years, Saba, I'll go through the same change. This is God's plan for us; it's not for us to try to alter it."

The suggestion that she was trying to defy God's will quieted Saba for the time being. Like many of the village women, she was pious, or eager to appear so. Her manner suddenly businesslike, she reported that another village woman was selling the pills Dr. Yasmeen had given her.

"Is that so?" the doctor said neutrally.

This was common, Dr. Yasmeen said later, villagers making

all kinds of accusations against one another, often for crimes they themselves committed. Saba's own vitamins would soon appear at the bazaar now that she knew they wouldn't restore her fertility.

Saba seemed to want to talk more, but Dr. Yasmeen ushered her out and called the next patient in. Parveen privately accused her of lacking compassion. Over the next hour, however, as the doctor saw a dozen patients—for ailments including bronchitis, diarrhea, hypertension, anxiety, and epilepsy—Parveen came to see that the doctor couldn't afford indulgence. She had to balance allowing the women to voice their concerns with treating as many as possible. Even though it was a women's clinic, mothers brought their children, for there was nowhere else for them to be treated, which meant that children with coughs and rashes and the runs were squeezed into the rotation too. Other children were simply placed in Parveen's care while their mothers undressed, as if she had flown here from America to babysit. In truth it was the most useful she'd felt since arriving in the village. But when a young woman named Anisa handed Parveen her baby boy, less than a year old, he began to bawl.

"Move him, sing to him," Dr. Yasmeen instructed a touch incredulously, as if she'd never met someone so untutored in infant care. Parveen had spent a lot of time with her nephew, but he'd never made her nervous the way these babies did.

Anisa's baby finally quieted beneath Parveen's bouncing and cooing. She nuzzled his soft head and inhaled his sweet-sour smell, thinking about Ansar, then looked up and gasped at the naked skin of the young mother. Pale as paper, it was splotched with bruises whose sickly gorgeous colors—violet, yellow, puce—were the most vivid thing about her.

"I'm dizzy, I'm tired, I can't breathe well," Anisa said.

Anemic, the doctor said, and she handed Parveen the stethoscope so she could hear the frantic heart for herself. Anemia was almost inevitable, the doctor continued, given how poorly the village women, even those breastfeeding, ate, with a diet of mostly tea, yogurt, and bread, perhaps dipped in a meat broth. She asked Anisa when she'd last eaten meat.

"Many weeks. I don't remember," she answered in a high voice. "We're poor people."

"And your husband? Has he also not had meat for weeks?" There was no hint of sarcasm in Dr. Yasmeen's tone.

"Not much more, but when we can buy meat I give it to him," Anisa said. "He needs strength to work in the fields."

"And you need it to work in the house and feed your child," the doctor said, this time with firmness, trying to transfuse strength into this weakened young woman as another practitioner might transfuse blood. She turned to Parveen. "This is common— they give the best food to their husbands, who then hold the women's fatigue, their inability to complete their household work, against them. You see the result," she said, pointing to the bruises.

"I bruise easily," Anisa said. "He's not a bad man."

Anemics did bruise easily, the doctor conceded, which made judging the strength of Anisa's husband's anger difficult. But he'd been angry enough.

AT LUNCHTIME, THE WOMEN vacated the clinic, and Naseer came in. In the waiting area he spread a mat on which he set kebabs, naan, and cucumbers for the three of them. Parveen, confident in the safety of the meat, consumed more than her share.

Naseer drove her to the village each week, the doctor said, the two of them leaving home at dawn and making sure to return to the highway by dusk. Though traveling the road to the village was excruciating, they used the hours well, discussing her cases and patients. Her great frustration was that, as a male, Naseer wasn't allowed to help her with patients, even though he'd been studying medicine for two years already.

He wanted to be a cardiologist, like his father, Naseer told Parveen, and he hoped to study in America.

"This is his roundabout way of asking if you can help him with this," Dr. Yasmeen said good-humoredly.

"I'll help if I can, but only if you promise to come back to Afghanistan to work," Parveen said to Naseer, then regretted her words. Who was she to decide where he should use his skills? "I'm joking," she added.

"It's my home and I'm needed here," he said, taking her seriously. "Of course I'll come back."

"Maybe you could work in this village," Parveen suggested.

Only someone like him, young and eager for experience, would come live here, Dr. Yasmeen agreed. But the women needed a female doctor, and too few women attended medical school, and even if they did, the culture would not accept them living on their own in a village. Nor was it clear that there was a salary for a doctor here, since Gideon Crane's foundation and the government each claimed the other should pay it. Dr. Yasmeen herself came as a volunteer. "That's why I was hoping you were a doctor or medical student," she told Parveen.

Parveen, self-conscious about having disappointed the doctor, tried to explain why she wasn't pursuing a career in medicine. The problem, she said, was that blood, all bodily fluids, made her queasy. She'd twice fainted as a child when the doctor had drawn blood. She preferred thinking about people to tending to them. In her physical anthropology class, she said, they had studied pictures of Neolithic bones, which demonstrated signs of tuberculosis such as collapsed vertebrae and lesions on the ribs. This fascinated her, the long history of such diseases, the telling traces they left over thousands of years. Why had tuberculosis come to be? How had it spread? Actual disease interested her only insofar as it presented questions like these. The treatment itself was best done by others.

"Like Naseer," she said, hoping to change the subject.

Embarrassed, perhaps, by her referencing him, Naseer fumbled his tea glass, spilling a bit, then spilled more as he leaped up to fetch a towel.

"But I've told you, Naseer can't help here." Dr. Yasmeen sounded exasperated. There was a brief silence, then she returned to her usual good cheer, impressing upon Parveen how extraordinary it was for the villagers to see a woman travel by herself to live among them. "You'll be in their stories for generations," she said, although she acknowledged that those stories might not be true. She herself had assumed, upon hearing that Parveen was coming, that she was meant to be another bride for Waheed. "But now I know that you have a fiancé in America."

Parveen had heard one of the women—who must have learned it from Bina or Shokoh—telling the doctor this, with great authority, as if Parveen weren't standing right there. There was no fiancé, she admitted to Dr. Yasmeen and Naseer, other than the one she'd invented. Seeing their astonishment, she giggled nervously and added, "I made him up so the men here would leave me alone."

There was an odd silence during which she sensed that they were both wondering whether she could be trusted, which made her wonder the same thing about herself.

Dr. Yasmeen stood and began to wrap up the leftover food. "I suppose it's for the best," she said. "This way you won't have villagers trying to marry you. Tell them your fiancé is a frightful man with a militia of his own."

"No one in America has militias. Well, almost no one."

"The villagers don't know that."

Capitalize on their ignorance, she seemed to be saying. Parveen found the notion slightly demeaning to the villagers, which didn't mean she wouldn't take the doctor's advice.

More women came after lunch. Ghazal, who was middle-aged and had a nose so large and magnificent it seemed to precede her into the room, entered and kissed both the doctor and Parveen

74

effusively. She was healthy, she said, patting her girth, and indeed Parveen hadn't seen a stronger-looking woman in the village; it was as if fat and meat had flown from the other women to her. The problem was her husband, she said. Lately he drooped like a dying flower; he had no strength for love. She mimed his failed erection by slowly curling a finger down. "He says he's tired from working so much, but I work and I'm not tired. If he cannot fix this I will have to go to his brother or the neighbor."

"My specialty is women's bodies, not men's," Dr. Yasmeen said, hiding a smile.

"In America there's a medicine to help men with that," Parveen volunteered, then wished she hadn't. She didn't want to make it sound as if America had solved all of its problems, down to erectile dysfunction.

"Ah, so the Americans make missiles as well as bombs," Ghazal quipped with a wicked smile. "Please ask your family to mail some."

Latifa, the woman who entered next, held a girl of less than a year in her arms. Another girl, perhaps a year older than that, toddled behind her, and behind her came yet another, perhaps four years old. And Latifa was three months pregnant. When she put her girls in Parveen's care, the older ones looked wary, as if sensing that Parveen was an outsider.

Latifa didn't know the sex of her unborn child, she told Parveen as the doctor examined her. But she was praying for a boy. Her husband often said he wanted her to bear children until she had one, and she wasn't sure whether he was joking. "As you can see, I've made only girls," she said, giving her brood a crooked smile.

The doctor offered a proverb: "Mothers shake the cradle with one hand and shake the world with the other."

"May it be so," Latifa said, sighing. She sounded unconvinced.

"Your own mother must be so worried about you!" Dr. Yasmeen said to Parveen once Latifa had left.

Not wanting to speak, Parveen nodded and felt the tears come to her eyes. When they began to leak down her face, Dr. Yasmeen hugged her fiercely, asking no questions, and Parveen sagged in her full arms, inhaling her scents of soap, roses, astringent alcohol. At last she described her mother's death. The doctor hugged her again, wiped Parveen's tears with her thumbs, as Parveen's mother used to, and ordered her to write to her father often, even offering to take pictures of her letters and e-mail them. (The Afghan postal service was better internally than one might imagine, she said, but international mail might be dicier.) She would print out and bring Parveen any replies.

Afterward, Parveen felt as if a space in her had opened up, some blockage cleared.

PARVEEN HEARD THE NEXT woman before she saw her, as the sound of unusual, high-pitched breathing entered the room. Unlike the other women, this one waited until she was in the examining room to remove her chadri. A large bump, like a balloon of flesh, swelled in the middle of her neck. Goiter, her ailment was called—a gross enlargement of the thyroid. It was common in the village, Dr. Yasmeen said, as were miscarriages, stillbirths, deafness, and cretinism (a child born with this condition was called *diwana*, "the mad one"), all resulting from a lack of iodine. The Afghans had a name for it, the "sadness sickness," and sadness did drape over this woman, Nadia. Barely able to swallow, she subsisted on yogurt and broth. Her affect was wan, her ribs pronounced. After the examination, she crumpled in a chair, naked but for the dress she clutched over herself.

"As I've said before, you need surgery," Dr. Yasmeen told her gently.

The high pitch of Nadia's breathing intensified.

"But you don't want to leave the village."

"No," Nadia agreed in a whisper.

Parveen asked why the surgery couldn't just be performed at the clinic.

It wasn't her specialty, Dr. Yasmeen said. Nadia needed a surgeon of the head and neck. Then she turned to Nadia to ask what her husband thought.

"That prayers and spells will cure me," Nadia said. The balloon jiggled a bit when she spoke. It was hard to look at but also hard to look away.

"Her husband is the mullah," the doctor explained, then crouched before Nadia and gazed into her eyes. "If I speak to him, will he let you go for the surgery?"

Nadia nodded.

The doctor adjusted herself from squatting to kneeling and took her patient's hand, as if in a parody of a marriage proposal. "And will you go?"

Nadia shook her head.

This was often the case, Dr. Yasmeen said, the women not wanting to leave their husbands or children or houses. They feared the long journey; they feared their honor being compromised.

"I fear I won't come back alive," Nadia rasped.

"MY MOST POWERFUL FEELING, most of the time, is helplessness," the doctor said after Nadia left. She began to tell Parveen about a pregnant woman in the village whom she had been monitoring and treating for preeclampsia, with typical symptoms: high blood pressure, sudden weight gain, swelling, little urine. Then, between the doctor's weekly visits, seizures began. This was an indication that she now had eclampsia, which would affect the placenta and be very dangerous both for her and the baby. But her family, without the doctor there to advise otherwise, believed the seizures indicated that she had become possessed.

Parveen opened her mouth to speak, but Dr. Yasmeen's hand

staved off the interruption. Even if they had known what was wrong with her, what were they to do? They took her to the mullah, Nadia's husband. "He choked her," the doctor said, with anguish, "and he beat her with a small whip to drive out the demons. The djinns." She paused. "He beat a woman who was pregnant and sick." Him, the doctor said, she condemned. Bruises disfigured the woman's neck, legs, and palms when she next came to Dr. Yasmeen. The seizures were continuing. In rural areas women were lost to eclampsia all the time, the doctor knew, so she and Naseer put the woman in their car to take her to a hospital where she could be induced or have a cesarean. The woman was in such grave danger that her family had agreed to let Dr. Yasmeen and Naseer take her.

"But why couldn't you deliver the baby here?" Parveen asked. "In that beautiful operating room."

"A beautiful operating room that has never been used," Dr. Yasmeen replied.

Parveen shook her head. "That's not true. They've done C-sections, fistula repairs, all kinds of things there."

"Who has?"

"I don't know, whoever the doctor was before you, I guess. Gideon Crane said so."

Dr. Yasmeen shrugged. "Well, I haven't done an operation here. I couldn't, because I have no one to do the anesthesia, not even a spinal, and I wouldn't do an operation here anyway because there's no one to give follow-up care, and what happens if an incision opens or becomes infected?" In Afghanistan, C-sections were very rare, she told Parveen, even in Kabul. In villages, they were almost never done. That was not the only time she and Naseer had driven a woman in trouble out of here to get care. "My son has scrubbed blood out of the back seat more than once," Dr. Yasmeen said.

Parveen was confused, but the doctor had more to tell. There was a heaviness to her face as she spoke, and she kept one hand on the exam table. Two hours into the journey with the pregnant patient, just when they reached the highway, the woman died. Parveen pressed her hands to her temples, trying to absorb this. This had happened only eight months ago, Dr. Yasmeen said, and, like Fereshta, the woman had left motherless children behind. Yet beyond the village, her passing had gone unnoticed.

All of these women dying, Parveen thought, their stories buried with them. A life flames out and the darkness rushes in.

"We had to turn around and bring her body home, two hours in the car, on that road, with the corpse of a woman we couldn't save," the doctor finished. "I don't think we spoke. After you pray, what words are left for an end like that? We spent the night in the mosque. By morning she was in the ground."

CHAPTER SIX

TWO MELONS

D R. YASMEEN AND NASEER WERE HURRYING TO PACK UP AND GET on the road when the door to the clinic opened, and a small figure in the head-to-toe green of the chadri glided in. When the garment lifted, Parveen was surprised to see Shokoh. Her panting suggested she had hurried. So stubborn at home, she seemed bashful here, although the doctor was quick to put her at ease. When Parveen explained who Shokoh was, the doctor, despite her eagerness to get on the road, became unhurried, patient. She made small talk, asking Shokoh how it was having a new friend in the house.

Shokoh swiveled in Parveen's direction, and as she did so, her face changed. Her eyes seemed to widen and glow, and a shy smile kept starting and stopping, but it wasn't Parveen she was looking at but Naseer, who in turn was staring at Shokoh's exposed exquisite face, which she made no move to cover. Her gaze, direct and lingering, seemed a radical act, as if within the walls of the clinic, the governing codes of the village had been suspended. And yet also ordinary, poignantly so—two teenagers paralyzed by attraction.

"My son, Naseer," the doctor said matter-of-factly.

When Parveen had asked him, over lunch, if he had a girl-friend, he'd shaken his head, dropping his long lashes. "He needs to finish his studies before marrying," Dr. Yasmeen interjected. "Besides, he only has eyes for his books now. I pity any girl who wants his heart."

When the doctor led Shokoh to the examining room, Parveen followed. The girl's body, small-boned and gently sinewed, was unspoiled by illness, poor diet, labor, or childbirth, other than her hands, which were tanned and chapped. Her stomach was nearly flat and her breasts buoyant. Only a few bruises on her torso and legs marked her milky skin, and Parveen wondered whether they were from a cow's hooves or her husband's hands and how she could find out.

On the examining table, Shokoh kicked her legs playfully and told Dr. Yasmeen that she'd been feeling more tired than normal, making it harder for her to do the milking and other work. Parveen assumed Shokoh was merely hoping the doctor could release her from the demands of Bina, who'd been making her grind wheat into flour, a task she considered tedious. The doctor checked Shokoh's vital signs and asked about her diet and about her relations with Waheed. "As often as he wants," Shokoh said resignedly, and Parveen grimaced. There were times she woke in the night wondering if Waheed was on Shokoh. She didn't want to visualize it, but she couldn't help it.

Shokoh's bleeding was irregular, she said in answer to another of the doctor's questions, but Parveen knew, from a day of listening to the women, that in the village this wasn't unusual. Cycles were easily disrupted by poor nutrition or hard work.

Shokoh dressed, then peppered the doctor with questions, including where she lived. The provincial capital, the doctor said, and Shokoh exclaimed that she was from there too. Did the doctor know her parents? No, the doctor said, laughing; the city had sixty thousand people. But if Shokoh wanted, she'd be happy to contact them.

Shokoh's face constricted and she mumbled that she would think about it.

When Parveen opened the door of the exam room, Naseer was in conversation with Waheed in the waiting room. "Your husband," she whispered to Shokoh, who yanked her chadri all the way down.

The doctor went out first. She told Waheed that Shokoh needed more rest, that she was still a girl, while Shokoh stood silent and immobile, unseen beneath a waterfall of green. Parveen was curious how Waheed would receive the doctor's admonition. Bina, as well as Waheed's own daughters, even those younger than Shokoh, worked harder than she did, and no one insisted on their rest. But he nodded as if to show he understood that possessing such a delicate flower was a prize that came at a cost.

They all walked to the courtyard gate, where the doctor's white car was parked, and Dr. Yasmeen embraced Shokoh in her green polyester envelope. The netting over her eyes made it impossible to tell whether she was looking at Parveen or Naseer. It was the one freedom the chadri bestowed: a woman could look where she wanted.

Behind her stood Waheed, oblivious. Done with talking, he turned and began to walk toward home, knowing that Shokoh would follow.

Dr. Yasmeen opened the door of her car and stared into its interior, sighing as if she were about to climb into her own coffin. She dreaded traveling the road, and yet time and again she did it. This was heroic to Parveen, who hugged the doctor goodbye. Then she ran to catch up with Shokoh, whose hand, from beneath the chadri, fumbled for hers.

This was her first time at the clinic, Shokoh whispered. She'd threatened Bina, saying that if she didn't let her go, she would tell Parveen, who would tell Dr. Gideon, who would be very angry. Bina, frightened, had relented. Parveen was mostly pleased by this. As she'd hoped, she was motivating the women to demand more freedom. She only wished the demand hadn't been made of Bina.

The morning after her visit to the clinic, Shokoh sat against the wall in the main room of the house, pulling the rope to rock the cradle. Her eyes had a faraway look; a smile played at the edges of her mouth. The cradle could have turned over and tumbled Bina's infant out without her noticing. Parveen was certain that Shokoh was dreaming of Naseer.

Despite her constant industriousness, Bina was observant and shrewd. She couldn't account for Shokoh's new degree of abstraction, but she clocked it. "You are more useless than usual today!" she said, and she leaned down to pinch the girl's arm. "Leave this. Go for water."

Shokoh hesitated. She wanted to escape the house, Parveen guessed, but not at the expense of having to lug back the full water jug. When Parveen offered to accompany her, Shokoh leaped to her feet, leaving the cradle rope swinging. The cradle slowed. The baby cried. Zahab, ever helpful, hurried to take Shokoh's place.

Shokoh snatched a chadri off a hook and made a face before slipping it over her head. Did Parveen want one? she asked with exaggerated politeness. Parveen demurred, feeling guilty that she had a choice.

As they left the compound, Parveen was struck, once again, by the view. Each time her eye found something new to praise— today, the stands of poplar trees that punctuated the valley floor, often clustering near the river's gentle curves, their trunks skinny and white, their leaves reflecting an almost silvery-green cast when the wind ruffled through. "Isn't it glorious?" she exclaimed.

"Not when it's the only view you'll ever see," Shokoh said, her voice swimming out from within the fabric.

Parveen kept quiet. Unlike her, Shokoh wasn't here on a lark. A marriage, in Afghanistan, was a life sentence.

"And to think that just last year I was still free," Shokoh said. "I lived in a city! I didn't have to wear this horrible covering whenever I went outside. I was in school. I could go to the shops with my mother or go see relatives or friends. Now if I leave Waheed's house once a week, I'm lucky. They say they're not Taliban, but what's the difference?"

Parveen wasn't sure herself. Because the village wasn't in the Pashtun south, the most conservative part of the country, she hadn't anticipated how homebound its women would be—hadn't expected that they would have to cover themselves completely when they left the house. Crane hadn't mentioned that. Then again, the village commander had fought for the Taliban, so perhaps it wasn't surprising after all.

As they walked toward the river, Parveen carrying the empty jug, they came upon Ghazal, of the imperious nose, berating one of her sons for letting their donkey wander off while he played with his friends. "The donkey has more sense than you!" she said as the boy cowered. "He came home and asked for breakfast. So I gave him yours! He even sat in your spot."

The boy's eyes grew enormous, and Ghazal laughed and tousled his hair.

"Even the commander's scared of her," Shokoh said, giggling.

They walked on, and Shokoh's story came in fits and starts. Waheed was her father's distant cousin, she said. Most likely he had seen her at a family wedding a year or two earlier, although, given the hundreds of relatives who'd attended, she had no memory of him. Her branch of the family had once lived in this village but it had left several generations ago. Now they resided in a bustling city where there were schools, a hospital, hotels, and people who didn't live with animals.

When her mother told her that Waheed had come to ask for her hand, she laughed. "I was still playing with dolls," she said. In villages, girls were considered marriageable early, but she was a city girl, still in school. She'd seen the internet, she told Parveen, by way of telegraphing her sophistication. She would never marry an old goat and go live in a village. It was unthinkable—but only to her.

While her family had escaped this village, they hadn't escaped poverty. Thirty years of war in Afghanistan had made sure of that. Her father worked at a government office, but his salary was low and the family large: Shokoh and three younger siblings, her mother, her unemployed uncle's family, her grandparents. Many months her father's salary wasn't paid. Waheed's proposal, while unexpected, also came with an unexpectedly generous bride-price, and so, although he was less educated than Shokoh and more than twice her age, the offer was hard to refuse. Her twelve-year-old sister could take her place as their mother's main helper in the house. Her father had sold her, in her words, into a life where there were no books to read, no paper to write on, no pencils to hold, only cow teats to grip. She was married to a man who was not only too old for her but also illiterate and dirty, who smelled of the fields and poked his corncob in her all the time.

"The day I came here," Shokoh said, flicking her hand at the valley, "my dreams died."

Parveen asked if her mother had agreed to this.

"It didn't matter whether she agreed."

"But surely your parents loved you."

They did or they didn't; another thing that didn't matter. Now Parveen understood why Shokoh had looked so conflicted at the doctor's offer to communicate with her parents. As Parveen had learned from Bina, when Afghan girls married, they often never saw their parents again, since the bride moved to her husband's home. Shokoh hadn't seen her parents since her wedding. Waheed would decide when or if she could. Parveen wondered how Shokoh's parents would tell this story.

When Shokoh had arrived in the village, she said, it was winter, a season she didn't think she would survive. Day and night she huddled by the woodstove and cried as the life of the house went on around her and the snow mounted outside the windows. Secretly she hoped that if she was troublesome enough, they would send her home, but this didn't happen. She was always cold and the air always smoky, and she felt that not just her lungs but her very soul was being tarnished. Soon sick, she ached for her mother, for anyone, to nurse her, but no one did. If Bina seemed fierce with her now, it was nothing compared to those early days. "Two melons cannot fit in one hand," Bina had muttered under her breath more than once, giving a dark twist to a common proverb. She accused Shokoh of faking her illness. At her worst moments, Shokoh said, she had prayed that the sickness would kill her. There was so little connection between the life she had left and this one that she was convinced that only one was real; the other was surely a dream. But which was which?

The sole mercy was that Waheed had never beaten her, not even when she raged at him or crawled away from him in the night. (She no longer bothered, she said, finding it easier just to get it over with.) This set him apart from many of the village men, who struck their wives at the slightest provocation. Waheed was prepared to wait her out.

But he wasn't nearly as different from the other village men as Shokoh's father had thought. Waheed had shown him "Dr. Gideon's book," which contained that picture of him with Crane. This had convinced Shokoh's father that Waheed was important. "Silly man," Shokoh said of her father. He couldn't read English to know what the book said.

Waheed had also boasted about being the only man in the village with a generator. Shokoh's father deluded himself into believing that she would still be able to study at night. But other than Dr. Gideon's book and the Quran, there were barely any books in the village, let alone in the house, nor was there a school for girls her age. When would she study, anyway, since all of her time was now conscripted by domestic work?

They'd reached the river, where the air was cooler. The water revealed every rock beneath. Shokoh knelt to fill the jug.

"When I'm out in the village, under my chadri," she said, "I look at the faces of other men and wonder what they'd be like as husbands. Some, maybe, are a little less ugly, others a little fatter. Some are younger. But otherwise they all seem like Waheed."

Parveen waited, sensing what was to come.

"The doctor's son—he has education. He lives in a city. Seeing him—I felt…"

Just that: *I felt*. There was something about the chadri that allowed for the discharge of greater intimacies, Parveen thought. Passion, shame, desire—all were hidden behind cloth.

Shokoh asked Parveen if Naseer had a wife, and on hearing that he didn't, she demanded that Parveen tell her everything she'd learned about him. Parveen relayed what she knew—that Naseer wanted to study in America, that he loved gadgets and machines, that he didn't have a girlfriend. But it seemed dangerous to feed a crush that could fester but never progress. Maybe she should be trying to persuade Shokoh to accept her unhappy lot.

But suddenly Parveen herself was sixteen again, looking out her bedroom window at the back alley, where, out of his parents' disapproving sight, Omar, a boy from the building next door, was changing from a conservative polo shirt and khakis into the motorcycle pants he preferred. Omar was eighteen. Parveen liked those motorcycle pants, and she liked the boy who wore them even more—she could still summon the shortness of breath she'd felt whenever they'd spoken. (Even if, as she learned later, to him she was only the smart girl next door.) What would it feel like to experience that tingle at the sight of someone, the compulsive need to say or hear his name, and already be married to a man more than twice your age, with no prospect of escape? Overcome with pity for Shokoh, Parveen wished she could spirit her out of the village, then wondered at her own impulse to be a savior.

"Naseer is very nice to his mother," she said finally. "And

also very clumsy." She imitated him spilling his tea, which made Shokoh laugh.

Parveen bent to splash her face; the water, descended from the snowy peaks far above, was bracing. Shokoh lifted her chadri and splashed her own face, then, seeing Parveen's surprise—there were men passing nearby—gave a saucy smile. "The village isn't quite as strict as everyone wants you to believe," she said, though she made sure to keep her eyes on Parveen, not the men. "I don't think women here even wore chadris much until outsiders started to build the clinic."

Parveen confirmed this later with Bina. When she'd first come to the village, Bina said, women rarely covered their faces, even in the presence of unrelated men. But when strangers began to arrive to help with or visit the clinic, the mullah, or maybe the commander, said that these people shouldn't be seeing the faces of their wives. The tailor started to stock more chadris, and he did a good business. Half the men in the village now insisted this was the way it had always been.

So this was why Crane hadn't mentioned the chadris. They hadn't really been worn when he was first here. His effort to help the women of the village had led to their greater cloistering, Parveen thought with consternation. Was idealism an experiment whose variables couldn't be controlled? She'd pondered how the village might change her but never given a thought to how she might change the village.

Now Parveen noticed the other women at the river also had their chadris pulled up. They'd been watching her—she was still a novelty—and when she smiled, just to be friendly, they began to approach.

Among them was an old woman Parveen had met briefly the previous day. She'd hobbled into the clinic's courtyard, then propped herself up beneath its single tree, leaning on the trunk for support. She looked a bit like a gnarled ancient tree herself, her spine twisted, her fingers tuberous, the backs of her hands spotted with brown as fungi patched bark. She was the dai, a title commonly rendered in English as "traditional birth attendant." For half a century she'd been delivering the village's babies. Parveen didn't learn her name; everyone simply called her "the dai."

The number of deliveries the dai had made would remain forever a mystery, for, being fully illiterate, she kept no records. This also meant there was no telling how many mothers or infants had perished along the way. Happy outcomes, tragic ones; all were fate, she believed, which was why she obstinately refused all efforts by Dr. Yasmeen to impart instruction or provide medicine that might save more women. To the dai the doctor was competition, and the dai would triumph using history, superstition, and, most of all, endurance. Her tenure testified to this. The doctor came and went. The dai never left.

She'd barely spoken to Dr. Yasmeen other than to greet her in a crinkly voice that seemed to contain a laugh. But now, by the river, she began to talk to Parveen, telling her how she had been married as a girl and borne five children, then lost her husband to illness. He had no brothers, meaning there was no one to marry her, no man to care for her brood. She had to work, and she believed she had a gift for bringing babies through the passage and into the world. She knew how to comfort the women; she knew the power of the herbs and where they grew; she knew the spells. "The lady doctor couldn't chase off the evil eye if it was staring her in the face," the dai said, although Parveen hadn't mentioned Dr. Yasmeen. The dai began defending herself against the doctor's imagined criticism. Who else had been there for the women, day and night, year after year, in winter as well as spring? she asked, not waiting for a reply. It wasn't her fault she'd been denied an education. And the clinic had changed nothing in the village. In the lonely hours when labor began, often at night, with a blanket of darkness over the village, the dai was still the only one there for the women. The only light, as she put it.

But the clinic had saved many women's lives, Parveen said.

Name them, the dai said, smiling, her mouth a checker-board of yellowed teeth and blackish gaps. Parveen, to her great frustration, couldn't remember the names, if Crane had even mentioned them. But they'd had cesarean sections, she said, and blood transfusions, and—

"Find me a woman who says the clinic saved her," the dai taunted. "Then I will believe you." No, the clinic had never done much of anything. Crane's foundation had sent a male doctor, whom the men of the village, but not its women, were happy to see. He didn't stay long. Ever since, only Issa had come, to maintain the equipment. "The machines have a doctor," the dai joked, "even if the women don't." At least Dr. Yasmeen unlocked it once a week now—the dai gave her that.

Parveen didn't like being baited by this unlettered woman, and she determined that she would find women the clinic had saved. What the dai said couldn't be true. Crane, in his TED Talk, had been so definitive about the clinic's accomplishments. And yet the dai also seemed certain, and Dr. Yasmeen had implied something similar. Was it possible that Crane's staff—Issa, most likely—had exaggerated or lied about what was happening at the clinic? Crane needed eyes and ears in the village, and Parveen would provide them. At the very least he should know that the doctor was not being paid and that women were still dying; for Parveen, this was the greatest shock.

In the meantime, she would defend Crane as if her own reputation were being assailed. "Dr. Gideon has done so much for the women of Afghanistan," she told the dai. "Don't make fun of his work until you've done as much."

"Be careful!" Ghazal warned Parveen. "She'll put a spell on you."

Unsure if this was a joke, Parveen told Shokoh they should go and hefted the full water jug. But it was as heavy as a small child, and Parveen was soon short of breath, and when Shokoh offered to take it, she didn't object.

CHAPTER SEVEN

A FLOWER HAS
NO FRONT OR BACK

THE FOLLOWING DAY, HER FIRST FRIDAY IN THE VILLAGE, PARVEEN went to the mosque for prayers. To be precise, she stood outside it. Friday prayers were for men, Waheed had made clear when she asked. Whatever "third sex" status she had at his house or elsewhere in the village didn't extend to its sacred spaces. Nonetheless, she moved toward the entrance after the men had gone in. She wasn't especially religious and never went to mosque at home in protest against the segregation of the sexes there. Here protest pushed her to try entry even though it was riskier. Having until now been treated more or less like the men, she wanted all of their rights.

Compared to the clinic, the mosque was almost ridiculously humble, a single story built from mud bricks. It was surrounded by a low wall and topped by a stubby minaret from which, five times a day, the mullah broadcast the call to prayer. Now he emerged from its precincts: a petite man with a bulbous black turban and a thick scar, shiny as a snail track, down his cheek. He wouldn't meet Parveen's eyes, even as he demanded to know her destination. Despite his rudeness she greeted him as politely as possible and introduced herself.

"I know who you are," he said, and again he asked where she was going.

"To the clinic," Parveen lied.

"It's Friday, it's not open," he said. "Nothing is open. I think it's Waheed's house you're going to." He pointed in that general direction and waited for her to turn.

Seething inside, she pretended to comply, walking slowly away, tossing a few glances back over her shoulder to see that he was still watching her. She couldn't stop thinking of his abuse of the pregnant woman with eclampsia, couldn't stop looking at his hands—small, pale, gnarled—and imagining them around a woman's neck. The double standard galled her; it was fine for the mullah to touch a woman in order to choke her but not for Crane to touch Fereshta to help her?

Until the mullah was safely inside the mosque she waited in the empty bazaar, then, feeling faintly ridiculous, walked over to the building to listen. The mullah was one of the forces, maybe the primary one, holding women back in the village. It was important to know what he was saying.

He wasn't hard to hear, as if he was amplifying his voice to compensate for his size. His sermon included a story about a village where an outsider brings in a disease that infects all the inhabitants. At first, thinking he was referencing the Europeans who'd brought smallpox to the New World, Parveen was impressed by his cosmopolitanism. Then she realized, with mortification, that she herself was his subject. The disease in question was immorality, spread by women in "Western dress" (if only he could see what passed for Western dress, or dress at all, in Berkeley). The danger, he said, was that the women of the village would take sick with the desire for freedom, the belief that it was fine to abandon their families and live among strangers.

When it became clear the prayers were nearly over, she scuttled away from the mosque and toward the bazaar. Waheed and

Jamshid found her outside the tailor's shop. She told Waheed, as if she'd just spent all of Friday prayers thinking it over, that she wanted to have some clothes made. "Clothes like Bina and the others wear," she clarified, not mentioning the mullah's sermon.

She was reminded, with some discomfiture, of an earlier transformation, during her first seminar with Professor Banerjee. Back then, feeling her professor sizing her up, Parveen had imagined a hint of disappointment in her gaze. Parveen was in her full California-girl phase, or rather the cliché of a California girl; she'd arrived at Berkeley with pale streaks in her hair, artful rips in her artificially faded jeans, hot pink on her lips, none of which was remarkable in Union City. But the friends she was making and the people, such as her professor, whom she admired dressed minimally, almost severely. Over that semester, she let her hair revert to its natural near black, traded her ripped jeans for intact black ones, dialed down the lipstick color, and bought a secondhand black pleather jacket (actual leather being out of her budget), all in an attempt to be taken seriously by Professor Banerjee and the other students in the class. It struck her, even at the time, that there was no self, no core, unshaped by others, that from the moment you're conscious that you're being viewed, you're being molded. Here was another reminder of that.

When the tailor reopened his stall, Parveen searched among several bolts of fabric standing against a middle shelf. She chose a terra-cotta hatched with black *X*s, then remembered that she hadn't brought money. Waheed said that he would settle with the tailor—her three months of rent, it seemed, had made him feel flush—and have Bina make the clothes. Parveen grimaced; this would give Bina another reason to resent her. No, she insisted, she would repay him, and the tailor should make the clothes.

"Fine," Waheed said. "Then he'll have to measure you."

As soon as he said this, Parveen guessed that she'd made a mistake, that having a male tailor take a women's dimensions simply wasn't done. But it was too late. Pretending nonchalance, she stood still while the tailor, embarrassed, applied the tape measure loosely so as not to touch her.

As they walked home, Parveen let on that she'd heard some of the mullah's sermon and that she knew it was about her.

Waheed laughed, then said, "He also likes to speak against me. When he talks about beggars becoming kings, that is me." There was something like pride in his voice.

Parveen asked what the mullah meant by that.

"I'm not as poor as I once was," Waheed said. "Not everyone likes that."

When they arrived at the compound, Waheed went upstairs, leaving Parveen in the courtyard with Jamshid. She went to the outhouse; he was still there, scuffing his feet in the dirt, when she came out. Newly hatched chickens, tiny downy clouds, were following one another around the courtyard, and he picked one up and handed it to her to hold. The donkey rolled in the dust. The breeze rippled through the drying laundry. Parveen, stroking the soft chick, was, for a moment, content. He and Bilal were going to take the livestock up to the meadow to graze, Jamshid finally said. Did Parveen want to come? He glanced at her as he said this, his shoulders hunching up toward his ears.

She wondered if she should ask Waheed's permission to go on this venture. But he wasn't her father or the arbiter of what was allowed in the village. "I'd love to," she said, both uneasy and excited about this possibly illicit trip.

The spry goats took the lead, followed by the donkey, while the cows brought up the rear. Leaving the houses behind, they took a narrow path that led up the slope. Above them a falcon turned, having detected their movement below. The path faded—the animals led the way around boulders—then returned, snaking upward. The plant life grew hardier at these heights, gripping on to bits of soil or emerging from cracks between rocks veined with rose quartz and verdigris.

It was afternoon, the day's peak heat past, but although the air cooled as they climbed, the exercise warmed Parveen. She realized how, cooped up in Waheed's house, she'd missed moving her body. The yoga mat had been used only to protect her bed from goat and chicken droppings.

In college, she'd jogged at least three times a week in the Berkeley Hills. The landscape had been exotic to her, a dirt track lined with silvery sagebrush and manzanita, mugwort and mule's ear, and, in one cool stretch, a row of eucalyptus trees with that pungent vaporous scent so vivid that it strung together, as if on a necklace, all the moments of her life in which she had encountered it. High in the hills, she felt she could really breathe. But the Berkeley Hills, while technically mountains, topped out under two thousand feet. The village's elevation was nearly double that, and these mountains stretched two or three times as high again. They were geologic epics, composed across millennia. After half an hour of ascension, they all passed through a gap and into an alpine meadow carpeted with wild grasses and flowers. At its edge it gave way to a vast plain of pale blue sky with the mountains rippling into the distance. Parveen, elated, extended her arms wide, as if to embrace the view.

The animals settled to their grazing. Parveen sat on a flat rock that still held the day's warmth, and Jamshid stretched out on his back nearby, propping himself up on his elbows. They stayed like that for a while, not speaking.

Bilal wandered off, and Parveen asked Jamshid about the boy's missing hand. It had been an accident, two years ago, Jamshid said. Bilal had been trying to help with the harvest and had sliced his left forearm with a scythe. The damage was so severe that the only choice was to remove the limb from the forearm down, leaving a sheared-off stump, knobby with scar tissue. Parveen shuddered at the pain he must have suffered. Already she felt affection for the boy. His large eyes, a mellow brown, dominated his face. His smile came rarely, which made it all the more lovely. He was observant and quiet, lacking the boisterousness and toughness that even the younger children possessed.

"You'll get used to looking at it," Jamshid said. "We all did." It had been hardest for his father. "He loves Bilal too much."

Parveen pondered this phrasing. Was there a danger in loving too much? "Your family has suffered a lot," she observed.

"Every family suffers a lot, at least in Afghanistan. Maybe not in America."

Not as much, she said. There was no war and much less hunger. But loss and grief, they were everywhere. Her mother had died too, she told him. From cancer, three years ago. Motherless children were a morose yet tight-knit tribe, she'd found, and she hoped that her disclosure might establish a bond with Jamshid. From the way he looked at her, as if truly seeing her for the first time, it had.

"I'm sorry, may she rest in peace," he said.

She asked Jamshid what he remembered of his mother.

"One day we had a mother, and the next we didn't; I didn't have time to memorize her." Parveen turned his words over. She'd had lots of time, months at least, to "memorize" her mother, but had it worked? The images she'd stored shifted in and out of focus all the time.

"This meadow was her favorite place," Jamshid said.

Parveen's first emotion, which she quelled, was a thrill at this glimpse of the dead Fereshta. "She came here often?"

Jamshid laughed. How could his mother have come here often? She'd been working all the time. But she came sometimes, he said, once he could walk. His sister Hamdiya, she would carry. Mostly it was to bring the animals. But sometimes as a family they came here for picnics. "Not much," he said, "just bread and leeks. Or walnuts and mulberries, like the mujahideen live on in the mountains." At his effort to sound tough, Parveen stifled a smile. "We had very little food then, much less than now. But we never thought about our stomachs up here."

Across the meadow Bilal was bending, then moving, then bending again, picking flowers with his single hand. Jamshid watched him too.

"I was the oldest. I would help my mother, when I wasn't making trouble for her. I could be very naughty," he said almost apologetically, but he insisted his mother had never scolded him. Parveen wondered if this was true or if it was just the haze of loss softening the edges. "She'd put me in charge of the younger ones. Mostly I just let them play in the dirt." He smiled at this. "She loved flowers. Bilal gets that from her."

"Was she like Bina?" Parveen asked, thinking of Bina's fondness for flowers.

Jamshid shook his head scornfully. Sometimes he didn't believe they were really sisters, he said.

Parveen had seen him take umbrage at Bina's treatment of Shokoh, if only Waheed wasn't around. Just that morning, Bina had sniped at Shokoh for forgetting to mind one of Bina's toddlers, and Jamshid had protested that it wasn't Shokoh's child.

"Shokoh isn't my child," Bina had countered, "yet I must take care of her."

"You're mean because you're jealous," Jamshid blurted.

"Oh yes, I'm jealous that she has a boy with no beard in love with her," Bina said, and Jamshid had fled in embarrassment.

"You didn't want your father to marry Bina," Parveen ventured now. She felt, unexpectedly, a little sorry for Bina.

"When has what I want mattered to my father?" Jamshid said. "'Feelings are like air to earth,' he says. Not solid. They do nothing to feed you." Besides, he added, Bina's coming was good for his sisters. Until she arrived, they'd had to do all the work his mother used to do.

Parveen shifted off her rock and lay down on the grass. She nibbled at a piece of it and briefly closed her eyes, lulled by the soft tickle of the air and the mellow afternoon light. How long had they been up here? Time had dropped away. When she was a child her family had sometimes taken day trips to the coast. The ocean's thunder and sparkle had thrilled her, but its monotony, its endlessness, had terrified her. The grandeur, the gravity, of the mountains was, for her, more profound, more provoking of ecstasy. For all their poverty, these two brothers were rich in a way she'd never thought to covet.

"I was there when she died," Jamshid said suddenly. "I heard it."

Parveen snapped to attention. He hadn't been near Fereshta when she died. Crane had taken her from the village to a hospital. But the agony she experienced before that had probably been seared into Jamshid's brain, and it wasn't surprising that a nine-year-old boy desperate to understand what had happened and trying to cling to his lost mother any way he could would mix things up. This grieved Parveen, but she saw no reason to correct him, nor was it her place. He was sitting up, arms wrapped around his knees, watching Bilal. Jamshid looked badly in need of a hug, but he seemed too old for one from her, which made her sad too.

"I'm so sorry," she told him. "You were too young to have that happen." After her own mother died, she added, she'd had all kinds of dreams where reality and fantasy seemed to mix. In one, for example, her mother was explaining to her and her sister how to cure her cancer, as if there were a recipe that they had failed to follow correctly. When he simply nodded, still glum, she tried to lift his mood. "You must be glad that the clinic is named for her."

"Yes, my mother died, and I must thank the American," Jamshid replied with unexpected heat.

Parveen said softly, "It's not Gideon Crane's fault she died." But to a child it would have seemed simple: an American took his mother away, and she never came back. He wouldn't be aware of the role the men in his village had played or how his own father had allowed his mother to die. Parveen wondered whether, at some point, she should explain this to Jamshid. He would be angry at Waheed. Did she want him to be? It wasn't fair for him to blame Crane.

The sky was turning pink, and vermilion backlit the clouds. Bilal returned with his bouquet, a ragged but glorious mix of scarlet, yellow, fuchsia, and blue, and presented it to Parveen. Him, she could hug, and when she did, he smiled bashfully. Later, in her room, she pressed the flowers between the pages of *Mother Afghanistan*, then turned the book over to inspect Crane's author photo. His pale blue eyes gazed out at her; she'd never noticed before, but they weren't exactly aligned, the left one slightly cast off into the distance while the right looked straight ahead. It was an imperfection that somehow seemed an advantage, as if he had a wide range of vision than everyone else. That night she wrote to him detailing everything she'd learned about the clinic.

THE TRIP TO THE meadow emboldened Parveen, and in the following days she started to venture farther on her own. In a house with a dozen inhabitants, she needed, on occasion, to escape. Although she'd given up many luxuries without complaint, she insisted on solitude. But it was awkward, always, leaving. The first few times Bina or Shokoh had asked where she was going. "For a walk," she said, unsure whether to invite them. They couldn't go as far as her; they couldn't leave their duties. She felt guilty about this, but not enough to stay home.

She began to wander regularly through the lanes of the village, down to the fields and orchards, up the slopes, though never as far as the meadow on her own. Each walk made her face less surprising to the villagers, more a feature of the landscape, so that eventually she was left alone. Her powers of observation grew microscopic. She noticed, as she climbed, the spring of tiny pink alpine flowers from a mountain crevice that had been bald just days before, or the lilac blossoms foaming from scree. Wild irises of a deep magenta. Wild geraniums, violet or pale pink. For plants she couldn't name she made lists of adjectives: *spiny, woolly, prickly, showy.* Leaves toothed or smooth. Stems fat or thin, hairy or nude. Weeds like unbrushed hair or brazen scarlet colonizers of wheat fields. She lost—gave—countless minutes to watching mother birds feed hatchlings and carry white balls of waste from the nest. Without the pressure to extract moments or memories and offer them up for consumption to friends, she found that time slowed, became sinuous.

She had been returned, almost overnight, to a pre-digital life, as if she had traveled back in time to 1990, or even 1930. In her first week there'd been a withdrawal period during which her yearnings for the constant drip of news from other lives, for diversion, was strong. She could feel it physically, a low-level irritability, this ache for more than what the present contained, for relief from the tedium of a given moment. But the immediate moment—the people in front of her, the experience she was having, her own thoughts, her own imagination—was all she had, and slowly her brain adjusted to this. Everything around her began to take on a startling vividness. Simultaneity, multitasking, that quintessential condition of twenty-first-century life in America, was no longer possible. Every channel was off but the one deliverable by her five senses and her own mind.

Her mind stilled, a tranquility derived as much from what wasn't in the village as what was. There were no cars, for one thing, no blaring horns, blasting radios, cursing drivers, backfires, traffic, or exhaust. A car door slamming here sounded like an explosion. No music, for another. Parveen's mother had once said to her father, as they trailed in the wake of a teenager leaking noise from his headphones, "Do you remember when you could walk around playing music only by holding an instrument?" In the village, it was still that time.

On the way back to Waheed's compound, she would sweep her hand along the village walls, dry and smooth, almost the texture of hands themselves, and try to imagine living within enclosures built by one's ancestors and that still, beneath layers of repair, held traces of their touch. Throughout the day the walls were repainted by shifts in the sun's position overhead—warm sand, then ocher, then amber. They were as smooth to the eye as they were to the hand. The village had no visual clutter. No billboards, no advertisements, no graffiti. No names on street signs, no numbers on the homes. The village was washed clean of words. What use did the villagers have for writing? Most of them didn't know how to read, and anyway they didn't need such guidance in the village where they'd lived their whole lives. The map of this place, the location of each family compound, had been laid down in every head in childhood, probably around the time language was. They could no more forget how the village was arranged than they could forget how to talk.

For Parveen the absence of written words was at first a shock. From the time she could read, she'd read everything that had passed before her eyes. Didn't everyone? she thought. It wasn't even a choice; reading was perhaps the only learned behavior that became as involuntary as breathing. It couldn't be un-learned, couldn't be switched off, she couldn't *not* read what was put in front of her: GOT MILK? on a passerby's T-shirt; GOT JUNK? on a speeding truck. Most of the time she wasn't even aware she was doing it. Her eyes flickered or jerked to wherever the words were, funneling them up to her brain to be sorted then mostly tossed. She passed newspaper racks and magazine stands, inhaling headlines on the move. She read when she went to the bathroom: PLEASE DISCARD SANITARY NAPKINS IN THE RECEPTACLE PROVIDED. EMPLOYEES MUST WASH HANDS BEFORE RETURNING TO WORK. She read when she walked down the street: STOP. 25 MPH. NO SMOKING. NO SKATEBOARDING. PLEASE USE OTHER DOOR. PLEASE USE REVOLVING DOOR. TENANTS ONLY. EMPLOYEES ONLY. NO

TRESPASSING. NO PARKING. VIOLATORS WILL BE TOWED. She read when she went to a restaurant or a supermarket or a movie or a class or on a drive. She read advertisements on billboards, on the sides of buses, on lampposts (in Berkeley, especially on lampposts). It was chaff, most of it. Word waste. She read it anyway. Her eyes were not her own, which was why only now could she truly see the blizzard of letters and digits she had lived in back home, the constant barrage of information and images to metabolize or ignore, process or discard. Only now did she feel, in the absence of this constant assault, how much work, how much filtering, her brain had been doing to withstand it. And that wasn't even counting the internet, that endless virtual bazaar, flat and bottomless at the same time.

She wrote a condensed version of this to Professor Banerjee. The response, which Dr. Yasmeen delivered a couple of weeks later, came in the slashing script familiar from seminar papers where it had accused Parveen of sophistry, insufficiently interrogating the hegemony of the gaze, and other intellectual crimes. Now Professor Banerjee worried that Parveen was romanticizing the village's pre-literate state. (She remembered, with a twinge, how she had recoiled at the DVDs in the bazaar, feeling that they didn't belong here.) Who in the village *could* read? Professor Banerjee asked. And to whose benefit was the illiteracy of the rest? What structures did the lack of knowledge hold in place as mortar holds bricks?

She received another letter too, this one, to her delight, form Gideon Crane. He was distressed by her report, he said, but in his experience, all those years ago, the dai wasn't the most reliable witness. Whatever was happening now, he knew that in the past the clinic had saved many women. Perhaps, as he was distracted by building more clinics and having to raise more funds (he'd been on the road for almost six months now and had missed the birthdays of both his daughter and his wife), the original clinic had suffered for a lack of attention. He would send someone to investigate or would come himself, and in the meantime he encouraged Parveen to keep writing to him. "Your idealism is an inspiration to me," he finished.

The praise warmed her. She imagined him coming to investigate and to meet the young woman who was so zealous about safeguarding his mission. She saw herself, clipboard in hand, translating for Crane as he spoke to Dr. Yasmeen and the village women about the clinic's history. She heard him praising her in his talks back home for saving him from the mendacity of his trusted lieutenant. Perhaps he would even include her in an updated version of *Mother Afghanistan*. Her faith had been restored.

Chapter Eight

Farther from Home

About two weeks into Parveen's stay, Shokoh began to vomit—mostly, but not always, in the morning. Parveen suspected the cause and was sure Bina did too. But they didn't discuss it beyond Parveen suggesting that Shokoh should return to the clinic and Bina agreeing. Only Shokoh seemed clueless.

Again Shokoh arrived at the clinic after the other women had gone, and again she boldly showed her face to Naseer, who again seemed undefended against her beauty. She entered the examining room glowing, heady with her effect on him. Dr. Yasmeen greeted her, listened to her symptoms, then asked her to urinate in a cup. Thinking this a joke, Shokoh laughed. The doctor raised her eyebrows and showed Shokoh how to do it while asking Parveen to hold up her dress. Afterward, Shokoh solemnly handed the cup to the doctor, mirth in her eyes. But minutes later, when Dr. Yasmeen had performed the confirming pregnancy test and delivered the news, Shokoh's face was defeated and white.

The baby would arrive in winter, the doctor told her. She was more than two months along. Yasmeen looked as downcast as Parveen felt. A child would be the final ligament binding Shokoh to Waheed, to his house and village. And the birth would be, as it was for every girl whose pelvic bones weren't yet fully developed, a trial.

"But Waheed told my father I could study," Shokoh whispered. Her naïveté—the belief that such an assurance was somehow contraceptive—tore at Parveen. So did her hopeful next question: "So I don't need to do any more housework?" As if Bina would spare her!

The doctor explained that for now she could carry on with regular activities as long as she made sure to eat well and rest.

"You should write to your parents," the doctor urged.

Shokoh, her eyes wet, shook her head, then nodded, then shook her head again. After a brief checkup she put her chadri on. Dr. Yasmeen nodded at Parveen to follow her. The girl trudged through the waiting room with her head bent, not even glancing at Naseer. It was as if she now belonged to this place, this village, and could no longer consider herself better than it. They walked home mostly in silence.

A hundred feet from the house, Shokoh stopped. When she spoke, her voice shook. "I will be like Fereshta or Bina, won't I? Child after child after child until I die."

Any possible words of comfort Parveen could think of seemed false. Again the notion of helping Shokoh escape came to her, a vision as absurd as it was unshakable.

It fell to Parveen to tell Waheed, since Shokoh seemed unable to speak. He was delighted by the news, as if this were his first, not his tenth, child, there being no apparent limit on the number he wanted. Parveen feared, on Shokoh's behalf, Bina's reaction, wondering what new cruelty her jealousy might spur her to. But Bina's face went as soft as Parveen had seen it. She kissed Shokoh three times and said that now there was much she would understand. Shokoh would know how it felt to care for another life more than her own.

*　　*　　*

THAT NIGHT, BENEATH THE single bright bulb, Shokoh did write, in a script so tiny it thwarted any attempt at reading by others. The children watched her but she made no effort to teach them. She allowed only Bilal, of whom she was fond, to use the pencils that she had brought from home and carefully hoarded. Parveen felt especially bad for Hamdiya, who tried to shuffle closer to Shokoh, only to be driven off with a scowl. Just two years younger than Shokoh, she clearly craved her as an older sister, a friend. There seemed to be so many possible configurations of unhappiness within this one family.

Using his remaining hand, his right, Bilal drew picture after picture of birds. To conserve the paper Shokoh dispensed, he worked on a very small scale, creating pages dense on both sides with avian life. Later, as Bilal and Parveen walked in the village or the mountains, he would show Parveen some of his real-life favorites—golden or azure, red-tailed or white-throated—and imitate their calls. Others he had invented. Birds were all he ever drew.

As for Shokoh, Parveen asked her the next day, while she was milking the cows, what she wrote.

Poetry, Shokoh said, and, after making sure that Bina was nowhere nearby, she recited fragments:

I keep hidden that
Thistles line my soul

Only when the light goes and
Night comes am I at home

These walls are mountains
Too high to be climbed

The falcon swallowed me
I flew in darkness

The hour of my wedding was time enough
To cross from child to old woman

And this, written the previous night:

My own cage
Grows within me

Shokoh milked as she spoke. Her face was averted and her voice flat. But Parveen was enthralled by the lines—their raw emotion, their play with images and language, their subversion. She told Shokoh her poems should be published so people could read them. Parveen imagined a joint book tour during which she would give interviews about instantly recognizing the girl's gift and be credited with having discovered the Afghan Emily Dickinson. Perhaps her father could write the introduction to the book; this would be good for his career and his confidence. Shokoh was present in this fantasy but blurry and rather silent unless Parveen was translating for her.

"Yes, I'm sure many people want to know about this life," Shokoh said, nodding savagely toward her hands, which were working the udders.

Into Parveen's mind intruded a memory of college boys manipulating video-game consoles. These irruptions always came suddenly, violently, as if her subconscious was still reconciling itself to being transplanted to this village. Parveen pushed the image off.

Lots of people would want to know, she insisted. All of the people who had read Gideon Crane's book, for example—they cared about the village. They didn't want to learn about its women only after they were dead. Her professor's words came to her: *I would read Fereshta's story told by Fereshta.*

Shokoh had talent, Parveen said. She should develop it, put it to use.

"You're not in America anymore!" Shokoh retorted. "This is Afghanistan. Not a place where a woman can do anything—fly to the moon or whatever. I can barely go to the river alone. For us, this is a prison without bars, and what good does it do me for you to come here and pretend otherwise? Better to tear up all of those silly poems."

Taken aback, Parveen weighed her words, hesitant to provoke Shokoh again. *Reconcile yourself to our reality*, Shokoh was telling her, but that was exactly what Parveen didn't want to do. She wanted Shokoh to believe that more was possible, that her life mattered. Again she brought up *Mother Afghanistan*. Did Shokoh know much about the book? she asked.

Shokoh had seen it when Waheed showed it to her father. In Waheed's house, it was kept in the aluminum trunk, and Bina had instructed Shokoh, as well as the children, never to touch it. "As if I want to," Shokoh sniffed.

Parveen said she had her own copy, and she went to fetch it from her room.

When she returned with it, Shokoh paused in her milking and wiped her hands on her dress. Then she took the book from Parveen and flipped with authority backward and forward through the pages, even though she couldn't read a word of English. She pored over the photos in the insert: Crane as a boy in Africa, then a teenager in America; Crane as a young medical student and husband, then a doctor, performing examinations; lurid newspaper headlines of his arrest; Crane examining the eyes of men, women, and children in Kabul; Crane posing with his Afghan colleagues at the hospital; Crane in a pajama kurta and blanket next to a donkey.

This last one made her giggle, but it gave Parveen an unexpected chill. Was that the same donkey that had carried Fereshta from the village?

Bina, as they spoke, came in and out of the edge of Parveen's vision. Ostensibly she was collecting the manure in the yard, but Parveen thought with annoyance that she was trying to eavesdrop on their conversation. Then Bina disappeared. When she rematerialized, she was gripping—brandishing, really—the hardback of *Mother Afghanistan*.

It was the family's precious copy, which Dr. Gideon had given to Waheed, Bina said. But no one in the family could read it; they didn't even know anyone who had read it until they met Parveen. Now Bina wanted to know what the book said about her sister.

"Oh, it says how wonderful she was," Parveen told her. "How special."

Bina looked almost puzzled. She said, without malice, her tone uninflected, "But she wasn't special. She did what we all do. Have children, cook, clean, sleep, wash, pray. Die." Bina sounded almost bored; to her, Parveen sensed, the statement was mere fact. She pointed at the cover of the book, at the photo of a woman in a head scarf over the shape of Afghanistan. "And that's not my sister," she said.

Parveen conceded it was not. How could it be when Fereshta was dead and no photo of her existed? Parveen explained that the publisher had just picked a picture to go on the cover.

But who was she? Bina asked.

Parveen had to say she didn't know, tried to say it didn't matter. But even she was curious now. Was she an actual Afghan, or perhaps a Saudi, an Indian, an Indonesian? Or merely a model posing as an Afghan woman? Did it, indeed, matter? Parveen had to credit Bina for making the photo, the very practices of book publishers, so strange for her.

"Is the book about this woman or my sister?" Bina persisted. "Waheed said it was about my sister, but he can't read, so how would he know?"

Parveen assured her that it was about her sister. Then Bina joined Shokoh in looking at the photo of Crane with Waheed, the same picture Parveen had seen in the various newspaper accounts of the clinic, the taller Crane with his arm over Waheed's shoulders, Waheed with his eyes half closed. The two women stared for a long time, as if drinking in, through a very narrow straw, the image of their shared husband.

"Can you read the book to me?" Bina asked abruptly. She looked so defiant, almost scowling, that at first Parveen mistook her words for a challenge. But when Bina looked away, chewing her lower lip and smoothing her hands, Parveen saw that the request was genuine.

"Of course I'll read it to you," she said. She explained that she would have to translate it first. And she wanted to read to Shokoh too.

"As you wish," Bina said with an uncharacteristic airiness, as if the power to grant something had ennobled her.

CHAPTER NINE

A DONKEY'S TAIL

As Parveen crossed the yard toward the grapevine, anticipation swelled in her. She'd spent the previous two days translating parts of *Mother Afghanistan*, her fantasies about how the reading would go coalescing as she worked. Once she read the climactic scene of Fereshta's death, she would ask Bina and Shokoh to explain, in their own words, what had happened. Why did Fereshta die? Who was responsible? They knew, she presumed, but asking them to articulate it, to name the forces oppressing them, was the first step toward changing the status quo. In her mind this had become a political project, one that she was sure Professor Banerjee would endorse. She wouldn't just fill Bina and Shokoh with knowledge; they would create it together.

MOTHER AFGHANISTAN, CHAPTER ONE

Perhaps the only thing worse than having a very bad man for a father is having a very good one, a saintly one, because you can never live up to his example. This was the story of my childhood.

When I was two years old, my family moved to a South African mission in KwaZulu-Natal, an area with hills as green and soft as Ireland. My father, along with my mother, who was raising five children, established and ran a hospital there. My father took neither salary nor payment from his patients. We lived off what they brought us (often chickens, once even a calf) and what we grew. My toys were fashioned from sticks and husks, and my friends were the African children who lived around the compound or, when their families needed help or refuge, inside it.

For me, my father was Mount Rushmore: impressive but untouchable. We were forever in awe of his selflessness, forever in want of his love. In his eyes, we were blessed, because we were fed, housed, and saved. We didn't need love. The Africans did...

Albert Schweitzer, the missionary who sacrificed the comforts of a European life to move to the jungle of Gabon so he could doctor Africans, was a hero in our house, a man who made our own service look paltry. I flipped through the Life magazine containing those dramatic black-and-white photographs of him, his mustache white as snow, until the ink smudged my fingers. I decided I would become another Schweitzer, and I practiced by pretending to be Schweitzer. I'm embarrassed to admit that I forced my African friends to lie down and be lepers, to affect horrific afflictions that I then cured. I even tried to treat their worms. When my sister reported this to my father, he punished me with a branch against my backside for pretending medical knowledge. That was the stated crime. The real crime, I suspected, was pretending greatness before I'd achieved it.

I would achieve real greatness, then. After I saved my best friend, Kumbalu, from drowning, I taught him to swim. Then I taught all of the village boys to swim, despite their fear of crocodiles. When I excitedly told my father this over dinner one night, he reprimanded me for boasting. He quoted Peter: "God resists the proud but gives grace to the humble."

Walking back to my house one day, I spotted a woman in labor in the bush—she'd been on her way to our hospital—and I sprinted *home to get help. My father duly followed me to tend to her, but he gave me no praise. His only comment was "I wouldn't expect you to do anything less." I was crushed, so badly did I want his approval. I began to exaggerate my good deeds, even invent them, all the while knowing I'd suffer his wrath for boasting and likely for lying as well. I invented stories of fending off snakes that were threatening livestock, of chasing off a lion that was stalking Kumbalu. Was this a rebellion of sorts? I vowed that one day I would achieve something true and so great that he would have to acknowledge it.*

And then, in a single night, he was gone. My father, who had saved so many lives, had no one to save him, although my mother tried. She found him slumped over at his desk, where he had gone after supper to attend to paperwork. He had been halfway through checking the hospital accounts when a massive stroke killed him instantly. I was bereft, naturally, but I was also furious. He'd gone while my backside was still stinging, before I'd had a chance to redeem myself, or achieve anything that would earn his respect, or stop being angry at him, or ask the question that occurred to me later: Didn't Schweitzer posing for those photographs and talking about his work amount to boasting? I didn't believe he was looking down on me from heaven, yet I was still determined, maybe more than ever, to accomplish something that would earn his esteem.

Our family returned to America soon afterward—we had no choice. My mother couldn't run the hospital alone. Another missionary doctor came with his wife and four children to take over, and we moved to North Dakota, where my mother had grown up and where her family could help care for us. She found a job as a nurse, and my siblings and I were enrolled in the local public schools.

I was thirteen then, an impressionable age, a "missionary kid" turned alienated and rebellious teenager. In Africa, I'd had nothing material to call my own, yet I'd wanted nothing, because I didn't know what there was to want. On our return to America, I saw what I had been missing—the games and books and clothes and cars and treats and plastic and electronics and drugs that are the diet of American children, at least those who can afford it, which we mostly couldn't. I felt deprived; in time I began to crave it all: Girls. Cars. Clothes. Money, and the freedom it would bring. For an adolescent, there were unlimited temptations. In high school I drank and smoked pot. I slept with girls and skipped school. I thought I'd given up on impressing my father. The truth was that I'd given up on myself.

A literal translation would be, in addition to exhausting, unnecessary, Parveen had decided after rereading this first chapter. There was too much the women wouldn't understand. Instead, in a notebook, she jotted down the outline of the abridged story that she wanted to tell. Once Waheed had left the house, Bina and Shokoh joined her outside, Shokoh eagerly, Bina reluctantly, even though it was she who had asked to hear Crane's book. She carried one child, the baby, and was trailed by two others. There was a new swing in the yard that Parveen and Jamshid had made by crisscrossing and knotting her jump rope and a piece of fabric around her exercise ball, then suspending the whole thing from a tree branch. The four-year-old, Haroon, demanded that Bina push him on it, which she did until Parveen called Hamdiya and Zahab to take the children away.

The three women sat together beneath the grapevine. It had to have been growing there for decades, so thick were its stems, like gray cables that intertwined to form a trellis above and around an old mulberry tree. The vine's wide, tooth-edged leaves resembled open hands, layered one atop the other to create an entrancing shade. Parveen placed *Mother Afghanistan* between herself and the women but with the front cover facing down, since it felt weird to have that stranger—that non-Fereshta—staring up at them.

"Is it a long story?" Bina asked. "We have work to do, even if this one"—she gave Shokoh a poke—"tells you otherwise." Parveen wondered if Shokoh's pregnancy was easing the tension between them.

Bina was fidgety, unused to leisure time, whereas Shokoh

did not seem in the least uncomfortable sitting still. She leaned against the vines, her face piebald with shadow and light. As Parveen talked, Shokoh reached over her shoulder to pluck leaves that she then tore into ever tinier strips.

Bina scowled. "Soon the whole vine will be naked."

Shokoh looked at Parveen, laughed, then returned to plucking and tearing. They were like siblings, Parveen thought, remembering the delight she had sometimes taken in needling Taara about her vanity or her habits or her fiancé. Bina and Shokoh knew, after only six or seven months together, exactly how to torment each other.

Parveen began: "One time there was a boy who grew up in a place called Africa."

"We've heard of Africa," Bina said dryly.

Parveen had forgotten their nightly steeping, via the BBC, in the world's affairs. "Of course," she said. "South Africa. Where that very old woman died." Then she continued: "The people were very poor. Even poorer than those of Afghanistan." She wasn't sure this was true.

"Do they eat dirt?" Bina asked. "In South Africa?"

"No," Parveen said uncertainly.

"Then they cannot possibly be poorer than us."

"More poor, less poor, I don't know," Parveen admitted. "But you don't eat dirt either. They were very poor. That's all you need to know."

She told them that Dr. Gideon's parents were very good people—doctors as well—and that his father ran a hospital. The fact that they were missionaries she left out. Instead, she presented his mother as an altogether different kind of proselytizer. She taught women how to space their children farther apart, Parveen explained, so the children would be healthy and the mothers less likely to die in childbirth. This seemed to Parveen a mild and virtuous emendation of the truth. Crane didn't mention contraception in his memoir, but Parveen felt compelled to; women delivering fewer children was the simplest way to reduce the number of mothers who died while giving birth.

Parveen continued with Crane's biography. When she talked about his desire to please his father even as he also chafed against his authority, Bina said, "It's like Waheed and Jamshid." Parveen eyed her, waiting for more, but Bina wouldn't expand on that. Parveen went on. When Crane was thirteen, his father died. His family moved back to America, where his mother worked as a nurse. Though his parents were American, until then he had never lived in the country and it was difficult for him to acclimate. Slowly, though, he learned.

Parveen tried to explain to Bina and Shokoh how she related to Crane's difficulty with returning to America, even though she'd moved to America at a much younger age. This was the power of books, she told the women, that you could see yourself reflected in someone not at all like you. "I know you've never moved from one country to another, but…" Parveen trailed off, not sure what she was hoping for.

"To leave your family and start over in another place," Bina said, "with a husband who's a stranger in a village you don't know—it's the same." Then to Parveen's surprise she asked Shokoh, "Isn't that so?"

Shokoh nodded miserably. "Worse," she said, "because you don't go with your parents. You go alone."

IF WAHEED WANTED TO speak to Parveen and she was in her room, he would send one of the children to fetch her rather than approaching her private space himself. The day after Parveen read to Bina and Shokoh, Zahab came to say that her father wanted a word. Parveen was sure that Waheed was going to admonish her for reading to his wives; she knew there were no secrets in the house, or at least none kept from him. She began to rehearse her arguments, seeing this as an opportunity to challenge the patriarchy. By the time she left her room, she was in a froth. She would tell Waheed that he had no business controlling what his wives heard or learned.

But when Parveen met him in the dirt of the courtyard, Waheed asked if she would read to them again.

Yes, she said when she recovered from her surprise. She would read to them again.

"Good," he said. "It's the only way they will ever travel."

Parveen sneaked a glance at him, mystified. "Why don't you just take them somewhere?"

"Where would we go?"

"Anywhere," Parveen said. "To see their families. To a city. Wherever *you* go. You saw—you met—Shokoh at a wedding, right? Where was that?"

His cousin's town, he said. Her cousin too. It was halfway between the village and the provincial capital.

"So go there. There's no reason they can't travel."

Waheed looked as if he'd never considered such a thing. "The khan's wife travels," he acknowledged, referring to the largest landowner in the village. The khan had a home in the provincial capital, and the family went back and forth.

"If the khan's wife can go, why can't yours? He's no better than you."

Waheed nodded slowly, stroking the nose of the donkey, who had meandered over.

"I could go with you," Parveen offered, already imagining the four of them—her, Waheed, Bina, and Shokoh—on a road trip. But he appeared more annoyed than pleased by that suggestion, and she wondered if she had pushed too hard. "Where did you meet Fereshta?" she asked, to change the subject.

Their marriage had been arranged, he said. "On our wedding day they held up the mirror and I saw her."

This was an Afghan tradition that Parveen knew well: the

bride and groom together read a passage of the Quran, after which a mirror was held before them so they could see themselves as a married couple for the first time. The ritual was performed—purely symbolically—even by urban Afghans who had met or dated before the wedding, even by Afghan-Americans who had slept together before the wedding. But in the case of Waheed and Fereshta, it really was the first time they'd seen each other.

"How did you feel?" Parveen asked.

He snorted, as if her question was too ridiculous to answer.

Before they parted, Parveen asked if Bina and Shokoh had told him they wanted to hear more of *Mother Afghanistan*. They had, Waheed said. They wanted to know why God had brought Dr. Gideon to this village.

MOTHER AFGHANISTAN, CHAPTER TWO

...My father's kind of poverty, his renunciation, his selflessness, was an achievement, the sort of asceticism and abnegation that put him in a club with Gandhi and Mother Teresa. It would have allowed him to hold his head high with the richest guy in our town had he ever returned there. I didn't think myself capable of that kind of selflessness, so I decided to impress people by amassing wealth. I look back on my own crassness sadly. I was earning a good living, yet it never felt like enough. I see now I was desperate for recognition. If I couldn't be the best, I wanted to have the most.

Which is what led me into fraud. Up-coding, double billing, possibly unnecessary diagnoses—I did it all, and Medicare gladly reimbursed it all. Sometimes it felt like the government wanted me to cheat...

My father often said that one kind of sin calls forth others. Cast off the first moral restraint, and the rest start to seem like paper chains. Still making up for what I'd missed as a kid (at this point I had been compensating for my childhood far longer than I had been a child), I felt entitled to do whatever felt good. It's limitless, really, what self-pity can justify.

I began to drink more. I strayed from my marriage. I had first one affair, then another, with nurses I worked with. Warm beds breed loose lips—isn't that what they say? I couldn't help but brag about my ill-gotten wealth, some of which was providing gifts for these nurses. One of them turned me in. She wore a wire. I was so consistent in my lack of ethics, so uniform in my sleaze, that it never occurred to me that a woman untroubled by having an affair with a married man might disapprove of stealing from the government.

I was served a search warrant at the clinic; my poor wife, Gloria, was served one at home. Then I was arrested, and that scene was replayed on both the six p.m. and ten p.m. local news. The feds were prosecuting me. My wife considered leaving me, and I wouldn't have blamed her if she had. Our daughter, thirteen years old, was humiliated.

I felt as low as a man can be. As sordid. I wanted to cleanse myself, redeem myself. Seeking a fresh start, my wife and I joined a new church, Crossroads, and I publicly repented for having backslid. Our pastor brought many good Christians to rally in my defense. Because of my cooperation, the government sentenced me to five hundred hours of community service and agreed to let me do it abroad.

God provides, and He guides too. I chose Afghanistan. Where else did America have such a strong interest? Where else was there such a strong need? In Afghanistan I could be a soldier without a gun. Perhaps I could help open the door for others who wanted to serve there in some way.

I said goodbye to my wife and daughter. My wife had stood by me with the utmost loyalty, what any man would hope for. But I'd hurt her. By going abroad I could spare Gloria not only the humiliation of a jailed husband but also the salt in the wound of my presence, the constant reminder of my mistakes and betrayals. I promised to return a better man.

I meant it from the bottom of my wounded, humiliated soul, but it was easier said than done. I had assumed Kabul would be a hardship. I wasn't prepared for its comforts, its mix of decadence and familiarity.

In the 1970s, it had been a stop on the Hippie Trail, the overland route that young Westerners took from Europe to South Asia. The mere name evoked a loose-limbed morality. Now, in the long wake of 9/11, it was inhabited by a new round of expats, do-gooders, and profiteers.

Each day I saw scores of patients, performed several surgeries, and trained Afghan doctors. The work, the unrelenting pace of it, exhausted and cleansed me. There was no time to think or err, only to do. By the end of every day I felt purified, but the night was full of parties to attend and bars to visit and I'd soil myself again, imbibing wine rather than the Spirit because drinking in a Muslim country had a frisson of transgression. Or because I was weak.

Then my five hundred hours were up, and it was time to go home. But what did home have to offer other than the tedious, painful work of reconstructing my marriage and my career? I wasn't ready. In Kabul I felt free, and I imagined that outside the capital I would find greater freedom still. I hungered for adventure. To go deeper into Afghanistan, I was sure, would take me deeper into myself. I wanted somewhere, something, harder to push against. What we think of as comforts are buffers, ways of not knowing ourselves, not becoming ourselves. I wanted to turn myself inside out, to empty my pockets, and so to learn what I contained.

I found a passable interpreter, A., to accompany me where I was going, which was admirable of him, given that I didn't know where that was. (I'm withholding his full name to protect his privacy.) "I will gladly go to anywhere, sir," he said, making "anywhere" sound like a state or city.

What I contained, at least in the beginning, was complaint. The driver whom A. hired proved unwilling to venture more than half a day from Kabul. Once he left us, we relied on a combination of taking "taxis" (beat-up cars and trucks whose drivers asked for money) and hitchhiking (beat-up cars and trucks whose drivers didn't). The less interesting a place, the more vigorously A. asserted its significance. I couldn't have been more bored. So one day when we were on a highway and I spotted an unmarked, unpaved turnoff leading up into the mountains, I told A. to stop the driver. The dust on the dirt road caught the light; the upward slant of it was arresting. It beckoned me, bred an inexplicable curiosity in me. A voice from within told me that was the road I had to travel. I didn't know that it would lead me to a mission that would transform my life and those of many others, that at last I would do something worthy of my father's approval.

But we had to get there first. The driver refused to take us, saying he wouldn't risk his trunkful of melons on a road to nowhere. My interpreter, A., was skeptical too. "I'm sure nobody lives up there," he said. "The road's probably just for grazing animals. Maybe there's a poor village. But most likely, there's nothing."

"Well, nothing is what I want to see," I retorted. I had become more and more certain that this was the path for me. We argued for a few minutes, and then, once it became clear to A. that I wouldn't change my mind, we got out of the truck. I settled in a shady spot beneath an over-hanging rock while he went off to find us donkeys. I didn't even mind the wait, which turned out to be long, so pleased was I at the prospect of an actual adventure. As I sat beneath my rock, various men—shepherds, drivers—stopped to investigate me in a friendly way. To one I tried, through body language, to explain that we needed two donkeys. He nodded and held up one finger, I held up two, he held up one, I held up two, then he left. Eventually A. returned, donkey-less and embarrassed. A few minutes later, my friend of the fingers arrived with two donkeys. He'd been trying to tell me he would be back in one hour...

Seven hours later, A. and I stumbled into the village, our donkeys so tired we nearly had to carry them ourselves. The valley glowed before us, as verdant, fertile, and harmonious a setting as I've ever seen. The sun kissed the tops of the mountains, which were ringed by clouds.

We found the bazaar. No foreigner, I learned, had ever come here before. Soon all of the villagers had gathered, climbing trees, crowding on rooftops, to stare at me. This is when I first saw Fereshta. Clearly pregnant, she emerged from the crowd to offer me water. I was struck by her beauty—her long-lashed black eyes, her rosy cheeks and creamy complexion, her delicate nose and small, perfect mouth. A luminous Afghan rose in the countryside. There was a grace to her. She told her *husband, Waheed, that he should offer to let me stay at their home, and he did.*

I spent much of my time in their house. Waheed was a bearded nebbish, a timid, nervously talkative man bullied by life, although he worked hard farming rice to provide for his large family. It was Fereshta who was the heart of the household. The children crowded around her like petals to a flower's center. There was joy in that home, laughter. Fereshta, heavily pregnant, would direct a son or daughter to bring me tea, or sometimes, waddling dreamily, she would bring it herself. She made sure I lacked nothing. She was a marvelous cook, her lamb always tender, her spinach mouthwatering, her beans savory...

Bina and Shokoh were silent as Parveen spoke, and she guessed they were trying to take it all in. She'd provided them a simplified version of Crane's actual chapter, dispensing with Crane's sordid history, which she found too complicated to explain and feared was too easy, in some fashion, to misconstrue. As she described Crane arriving in the village, she scrutinized their faces, looking for signs of emotion or recognition. Given that they didn't often leave the village, did it feel strange to have an outsider describe his arrival here? Parveen had expected Bina to be moved by the description of Fereshta, and indeed this was when Bina interrupted.

"Fereshta wasn't beautiful," she said in the same matter-of-fact tone she'd used to say that Fereshta wasn't special. Parveen, caught off guard, tsked to show her disapproval of Bina's jealousy.

"What's wrong with what I said?" Bina asked. "She looked like me."

Shokoh laughed, a little too appreciatively. Parveen found Bina's honesty about her own homeliness plangent.

"Waheed was very poor," Bina went on. "He couldn't even buy a donkey's tail. How would he marry a great beauty?"

Parveen considered this. Bina had hit on a near-universal truth: the higher a groom's status (as determined by his wealth, education, career prospects, and family lineage), the prettier his bride. Parveen had often seen and critiqued this phenomenon in Union City.

"Maybe he forgot what she looked like," said Shokoh. Her lashes cast shadows on her cheeks, which were flushed from the warmth of the day.

Shokoh's face would require no enhancing on the page, and Parveen wondered how Waheed, a humble farmer, a small land-holder, had mustered sufficient funds to pry her from her family. What change in his circumstances since he'd married Fereshta and then Bina had made this possible? Already inclined to dislike him, she now began to suspect him.

As to Crane, Parveen didn't fault him for making Fereshta out to be comelier than she was, if that was in fact what he'd done. He knew his readers, maybe better than they knew themselves. If you wanted people to weep at the death of a tragic heroine, you didn't make her plain. She had to glow.

PARVEEN WASN'T DONE WITH her reading, but Bina insisted that she had to get back to work.

"Just a few more minutes and we can finish the chapter," Parveen said. She wanted at least to get through the part about Crane in Fereshta and Waheed's house, although she worried that the flattering portrait of Fereshta's cooking and mothering might irritate Bina. Maybe she wanted to irritate her, a bit.

"My work won't do itself while I sit and listen to this," Bina said. Parveen folded her hands and watched the leaves move and said nothing for a few moments. Then she told both of them that anytime they wanted to look at the book they could come into her room.

You can come into my room. This message soon reached the

rest of the family too, and, except for Waheed and Jamshid, come into her room they did. (Waheed's orders, she knew, had previously held them back.) Parveen would return home from walks and, upon entering the compound, see that her door—which Waheed, after a few not-so-gentle reminders, had built from poplar wood—was open, meaning another pillage was under way. Adeila and Aakila tried her lipstick (on their cheeks and noses as well as on their lips) and unraveled her tampons; Shokoh spilled her lotion, whose lavender scent at least improved the odor of the room. Parveen adopted the only sensible response—she became less protective of her things. Most she didn't need anyway. She no longer wore makeup, barely bothered with sunscreen. She bathed less often, hardly brushed her hair. Her eyebrows went untamed, which, after years of wrestling with them, was a relief. When she glimpsed herself in the stillest part of the river, where the village women, having few mirrors at home, went to examine themselves, her own appearance always surprised her. She looked free. Unbridled.

Shokoh began to take paper from Parveen's room. She tore it carelessly from the notebooks, then wrote on the pages in front of Parveen. There was a silent challenge in this, Parveen thought—Shokoh's way of saying, *You want me to write? Fine, then make it possible.* On occasion Shokoh would leave poems in the notebook. In them Parveen detected new glints of optimism:

The morning light wakes me.
I open my eyes and dream.

Parveen was always pleased when she found someone perusing a book in her room. The children's favorite was Louis Dupree's comprehensive anthropology of Afghanistan, with its grainy gray pictures of things both known and strange. Parveen had read it during the hasty survey of the anthropology of Afghanistan that she'd undertaken before her journey here. The book was more than thirty-five years old, but there wasn't much recent literature, which made sense; the country had been at war for the past three decades, since the Soviets had invaded, and thus inhospitable to anthropological research. She'd found Dupree's book fascinating and useful, but it also underlined the broad appeal of Crane's memoir, although she would never say so to Professor Banerjee. We were wired for stories, she thought, all the more when they contained a protagonist we could relate to. Crane was a stand-in for his readers.

One day Parveen came home from a walk and noticed the slight movement of a shadow as she rounded the corner to her room. Feeling playful, she decided to catch whoever it was— probably one or more of the children—by surprise. She crept toward the doorway and then, a few feet away, stopped. It was Bina, whom she had never seen in her room before. Bina, so absorbed in a book that she didn't sense Parveen's presence, was moving her index finger across the page as if she were reading, but Parveen knew that was impossible. She craned her neck to see better and realized that the book was *Mother Afghanistan;* Bina's finger was tracing its photographs as if they were lines from a lover. Slowly, noiselessly, Parveen backed away. It seemed worse for her to trespass on Bina's reverie than for Bina to trespass on Parveen's space. If caught, Bina would be, at the very least, embarrassed or defensive. Parveen went up the stairs to the main room of the house, and when Bina came up a few minutes later, she pretended to be absorbed in rocking the cradle.

"The baby's not in there," Bina said.

"Oh, how silly of me," Parveen said.

Those photographs contained no trace of Bina's sister; it was as if Fereshta had been blotted from history, Parveen thought. Yet the text around them enshrined her there. Parveen still thought it admirable, most of the time, that Crane had kept Fereshta's story alive. Maybe only someone who'd been low in the eyes of men could see what was so special in her. Yet in the village, the nature of that specialness was so elusive, its details so obscure, that Parveen was beginning to question an American man making use of it. To what degree was it legitimate to fill in the blanks in an Afghan woman's life and to what degree had Crane done so? It seemed to Parveen that, just as with the war, the closer she got, the blurrier Fereshta became.

CHAPTER TEN

THE DOG AND THE COBBLER

VERY EARLY ONE MORNING NEAR THE END OF JUNE, PARVEEN wandered down to the river. She loved this time of day, before most families stirred from home, when the sun, still more suggestion than observable fact, banded the sky with navy and pink. The fields were wet with dew, and the birdsong had a lonely sound that Parveen found perversely pleasing.

But on this morning, Parveen found her path blocked by Ghazal. Usually Ghazal made her laugh with jokes about her husband's impotence or her own sexual appetites, which, it turned out, were legendary among the villagers whose sympathies tended to lie with her husband. So far, Ghazal was the only woman who'd agreed to answer Parveen's survey questions, the others having either demurred or directed Parveen to talk to their husbands. With Parveen taking notes, Ghazal had graphically described her sex life, back when she had one; her pregnancies, complete with incontinence, constipation, heartburn, and farts; her deliveries and the condition in which they'd rendered her vagina. Given that Ghazal's youngest child was already ten, her memory for these details was extraordinary, Parveen thought as her hand cramped from writing. When she suggested they stop, perhaps to resume another day, Ghazal said, "You don't have more questions?"

But this morning Ghazal was distended with anger. Shokoh had been boasting about Parveen reading to her and Bina, and Ghazal wanted to know why Parveen wasn't reading to all of the women. "Don't we deserve to learn too?" she asked. It was bad enough that Parveen was living with Waheed; now his wives would have another reason to feel superior.

Parveen apologized for not having considered this and started to explain why it wouldn't be practical, but the look of disappointment on Ghazal's face stopped her. "You're right," she said, "I should read to all of you." And without bothering to think through how, she promised that she would.

Ghazal squeezed her hand in glee, and they walked back from the river together.

Over bread, eggs, and tea that morning, Parveen told Waheed that she wanted to begin reading to all of the women, not just Bina and Shokoh. Both wives looked peeved, but Parveen ignored them. There was no reason why they alone should receive her attention, and she refused to feel guilty.

Waheed took a long slurp of his tea, which she took to mean that he wasn't opposed to the proposal. "The mullah will be the biggest obstacle," he said, then laughed because of the mullah's diminutive size. He was sure to resist the idea, Waheed said, and while the men here didn't really like him, much less respect him, they wouldn't go against what he said.

I know, Parveen thought. *You listened to him when he said Crane shouldn't help your wife.* Still, she was pleased not to have Waheed opposing the plan, and she asked him to accompany her to petition the mullah. "My presence won't help you," he said. "He's jealous of me. Better that you go alone."

She tied her dark blue head scarf tightly and set out for the mullah's. Even by the standards of the village, his house was tiny, his chickens scrawny, his cow bony. He was poor; his faults, apparently, did not include corruption. Afghan mullahs, she knew, were often itinerants who relied on villagers to provide their food and housing. "If the mullah invites himself to dinner, you must accept" was a popular joke, one of many Parveen had heard about village mullahs, whose spiritual authority was checked by their unfortunate need to eat.

The mullah answered the door with a Quran in hand, no doubt to show off his literacy, then called for his wife. When Parveen said that it was him she had come to speak to, he reddened. Nadia greeted Parveen with warmth, and Parveen noted with a pang that even at home, Nadia kept her goiter covered; she had a piece of fabric wrapped almost stylishly around her throat.

While Nadia made tea, Parveen laid out her plan. The mullah found it disturbing. The men of the village didn't know what Crane's book contained, he said. Why should the women? "The only book the women need to hear is the Quran."

"Why can't they know both?"

He took offense; was she suggesting the two books were equal?

Of course not, Parveen assured him, and she reached for analogies. Was the ant equal to the yak? The pebble to the mountain? And since Crane's book was so insignificant compared to Islam's holy text, what was the harm in allowing the women to hear a little bit of it?

The book was not insignificant, the mullah said. It had changed much, too much, in the village. In building the clinic, Crane had privileged the healing of the body over the care of the soul. The clinic was literally twice the size of the mosque. Why hadn't Crane given money for what mattered more to both the villagers and God?

Parveen thought: *Because you have Fereshta's blood on your hands.* She said: "But the clinic helps your wife. The lady doctor is treating her sadness sickness."

"The clinic didn't save my first wife. She, too, died in childbirth."

"But not in this village," Nadia dared to whisper as she knelt with the tray of tea.

Parveen feared the mullah might punish Nadia for correcting him. Instead, he ignored her. "For two years," he said, "until I remarried, I was both mother and father to my children as they cried." He added, almost parenthetically, "It's not easy for a mullah to find one wife, let alone two, with so few funds." Then he returned to his dead wife: "No one wrote about her in a book. No foreigners came to offer me condolences."

"I'm sorry," Parveen said.

"That clinic has made kings of beggars."

Again, that phrase. "Isn't that better than making corpses of women?" she said, surprised by her own quickness and boldness. "Besides, who here is a king?"

"You live in his palace."

"Waheed hardly lives like a king."

"Then how is it the moon shines for him alone?"

Parveen had no idea what he was saying, and she told him so.

"The dog and the cobbler know what's in the sack," he replied.

"So does the mullah!" Parveen said, hoping to bait him into explaining himself.

It didn't work. Instead, he began to lecture her, growing so animated that he forgot not to look at her face. Foreigners worried only about trying to prolong life a little more, he said, but that was in the hands of God. When the day of judgment came, it was the condition of the soul that would matter. What were a few more weeks of life next to the eternity of hellfire? "You look at a woman and see only a body," he accused Parveen. "I see a soul and evil spirits trying to possess it. There are forces. A much more powerful battle under way. Not all answers, not even most, can be found in your science."

As he droned on, Parveen's mind drifted. There were echoes in what he said of what she'd been taught in her medical-anthropology courses, that the medical profession didn't have all the answers, that it only pretended to, which was why it was essential to question doctors who would never admit doubt, whose neat narratives reinforced their authority. It was only natural that humans, when faced with the inexplicable, posited complex theories dense with jargon, then conveniently forgot they were theories. Not so long ago surgeons had hacked away at women's chest muscles to remove their breast cancer. Was it less chauvinistic to believe you could beat an illness out of a woman? At least the mullah admitted to the power of what could not be seen or known. Here was Foucault's priest, but a humble one, and Parveen told herself to listen deeply, to ascertain his worldview.

The problem with trying to enter into the head of the Other, though, was that the Other was always more than one. No sooner had she tried to see the world through his eyes than she began seeing it through the eyes of the pregnant eclamptic woman he'd whipped and choked to evict the djinns. Did she cower as she was beaten? Did she gag as she was choked? He persisted through her pain. How she must have cried out, how she must have feared for her child's life, for her own. Or had he made her, too, believe that she was possessed? No doubt any resistance would have been taken as further proof of the djinns' occupation of her body, the inability to meet an absurd test of innocence confirming her possession. His imagining of this great spiritual battle had been more real to him than the woman before him. He was a superstitious simpleton as arrogant and power-drunk as any Western practitioner, another man experimenting on a woman's body just as men always had. If Western medicine was too willing to reduce illness to the body alone, here was the countervailing, and even more dangerous, reduction to spirit, in which a man had the power to make a woman's loved ones stand by while, in the name of God, he choked her.

All the tea Parveen had drunk was straining her bladder, and she wanted the meeting to end. She tried flattering the mullah by telling him how much he was teaching her, how much she had to learn, then hit on another idea—she promised to write to Crane's foundation about donating funds to improve the mosque. Crane would never do this, Parveen knew, but she implied she had the power to make it happen. She felt sordid, lying in this manner, but she did it anyway.

The mullah thought for a few moments while Parveen studied her dirty fingernails. "You can read to the women," he said. Then he ordered his wife to follow him into another room.

Alone now, Parveen heard them whispering. She wondered if she was meant to show herself out. But they returned.

"We want to give you something," the mullah said.

He motioned, with sudden formality, for his wife to hand Parveen what she was holding—a folded cloth the color of celery. Parveen spread it open. It was one of Nadia's shawls, begrimed by use and faded in places to gray. Parveen swallowed hard before thanking them. They had so little to give.

PARVEEN WALKED HOME FEELING triumphant and eager to tell Waheed about her success. She realized that, despite herself, she was warming to him. He kept confounding her expectations, first by encouraging her to read to his wives, now by helping her with her plan to read to more women. But she told herself to remain wary, that perhaps this was how patriarchy was maintained, through small liberal concessions that did nothing to diminish the control men had.

"So where will you do this?" he asked when she told him of the mullah's agreement.

She hadn't thought about that. To choose one house, including Waheed's, would create envy among the others, and envy was a force she was learning to respect. There was the clinic's court-yard, but it lacked shade beyond its single tree, which looked more like a prop than a shelter.

Waheed suggested that Parveen ask the khan, the one person

who might have land to spare. In addition to being the village's largest property owner, he also controlled the water rights and acted as the liaison to the district government. These privileges, as well as most of his land, had been inherited from his father, who had inherited them from his father, who had inherited them from his father, and so on. Distinguished-looking, with a leonine face and a neatly trimmed gray beard, the khan had the supercilious air of one who believes his advantage stems from his own virtue. The gold watch he wore had also come from his father.

The khan, as Waheed had told her, lived mostly in the provincial capital, but he often came to the village on Fridays. After prayers she went to his house and found his expansive reception room crowded with village men—friends, courtiers, petitioners.

"The American girl has come to study me," he told them. "Or maybe she wants accommodations more comfortable than a storeroom!"

His audience laughed as if they were being paid to. Later she would imagine delivering quick, devastating comebacks, but now she stood mute, a frozen smile on her face. The khan dismissed everyone and invited her for tea with himself and his wife.

By the standards of the village, his house was palatial—airy and well-proportioned, shielded from the sun by a row of stately poplar trees. The glass windows were clean; the carpet where they sat was velvet-soft. The khan cocked his head at her, a possibly lewd twinkle in his eyes, and waited for her to speak.

Parveen's idea bemused but did not especially interest him, since there was nothing for him to gain. But he had an orchard she could use until the apricots came, he said. How long that gave her, Parveen didn't ask.

She should have known that the khan was not a man who gave anything away for free. His first price, in her case, was information. How much was she paying Waheed in rent? he wanted to know.

A ransom, she gathered from his expression when she named the sum. It hadn't seemed much in Berkeley.

"Waheed's good fortune was to lose his wife," the khan said.

"And was it also good fortune for six children to lose their mother?"

"No, no, it wasn't," he said with what Parveen mistook for contrition. "Luckily they have been blessed with not one new mother but two."

Parveen gritted her teeth. Coarse words were worse when they happened to be true.

The khan directed his wife to prepare food, although Parveen insisted she wasn't hungry.

"In our culture it's rude to refuse hospitality," he said.

"I know; it's my culture too," Parveen replied. "Of course I'll eat."

They sat quietly. His steady gaze on her made her uncomfortable. Abruptly he said, "Come, let's go see the orchard," and without bothering to inform his wife they were going, he ushered Parveen outside.

"What about the food?" she asked, but he didn't answer.

As they walked along the valley, his long finger worked overtime to point out all the fields that were his. They came to the orchard. Its mud walls were crumbling like stale cake, but inside it was lovely, cool, tranquil. The apricot trees twisted and leaned out of the grid in which they'd been planted, their branches bent and curved like dancers' arms sleeved in vivid green. Shadow and light trembled against each other on the orchard floor, where grass and clover grew calf-high. A fruit-sweet scent perfumed the air and the bees circled dizzily.

Would it do? the khan asked.

It would, Parveen said blandly, not wanting to betray her excitement.

"I'm glad," he said.

When he held out his hand for her to shake, by reflex she took it, not stopping to think how unorthodox it was for an Afghan man to offer a woman his hand. In a single motion he pulled her to him, put his other hand on the back of her head, bent his face to hers, and forced his tongue into her mouth. He thrust his groin against her and she felt him harden. She reared back, rebelling so strongly against his hand that she felt a stab of pain in her neck. "If you do that again, I'll tell!" she sputtered.

"Tell who?"

He said this with infuriating innocence. He wasn't taunting her, she realized. The threat of exposure meant nothing to him because he was right; who would she tell? His wife, who could do nothing? The village men, who would likely think that if anyone had done something wrong, it was Parveen, coming to this village—and now this orchard—on her own? She had no protection except her own instincts, which were in urgent need of sharpening.

THE ENCOUNTER RATTLED HER enough that she thought about abandoning her plan to read to the women. She considered herself lucky not to have been raped, and she didn't want to be in any way indebted to the khan. But if she changed her mind, she would have to explain why to Waheed. And the argument for empowering the women was even stronger now. They needed to recognize injustice as it happened so that the next time a man tried to take advantage of them or deny a woman medical care, they would fight. She remembered *Lysistrata*, the Greek play in which women banded together to stop a war by withholding sex. Maybe, little by little, she could foment a similar kind of collective action.

And so Parveen began to tell the women about her plan to read to them, giving Ghazal credit for making it happen. Parveen spoke to their husbands too, assuring them that the mullah approved. But one day Waheed came home to report that Commander Amanullah was trying to turn the men against her plan. Waheed agreed to accompany Parveen to speak to Amanullah. They found him sitting, as usual, with the blacksmith, sipping tea from a tin mug. A group of men gathered when they began to talk.

"It's only an hour," Parveen told him. "The women could get a little sun on their faces. They could learn something. Then they'll be back home."

"The honor of our family, of my name, is more important than the sun on my wife's face," Amanullah boomed as the men around him nodded.

Parveen wondered why he was referring to only one wife. She knew from *Mother Afghanistan* that he had three.

Amanullah continued: "If our honor is lost, it's as if we are in shadow forever. Besides, she gets plenty of sun inside our compound."

"Then don't send your wife."

Startled, Parveen gulped; had she let slip words so blunt? But no, this time it was Waheed, standing next to her, who had spoken calmly, directly, to this bull of a man.

"Then don't send your wife," he repeated. The meaning was clear: *Decide for yourself, but you won't be deciding for the rest of us. The reading will go ahead with or without your consent.*

Parveen tensed, sure that Amanullah wasn't often challenged like this.

"If I don't send her, how will I know what's being said?" he asked, to laughs. But it wasn't a joke; he seemed genuinely befuddled. He proclaimed that his wife would attend, and the other men looked at Waheed with new respect.

On the way home, Parveen thanked him.

"That which thunders does not rain," he said, presumably in reference to the commander. There was a time, he went on, when he, Waheed, was a "smaller man," and he would have been afraid to be so bold. He didn't need to spell out what he meant, which was that Gideon Crane had made him someone important.

Parveen wondered if he'd agreed to accompany her in order to demonstrate this. His story, when she thought about it, was extraordinary. This village was a static place. A family's standing could easily diminish, but little other than finding a way to profit from war could improve it. She was quite sure that no one here had ever sprung from his low place the way Waheed had. He hadn't come into land, gotten an education, or shown a knack for agriculture or business or politics or battle. Nor had he grown opium, bred a militia, or bartered with the Taliban. He'd become a celebrity, which made his a very American story—one authored, fittingly, by the American Crane.

Chapter Eleven

The Orchard

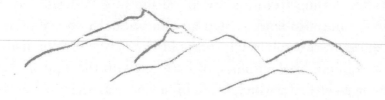

Mother Afghanistan, Chapter Eight

I woke one morning in the village to a knock on the door. Two men stood there with Kalashnikovs slung over their shoulders, which told me that when they said, "Come," it wasn't a choice. Outside, one hoisted me by the arms while the other placed a black bag over my head. In such a moment it is not just the inability to breathe that you must fight but the fear of the inability to breathe. For the panic is as much a threat to you as the bag itself. It was the panic that drew the bag to my nostrils, making me suffocate, making me panic more, until I forced myself to calm down and could breathe again.

They bundled me into the back of what I thought was a pickup truck. I could feel cold metal beneath me, open air above.

"Where am I being taken?" I cried through the bag.

"To Commander Amanullah" came the answer, and I began to shake with fear.

Amanullah was the local Taliban commander. Here is what they said of him: That he had wielded his whip on women who dared to leave their homes. That he beheaded anyone who defied or betrayed him. That he ran a personal dungeon where those he arrested for petty infractions were hung by their elbows from a bar until their families paid to have them freed. That he should have been sent to Guantánamo but escaped by bribing local Afghan officials. That he flaunted his liberty and terrorized the villagers and abused his three wives.

I'd never laid eyes on him, but from the time I arrived in the village, he'd pressured the mullah to issue a fatwa calling for my death, even though at any moment he could have executed me himself. Perhaps since he was a Talib—which meant, in theory, that he was or had been a religious student—his standing with the villagers would require legal cover for his sins. The mullah, a generally cowardly man, had so far refused.

Now it appeared that Commander Amanullah had decided to take matters into his own hands. My legs were jelly; my hands, bound, were numb. I prayed and tried to think of any arguments that could stave off my death. The pickup truck rattled along terrible roads, and in the back, with my hands tied, I banged and rolled like a loose marble until I found a way to curl up and use my feet to steady myself. Then the truck jolted to a stop.

I was taken out, and the men walked me a short distance. I had to be supported on both sides so I wouldn't collapse. When the bag was taken off my head, I was inside a compound with a dirt floor and high walls. Such a plain, sad place to die, as if it mattered. Would they bother sending my body back to Gloria? Could I ask them, at least, for that? Strange how the mind turns to practicalities at a time like this. It did not occur to me to beg for my life, only for the small dignity of having my body, even bullet-riddled, even separated from its head—at this I shuddered—returned to my wife. Then I thought about my daughter, about her having no father, and what nearly made me weep was realizing that she already barely had a father, that I had been absent even when I was present, busy with my affairs and my fraud (which I had rationalized by saying it was for her, for her future), then consumed with my exposure and humiliation. She was hazy in my mind during that time. I think she mostly retreated to her room; she must have been embarrassed to see her friends. Then I left for Kabul, and I'd hardly spoken to her since. If I were to die, would it feel any different for her? I vowed that if, by some miracle, I made it out of here, I would become a much better father to her.

I was led to a long narrow room with a few tables and chairs and one window. Two young teenage boys came in and began to take pictures of me with their cell phones. This alarmed me; I had seen the images of executed foreigners that appeared on the web after their deaths. Never had I imagined that children might be the photographers.

"Can you help me?" I asked. "I've done nothing wrong. I have a daughter about your age. She wants a father too."

They looked at each other and giggled, took more pictures, then vanished. Eventually I was led to Commander Amanullah. It was all I could do not to urinate on myself when I saw him. He had the build of a giant, a black turban, a black beard, and black eyes; there was black beneath his fingernails and a bile-yellow coating on his teeth. Black beneath the fingernails on one hand, to be precise. Where his other hand would have been, there was a steel claw. He alone among his men held no weapon. This scared me most of all.

"I have three wives," he began with no preamble. "Gulab is the newest, but she is losing her eyesight. You are an eye doctor. You will treat her. And if you help her, you'll live."

This was not a scenario I was prepared for. "I-I-I'll do my best," I stuttered. "May I examine her?"

"No!" he thundered. "You're a man, a foreigner, an infidel. You cannot see her."

"Then I have no hope of fixing her eyes, which means..." I didn't finish the thought.

I should tell him how to help her without seeing her, the commander said.

This was impossible, I told him. He needed a female doctor.

How many female doctors of any kind did I think there were in Afghanistan? he snapped. And of those, how many would be willing to come here? "You're an American," he went on, "you have the best medical training. All of our commanders who went to Guantánamo Bay came back with many of their medical problems solved, even if they'd also acquired new ones. Your doctors and your torturers, it seems, are equally advanced."

Under more congenial circumstances, I might have appreciated his wit. But my life was at stake; I had to be cunning, buy time. I asked him to describe the problem, when it had started, how it had progressed. The more we talked, I reasoned, the harder it would be for him to kill me. I didn't have the exotic tales of A Thousand and One Nights at my disposal, but I could bore him with several years' worth of dry material from medical textbooks.

Instead, it was he who began to tell a story, of the beautiful young girl—probably not much older than my own daughter—he had taken as his third wife, his sweetest wife, and how her eyes had begun to hurt. In bright light she cried out, and even opium didn't relieve her pain. She was losing her sight. Her household duties had become difficult for her to manage. The other two wives, already resentful of her favored position, had started to complain. Commander Amanullah wanted to protect her, to heal her, to save her from this agony. If she didn't recover, he couldn't ask his other wives to care for her. She would have to return to her family, and this would be a shame upon them, upon her, and upon the commander himself.

"Fix her," he told me. "You must fix her eyes."

It was clear not just from what he said but from how he spoke that he loved her. The thought flared across the darkness of my predicament and made the commander harder to hate. Love among those we label barbarians should not surprise us. They are as human as we are. I realized my own eyes were wet now.

"I want to help," I said finally. "I can guess at the problem. But I cannot prescribe a solution without seeing her eyes. I could do more damage, and I would never forgive myself for that. If you don't want me to look, it's better to leave them be and just kill me now."

He was silent for a long while. Then he uttered a few words and waved his hand. Two men grabbed me and returned me to the small room. Here were my last minutes, and here came my last meal: a huge hunk of pale brown, roughly hewn meat. If Commander Amanullah didn't kill me, this would. I eyed it warily, as if it might move. Then I ate. My hand reached out, as if of its own volition; it tore off strips and brought them to my mouth. The meat was as tough and flavorless as leather. Still, I worked my jaw. If I was going to die anyway, why die hungry? But also, I couldn't help myself, and as my blood sugar rose, a great peace—as in the wake of a migraine—came over my body. I was relaxed enough to sleep.

Then the door opened. My guards barked at me to move.

"What's happening?" I cried. "Where am I being taken? Please let me finish my meal." Ridiculous, but those few bites had left me ravenous. At death's threshold, I could think only of that meat.

I was led into a pitch-black room. I heard rustling—whether rats or humans, I couldn't tell. Fear sickened me, as did the stench of manure, and I gagged. My eyes adjusted to the lack of light, and a candle flared, glinting off the shiny polyester of a woman's burka and also the hook hand of Commander Amanullah. There was no one else in the room.

"This is Gulab," the commander said. "You will examine her eyes, nothing more, and then you will make her better." He held the candle up and I saw that the burka's netting had been delicately cut away. I had a rectangle to work with.

"It's not enough light," I told him. "I can't see properly."

He moved the candle closer, so close that I feared either the cheap fabric or my hair might catch fire. The heat cooked my cheek. Drops of wax pocked the floor. I heard our mingled breathing and the rustle of fabric when she moved. I smelled sour breath, sour meat, sweat, and, most significant, the discharge of pus from her eyes. The light had made Gulab cry out in pain, but when I dared look into her eyes, they merely reflected the flame, along with a miniature version of my terrified self.

"I'm sorry, but I can't see anything this way," I said to the commander. "I need my equipment and more light."

To my surprise he agreed to allow that. He went to the door, called

142

one of his men, and returned a minute later with my medical bag, which had been kidnapped from my room along with me. Lanterns were brought. I removed my binocular loupe and ophthalmoscope from the bag and examined first Gulab's eyelids, then her corneas, which were slightly opaque. I suspected trachoma. But to confirm my hunch I needed to evert her eyelid, to turn it inside out. I needed to touch her.

When I told the commander this, he hesitated. Then he said, "Go ahead. But only the eyes." I wondered if he would have me killed afterward so that no one would know I had touched her.

I put on sterile gloves, taking my time. I have performed hundreds, maybe thousands, of eversions during my medical career, but never with hands trembling as they were now and never on a patient who flinched so dramatically at my touch.

"Hold still," I murmured, as much to myself as to her.

Normally the conjunctiva, the membrane lining the inside of the eyelid and the forepart of the eyeball, is a smooth transparent pink. But Gulab's conjunctiva was so thickened and inflamed that it was spotted with white follicles, like little tapioca beads, and it glistened with fibrous scars, also white. Without a doubt, this was trachoma, which comes from the Greek word for "rough." Luckily for me, and of course for her, Gulab's trachoma was still at a treatable stage. If I'd seen her much later, her eyelashes would have begun to turn in and rub on her eyelids, which is excruciating and correctable only by surgery.

"I can treat her," I told Commander Amanullah, and in the dim light I saw tears of relief well in his eyes. So powerful was his love that it felt like another presence in the room with us.

A single dose of azithromycin, two 500-milligram tablets, would cure her, and I had snared a few extra from the eye hospital in Kabul. I gave Gulab the two pills. Commander Amanullah wanted more. He assumed, as ignorant people do, that more medicine would kill more disease. I refused, more confident now about standing up to him. Then I insisted on examining all of his men, his two other wives (through the same method), and his children, to look for signs of trachoma. I put drops to battle infection in the eyes of the children, and I taught all of them how to keep their eyes, faces, and hands clean. They needed to be more intolerant of flies, which spread bacteria. And the women were not to use their burkas or dirty rags to wipe the eyes and faces of the children.

Gulab's pain began to abate within a day. There followed a feast of celebration, a sheep slaughtered in my honor. The commander and I sat together and talked man to man of what it means to love your wife. I thought of Gloria, of my infidelities and indiscretions. Commander Amanullah was not the only one changed by our encounter. For all of Gloria's freedoms, could I say the commander treated his wife worse than I did mine? It was my freedoms, not Gloria's, that were the problem. I'd abused them and, through them, her. I wasn't at her side...

I was sick for three days afterward. I don't know if it was the meat, the feast, or the stress, but it was worth it to learn this lesson: how easily we can win these people over if we recognize their common humanity, if we see ourselves in them, if we use our power and skills to solve their problems rather than to rain bombs on their heads, and if we help the men help their women. What is the cost of a dose of azithromycin compared to a cruise missile? Love is universal. We forget this at their peril—and ours.

PARVEEN CHOSE THIS CHAPTER, about Crane's encounter with Amanullah, as the first one to share with the women in the khan's orchard. It had a meaty mix of drama and emotion, and it had the flavor of a folktale—colorful, sometimes comical, with a moral attached. As the protagonist, Crane could be both crafty and vulnerable, succumbing to, then outsmarting, then befriending Commander Amanullah. She might have thought better of making the most vocal opponent of this enterprise its first subject, but Waheed's boldness had emboldened her too.

Parveen again created a simplified version of the chapter in her notebook. Only the boys with cell phones struck her as odd, since no one she'd met in the village had one.

She worried no one would appear that first morning other than Bina and Shokoh, who had promised, but soon women, perhaps fifty in all, began to enter the orchard in small groups. They molted their green chadris, which disappeared into the grass, then patrolled the orchard with an inspecting air. When, at Parveen's behest, they finally sat, they remained restless and talkative, too excited to still themselves.

"We must start our reading to take advantage of the time," Parveen called out. "We can only use this orchard until the apricots come, and we'll need a number of meetings to get through the whole book."

There was a pause, then a burst of laughter.

"And what is so funny?" she asked.

"The khan is playing tricks on you," Ghazal called out. "This orchard gives no fruit. It hasn't for years. It gave sweet apricots for twenty or twenty-five years—"

"Then it got tired," the dai said.

"Are you trying to make us all barren, putting us in an orchard that doesn't give fruit?" This was Saba, who had been so distraught about menopause. Her tone was pointed.

"I'm going to tell my husband this place is full of fruit," Ghazal said, as if here was the aphrodisiac she had sought.

"Juicy fruit—"

"Plump fruit—"

"Sweet-smelling and -tasting fruit," said Anisa, the anemic woman who had seemed so exhausted when Parveen met her at the clinic. She licked her fingers, and the others laughed.

At the clinic, Parveen had seen Anisa and many of the others naked, recumbent, even battered. But here, savoring a rare morning of freedom and leisure out of their husbands' shadows, they were neither patients nor victims. Here they were lordly.

"Then the khan will hear there is fruit here and come kick us out," Latifa said fretfully, "for what value do we have against a bushel of apricots?"

By "we" she meant women, and Parveen found this especially painful coming from the mother of three girls with possibly a fourth on the way.

"He got greedy, that's what Waheed says," offered Shokoh, with a taunting glance at Bina. "He planted clover, which takes too much water, and the fruit won't grow."

"The khan got greedy?" Saba said with mock innocence, and everyone except Bina laughed.

"Fruit or no fruit," Parveen said, "we must begin."

She had the women sit in a semicircle. Some held hands, some nursed infants, some sewed. Children wandered in and out of the orchard, but they were more quiet than usual, as if they too had fallen under its spell.

Parveen glanced down at the notebook she'd brought. She would tell a story of something that happened to Dr. Gideon in the village, she explained to the women. This was six years ago, but possibly some of them had heard this story themselves. "One morning, as Dr. Gideon slept," she started, "he heard a knock on the door. Two men with guns stood there, and they covered his eyes and forced him into their pickup truck. They took him to see Commander Amanullah, the Taliban chief in the village. He was a terrifying man. He had a hook for a hand. He kept a dungeon. He was said to have tortured people and chopped off heads—"

Squawks of protest echoed through the orchard. Parveen stopped, alarmed. The women were all talking at once, making them impossible to hear, until they elected one woman to speak for them. Saba asked if Parveen was talking about their Amanullah.

Yes, said Parveen, feeling slightly faint.

"But he isn't Taliban," Saba said. "We've never had Taliban

here." The other women made loud noises of assent. "He was a mujahid."

"Well, yes, he was," Parveen said carefully. "But then, according to Dr. Gideon, he changed..." She trailed off.

"Amanullah fought against the Soviets—"

"That's how he lost his hand."

"Then he went away to fight the Taliban—"

"There are no Taliban here!"

"Why are you saying such things? You'll get Americans to start dropping bombs on us."

Parveen took a deep breath and said there was nothing to worry about from the American soldiers, who were far off and would never come to this tiny village. Nor was she asserting that there were Taliban here. "This is what Dr. Gideon wrote in his book," she said, then suggested that there might be a different commander to whom Dr. Gideon was referring.

"There's only one commander here with a hook," the dai said. "Ask Amina how many times in the night that cold touch has woken her up!" She pointed to a haggard woman whom Parveen hadn't met yet.

"These years I wish it woke me up more often!" said Amina, who was delighted by her own quickness. The women roared with recognition.

Parveen asked Amina if Dr. Gideon had ever treated her eyes.

"It's my stomach that's troubling me," she answered. "Why would I need a doctor for my eyes?"

"Because when your mother-in-law waves her arm for tea, you never see her," Ghazal said, to more laughter.

"It was another of his wives," Parveen corrected herself. "It was Gulab."

"Who's Gulab? He has no other wife!" Amina spat, now electric with anger.

"Oh," Parveen said, bewildered. "Oh. Well, all right. I'm sorry." Parveen wondered if, as with Fereshta, Crane had transformed plain Amina into a more glamorous figure. If so, this habit was starting to make her uncomfortable. It suggested women weren't enough as they were. "Maybe your eyes bothered you then?" she tried. There was an atemporal quality to the women's lives, a lack of chronology. What mattered was what ailed them in the present. Since Crane's initial visit, he'd returned often to build, then rebuild, the clinic. Perhaps this was increasing the women's confusion. "When Dr. Gideon came that first time," she asked Amina, "did he give you pills to help your eyes?"

"I've never seen Dr. Gideon," Amina insisted, "and I told you, I have no problem with my eyes."

Parveen, flustered, wished the women gone so she could think. They would stop for today, she said, and she would write to Dr. Gideon to ask about this. In the meantime she suggested that it might be best for them not to mention it to their husbands. She didn't want to stir up trouble in the village.

The women drifted off. Parveen lingered alone in the quiet of the orchard, trying to parse what had just occurred. Outside the walls, Bina and Shokoh were waiting for her. In their presence she felt embarrassed, uncertain. "I'm sure this can all be explained," she said.

"Why does it need to be explained?" Bina said. "It's just a story Dr. Gideon made up."

"He said it was—is—a true story."

"Why does that matter?" Shokoh asked.

"Because it does," Parveen said impatiently, then tried to explain. "In life, in history, it's important to know what happened to us."

"But we know what happened to us," Bina observed. "Whether the story you tell about it is true or not true doesn't change what already happened."

Parveen hesitated, searching for a rebuttal. "We make decisions about the future based on the stories we tell about the past," she said.

"We're women," Shokoh replied. "We're not allowed to make decisions."

BACK AT WAHEED'S, PARVEEN crouched in her stall, studying *Mother Afghanistan*. What Crane had written about the commander, what he'd inscribed on the page for posterity, was unequivocal. Perhaps that was why people wrote, to close off other versions of the past. Yet whereas the women might want to hide that there'd been Taliban in their midst, she could think of no reason for Crane to have lied.

Suddenly there was a banging on the compound door and Commander Amanullah was bellowing outside it. With Waheed in the fields, Parveen couldn't let the commander in even if she wanted to, which she didn't. Full of dread, she slipped out into the lane to speak to him.

"I am not Taliban!" he roared in a voice loud enough to scare off a platoon of them.

His success on the battlefield made new sense to Parveen. Bullets of spittle flew toward her; she closed her eyes as they landed on her forehead, eyelids, cheeks.

"I fought against the Taliban just as I fought against the Soviets," he said. "I am a mujahid!"

When Parveen opened her eyes, he was punching the air with his hook, as if to remind her of what combat had cost him or hint at what her smears could cost her. Amina, in her chadri, stood just behind him.

"I know, I know," Parveen said. "It was Dr. Gideon's story. I don't know why he put your name in it. It's all just a misunderstanding."

"You said that my husband had a dungeon and beheaded people," Amina trilled.

"Crane—Dr. Gideon—*he* said that. Not me."

"Then tell him to come here and answer to me!" Amanullah shouted. "Be glad you're a woman."

"I'm sorry," Parveen said. She was woozy and shaking and close to passing out. She wished she could sit on the ground. She'd never had anyone this angry with her, never been yelled at this way. He was going to hit her, she feared, and she flinched in anticipation.

"Get the book," Amanullah said. "I want to see it."

He wouldn't be able to read it, but Parveen went to retrieve the book. Inside, Bina and Shokoh were huddled against the wall, listening. Bina whispered that she'd sent Bilal for Waheed. Parveen, who now remembered seeing the boy slip past when she'd gone out to greet the commander, nodded gratefully.

It was tempting simply to bar the door until Waheed's return, but Parveen forced herself to take *Mother Afghanistan* out to the commander, who nestled it in his hook while paging through it with his other hand. He, too, stopped at the pictures, mesmerized. He was staring at the one of Waheed and Crane when Waheed came running up. The commander, seeing him, exclaimed in amazement, his expression incredulous, "That's you!" When Waheed asked him in for tea, Amanullah acted as if he'd received an invitation to a royal wedding. "I'm in this book?" he said to Parveen once they were inside. He no longer seemed concerned with how it presented him. He paged through the pictures, looking for himself.

Parveen took the book and found a reference to him. "That says, in English, 'Commander Amanullah,'" she explained. "Millions of Americans have read your name."

This was tawdry of her, since his name in the book was connected to a description he disputed. But the confirmation was pacifying. He grew respectful. He asked if he could keep the book. No, Parveen said, but she promised to try to obtain a copy for him.

Amina was sent to help Bina and Shokoh. Over tea, Waheed told Parveen, "Amanullah was never Taliban. He fought against them, just as he fought bravely against the Russians—I've told you about that. He's seen much more of the country than I have. He has lost a great deal; his sons were martyred fighting the Taliban. The three of them left the village to fight together. Only he came back."

Parveen said meekly that she'd assumed his sons had died fighting the Soviets.

"There's a lot of history here you don't know. And even to know is not always to understand."

"Crane wrote it, not me," she said weakly. But she still felt it was somehow her fault.

After the commander left, Waheed said, "They say his sons' deaths were terrible," and she felt even worse.

That evening, she sat with Waheed and Jamshid while the women cleaned up after dinner. With her back against the cushions, she scribbled away in one of the spiral notebooks she'd brought, describing the day's events in a letter to Professor Banerjee. Each time she wrote in English, she felt the strain of changing languages a little more.

"Will you write such things about us too?" Waheed asked from across the room.

"Anything I write will be the truth," Parveen told him. But she put the pad away.

THAT NIGHT, BESET BY ANXIETY that the uneasy truce with Amanullah wouldn't last, she barely slept. She kept searching for explanations. Perhaps Amanullah had a daughter whom Crane had treated, and he had misunderstood and thought she was the commander's wife. Except Crane, she realized, wouldn't have understood or misunderstood anything; he spoke no Dari. The translator he relied on, A., would have been the filter through which he experienced the village, its people, the commander. The errors had to be the translator's. But had A. even been there for the kidnapping? she wondered. Crane hadn't mentioned him.

The next morning she went to Amanullah's house. She expected to encounter a fort, since Crane had so vividly described the high walls. But to her the commander's compound looked no different than Waheed's. Fear can profoundly distort perception, she concluded. Today she would likely find the commander, so terrifying yesterday, comical once again. But she didn't find him at all. Amina informed her, from behind the door, that he was already at the bazaar.

Parveen asked permission to come inside so that they could talk. Amina agreed but kept her eyes on her feet, leaving Parveen to apologize to the part in her hair. "I hope both you and your husband can forgive me," she said.

"He's forgiven you," Amina answered, then she raised her head to look squarely at Parveen and revealed the large purple-red bruise on her face. That sickening instant when Parveen had feared she was about to be struck—the blow had landed here instead. Amanullah had forgiven Parveen, he had forgiven Crane, but someone had to pay.

PART TWO

CHAPTER TWELVE

THE SMELL OF MILK

THE WHEAT DIVESTED ITSELF OF GREEN UNTIL IT WAS HIGH AND tan and ready for harvest. In the fields, under a scything sun, the men crouched with sickles in hand, using the same tool, the same motion, with which farmers had been reaping their crops for millennia. The stalks were gathered with the left hand, then severed at the base of their stems with the right, so the sharp curved blade sliced toward the body again and again. Gathering, cutting, gathering, cutting; the men worked for hours, the labor leaving bodies sore and minds numb and skin coated with the chaff that floated snow-like from the yellow-gold stacks of wheat. Parveen, not oppressed by the labor, was content to savor the beauty, the harvest against its backdrop of purple-gray mountains and austere white clouds. This was what she was doing on the July day Colonel Trotter first came to the village.

Three children raced toward Waheed shouting, "Americans! Americans!" As if Parveen weren't one herself. Shielding her eyes, she saw a group advancing along the valley floor, with more children behind. Their approach through the heat and haze of the day seemed to go on forever, as if something momentous was about to occur. They wore military uniforms the color of sand, which set off an alarm in Parveen. Her fear was that the war had arrived.

This apprehension diminished somewhat as the soldiers drew closer. They were sweaty and pink-faced from the walk, and the tallest of them, at the center of the group, was not in uniform at all. He wore instead a navy-blue *perahan tunban*, the knee-length shirt and baggy pants customary to Afghan men. Parveen guessed he was trying to convey cultural respect, but the attempt was so blatant she couldn't help feeling a little embarrassed for him. In his military haircut and Afghan garb, he looked like a frat boy dressed for a costume party.

He waved and called a hello to Waheed. The sound of English jarred Parveen after weeks of hearing only the lilt of Dari. Upon reaching Waheed, the man held his hand out—it was tepidly received—and introduced himself as Lieutenant Colonel Francis Trotter. "Call me Frank," he said in the flat cadence of a Midwesterner. His long face was sunburned and ruddy. His hair, thick and dark on top, speckled here and there with gray, was shaved almost to the scalp on the sides. This made his ears, which were prominent, appear nearly perpendicular to his head.

The colonel had a good eight inches on Waheed and an entirely different build, broad-shouldered and strong, the product of gym repetitions, track miles, and carbo loads, whereas Waheed's spare physique testified to years of fieldwork and a meager childhood diet. Parveen guessed the colonel to be around forty, slightly older than Waheed, but it was Waheed who seemed, after decades of eking out a living from the land and battling to keep his children and wife alive, ancient.

The interpreter was an Afghan in the same uniform as the soldiers. In a glance, Parveen registered instinctive approval of his body—lean and broad-shouldered—and his dark eyes. He greeted Waheed in Dari in a way that suggested they'd met before, which surprised Parveen. The interpreter told Waheed that "this American" wanted to visit "the grave of Jamshid's mother." Afghans rarely used women's names—they usually referred to them in relation to their sons—but Parveen wondered how the interpreter knew Jamshid's name. Jamshid was standing well behind Waheed, but she realized that the teenager and the interpreter were, even at a distance, staring at each other, as if a line were pulled tight between them.

Waheed pointed the way, and Colonel Trotter and the others began to walk toward the graveyard. Parveen followed behind, with the children, close enough to hear what was said. No other women were in sight. Through the interpreter, Colonel Trotter asked Waheed about the canals, hewn from hollowed-out trees, that carried river water to irrigate the fields. He asked about crops and crop yields, about livestock grazing and the village population and family structures and what kinds of foods they stockpiled for winter (dried mulberries, dried and salted yogurt balls, called *kurut*, flour, nuts, and so on). He asked about the political structure in the village, about how the shura, the village council, was chosen. The man guzzled information. Parveen imagined it all being sorted into relevant headings in his brain: Agriculture, Governance, Commerce.

The graveyard sat at the narrow opening where the valley fanned out from between the foothills of the mountains. The graves were mounds of stones and rocks, one looking like the next, other than a few with faded, ragged green flags honoring those martyred while fighting the Soviets, and the tiny mounds that signified lost babies. Parveen had visited several times and always found the site unnerving. Graves generally went unmarked here, just as official birth and death certificates were rarely written. Villagers' lives and passings were registered only in memory.

There was, in this cemetery, one exception: Fereshta's grave. She had a marble gravestone that looked, amid the gray rubble, like the last good tooth in a rotted mouth. The tablet, complete with inscription, had arrived in the village without advance notice two or three years earlier, Waheed had said. Gideon Crane had paid for it. For visitors—for pilgrims, among whom Parveen reluctantly numbered herself—finding Fereshta's grave was easy now. Her name was carved in both Persian and English, although the graveyard's pervasive dust had silted into the letters. The American soldiers gathered around the grave and bowed their heads as if they were praying.

Parveen imagined Fereshta as a goddess at whose shrine visitors came to light votive candles. She asked Jamshid, who was standing next to her, if other foreigners had come to the grave.

Yes, he said. Many had come, usually by helicopter in the first couple of years after Dr. Gideon wrote his book. More recently, there'd been far fewer; Parveen was the only one they'd seen this spring. Still, he said, his mother was the most important person here.

Parveen couldn't tell if he was being sarcastic. Envisioning foreign soldiers making a pilgrimage to her own mother's burial site in California, she wasn't sure whether it would feel like an honor or an invasion.

"More people care to know her when she's dead than when she was alive," Jamshid said.

Parveen didn't think his comment was directed at her necessarily, but it shamed her nonetheless. Would Fereshta, alive, have held her interest? She found Bina nowhere near as compelling as her dead sister.

"At least he met her," Jamshid said. He was talking about the interpreter, she realized, who was now deep in conversation with Waheed. Every once in a while, he would glance toward Jamshid, and occasionally his eyes would find Parveen. She sensed that he could tell she wasn't from the village.

Who was he? Parveen asked.

That's Aziz, Jamshid said. He'd been to the village before, years earlier, as Gideon Crane's interpreter.

"Are you serious?" Parveen couldn't believe her good fortune.

In the two weeks since she'd recounted Crane's chapter for the women and faced the commander's outrage, she'd grown certain that Crane's translator, A., was to blame for the mistakes in *Mother Afghanistan*. She'd even mentioned this theory to Waheed, who'd replied that the interpreter was a decent man. But since when were decency and incompetence incompatible? Now, with A.—Aziz—here in the valley, she could find out what had gone wrong.

THE AMERICANS, AFTER A cursory examination of the rest of the graveyard, marched back across the valley floor. Sagging from the heat, they arrived at the clinic, where Waheed led them on a tour, offering garbled explanations about the equipment and the donors of which the interpreter made garbled translations. To the Americans it all seemed to make sense. They offered admiring remarks, then exited to wait for the gathering of the shura, with which Colonel Trotter had requested a meeting.

Little happened fast in the village—there was no reason it should—and the tension between politeness and efficiency was evident on the colonel's face. Speaking in low tones to the men who'd accompanied him, he pored over a map and checked his watch every few minutes. At last the interpreter, Aziz, called the soldiers. The council had assembled, and Colonel Trotter and his team moved to join them. Most of the village men—no woman other than Parveen was present—had seated themselves beneath and around a stand of poplar trees near the river, with the elders at the front. The mullah had come, as had Commander Amanullah, who lifted his hook to greet Parveen. She pretended not to see.

A woven plastic mat was spread on the grass, and the Americans sat together on one side of it. One boy dosed small glasses with pale clear tea while another piled sugared almonds onto plates. The soldiers were careful to cross their legs and not present their feet and to lay their weapons down next to them or prop them against trees. Light dribbled through the leaves above, patterning the faces, landing like lace on the guns. Afghans were used to guns, of course—many kept them in their homes—but they hadn't brought any to the meeting. The Americans' automatic rifles, so casually displayed, seemed to create an imbalance, a disturbance, in the air.

Colonel Trotter ostentatiously removed his watch and handed it to one of his soldiers as if to suggest he had all the time in the world. A nearly toothless elder gave a long, florid welcome during which he praised both God and the American presence in Afghanistan, even as he also thanked the colonel for respecting the wisdom and authority of the shura.

"He welcomes you to the village," Aziz told Colonel Trotter.

It was an honor to be here, the colonel replied. He said he was from an American state called Kansas and that his father had been a soldier, then a farmer, so he understood what it meant to earn a living from the land. As the elders surely knew, the Americans had come to Afghanistan because there were bad actors who were threatening the United States and harming the Afghan people, and the Americans had stayed in Afghanistan in order to help to rebuild it. To make it prosperous and strong as well as safe. They were here to serve the Afghans, to listen to them, to work together on delivering what the people needed. He commanded a battalion of five hundred soldiers who were doing everything from training the Afghan army to practicing counterinsurgency to working on development projects.

He used a lot of superlatives in his speech, Parveen noticed. His soldiers were "outstanding"; the governor of the province, a man the villagers had never seen, was a "tremendous friend"; and Gideon Crane's book *Mother Afghanistan* was, as they all surely knew, "magnificent."

It was the book that had brought him here, Colonel Trotter said. A lot of Americans had read it. The former president of the

United States, who in 2001 had ordered the American military into Afghanistan, had read it, as had his wife. All of those readers had come to care about the village. They knew there was a clinic, but was there more that the people of the United States could do to help? The answer, he said, was the road to the village. Crane had written about how God-awful it was, and traveling it for the first time today, Trotter could confirm he was right. "Right now, it's a real impediment to progress, not to mention a real nightmare for my back."

This joke, once translated, earned a polite laugh or two.

Colonel Trotter grew serious. The road was going to be widened and paved, he said, so that cars and trucks could drive in and out, which would allow women in medical peril to get help. This was why he had come; this would be a gift from the American people to the village. Not just its women; farmers would benefit too, because they'd be able to sell their crops all over the country. Roads had transformed the lives of earlier Americans, linking them into a market economy. They'd do the same for Afghans. No more losing whole days going to a town to get seeds or tools, Trotter said. "Bam, you can do it in just a morning, drive right back. Your productivity goes way up. Your incomes go way up. Progress." He nodded at his own words.

Parveen, hearing the reason for the visit, was relieved, partly because it wasn't about the war at all and also because it turned out that she hadn't been the only one to come because of Crane's book. A road, an easily traversable road, would change so much here, she thought with growing excitement. Dr. Yasmeen, or any doctor, could drive in much more often. The woman who'd died from eclampsia in the doctor's car would probably still be alive if the road had been paved and the journey along it a half an hour instead of two hours or more. Fereshta would still be alive; Colonel Trotter was saying this now, pronouncing her name "Fresh-ta," like a soft drink. Parveen waited for the reaction of Waheed and Jamshid, who were sitting together, but Aziz, when he translated, left out the part about Fereshta.

For a few moments the only sound was the clicking of prayer beads. Then the elders began murmuring among themselves.

"Will every village nearby also have its road paved?" one elder, his beard as white as a burial shroud, finally asked, and the others nodded as if this were the question on all of their lips. The question, which seemed so provincial, disappointed Parveen. Colonel Trotter was talking about changing their lives!

They'd been paving roads all over Afghanistan, the colonel said, but this village—well, Americans knew about this village, they knew its story, because of Gideon Crane's book. So in this area, they wanted to start with this village's road, because it would mean a lot to the American people too.

"The president of the United States wants your road to be paved," Aziz said, and more murmuring among the elders ensued.

Parveen was surprised by how much the interpreter abbreviated. Yet even with the shortened renditions, it felt interminable. Because Parveen spoke both languages, it was like waiting for a slow student in class to finish his math problems. While the words were translated, her mind moved on, so when the reply finally came, after its own translation, it seemed to have arrived from the past.

Colonel Trotter estimated that the project would take about four months to complete. Unlike in many parts of the country, they didn't have to pacify the area before starting work; it was already peaceful. He introduced his team's civil engineer, who described how they would use excavators and rock hammers to widen the road and, where that was insufficient, blast the rock away after drilling holes into the mountain. There was always a danger of triggering landslides or creating instability, he went on, but this would be managed. Controlled violence, thought Parveen. The engineer described how the debris produced by cutting into the mountain could be used as fill to widen the road on the river side if the ground was stable enough. He made the terrain that Parveen had conceived of as solid and permanent sound like a room to be renovated.

"He still has the smell of milk on him," one elder said of the engineer, to laughter.

Parveen laughed too; he looked barely older than a college student.

Colonel Trotter glanced toward Aziz, who said, apologetically, "To the elders he appears very young."

"Old enough to have a master's degree and be on his third tour," the colonel said tersely. He took over the talking to say that any villager who wanted to be employed on the road project would be hired. The road would be paved before the snows came. Were there any questions? Anything he should know?

No one answered this solicitation because Aziz didn't translate it, and the colonel unfurled a large map. Everyone shifted back on the mat to make room. "This is your neck of the woods," he said.

Parveen stood up to see. The map had Cyrillic lettering, which suggested that it had been made by the Soviets during their invasion. With the heart of their conflict much farther south, apparently the Americans themselves had yet to map this region. On the Soviet map, the mountain altitudes were captured in concentric waves, the paths in spidery lines, the highway in a solid one. The Americans had added a red star to show the village and a dotted red line to show the road that led from it to the highway.

The elders stared at the map; some of them, Parveen discovered later, had never seen one. They'd learned the area on foot or by donkey, and they remembered it by landmarks, judged distances by time, not kilometers. They lived in three dimensions, they had no reason to translate into two. Maps were for going places you'd never been or recording places you'd left behind. The elders did neither. With their fingers they jabbed at features on the map that were inscrutable to Parveen and argued about the locations of other villages, villages they knew by walking.

Why pave the road to *this* village? They asked the colonel again. Why not all the others?

"Star, star, star, star, star," one elder said, placing his finger on the map again and again in different spots to show the locations of other villages.

It's a funny thing how men will fight to the death for an advantage, Parveen thought, but when handed one may retreat from it as from a live grenade. These elders and their ancestors, she knew from Waheed, had joyfully schemed to annex land from or interfere with the water rights of other subtribes. Yet now they seemed to be resisting—at least, Parveen interpreted their questions as a way of indirectly declining—what would be an obvious boon to their village.

With effort Colonel Trotter repeated his explanation. Simply by allowing the Americans to pave the road, the villagers would progress from a subsistence economy to a market one. They could buy plows, tractors. Clothes for their wives. *Longer lives* for their wives. A better future for their children.

"Everything will change with this road," Aziz told the elders.

In response, the white-bearded elder began to recount the history of the village, taking a route from past to present as winding as the road itself. Herders seeking land to graze their animals had first discovered this valley, and their goats had made a track barely wide enough for a man to follow through the mountains and along the river. With time, houses were built and fields were laid out to make use of the abundant water and fertile soil. Here another elder picked up the story. The track widened so that a donkey could pass, then widened still more for its cart. And this was sufficient. A better road was not what they needed. No one in the village even had a car. They needed help with their aging irrigation systems; they needed a schoolhouse and teacher for their children, who were currently educated in the mosque. To pave this road and not do the same on roads leading to villages nearby could create envy and therefore lasting enmity between tribes. This point, of course, required a genealogy of all the local tribes and subtribes...

Parveen had crept around to the other side of the assembly to see Colonel Trotter's face more clearly. His eyes were gray and shrewd. He kept sneaking glances upward, as if anxious, or maybe hopeful, that rain might intrude. The sky was clear. The speeches of the elders ran their long courses, only to be reduced by Aziz to a three-minute history and a list of concerns, which the colonel quickly dispatched.

They shouldn't fear change, he lectured them, his knee jiggling slightly. By paving roads, the Romans had vastly expanded the reach of their empire. By building an interstate highway system in the 1950s, America had cemented its status as the greatest country on earth, Trotter said. And decades back, the Americans and especially the Soviets had built many of Afghanistan's highways; this was nothing new.

Aziz did not talk of the Romans or the Russians or of America's highways or its greatness. He repeated that the road could help transport goods to market and ill family members to a hospital. The village men again agreed that this was important but again insisted that the road was not the aid most needed.

Parveen was beginning to suspect that the villagers' true sentiments lay hidden beneath their words, their speeches like long tangled vines covering the trellises supporting them. They were talking around the real source of their stubbornness—whether because it couldn't be spoken aloud, because words couldn't properly convey it, or because they couldn't even identify it, she wasn't sure. Perhaps it was simply that they would feel anxiety about any foreign power rolling into the valley and telling them what they needed. The gun on the grass.

"They agree that to save the life of the woman is important," Aziz said, "so I think they'll work with you."

This stunned Parveen. Nothing she had heard the elders say could be interpreted this way.

"Terrific," Colonel Trotter said, visibly relieved. This was a tremendous day for the village and he looked forward to their cooperation. "This is just the beginning of the relationship with us," he said, hooking his index fingers together to symbolize their intertwining. Once there was a functioning road, there would be much more that his engineers, various NGOs, and, of course, the Afghans' own government could do for them.

Aziz told the shura that the American engineers would do a lot for the village, that they would work on their irrigation canals and whatever else was needed. Now the villagers also looked pleased. Each side had the sense that it had achieved what it wanted but only because this interpreter had created the illusion of agreement where there was none. Now what?

It all made a kind of horrible sense to Parveen. If Aziz's behavior today was any indication, he hadn't just made mistakes when he was working for Crane. He had twisted, even invented, information. Whatever game he was playing, both Crane and Colonel Trotter needed to know about it.

"Who will guard the equipment for paving the road?" Commander Amanullah was saying.

When Aziz translated this, the colonel stared at the commander as if trying to remember where they'd met. "We have a saying in America—we'll cross that bridge when we come to it." It was hard at this point, he said, to know what or who the equipment would need guarding from.

"The guarding will be negotiated later," Aziz said.

There was a bit more small talk, and then, with a brief prayer, the elders ended the meeting. All the men stood to extend their hands and stretch their kinked legs. Colonel Trotter and his team walked back up toward the clinic, where their vehicles, a band of Humvees, were parked. A couple of the soldiers were reporting on the body language they'd observed during the meeting—who'd seemed enthusiastic and who querulous, who'd stayed quiet and what that might mean. No one mentioned the two elders Parveen had seen yawning behind their hands. She followed, eavesdropping. It was amazing, she thought, and sometimes quite useful how invisible a woman could be.

"The guy with the hook, he's the Talib in Crane's book," the colonel said. "Did he think I was going to hand him a bag of money right there for protection?"

Amanullah might be capable of extortion, but Parveen knew now he wasn't a Talib and wanted to prevent that misunderstanding. She hurried up to Colonel Trotter, who stepped back at her approach. "Hello, Lieutenant!" she blurted out.

At first startled, he recovered his composure and said dryly, "Lieutenant colonel, actually. It's just a rank or two higher." She winced at her mistake, and he smiled to show he hadn't taken offense. "I thought you were—never mind," he said, and he held out his hand. He asked where she'd come from, and when she told him, he laughed. "A Berkeley grad here? What, are you going to train them to grow arugula? Sorry, that was too easy. You're Afghan?"

"American."

"Right, I meant—you speak the language."

"Dari, yes."

"I've had *Dari for Beginners* on my desk for months," he said ruefully. "I should be better than I am." He asked what had brought her to the village.

Mother Afghanistan, she said.

"The power of that book," he said, shaking his head to show his respect. It was really something, he went on, the way Gideon Crane had managed to figure out what everyone from Alexander the Great to the British to the Soviets had missed, which was that, while Afghans couldn't be subdued, they could be understood; they could be respected. Crane had given the military a road map to succeed where every empire had failed. They just had to follow it, Trotter said. That's what this road project was about. Kind power.

"About the book," Parveen said. This was her chance. Aziz was some distance off, smoking and watching them. His eyes were as black and restless as carpenter bees. They looked like they didn't miss much.

Yes, Trotter said again, the book was really something. This time it almost sounded, to Parveen, as if he was trying to convince himself of this. His wife had read it in her book club; they'd gone whole hog for it, and she'd pressed it on him—this was before all the generals were reading it, he said modestly. In fact, his wife's words had sparked the idea of doing the road, although he wouldn't tell his superiors that. One day when they were Skyping, she said that she hoped it was easier to get in and out of that village now than it had been for Gideon Crane. A light bulb went on, he said. Here was a project that would not only benefit Afghans, Afghan women, but also resonate back home. Thanks to Crane, this was the one village in Afghanistan a whole bunch of Americans had an interest in; they cared about it, even if they didn't care about Afghanistan itself. Heck, this village was more real to them than the country as a whole was. The road would create goodwill with the Afghans and good feelings among the Americans, real bang for the buck.

"Yes, but can I tell you—" Parveen tried to interject, speaking quietly so that Aziz wouldn't hear.

Unfortunately, Trotter seemed not to hear either. How long did she plan to stay in the village? he asked. "Your family must want you home."

"I promised I'd be home for Thanksgiving," she said, "but— now I want to stay long enough to see the road built." She hadn't realized this was true until the words barreled out of her mouth. It was more than wanting to see how the road would transform the village. It was that, seeing her idealism mirrored in Trotter's, she felt less alone. It no longer seemed quixotic to believe change could come.

"Don't worry, you'll drive out of here on a paved road and be home in time to cook the turkey. Or eat it." His own deployment ended in early December, he added, which meant that, unlike last year, he would be home for Christmas.

In America, Parveen said, she'd imagined soldiers staying in Afghanistan for years on end—going gray here, going native.

Not so, Trotter said; deployments were for six months or a year, although by now the war had gone on so long that many soldiers had returned two, three, or four times. He himself had been deployed twice to Iraq before coming here. And there'd been stop-losses, which meant that soldiers who were due to rotate out couldn't because there weren't enough soldiers to replace them. But in general, the equipment stayed while the units turned over. The equipment and the interpreters, Trotter said. Their war had been longer than any of the soldiers'. "Right, Aziz?" he shouted.

Aziz, still smoking, gave a quick nod. Had he head what they were talking about, or was this reflexive affirmation for his boss?

"It's not really fair that he doesn't get combat hash marks," Trotter said. "He's probably seen four deployments come and go. Get over here, man, and meet Parveen," he called. "Actually, finish killing yourself with that cigarette first."

Yes, Parveen thought, *take your time.* She didn't want Aziz coming over yet; she was enjoying her conversation with Trotter. She knew so little about the military, and the colonel seemed eager to educate her.

"Generals turn over too?" she asked.

"Absolutely," he said. "We're on our third Joint Chiefs chairman since 2001. The third army chief too." He spoke almost gently, as if trying not to call attention to her ignorance. In

Vietnam there'd been four commanders in chief and three generals, he said. "Hopefully this war doesn't go on as long."

So if he left, Parveen said, someone else would finish the road?

"I'll finish it," Trotter said, less gently. But yes, if necessary, his successor would take over where he'd left off. He couldn't pretend there weren't occasional complications, the main one being that every leader assuming command tended to think that his predecessor was an idiot, he said with a smile. It made her think of sunlight hitting a rocky cliff that spent most of its life in gloom. The muscles of his face seemed surprised whenever he worked them.

The military was like a superorganism, she thought, a giant body constantly shedding cells and generating new ones. Aloud she wondered: if everyone was changing all the time, if every soldier was always being replaced, was it even still the same war, philosophically speaking? She worried that she sounded stoned (she'd never actually been stoned; all her knowledge of that state was secondhand) and so was confirming his stereotypes of Berkeley.

To the contrary, he seemed to embrace her question. "It's the Ship of Theseus," he said.

She nodded as if she understood, then eyed him. "What was that again?"

"Theseus. He founded Athens, killed the Minotaur in his labyrinth, did a few less savory things. But that's what's great about Plutarch—he wrote about Theseus in his *Lives*—he doesn't sugarcoat, gives you warriors with their warts and all. The *Argos*, the ship Theseus returned to Athens on after killing the Minotaur, the citizens put it in the harbor as a memorial, and they would take away the old timbers as they rotted and put new ones in their place, so it became a puzzle for philosophers: Was it the same ship if over time you swapped out every plank?"

Parveen must have looked surprised, because he smiled.

"Listen, Berkeley, not everyone in the military is a moron,

despite what your college may have brainwashed you into believing." He had studied classics at West Point, he said. "And I took quite a bit of philosophy, so I can also tell you about Neurath's boat. Otto Neurath, German—no, Austrian—philosopher. We're like sailors on the open sea, Neurath said, who have to rebuild and repair their ship without ever being able to start fresh from the bottom to the top. But any part can be replaced as long as there's enough of the rest for support," he went on. "Neurath was talking about the foundations of knowledge—arguing there was no such thing because any plank could be swapped out—but it could be applied to many contexts. Identity, for one; how do you replace the rotted parts of yourself while still staying intact as a person? And war, for another."

As he talked, his men began exchanging winks and stroking their chins, tipping their heads back and gazing contemplatively at the sky. Trotter didn't seem to notice. Clearly this wasn't the first time he'd pontificated, but it was the first time for Parveen, the first time meeting anyone in the military at all, and almost against her will she was impressed. Transfixed. Excited. Even, she had to admit, a little aroused, though he was basically old enough to be her father. She couldn't help but contrast his barely camouflaged impatience with the elders with his interest in schooling her.

And he wanted to learn from her too. He began asking her questions about the village women, drilling for information like a farmer in search of groundwater. What were the women's days like? How much education did they have? Was the clinic helping them? Had it saved lives? Not being able to talk to women, he said, was like being blind in one eye.

The problem with the clinic, she said, was that it didn't have a full-time doctor, and no one seemed to want to pay for one. He nodded knowingly and said that most likely Crane had made an agreement with the government to staff the clinic, and they hadn't followed through. The military often had the same problem with the schools and clinics it built; the government didn't pay salaries to staff them.

Now it was Parveen's turn to show off. She told him about a medical anthropologist studying child mortality in Brazil who had been perplexed about why families were so accepting of their infants dying. A key reason, the researcher found, was that the state—the bureaucracy—was completely indifferent to these deaths. If the government treated high rates of maternal mortality—or child death or hunger or whatever the issue was— as normal, it became normal to the people too. They assumed that is how things were meant to be.

"Especially when you have a religion as fatalistic as Islam as your guiding principle," Trotter agreed. "It just about killed me in Crane's book when our friend Waheed there kept calling everything God's will." He caught himself for a moment and paused. "Sorry—you're probably Muslim, but you grew up with a different mentality."

Parveen had no idea how to respond to this.

Anyway, he said, once the military paved the road, there would be no more excuses. It would be easy to get a doctor in here every day, he said, and he inquired further about Dr. Yasmeen.

Parveen had his ear, and she poured as much into it as she could, everything she'd been told about the ailments of the women and much of what she'd seen in the clinic. She forgot about protecting patient confidentiality; she saw the women less as patients than as stories, stories that would horrify and move Trotter as they had her. It was probably safe to say that the colonel had never heard so much about female parts before, but Parveen wanted to spare him nothing, including embarrassment. She imagined him reporting all of this on some occasion to the First Lady, maybe even to the president. Only later did she understand that anecdotes did not travel up the chain of command. Which wasn't to say they couldn't influence the course of events.

Although she worried that it would cement an image of the village as backward and primitive, she told him about the mullah choking the eclamptic woman and her subsequent death. The story was too good—too important, she thought—not to tell. And it was true. Perhaps she was also attempting to separate herself from "that kind of Muslim," even as she felt queasy at her impulse to do so. It was a sort of juvenile betrayal, as if she were back in school trying to ingratiate herself with the cooler kids.

Trotter shook his head in disgust. "Another good reason to pave this road, to strip guys like him of power."

With this, Parveen agreed. The mullah wouldn't be able to control a village where people could come and go as they pleased, where they were exposed to much wider influences. Even the khan would have less power, she thought with delight. But she hadn't forgotten the elders' hesitation, and she raised it with Trotter.

"Oh, the elders came around," he responded. "We just need to make them feel ownership. And get it done—they're used to promises being broken."

But they hadn't come around—that had been his interpreter's intervention. She wanted to tell Trotter this, but Aziz had been edging closer as they talked, preceded by the smell of a thousand cigarettes. He wasn't as tall as Trotter but he wasn't short, and his features—those dark eyes, a Roman nose and sensuous mouth—made for a face that was intriguing and therefore unnerving.

She greeted him in Dari.

"I speak English," he replied in English, showing badly yellowed teeth.

"And you probably want to practice it as much as I do my Dari," Parveen said in Dari.

"I'm an interpreter, I don't need practice," he said, again in English.

She considered informing him that he did need practice but

thought better of it. Under Trotter's gaze, they were both stiff, like under-rehearsed performers.

Where was Parveen from? he wanted to know.

Kabul, she told him in English. She'd been born in Kabul.

He asked where her family lived now.

Parveen didn't want to simply say "California," a place so much easier to grow up in than Kabul in wartime would've been, so she told him that her family had left in 1988 and with great difficulty found their way to California. She knew she sounded defensive.

"I live in Kabul, I've always lived in Kabul," Aziz said, emphasizing the word *always*, and she knew that he was shoving in her face everything that he'd endured and that she'd escaped. Between her and Aziz a whole conversation was happening beneath the conversation that Trotter could hear.

Oblivious to this tension, the colonel broke in: "Parveen changed her life because of Gideon Crane's book, Aziz. She left America and came back to this country. She's living here, working here, because of that book."

"You're A.," she said, hoping her voice conveyed accusation.

"I'm Aziz. I don't like that he called me A."

"He was trying to protect your privacy. He says that in the book."

Parveen didn't say that, given his descriptions, perhaps Crane had done Aziz a favor by withholding his name.

A. seemed to be having a harder time in the village than I was. He would begin each day with a litany of woes. His bones hurt from sleeping on the floor. His nose ran from the altitude and his rear end from the food. He missed his mother's cooking. He insisted that the villagers, illiterate and uneducated, were little better than the animals that lived in their compounds. I couldn't say they were much fonder of him; people don't like to be judged, especially by someone who fails their own tests of manhood. A. could not chop wood or harvest wheat or butcher an animal. He had

*no children and no wife. His only skill was interpreting, and I'm being
generous in calling it a skill. But I liked him. And he didn't snore.*

She wanted to keep talking about the book, thinking she
could at least hint at Aziz's mistakes—or fabrications. But Trotter asked her to explain to Aziz what she'd been studying. As she
spoke, Aziz folded his arms and stared down at her, making his
boredom clear. *Asshole*, she thought, imagining telling friends
back home about him. They would get his type exactly: both
arrogant and insecure, probably a misogynist, nowhere near as
good-looking as he likely thought himself.

"So could a medical anthropologist look at, say, how protocols
for treating battlefield casualties have evolved?" Trotter, ever the
eager student, asked.

"Perhaps," Parveen said hesitantly, unsure whether this would
actually be a legitimate subject of study for her discipline.

Trotter ran with it anyway. In this war, he said, they'd reduced
lethality—soldiers who died from their wounds—to about 10
percent, whereas in Vietnam it had been 24 percent. "When you
consider the tremendous advances in firepower," he said, "and
the junk they keep thinking up to put in goddamn IEDs, it's that
much more impressive. Outstanding, really."

Mostly to be polite, Parveen asked how the improvements had
happened, which started Trotter on a long disquisition. There'd
been advances in equipment and armor, he said, but mainly the
evolution in the medical system on the battlefield, with field
hospitals going into battle right behind the troops, carrying
everything from anesthesia packs to ultrasound machines. The
goal was basic triage that would get the wounded as swiftly as
possible to a combat-support hospital, usually Bagram. If they
needed more than three days' treatment, they'd be sent out of
country. To Germany, usually. All high-level hospitals. And if it
would take them more than a month to heal up, they were sent
home to the States.

The more Trotter talked, the more any attraction Parveen felt to him fizzled. And when Aziz glanced at the afternoon sun, dropping glacially but perceptibly, and said, "Colonel, we should—" she realized that it was the interpreter with whom she wanted more time. Some part of her craved the vexation he provided.

"And the Afghans, how are they treated?" she interrupted before Aziz could convince Trotter to go. She felt Aziz's attention shift ever so slightly toward her, the incremental turn of a weather vane.

"The same," Trotter said. "With the best we've got."

"Meaning field hospital, combat-support hospital, then, if needed, Germany or wherever?"

"Yes," Trotter said. "Well, no," he clarified, "they're not flown out of country."

"Because..."

"Because this is their country. They want to stay here." Trotter didn't look at Aziz as he said this. "They have—they need to develop—they have their own medical apparatus."

"So what's the setup for them here?" Parveen said, as neutrally as possible. "Can you walk me through the process?"

"Not my ambit," he said, looking toward the vehicles. "You're better off talking to the medical folk. And we should hit that road so we're not trying to take it in the dark."

I took that road in the dark, Parveen wanted to boast. Instead she persisted with "Just a few more questions, if you don't mind." What were the Afghans' hospitals like? Trotter hadn't seen them. Was the lethality rate for Afghan soldiers and interpreters about 10 percent, as it was for American soldiers? Trotter didn't know. So he couldn't say for sure they were receiving anything close to equivalent care? No, he acknowledged, he couldn't. Then he cut off her questions and said they had to depart.

He seemed peeved not just by her queries but by her tone, which perhaps had grown overly interrogatory. To take this tack with a military man was tricky; she worried that Trotter might question her patriotism. But she reminded herself that Professor Banerjee had taught that to be a radical anthropologist was to alienate and be alienated, from your nation as well as your race, your class, your gender, your subculture, even your family. "No loyalties" was her professor's mantra. Loyalty was the enemy of dispassion. Loyalty could prevent clear sight, the demand for truth, the exposure of injustice.

Parveen wanted to show Aziz how concerned she was for the welfare of Afghans, and she also wanted to impress her professor, to whom half her brain was composing a long account of the conversation with Trotter as they were having it. It was Professor Banerjee who had drummed into Parveen these fundamental questions about who would live, who would die, and why. "Power, not fate," Professor Banerjee would say over and over during her lectures. It was power that dictated that wounded Americans would be flown out of country to ever more sophisticated levels of care, just as it was lack of power that dictated that Afghans would eventually be consigned to their own country's broken health-care system. This was why Parveen was ethically obliged to interrogate. It wasn't just so that she could know but so that Trotter would see. He had the power, possibly without even being cognizant of it.

Yet she regretted that she'd alienated him even as she'd failed to warn him about Aziz. The look of vague disappointment on the colonel's face made her cringe, and she tried to smooth things over by asking, as Trotter and his men climbed into the Humvees, how their vehicles had managed the narrow road.

"Oh, we've got inches to spare," Trotter said with another smile, this one tight. "We're comfortable with small margins." But, he added, one benefit of widening the road was that it would become easier for the Americans to pass.

CHAPTER THIRTEEN

IN THE HOUSE OF AN ANT

THAT EVENING, THE WHOLE FAMILY CLIMBED THE LADDER TO
the roof. They did this frequently in summer, treating the flat
surface almost as another level of the house. It was cooler up
there, and the view at dusk was lovely, the whole valley infused
with lilac-hued light. Other families, too, were on their roofs,
and the sounds of their voices floated toward Parveen.

She asked Waheed what he thought about the Americans'
plan. The others listened deferentially, as if his answer would be
oracular. He was unequivocal: the elders were right to oppose
the road, and the Americans should listen to them.

"But how can you not want a better road?" Jamshid spoke up.
The elders wanted nothing to change, he said. They would keep
the village a "dead place." Why didn't they see that the village
was lucky to have been chosen by the Americans?

It hadn't occurred to Parveen until then that while the shura
might speak for the village, it didn't speak for every villager. She
wondered if other young people felt the same, if the prospect of
an easy exit would stir new aspirations for them.

Still, it was rare for any of Waheed's children to argue with
him, rare for Jamshid to express a dissenting opinion so strongly

to his father. Hamdiya elbowed him as if to say, *Watch it*. Waheed said nothing, which was sufficient to convey his displeasure. For a while no one else dared to talk. Then, tired of the silence, Parveen brought up how Aziz, the interpreter, had, in the face of the elders' clear objections to the road paving, told Trotter that they were fine with it. He'd made things up, she said, and she suspected that he'd done the same with Gideon Crane, which would explain the problems in his book.

"I told you, Aziz isn't a bad man," Waheed said.

Fine, Parveen said—although she didn't necessarily agree—but wouldn't this false sense of agreement cause problems?

"He knows from experience that the Americans will do what they want anyway," Waheed said. "They'll talk about how much they're helping you even as they're breaking what's most dear to you."

The causticity of this comment caught Parveen off guard, but before she could reply, Jamshid spoke, his voice cracking slightly from puberty or from feeling. "But if they finish the road, we won't need their help again."

"Do you think this will be the end of it?" Waheed said. "That they'll finish the road and leave?"

"Listen to your father," Bina said. "He's correct."

He was always correct in Bina's mind, Parveen thought bitterly. Like Bina, she'd been raised to respect her elders, but in her case, she'd been allowed to have her own opinions as well. The members of this family could do with more of that.

Again, however, no one spoke. Faces disappeared into the dimness as stars emerged across the indigo sky.

Shokoh crept near Parveen. "Ask him," she whispered. "Ask Waheed if I'll be able to travel."

Shokoh's morning sickness had mostly passed by now, and the pregnancy was enlivening her. Her enervation—her depression—had lifted, at least most of the time. She looked vital, aglow. She complained less and laughed more, and not always in the sarcastic way that Parveen had become accustomed to. Sometimes Parveen would hear her soft humming. No melody, no tune, just happy sound. She talked about how she would teach her child to read and write. This chatter amused Waheed.

Hearing about the road project that afternoon, Shokoh had clapped her hands and asked Parveen questions about the Americans—what they looked like, how they spoke. Then she'd asked if, after the baby was born, Waheed would take her and the child to see her parents, whom she seemed, for now, to have forgiven. How easy it would be to go to her old home! Imagining the paved road, she seemed to envision caravans of buses, honking taxis, and motorbikes speeding along it, filling the sleepy village with the conveyances of her old life, her old city.

"I don't know," Parveen had answered cautiously, afraid to encourage her hopes. They would have to ask Waheed.

Now, on the roof, Shokoh was prodding her to do just that. Perhaps Parveen drew strength from not being able to see Waheed's face. Or perhaps, frustrated at his petty tyranny, she wanted to provoke him. "When the road is done, will you take Shokoh and the baby along it to see her parents?" she asked, her voice ringing loudly.

"Maybe," Waheed said.

Certain this answer would disappoint Shokoh, Parveen pushed harder. "The other men look to you. They're likely to follow your lead. Even if you don't agree with the road, will you use it once it's finished?"

After a long pause he said that when the baby arrived and the road was paved, there was no reason they couldn't visit Shokoh's parents, which wasn't, Parveen noted, the same as promising they would. He sounded grumpy, as if it was dawning on him how much the road might change and what these small challenges by his son and impudent houseguest might portend. Soon after, he went downstairs, and the others trailed behind, until only Parveen and Jamshid remained on the roof.

"That was impressive, that you stood up to your father about the road," Parveen told him. "He's not used to anyone ever disagreeing with him!"

"It's not impressive to challenge your elders," Jamshid said dispassionately. "He's a good father, he deserves respect. I often disagree with him, but I rarely say so." He was a faint silhouette to her, his head tilted back, and she couldn't tell whether he was chastising her. For what felt like a long time, he was quiet. Then he said: "I sometimes look at the sky and think how much there must be beyond this valley."

Seen through his eyes, Parveen imagined, the pattern of stars might resemble the map the Americans had brought, a topography of mountains, rivers, roads. Of possibilities. A similar restlessness had brought her here. But now she knew that the stars were the same everywhere—only in most other places, the view of them was obscured. The world beyond the valley held no attraction for her. Everything that mattered was here, contained in this small patch of earth. This as much as anywhere was the center of things, but perhaps Jamshid needed to discover that for himself.

A FEW DAYS LATER, he accosted Parveen as she was leaving her room. It was clear he'd been loitering, waiting for a chance to catch her alone. His question wasn't one she'd anticipated. He wanted to know if she would teach him to read. "I've wanted to, but I can't," he said. "I only learned a little in school. Shokoh can read."

"I know."

"She thinks I'm stupid. I'm sure you do too."

"No, no," Parveen said. In truth, until the night on the roof, she'd thought him pitiable, so deeply was he tucked beneath his father's shadow. When Waheed went to the fields, Jamshid went; when Waheed came home, so did Jamshid. They prayed together. They ate together. He was yoked to his father's farming life as surely as Waheed's oxen were yoked to the plow.

"I'd like to marry a beautiful educated bride," Jamshid told Parveen. "As my father did."

It struck her that he might be as jealous of Waheed as Bina was of Shokoh. After all, Jamshid made more sense as a mate for Shokoh than his father, who was some two decades her senior. But Jamshid would never be able to earn the bride-price for such a bride—this was what he was telling Parveen now. Which made her wonder: How had Waheed found the money?

"If I'm at least a little educated," Jamshid said, "a father may appreciate that for his daughter."

"Is that the only reason you want to learn?"

"Until I can read, how do I know what I'll learn? Can I look at the ground in winter and guess what will grow from it?" The sunlight was hitting his eyes, and the tiny gold flares around his pupils seemed to suggest an inner light that Parveen hadn't recognized until now. With the road, Jamshid added, more would be possible. If he could read and travel, maybe his life would change.

There was upheaval within him, Parveen sensed, ever since the Americans' visit. Yearning, once released, was hard to re-bottle. She asked what he would want to do instead of farming if he had a choice.

He thought hard. "A shopkeeper?"

His knowledge of professions was limited, but to him, Parveen saw, this was a step up.

Or a trader, he said, so he could visit a lot of places. With the road, it would be easy.

Jamshid, she was learning, was not alone in his aspirations. The Americans' visit and the prospect of the road had cracked something open in the village, at least among its youth. For all the valley's isolation, its teenagers were more aware than Parveen had realized of what they were missing. At the river and at the clinic, women were reporting exchanges similar to the one between Waheed and Jamshid between their own excited sons and reproving husbands. The fathers and, especially, the elders had memories of the Soviets, who had also started by helping, by building roads and highways, even. Later, behaving themselves like fathers angry with rebellious sons, the Soviets had invaded and broken the country on the very same roads they'd built for it. It was better to remain independent from any hand that offered help, the elders believed, because it was usually control that was wanted in return. But the sons insisted that the Americans were different, they didn't want to stay, they didn't want to rule.

Parveen agreed. She thought the village graybeards too suspicious and asked Waheed why it was fine for an American to build a clinic but not for Americans to pave the road.

"The clinic barely changed anything," he said.

She wrote that line down in her notebook. Was the clinic nothing more than a stone dropped in the river, a brief disturbance that the onrushing water soon rendered immaterial?

She wanted to teach Jamshid, but it wouldn't be easy to find a time. He left early for the fields, stayed there most of the day, and returned home sweaty and spent. Location was a problem too. After dark the only usable light in the house was that single bulb in the main room, but he refused to take his lessons in front of his family, especially Shokoh, who he was convinced would mock him.

Parveen suggested lunchtime at the fields, when most of the men took a rest. They might tease him at first, she said, but they'd grow used to it. And—who knows?—maybe some of them would end up wanting to learn too.

To Parveen's dismay, it wasn't Jamshid's peers who teased him but his own father, and before the lessons had even begun. When they suggested the idea to him that evening, he asked Jamshid what he would do with this knowledge. Write letters to the cows? Waheed never minded getting a laugh at others' expense,

Parveen had observed, but beneath his sneering question she suspected hid fear—the fear that if Jamshid learned to read and write, his willingness for fieldwork would diminish, as might his respect for his unlettered father.

"What's the harm?" Parveen asked.

Waheed shrugged. "No harm. And no help."

She took this as permission. The next day when Bina carried lunch to Waheed and Jamshid, Parveen went along, and when the men stretched out to rest, she and Jamshid found shade. They nursed watermelon slices down to the rind, the juice soon a sticky coat on their fingers. The seeds felt foreign in her mouth, and she told Jamshid that in America most watermelons no longer had them—they'd been bred out. Scientists were working on doing the same thing with humans—getting rid of the things people didn't like. Illnesses passed from parents to children, for example.

"God should change things," he said. "Not people."

That was debatable, Parveen said. Some argued that man was assuming divine powers, others that if man had the capability to invent such things, it was because God had granted it. And still others—she took a breath—said there was no such thing as God at all.

He looked at her, curious. "Infidels," he said.

"Infidels," she agreed, wondering if that's what he would call her if he knew of her own doubts.

She had borrowed the twins' primers, which, it turned out, had once been Jamshid's, from his own time of schooling in the mosque. He knew the basics, but he'd had almost no occasion to use them. Parveen made him copy the letters of the Dari alphabet over and over, as her father had once made her. Jamshid was reluctant to read out loud to her because there were so many words he didn't know, but she insisted and he relented, although he wouldn't look at her when he read.

They agreed to meet twice a week. Their sessions took place in full view of his father and any of the other fieldworkers who cared to observe, which, after some initial curiosity, they mostly didn't. After a few lessons, Parveen tried to probe more deeply into his hopes, especially those unleashed by the prospect of the road.

He wanted to earn enough money to woo a beautiful bride, he said, as he had before.

Parveen suggested, as delicately as she could, that maybe the village wasn't the best place for a girl like Shokoh.

But the road would change the village, Jamshid insisted—it would become more like the district center. He spoke as if the district center were a booming metropolis when Parveen guessed it to be a paltry town.

When Parveen asked how much it would cost to get the bride he dreamed of, he named a high sum. How then, she asked, had Waheed managed to raise the bride-price for first Bina, then Shokoh, while being just a farmer himself?

To earn Bina's bride-price, Waheed had sent Jamshid out to tend other people's cows, he said. He would take them up to the meadow in the months after his mother's death. It made him feel closer to her.

"And for Shokoh?" Her beauty and education would have made her price much higher than Bina's, Parveen knew. Shokoh herself had said the price was too high for her family to turn down.

Jamshid looked over at his father, stretched out some distance away, an arm over his eyes, apparently asleep beneath the baking sun. "He would say it was God's will."

"You don't agree."

"It's a way to take what you want. If you can get it, God meant you to have it."

"What does that have to do with Shokoh's bride-price?"

"Clearly God meant him to have her."

"Okay, fine, but it's not like money just fell from the sky."

Again Jamshid looked toward his father. "He would say that God sent Gideon Crane here."

Parveen, confused, asked whether Crane had given Waheed money.

"Don't you notice anything?" Jamshid said bitterly. How, he asked, was his father the only one in the village with a generator when not even the khan had one? How did they eat so well when his mother, during her life, had probably eaten meat no more often than he could count on two hands?

So Crane gave the generator to Waheed? Parveen asked.

"I don't think he gave it," Jamshid said. Then, seeing his father stir and sit up, he stopped speaking.

With the lesson concluded, Parveen walked back to the house, replaying in her mind her arrival in the village that first night, fumbling through the darkness, only to be blinded by Waheed's light—the only light in the village. She was fumbling still, it appeared. She remembered the mullah's comment: How does the moon shine only for him?

As she entered the courtyard, her eyes caught on the empty diesel cans neatly lined up against a far wall. She'd seen them every time she came into the compound but had never truly registered them. Now she picked one up, then another, then another; on the bottom of each was a sticker identifying it as the property of Gideon Crane's foundation. It made no sense that Crane's foundation would provide Waheed with fuel when at the clinic it was so carefully rationed.

Waheed arrived home late in the day, basted in sweat and chaff, drained from working in the heat. Parveen had to subdue a spasm of compassion to interrogate him. How had he gotten a generator? she asked. Only him and no one else. How come?

"It seems my son has been gossiping like a woman."

Jamshid wouldn't tell her anything, Parveen lied. She'd asked him how Waheed had raised the money for Shokoh's bride-price and had started thinking about the generator herself. Then she'd noticed these cans from Crane's foundation. "Are you taking fuel from the clinic?" she asked, staring him in the face.

"We have a proverb: do not stop a donkey that isn't your own."
Parveen folded her arms.

"Should everyone profit from my wife's death except me? Everyone but her children?"

"No one should profit from a death," Parveen said righteously.

"In Afghanistan, most often, no one does. Otherwise we would be a very wealthy nation."

So how had he profited? she said, refusing to yield.

"I'm renting a room to you."

"Now, yes. Did you do that before? Did Crane pay when he stayed with you?"

"Dr. Gideon did not stay with us—"

"But he did," Parveen said, then paused. "Or the book says—"

"The book, the book. You act like it has the truth of the Quran. Dr. Gideon stayed at the mosque, like all travelers do. Only because you're a woman did I allow you to stay in my house. But you're our guest, not our minder. I know Americans think the whole world is their business, but my house is not."

He stalked off to go inside. Parveen stood where he'd left her, torn between the politesse of a guest and the ruthlessness of a snoop. No, of an anthropologist, she corrected herself. How could she understand the village if she failed to see its inhabitants clearly, to decide for herself what she was seeing?

She went and sat under the grapevine. After some time, Waheed, clean and calm, joined her. For a while they sat not speaking, enjoying a wisp of a breeze. She surreptitiously studied the deep lines etched across the leather of his face.

Then he began to talk. Perhaps his family looked poor to her now, he said, but they were much poorer when Fereshta was alive. Waheed had far more debts than land, of which he had barely any. On most days the family ate only bread, yogurt, and tea. There was one cow. When Fereshta died, Dr. Gideon gave the family money for her burial, but it was soon exhausted. His children hungered for everything, Waheed said. For a mother, for food. The twins were so young they quickly forgot their mother, but they needed one, and the older ones wanted one; they cried for Fereshta wherever they were—outside, in the fields, or in their beds at night.

Parveen's throat constricted as she remembered the weeks and months after her own mother's death, and as she thought of her father, how alone he still often seemed. Why judge Waheed differently?

He needed a wife, Waheed continued. It was true that Jamshid had helped earn the money for a bride-price by tending the cows, but according to Waheed, the final installment came when Crane returned to the village, less than a year after Fereshta's death, to build the clinic. He had Issa with him; they hired Waheed and other men to help. So he had a little money again— enough for a bride-price—and Bina came. She was a good mother to her sister's children, but she soon bore a child too, and even the best mother cannot make bread from air. Their poverty was worse than ever. Then, a couple of years after Bina's arrival, Issa returned. Dr. Gideon had written a book about the village, he said, and as a result a lot of money had been raised. Once again Waheed had work, this time taking down and rebuilding the clinic on a much larger scale. Thereafter, again, there was no work, but in other respects Waheed's life began to change. Important visitors came to the village, and all of them wanted to meet Waheed, just as Colonel Trotter had. Issa explained that it was because Waheed and Fereshta were featured in Dr. Gideon's book; he showed Waheed the picture of himself with Crane.

Waheed was honored by this, and moved, and also perplexed; these people had never met his wife, yet they were sad for her, for him, for their children. They all wanted to meet him and take his picture. He let them take it every time but was given nothing in return. Or just some useless things, like clothes the family wouldn't wear; these were used instead to plug holes in the outhouse walls. Meanwhile the khan was growing richer and richer, renting his field for the helicopter landings, and others were profiting too by stealing medicine from the clinic to sell, which Waheed refused to do.

Then Bilal had his accident. Waheed took him to the provincial capital, to the hospital there. The doctors severed the limb from the forearm down, but they saved his life. The operation was costly. In the house of an ant, Waheed said, a dewdrop is a storm. He had to sell some land to the khan. Bina, meanwhile, had given birth to a second child and was pregnant with a third. Whenever he caught up, Waheed said, he fell down again. Some days the pressure was so great he thought he couldn't continue. It was a shameful thing for a man not to be able to bring his children food. As they thinned to barely more than bones, his anger grew. A man could endure anything if he had hope that things would get better. Hope, maybe, was as important as bread. But Waheed had no hope.

Parveen didn't know where this story was going, but she let him spin it out. She couldn't tell if he was unburdening himself of years of trauma or trying to anticipate and ward off her judgment. Whenever she softened toward him as he spoke, vigilance would rear up in her, but then she would conclude she was being too harsh. The correct emotional calibration seemed impossible in the face of such a story and the way it touched, however obliquely, on her own.

Had the clinic been no help to Bilal? she asked.

The clinic was almost never open then, Waheed said. Most of the time it had no doctor. There'd been the man—useless to the village women—sent at first, then occasional guest doctors brought by Crane's foundation for a day, usually with a photographer in tow. Then, for a long time, no one, then Dr. Yasmeen. As Waheed talked, Parveen tried to absorb what he had just offhandedly confirmed—that, as the dai had claimed, the clinic had barely ever been operable.

This was why, Waheed was saying, Issa had gotten the idea to give Waheed the clinic's backup generator and provide the fuel. The accounting at Dr. Gideon's foundation was poor, Issa had told Waheed. People there sent money to him without asking how it was spent. If Issa told them the clinic needed more fuel, they sent more money.

And they didn't know that the clinic was hardly ever open? Parveen asked.

Waheed didn't know what they knew.

Why hadn't Issa just told the foundation he needed fuel money and kept it all for himself? Parveen asked. Why bring in Waheed at all?

Waheed didn't know. "Ask Issa," he said simply. Issa gave him money too—sometimes the equivalent in afghanis of a hundred dollars a month. Waheed, grateful, had never asked why. He assumed Dr. Gideon had directed Issa to help Fereshta's family. The money had changed their lives, he said—among other benefits, he'd bought more land—but so had having lights and electricity. When night fell they no longer had to just sit and look at one another through lantern light, then crawl to their beds. They'd become addicted to light. "Before Dr. Gideon arrived here I was a simple man. A good man," Waheed added, almost helplessly, as if Crane's virus of want was an infection he'd caught.

Parveen couldn't tell whether Waheed was seeking absolution or daring her to report him to Crane. Who would blame the husband of the dead woman for wanting to give her children food, give them light?

"The fuel could be used to keep the clinic open more," she said at last.

All the fuel on earth wouldn't help the women here when there was no doctor, he said. Besides, he'd told her already—there was no shortage of fuel. He could get as much as he wanted from Issa. And anyway, none of this—not the clinic, not the generator—would be here if he hadn't lost his wife.

He was hardly the only man in the village who had lost a wife, Parveen fumed to herself. She felt strongly that Waheed and Issa were committing a grievous moral harm. Yet she couldn't say against whom. "You don't see how this is wrong?" she snapped.

"You sound like my son. A boy with no family to support can afford to be pure, as can an American girl. My children eat better than they ever have. Should I apologize for that?"

He had done more than buy food, she said. He'd used his gains to get Shokoh into his house, his bed.

"In marrying Shokoh I helped her family," Waheed insisted. Parveen was taken aback but said nothing, and Waheed continued. "Her father was sick—he is sick—but she doesn't know. When he dies, the family will have no one to provide for them. So I offered to marry Shokoh. She is settled here; she'll be taken care of." He'd paid a very high bride-price, he said, which would help support the rest of the family after Shokoh's father was gone.

So while Shokoh believed that her father had sold her, more or less, it seemed less mercenary reasons drove his bartering. If the truth was that her father was dying and hoping to make sure his family was provided for, then in this telling, Waheed was coming to their aid. But how was Parveen to know what was true?

"The sum was much larger than a more suitable mate would have had to pay," Waheed said. His humility reminded her of Bina, so confident about her lack of beauty. Both refused to partake in self-delusion.

"And her father?" Parveen asked, refocusing. "How is he?"

Waheed said he didn't know.

"And you're not going to tell her?"

"When the time is right, I'll tell her."

"What, when he's dead?"

"No, before."

"But you don't know when that will be. What if I tell her?"

"Then she'll know. Nothing will change except her happiness."

Was it possible he believed Shokoh happy? "If you were so worried for her family, why not just give them money and let her stay there and finish school?"

"But then what use would she have for a village man like me?"

What use did she have for him now? Parveen thought angrily. The urge to somehow pry Shokoh free returned. "So it wasn't just from charity that you married her," she accused. "You wanted her."

He looked straight at Parveen. "You thought there was only virtue here?" When, embarrassed, she didn't answer, he said, "I've been working almost since I took my first steps. My belly has been empty more days than it has been full. Should a man never take into account his own wishes? I married Bina to give my children a mother. Shokoh, I married for myself."

For all the differences between Waheed and Crane, Waheed's words reminded Parveen of the way Crane had tried to make up for the privations of his childhood far longer than that childhood had lasted. As Crane had suggested, self-pity was a blank check that would cover the costs of almost anything. It wasn't that Waheed lacked a moral calculator. No, he had conceptions of fairness, and he believed his behavior comported with them. The problem, hardly unique to him, was that he had narrowly constructed those conceptions to favor himself. Was he a hard-working, long-suffering widower or a lascivious oldish man? Could he be both? You could view a man from so many different directions and never see him whole. Parveen wanted someone to tell her how to judge, how to think about Waheed. She would write to Professor Banerjee.

That night Waheed didn't switch on the generator. It needed a small repair, he told his family. The small repair, he did not say, was Parveen. "You decide what to do," he had told her at the end of his confession. "Would you rather we all stay in darkness?"

Little by little, like a line being reeled in, the day's light went.

They sat in the dark then. Lanterns, once lit, cast a spooky romantic glow on the half forms of the family. Everyone moved more slowly, talked less. Shokoh didn't write. Bilal didn't draw. The children whined at first, then grew silent. Parveen said good night and descended to bed, shuddering as she imagined the village from above, hooded by mountains, the light from this household extinguished.

CHAPTER FOURTEEN

THE COVENANT

Parveen had shared nothing from *Mother Afghanistan* with the women since her run-in with Commander Amanullah nearly a month before. Now, perhaps because of her tutorials with Jamshid, they began accusing her of neglecting them. The orchard beckoned and they wanted to return—mostly, she suspected, because it gave them a reason to get out of the house. Seeing the khan at the bazaar one Friday, she told him, while making sure to stand several feet away, that they would be using his orchard again. He smiled and glided his hand, palm up, in front of himself, as if to say, *You're welcome*.

The day on which they gathered was warm, but the orchard was pleasingly cool, suffused with watery hues of green. As a joke, the women had brought basketfuls of apricots harvested from their husbands' orchards. The apricots were, like the rest of the valley's fruit, extraordinary: silky to the touch, a gorgeous pale yellow in color, and intensely sweet.

Parveen ate her share, but she nearly choked on the one in her mouth when Ghazal called out, "How is your fiancé?"

"Fine, fine," she said.

"You'd better marry him soon," Ghazal said, then looked

194

around saucily for the best moment to land her punch line. "Because if you don't hurry and bear fruit, your womb will look like this." She held up a pit to whoops of laughter.

"Very funny," Parveen said. She would never admit this to the women, but she'd begun to think about, even dream about, children of her own; being twenty-one in a village full of teenage mothers was doing that to her. Twenty-two, actually; her own birthday, July 25, had just passed, unmarked by anyone but herself. No one in the village celebrated birthdays because they often didn't know when they were.

"I won't be sad when my womb looks that way," said Latifa, who held one infant while her two tiny girls gamboled around her in the orchard. At her most recent checkup with Dr. Yasmeen, she'd learned from the ultrasound that she was most likely going to have another girl, her fourth. She had told the doctor and Parveen that she wasn't going to tell her husband in the hope that the machine turned out to be wrong. Massaging her belly now, nearly five months along, she appeared uncomfortable to Parveen, perhaps even miserable. In her implicit complaint, Parveen saw boldness. Unlike some of the women, Latifa never pretended to enjoy being a vessel for reproduction.

"You'll change your mind after the baby comes," Bina said. "We always do." She smoothed the head of her youngest, six months old, who was nestled in her lap. Parveen had to acknowledge that Bina was a tender mother. Latifa tilted her head in half-hearted agreement.

As for what to share this time, Parveen had settled on Crane's chapter about getting the clinic built, mostly because it didn't seem to cast anyone in the village in a bad light.

Mother Afghanistan, Chapter Eleven

Back in America, haunted by Fereshta's death, I went into a deep depression. Like a platoon leader who has lost a soldier in battle, I relived the sequence of events—her ride on the donkey, those hours of torment—again and again, wondering what I could have done differently. I railed against cruel fate, which had exiled the women of that village from medical care.

One night I dreamed of my father, a dream so vivid it stayed with me for days afterward. In it he beckoned me to follow him, and we passed through a wall and into Fereshta's village. There before us stood a white building, tall and strong. "Look what you built," my father said, and for the first time I heard pride in his voice. When I woke, or when Gloria woke me, I was sobbing. Soon after, I told her that I had to return to Afghanistan and build a clinic for the women in Fereshta's village, that by doing so I could make her death serve a purpose. It was a covenant with myself, or perhaps God had found a path for me after all. My pastor and the members of my church—God's flock, some would say—raised the money for me to return to Afghanistan and build the clinic . . .

. . . On my way back to the village, I stopped to ask directions from a Kochi nomad. Dressed in white, with a white turban, he was leading a camel piled high with his possessions. Except he turned out not to be a Kochi nomad but a man disguised as one. His name was Issa, and he made his living by raiding archaeological sites and selling their antiquities on the black market. He looked as ne'er-do-well as he was, with a black mustache and impish eyes. But inside he turned out to be a softie. As soon as I told him of my mission, he announced that he was going to join me. His own mother had died giving birth to him. As a boy he had slept with her shawl, the only item of hers he had. As a man he still dreamed of her touch. We were two black sheep trying to make good on our lives.

Getting the clinic built would turn out to be by far the hardest thing I have ever done. On the highway to the village, we came upon a roadblock placed by bandits. They surrounded Issa's jeep and demanded money, and we got out with our hands up. I was less afraid for myself than I was for the as-yet-unbuilt clinic. If they took our cash, we would not be able to buy materials or hire laborers. Then Issa did something remarkable: He told them where we were traveling and why. He said I had come to build a clinic that would save women from dying in childbirth. He told them about his own mother dying, how he, like so many other Afghan children, had grown up without a mother's love. As he spoke I saw tears come into the eyes of some of the bandits, and several told Issa that their own mothers or wives or sisters had died giving birth. Then not only did they let us pass—they gave us money, no doubt stolen from other travelers. I didn't think we should take it, but Issa said it was better if we did. He didn't want to anger or offend them, and it was possible that this act of generosity might set them on a more righteous path. And so we sailed on toward the village . . .

. . . Our travails weren't done. A petty provincial official—is there any other kind?—saw profit in our plans. He and his flunkies intercepted us during our rest stop at the provincial capital and insisted that we needed a permit to do any kind of building in a village. This was bunk, since the villagers had been building without permits for probably thousands of years. But it was different for me, he said. I was a foreigner wanting to build a health facility. And he was a corrupt official wanting a bribe. The "permit-application fee" would go right into his pocket. Issa argued that we should just pay him so we could move on. But on principle I objected, and I also suspected that once we paid off one official, we would confront a long line of others seeking their ounce of flesh. We sneaked out of our hotel in the early morning to leave for the village.

But on our way we ran into a fierce bunch of local Taliban in huge turbans and foot-long beards. They didn't want me building in the village. Here, again, Issa proved indispensable. His personal tragedy, the mother lost before he knew her, fed his perseverance and ingenuity. He was relentless; this wasn't merely a job for him, it was a mission. He found out how much the Taliban were paying their fighters, then offered them one and a half times that amount to come work for us building the clinic. Fereshta's clinic may be the first joint venture between the Taliban and an American...

Parveen had skipped this last paragraph when making the outline of the story in her notebook, as she didn't want to provoke the women by talking about the Taliban again. Nor was she sure any longer that the men Crane had run into actually were Taliban—it seemed unlikely, given their lack of presence in the area. Her best guess was that Issa had told him they were Taliban, and Crane perhaps had been too willing to believe him.

There were more logistical challenges to overcome. I wanted the clinic to have a wood frame beneath the traditional mud-brick construction (and I planned to insist on white paint, the color of health and sanitation, over that), but trees with strong enough wood didn't grow in the village. We had to buy them just outside Kabul. But hiring trucks to transport them was going to break our budget. Plus even if we could persuade a driver to travel the road to the village in his truck, the truck would probably plummet over the road's edge. Issa and I were confounded. But as we stood at the lumberyard where we had bought the logs, we saw the Kabul River, and—hit simultaneously by the same stroke of inspiration—we quickly consulted a map. That river traveled through three provinces, eventually passing alongside the road to the village and then into the valley. We would float the logs to the village. And we would ride partway. We lashed them together, put them in the river, climbed on top, and crossed our fingers. Soon we were moving, leaving the city behind. The journey was transcendent. The peace of the soothing water combined with the prospect of building the clinic helped me begin to heal from the trauma of Fereshta's death.

When we reached the village, a joyful reunion took place. Waheed wept with gratitude that his late wife had not been forgotten.

"I have never seen Waheed weep," Bina said sharply. It was the first interruption and one that Parveen had no polite answer for. So she simply kept on.

The men of the village rallied to help us build the clinic, working fourteen or more hours a day, refusing any pay.

Here, Parveen herself stopped, as she remembered Waheed saying explicitly that he was paid for working on the clinic. She asked the women about this; did they know whether their husbands earned money for helping with the construction?

"Of course they were paid," Saba said. "Why would they build it for free?"

"Because the clinic was meant to help their wives—to help you," Parveen said thinly.

"Well, their wives also needed to eat!" Saba said. "Their children too. That was a good time in the village," she added, almost wistfully.

The women who'd been married then remembered not just that their husbands had been paid but also, in moving detail, what they'd done with their respective windfalls: a feast of lamb; a new plow; a fibroid as big as a watermelon removed; medicine for a child's epilepsy; money for a wedding.

Parveen didn't know what to make of this discrepancy. It was certainly more heartwarming to have them volunteer, and she guessed that Crane would have preferred that gauzier version of reality. Perhaps Issa or Aziz told him the men had turned the money down, or perhaps Crane had convinced himself that was the case. She was coming to understand how superficial his understanding of the village had been, even as so many Americans looked to him to explain, to define, the Afghans, who in this adventure abroad were both enemy and friend.

The Afghans were used to such hard labor, but the American with them, white-collar soft, was not. I crashed into deep sleep each night until my sore muscles began to adjust and strengthen. The women of the village, in a lovely gesture, brought us meals as we worked. We probably consumed five hundred watermelons among us. We sang and joked as we worked—imagine dozens of Afghan men singing "Mammas Don't Let Your Babies Grow Up to Be Cowboys"! It was like a barn raising. In twenty-two days, the clinic was finished. Fereshta's clinic; I wouldn't allow it to be called anything else.

"SING THE SONG!" GHAZAL called out.

"What?"

"You said the men here sang a song with Crane. Can you sing it?"

Parveen demurred, saying she couldn't sing and didn't know the words. But the women insisted, their calls ringing through the orchard. Finally, in halting fashion, she sang, to laughter and applause, what few lines she could remember:

Mammas don't let your babies grow up to be cowboys
Don't let 'em something something...
Let 'em be doctors and lawyers and such

Then she had to translate the words, explain what a cowboy was and what a lawyer was, convey that the singer didn't really mean what he sang, and so on. It was exhausting. Worse still, the women, after trying and failing to sing the first line of the song, concluded they were stupid; how else to explain that their men had learned it when they could not?

"I'm sure the problem is with your teacher," Parveen said, but the women looked unconvinced. Then they began squabbling over when the clinic had been built. The dai insisted it had been in the fall, which meant watermelons wouldn't have been in season, and someone else said it depended whether you were talking about the construction of the clinic the first time or the second, and with that Parveen dismissed the gathering.

She needed to talk to Issa and wondered if he'd be back soon. He'd returned to the village several times since bringing her, but she'd avoided him and he, apparently, her, since he never came near Waheed's house. No one else from Crane's foundation had visited, not even to investigate what she'd written him about the clinic, and she no longer believed that Crane himself was going to make an appearance. She'd responded to his letter, then written him another one after her run-in with the commander. There'd been no reply.

Chapter Fifteen

An Arranged Marriage

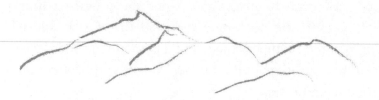

I AM ON FIRE," THE PATIENT—A WIFE, MOTHER, TEENAGER—announced. Her vagina was burning. Her back hurt, too, and she had fever and chills, nausea and vomiting, and unbearable pain during intercourse, which didn't make it any less frequent. "The whole time," she told Dr. Yasmeen, "I am screaming in my head."

The doctor helped her lie down on the examining table and place both feet in the stirrups, then she snapped on gloves and began the pelvic exam, apologizing in advance for the pain she was going to cause. She inserted her hand, removed it to show Parveen a finger thick with discharge, then slid in the speculum, and the woman, Reshawna, cried out. Parveen shivered, remembering her own less traumatic but still unpleasant encounters with the cold metal, and remembering as well what she'd learned in one of her medical-anthropology classes about the speculum's origins. It had been devised by a doctor who'd experimented, repeatedly, on his female slaves.

Parveen was holding the patient's baby, and the infant smiled up at her with his mother's face—broad, with wide-set eyes and a spud of nose.

Had Parveen ever had a urinary tract infection? the doctor asked.

She shook her head.

It does feel like a fire inside, the doctor said, and what Reshawna had—pelvic inflammatory disease—was worse. It was common in the young here, because they began having children before the uterus had properly developed and because infections were so easily acquired (the village women, for example, believed it was wrong to bathe during menstruation, though the doctor was slowly educating them otherwise). If left untreated it would recur until it caused infertility. Dr. Yasmeen injected Reshawna with antibiotics and said it would be best for her husband to stay off her for a few days so she could recover.

"He won't," Reshawna said.

"I know," the doctor said, sounding fatigued. "But tell him I said it would be best."

Parveen wondered how the village men took such advice when delivered by their wives. Reshawna's faint laugh suggested it might not be delivered at all. She asked: "Should I wait until he has opened the door"—she meant penetration, Parveen realized belatedly—"then say, 'Oh, I just remembered, the doctor says you aren't to do this!'" Even through her pain she was a natural comic, circling the fingers of one hand around an invisible penis and with the other waving a finger in her husband's imagined face. "Or will you write him a letter saying he should leave me alone? Remember, he can't read!"

Dr. Yasmeen curled her plump hand into a fist. "Can he read this?"

All three women laughed, too hard. What could be said or mimed or imagined in the clinic could not be repeated or enacted outside of it, which meant the wit packed an extra punch.

"Sometimes I wish I could implant an IUD in every fourteen-year-old in this village," Dr. Yasmeen said with a sigh after Reshawna had left. But the women tended not to agree to contraception until they were six or seven children in, by which point their health was already damaged.

There was a knock on the examining-room door. A woman entered and handed Dr. Yasmeen a piece of paper. It was a note from Naseer saying that the Americans were outside the clinic and wanted to speak with her.

"What do they expect, that I should walk out on my patients?" she said, half to herself, half to Parveen. She wrote that she would come out at lunchtime. This was at least an hour away. Parveen imagined Trotter checking and rechecking his watch.

This was the first time the Americans had returned since their initial visit a few weeks earlier. In the interim, an Afghan recruiter had come on their behalf, looking to hire laborers, but after a couple of hours he'd left without a single villager having signed up. It was too far to travel, Waheed had explained to Parveen. The work on the road was starting at its far end, where it peeled off from the highway.

Excavators and rock hammers had begun attacking the mountainside, the doctor and Naseer reported on their visits. Naseer's eyes had gleamed; he loved machines. If he had the chance to talk to the engineers about their work, he asked Parveen, would she translate? His English wasn't good enough for a technical conversation.

Dr. Yasmeen was, of course, pleased by the American project, since she and Naseer would so clearly see the benefits of it. Yet she also seemed slightly amused by it. A superpower bringing its resources to bear here was, she joked, like putting a stent in a capillary. She captured, in her lighthearted way, the arbitrary nature of the Americans' ambitions, how her country was being remade by their whims. It was a different version of the elders' "Why here and not there?" objection, yet not completely at odds with it.

At her lunch break, Dr. Yasmeen went outside to meet Trotter. He was in uniform this time, like his men. He'd come by helicopter, he said, landing in the field of the khan, whom Parveen imagined, with a shiver of disgust, counting his new riches. Accompanying the colonel was a camera crew, part of a public-affairs team producing a piece about the road project.

"I've heard so much about you from Parveen, from others," Trotter told Dr. Yasmeen, who smiled warmly and introduced Naseer.

Aziz was there, looking nowhere near as villainous as Parveen had convinced herself, in his absence, that he was. He gave her a passably friendly greeting. Trotter told Dr. Yasmeen she was doing wonderful work and that he wanted Americans to know more about it and about how she might benefit from the improved road. Would she mind if they recorded a short interview with her?

She didn't mind, she said.

Parveen, worried that the video might somehow be seen by the judging gaze of her professor, made sure to move out of camera range. The crew asked Dr. Yasmeen about her commute, about the brutality of the road, and after Aziz translated, she replied plainly, "If you drive the road you will see its condition."

Parveen fretted; she wanted Dr. Yasmeen's heroism, her grit, to be clear. "Show them your car," she suggested.

Splattered with mud, coated in dust, the vehicle was the perfect prop. Dr. Yasmeen stood next to it with the camera rolling and spoke stiffly about how the widened and paved road would make her commute so much easier and allow women who needed help to get to the hospital, to specialists. She said all the right things, yet the interview made Parveen uncomfortable, maybe because the doctor was put in the position of being an unwitting prop herself, called forth to justify and praise the American decision to improve the road.

Perhaps Dr. Yasmeen also felt this, for she said, "But this road won't help most villages." It was more important, she insisted, to train more women from villages like this one to be midwives so they could offer decent and consistent care.

Aziz's interpretation for the camera crew left out the part about how the road wouldn't help most villages, which irked Parveen.

Trotter signaled that they had gotten enough footage. Then, with the camera off, he began to question the doctor himself, with Aziz translating. Were there any medicines she lacked? What vaccines did she give?

None, she said, because they required refrigeration.

But the clinic had refrigerators, he'd seen them, and a generator, so why couldn't such medicines be stored there?

Her understanding—she looked at Naseer for confirmation—was that it would take much more fuel than the foundation could provide to keep the refrigerators on all the time. She'd asked about it when she first came and was told it wasn't possible.

Trotter asked if his men could take a look at the generator. He thought they should consider solar panels. He talked at length about the success of photovoltaic technology as Aziz tried futilely to keep up. The doctor, who valued her time as much as Trotter did his, didn't camouflage her impatience; she cast her eyes frequently toward the door to the clinic courtyard, where women were waiting for her. She wasn't going to have a chance to eat.

But Naseer was thoroughly interested. He wanted to know exactly how the technology worked, and when Aziz ignored his questions, Parveen took over translating, ignoring, in turn, the annoyance on Aziz's face. She made sure to say those were Naseer's questions and was pleased with herself for making Trotter see what an intelligent, curious young man Naseer was. The particularity of a person, once you saw it, couldn't easily be erased.

They all walked to the back of the clinic, where the generator was kept. Trotter was surprised there was only one generator. What if this one went out? he said. They needed a backup.

Parveen's face grew hot; should she tell Trotter where the backup generator was? She looked down at her feet, seeking time to think, to weigh her obligation to be honest against the possible repercussions.

Trotter was rambling on about the steps necessary to get photovoltaic, about how the village ought to be making more use of a clinic so advanced. "I heard about the woman who died in your car," he said to the doctor. "The one the mullah choked."

Suddenly Parveen was preoccupied not with Waheed's sins but her own. Dr. Yasmeen had told her on the first day they met that what was discussed in the clinic should remain confidential. It was a condition of Parveen's presence, laid down so that the women would feel safe sharing the most intimate details of their lives and also so the villagers wouldn't think the doctor was gossiping. This would be evidence that she'd violated the doctor's injunction. Now, as the translator, she had to decide whether to confess her transgression or hide it. Squirming inside, she rendered Trotter's words as "I know it's been hard to get women to hospitals in time," then darted a glance at Aziz. She'd always conceived of herself as a straightforward person, but she'd sided with dishonesty twice in quick succession. Maybe it was time to stop being surprised at her own evasions.

Trotter asked Aziz to tell the doctor that as they began to blast the mountainside, the road would become impassable at times. He didn't want this to curtail her visits to the village in any way, so when the road was impossible to drive, the Americans would fly her in by helicopter.

Her face paled. She'd never flown, she said. Not in an airplane, not in a helicopter. It scared her.

"We'll be fine," Naseer said. He looked excited to escort her—what young man wouldn't be? Besides, he was the one who drove them on the grueling road. Parveen couldn't blame him for wanting a break from it. "They have the best engineers," he told his mother, "the best equipment."

"They still crash," she insisted.

Aziz didn't relay the doctor's concern to Trotter, and Parveen decided not to either. There would be no other way into the village once the roadwork was in full swing, she reasoned, and the women needed Dr. Yasmeen to come as did Parveen. In fact, she suggested to Trotter that he could fly the doctor to other villages also.

He shook his head. Right now he wanted her to reach one place, which was here.

THAT AFTERNOON PARVEEN ASKED the doctor how she felt about the Americans. The patient visits were finished. Dr. Yasmeen was sterilizing her tools; Naseer was mopping the floor in a systematic way, as if he'd mapped it into rectangles. He had an organized mind, Parveen concluded; her mother had always said you could learn a lot about people from the way they performed mundane tasks.

"How do I feel about them?" The doctor smiled. "This is like asking a bride on her wedding day about the groom her parents have arranged for her to marry." Which, Parveen remembered with some embarrassment, was more or less what she'd asked Waheed about Fereshta. "This marriage between us and the Americans was arranged, and my feelings about it don't matter," Dr. Yasmeen said. "Of course I celebrated when they came. I was in a prison, and they freed me."

The prison to which she referred was her house. Once the Taliban had taken over, she said, she was essentially incarcerated there, even as her husband continued to work. Dr. Yasmeen had started medical school after Naseer was born and finished just before the Taliban came to power. They'd exiled her from her profession. Only when a powerful Talib wanted a doctor for his wife was she able to work.

"You can imagine how grateful I was when the Americans came. But remember—unlike the Afghans with the Americans, I chose my husband. I didn't have an arranged marriage."

Straining for her meaning, Parveen asked if she wanted them to go.

"I don't want them to stay forever, which is different. Or so I tell myself. Then again, it's easy to congratulate ourselves for our courage when in reality all we've done is survive."

"I'm not understanding."

It wasn't clear what would happen, the doctor said, if the Americans left Afghanistan. Everything was precarious. Even when the surface looked smooth, there was great tumult beneath it. "Once you've lost your freedom, or home, or stability," she told Parveen, "you never take anything for granted again. Your parents must have felt that."

Parveen didn't know what her parents had felt, since their feelings about either the past or the possible instability of the future were never a topic of conversation. They had given her the gift of innocence. She sometimes had a hazy sense of adult difficulties, as a child at the beach might note a ship sailing along the horizon before she returns to playing in the sand. But because her family's circumstances had seemed so immutable—when she was young, she was sure that her parents, and possibly her sister and herself, would forever live over the dollar store—Parveen often forgot that they'd ever lived anywhere else. Of course, when her mother died, she learned that nothing was immutable. Change was an insurgent. Whether it was a death or a war, it most often arrived when you were looking the other way.

And yet, the doctor continued, the health of a country could never be good as long as it was dependent on other nations. With all the help, the money, had come so much corruption. "You don't see it here," she said, "but in the cities—"

Parveen took a deep breath. "I know where the second generator is," she said in a rush.

Naseer stopped mopping. His mother looked at him as if to confirm what she'd heard. Then they both looked at Parveen, who was reminded of when she'd confessed to her fake fiancé.

She told them the whole story. "The work and risk that went into getting this place built," she said, all of it fresh in her mind from the chapter she'd shared with the women, "and then Issa and Waheed treat it like a bank." She told them about the thousands of idealistic Americans, some as young or younger than Shokoh, who'd raised money to save Afghan mothers. How would they feel if they learned that some of their donations had allowed Waheed to pry Shokoh from her family and school? She didn't want to imagine what Issa had done with his gleanings.

Dr. Yasmeen's frown deepened as Parveen spoke, and when she finished, the doctor urged her to tell Waheed to return the generator.

But if she did, Parveen protested, he might send her from his house or even the village.

The doctor didn't want Parveen to leave, but this country's greatest problem, she said—perhaps even greater than war— was that no one took corruption seriously. Waheed's ill-gotten wealth might appear to elevate him, but it actually debased him. "I suspect he can be brought to understand this," she said. He struck her as a simple man, not a greedy one.

As for Issa, Dr. Yasmeen had had her own dealings with him, none of them pleasant. She'd begun coming to the village after meeting the khan's wife, who'd been at her hospital for a medical procedure. The woman had described a beautiful clinic that had had no doctor for several years. Curious, Dr. Yasmeen visited, assuming it would be decrepit. Instead, it was well kept, nearly immaculate. A ghost clinic. She'd found it eerie. She volunteered to travel there weekly to see the village women. One day Issa showed up at the clinic and told her to go; it turned out he was worried she would want to be paid. When she said she didn't care about the money, she only wanted to help the women, he started haggling with her over how much fuel and supplies she could use. Finally the villagers intervened on her behalf—they wanted her.

She'd never met Crane. "Sometimes I don't believe he exists," she joked. Still, she thought Parveen should write to him about Issa's finagling, because to keep this secret would debase Parveen as well.

Professor Banerjee had a different take. In an e-mail that Dr. Yasmeen had printed, folded neatly into an envelope (without reading, she stressed), and brought to Parveen, her professor pooh-poohed her discovery about Waheed, though in higher-flown language. Like Dr. Yasmeen, Professor Banerjee saw this as a story of post-9/11 Afghanistan writ small, a narrative in which American aid created dependence and fed greed, but they differed on the question of whether Waheed should be held to account. From Professor Banerjee's perspective, such "amoral familism" was a common, and essential, survival strategy of the impoverished. All corruption by the poor was necessary, since the state and elites afforded them so few opportunities for advancement. *Of course,* she went on, *"amoral familism" is itself a contested concept with a long history in anthropology...* Blah-blah-blah; for the first time, Parveen found her professor's erudite lecture of little comfort and even less use, and she put the letter aside.

SOME DAYS LATER, BILAL reported to Parveen that Issa was at the clinic. Ordinarily, this would have caused her to stay home until he was gone, but this time she hurried there. Inside, he and Waheed were sitting in the waiting-room chairs, which the women never used. Cans of diesel were set neatly in a row in front of them.

Issa invited her in as if there was nothing to hide. "I was just telling our friend Waheed that with the roadwork, I may not be able to come for a while." If he could, he said, he would finagle rides on the Americans' helicopters—someone had to check on the clinic, after all—but they might not allow him to transport diesel. And even if he were to to ask the soldiers to bring it by road, for the sake of the clinic of course, he couldn't send too much lest it attract attention.

Preparing for moral combat, Parveen balled up her fists. People, Americans, hadn't raised money for Issa to enrich Waheed just so he could get another wife, she said.

Issa's cold eyes showed the faintest flicker of surprise, and Parveen feared, for just a moment, that he might harm her. But the thought felt like something out of a bad movie, in part because she realized that she trusted Waheed to protect her—Waheed, whose life she had just splayed out as evidence for her prosecution and who was now looking at Issa apologetically. Maybe it was Waheed who needed protecting from her.

When Issa spoke, it was in a leisurely voice. Was it better, he asked Parveen, for Waheed's generator to be buried in cobwebs and dust because it was never used? And was it a sin, here in Fereshta's clinic, to help Fereshta's husband? The sin, he said, was how little attention Dr. Gideon and his foundation paid to what was happening to their money. It was almost a pleasure to take it from them.

But why was he helping Waheed? Parveen said. Out of the goodness of his heart?

"I wouldn't say, nor likely would you, that I have a good heart," Issa replied, and Waheed gave a sage nod of agreement. No, Issa said, it was that Waheed was helpful to him. He explained the details of his schemes: He requested far more fuel money from the foundation than any clinic could ever use, and the staff never balked. "They toss out money the way farmers do seeds." The extra money went to himself or Waheed. But occasionally some new employee—they never seemed to last long—would ask for receipts for the fuel Issa was supposedly buying. This was inconvenient, because then Issa had to buy the fuel and sell it to get cash. Some of the fuel he would bring to Waheed for use in his generator. The village hadn't seen an auditor or staff member for years, but this way, in the unlikely event that one did come, Issa would have enough empty canisters to show them.

All of this he freely admitted, showing no fear that Parveen might expose him. She wondered if this was because he thought no one at the foundation would care.

It sounded awfully complicated, she said, and Issa agreed. Perhaps he missed the challenge of his old life, he mused, almost wistfully. He described for Parveen the improvised bricolage of obtaining and transporting antiquities. The knowledge he possessed of the many civilizations—the Greco-Bactrian, the Kushan, the Ghaznavid, the Ghorid; he could go on—in whose shards he trafficked. The complexity of the black market. To smuggle artifacts in unlikely ways, including in jugs of freshly harvested honey, required real cleverness. Working for Crane, much less so.

As to why he also gave money to Waheed, that was partly because Waheed was helpful to him with the fuel. "But also there's more money than I need. Much more. And I like Waheed." He recounted coming here with Crane to build, then later rebuild, the clinic and getting to know the villagers. Waheed had so little, yet he didn't ask for anything. Everyone else did. The mullah wanted money for the mosque, the commander wanted money to provide protection, and the khan—well, the khan wanted money for everything: for the land, for water, for the procurement of laborers, for the use of his field as a helicopter landing. "But Waheed, whose wife, may she rest in peace, was the reason all this money was pouring into the village, demanded nothing. So he was the one I gave to. I haven't made him rich but I've made him richer. And this has driven the khan nearly mad!"

Issa laughed. "He doesn't understand where Waheed's money is coming from, why he's not poor anymore. He hates that Waheed has a generator."

Parveen, despite herself, was starting to laugh too.

It wasn't the point, Issa said, but it was nevertheless a nice reward to baffle and irritate the khan. And it was even more enjoyable to take a humble man and raise him.

Issa was, or saw himself as, a social engineer, Parveen thought, a Robin Hood redistributing this negligent foundation's wealth. She remembered the mullah's words: *That clinic has made kings of beggars*. It wasn't Crane who had done so, but Issa.

Of course, once Waheed began getting Parveen's rent, he didn't need Issa's money as much. In fact, Issa argued that Waheed should now be giving him part of his earnings, a kind of commission. "But you don't need it," Waheed said.

"This is true, but shouldn't brothers share everything?"

"You're too ugly to be my brother," Waheed said.

"This is why I trust him," Issa said to Parveen. "Everyone else tells me I'm handsome."

She tried out the doctor's argument on him, that corruption was Afghanistan's greatest problem, that it was tarnishing Waheed, realizing as she said this that she was talking about Waheed as if he weren't there.

Issa shrugged. The country's corruption wasn't his creation or his problem. Others could lead that jihad. As for Waheed—here, Issa placed his hand on Waheed's shoulder and left it there a few beats—he wasn't a child. He could make his own decisions. "Like all of us," Issa said, "he will face God on the day of judgment." He turned to address Waheed. "Perhaps you will have a conversation like this one, although I hope it will sound less like a mullah's sermon. And if he took another wife"—he leveled his gaze at Parveen—"that's his headache. I myself prefer to be unmarried—women bring difficulties."

Issa's misogyny was so blatant that, counterintuitively, it was almost hard to take offense. But it did make him an odd choice for Crane's crusade against maternal mortality. *Mother Afghanistan* had made it sound as if Issa took saving each woman's life almost personally, when in fact he seemed to take nothing seriously. Though perhaps by now she shouldn't have been, Parveen was surprised at how little sentiment, how little investment—other than the financial kind—he seemed to have in Crane's work. He was having fun, that much was clear. Was this, so different from her own gravity toward everything, a better way to be? "I don't like the khan either," she said.

"They say that my enemy's enemy is my friend, so I suppose that makes us friends." Then again, Issa said, ticking off the unpopular, unsavory warlords whom the American military had empowered to help it fight the Taliban, an alliance born of a common enemy wasn't always the best approach. "One must be careful in choosing friends." And with that, he said he needed to go. Dr. Gideon would be in Kabul in a week (or so he claimed; he often canceled these trips) and Issa had to prepare.

Would he come to the village? Parveen asked, remembering all the questions about his book she meant to ask Issa.

Why would he? Issa answered. There was nothing for him here.

Issa departed in his Land Cruiser in time to reach the highway before dark. Within a day or two, Parveen heard booms in the distance, the sound of the Americans blasting the mountainside away.

Chapter Sixteen

Half a Loaf

WHEN TROTTER CAME TO THE VILLAGE IN MID-AUGUST, HE'D added a protective vest and helmet to his military uniform. This made his sitting with the shura more awkward, but he managed it, right down to the crossing of his legs, although it gave his face a constipated look. Across from him sat a soldier wearing, over his armor, a backpack from which antennas protruded, as if he were an insect complete with exoskeleton. The other soldiers didn't sit at all, nor did they lay down their guns. Instead, they spread out in a perimeter around the meeting, their backs to the shura and their weapons aimed outward. Aziz, who crouched near Trotter, had hidden his eyes with dark wraparound sunglasses.

It was an unusually hot day, even in the shade. Moisture pooled on Parveen's back and dampened her dress. Flies blackened the plates of sugared almonds, which grew sticky in the sun. Trotter left his tea mostly untouched, and irritability seemed to float in the air like an allergen.

Trotter began to talk. The construction of the road was going well, he said, and he offered a litany of statistics to prove it: tonnage of rocks cleared, feet of dirt graded, number of laborers employed, amount of equipment used, and so on. Then he said, almost casually, that there had been one wrinkle, unexpected in this peaceful place. During the preceding week, the road laborers had come under attack—he left its nature unspecified—as had the soldiers who'd gone to protect them.

When Aziz translated, the faces of the elders betrayed no surprise. Or any other emotion.

Trotter continued. Those perpetrating these attacks were enemies of Afghanistan, determined to prevent its progress. They would fail; they would be defeated. The villagers could help by sharing any information, anything they'd seen or heard, about who might be behind the attacks. Trotter spoke placidly with neither anger nor frustration, and in doing so he conveyed his confidence that any resistance to the road would be subdued, because those resisting were on the wrong side. He didn't speak like a preacher—his flat Midwestern tones and his evenness precluded that kind of delivery—but the villagers listened first to him, then to Aziz's fairly scrupulous interpretation, with the rapt concentration a good preacher commands.

But when that raptness, that utter stillness, held firm even after Aziz finished, it began to seem less like the giving of attention than the withholding of something. As Trotter looked from face to face, the silence gathered until it seemed to overflow.

At last an elder spoke. No one in the village knew anything about this, he said. They farmed their fields, nothing else. But he reminded Trotter they had told him that to do this village's road and none of the others could stir up bad feelings. He repeated their previous counsel: progress was important, but so was peace, and to favor one son over another would create division in a family.

"Other tribes and subtribes, other villages, might have jealousy that only this village gets a road," Aziz explained to Trotter. "Afghans have a saying: Half a loaf, but a peaceful body. They're quoting this."

"I understand that," Trotter said with a flash of impatience.

The army was reaching out to the leadership of other nearby villages and tribes, he said, so that they understood this project was a beginning, not an end. The Americans wanted to connect all of Afghanistan. But anyone sabotaging this road, whatever the reason, was going to be held to account for his actions. Also, Trotter said, did the elders remember that he had offered employment to the whole village? That any man here could be put to work on the road?

Yes, they remembered.

And yet not a single villager had taken a job, Trotter said. Not one. That surprised him. These were good jobs, well paid, as he was sure they knew. Men were coming from all over the district asking for work. They were being put to work. Yet no one from this village had come. Trotter waited a few beats, then said, "I trust that's not because anyone here knew that there might be attacks. I trust that anyone in this village who knows anything will reach out to us."

The colonel hoped the villagers would share anything they learned, Aziz interpreted.

There were nods, nearly enthusiastic, all around.

"Good," Trotter said. "Good. Let me tell you, we get this road done, a lot else flows in here—all kinds of development. Schools. Help with agriculture and irrigation, which I know you want. The road doesn't get finished? None of that happens."

Aziz tried to leach the colonel's words of their threat, and Parveen had a flash of insight into the interpreter's work, into the cognitive compartmentalization required to be an emissary of unpleasantness. You were being paid to act as a ventriloquist's dummy when you had thoughts and feelings of your own. This gave her newfound compassion for Aziz.

When the meeting broke up, the elders formed small huddles. Trotter greeted Parveen distantly. A weight seemed to be drawing his features down even as his well-exercised optimism fought to hold them up. He gave Parveen the gruesome details. An improvised explosive device packed with ball bearings, nails, and rocks had taken divots out of a laborer working the road; he'd been left a bloody pulp. When Trotter's soldiers rushed to help, they'd come under fire, and one of them had taken a bullet in the thigh. That soldier had been medevaced to a combat hospital and was stable. The laborer, although taken out on the same medevac, was dead.

"We heard explosions," Parveen said. "We thought it was you, blasting for the road."

"Could've been," Trotter said grimly. "Or it could've been the IED. It was a doozy." But this was a sign of the American-led coalition's success, he insisted. The militants were being squeezed elsewhere, so they'd come here. He paused, and his gaze wandered upward to the mountains, then out to the pastoral tableau of fields and orchards, as if all of it was, in the end, just vegetation for trouble to hide in. "You know, when people talk about Afghanistan being tough terrain, they talk about the mountains, but it's really the valleys. Our biggest battles, the worst kill zones—all valleys." He reeled off a list of places she'd never heard of: Pech, Shok, Korengal, Ganjgal, Tangi. "Real death traps. It's the damn geography."

"Aren't the damn people the problem?" Parveen tried to joke. "They're the ones planting the bombs."

Trotter didn't take the bait. "Plenty of good people here," he said. "They just need to stand tall." He'd asked Aziz to go around and quietly encourage the villagers not to be afraid to tell him or his men what they knew.

"But shouldn't they be afraid if the enemy"—the word sounded strange coming out of her mouth—"is nearby?"

"The enemy's days are numbered," Trotter said with confidence.

Parveen lost his attention then to a mechanic. This time the Americans had come not in Humvees but in mine-resistant all-terrain vehicles—M-ATVs, in Trotter's parlance. They were rectangular, sand-colored, and—although they could hold only five people, driver included—huge, higher than the Humvees and slightly broader too, which meant the road had to have been widened in places already to permit their passage. Their metal armor was meant to defend against IEDs and their V-shaped hulls to deflect the force of an explosion. Parveen felt claustrophobic just looking at them; they reminded her of rolling tombs.

One M-ATV had overheated on the way into the village, which didn't surprise Parveen. It seemed inevitable that, like obese hikers, these cumbersome giants would regularly conk out. The mechanic was telling Trotter that they might have to attach a towline from another M-ATV to pull the vehicle out.

It was the same problem the British had experienced getting their wheeled guns to these villages, Trotter said with what sounded almost like satisfaction.

Parveen decided to search for Aziz. She hadn't yet confronted him about the untruths in *Mother Afghanistan*, although she thought often, maybe too often, about doing so. Almost against her will, her eyes had roamed toward him during the shura meeting. She couldn't tell if Aziz was watching her from behind his sunglasses.

He wasn't in the bazaar drumming up courage or whatever Trotter had asked him to do. A couple of village men directed her down to the river, where she found him alone, cross-legged, smoking. His armored vest and helmet lay next to him, and his sunglasses were atop his head. He was silently examining his own reflection in the water, and when Parveen sat down next to him, their reflections appeared side by side. It reminded her of the moment an Afghan bride and groom saw each other for the first time in the mirror.

Rather than turning to Parveen, he nodded at her watery avatar. Neither spoke. Smoke curled up from the cigarette in his right hand. She studied her own face, the changes in it since her arrival—eyebrows bushy, skin browned, cheekbones emerging as she lost weight—then, more discreetly, Aziz's. There was something comforting in his presence. He looked like half the guys she'd grown up with.

Suddenly he smiled, a wide grin that rippled over his face and created the illusion that the water was rippling as well. "Our wedding," he said.

She laughed, not telling him how their thoughts had overlapped. To joke about such things was what children playing adults might do. But they *were* adults, and at the freedom suggested by that, she tingled. It was an instinctive reaction, and like an intelligence officer in her own body, she tried to read what it might signal.

For want of a fitting reply, she mentioned that the soldiers were trying to fix the vehicle.

"They love to fix things," he said.

She laughed again, because again she'd had a similar thought, that rather than dispiriting Trotter and his men, the challenge of the disabled vehicle seemed to energize them. Unlike negotiations with cagey villagers, it had a concrete solution. Suddenly she felt shy, though, which wasn't usually her problem. "Trotter thinks you're talking to the villagers. Are you hoping they'll come see you here?" The question sounded snotty, though she hadn't meant it to be.

"What's the point? They won't tell me anything even if they know everything."

Without discussing it, they'd slipped into the perfect way of conversing: Aziz spoke Dari and Parveen spoke English, each of them using the tongue that came most easily while still understanding the other. It was the opposite of their first meeting, when she'd tried to insist on Dari and he on English.

If the villagers informed on the insurgents, Aziz said, or on whoever had carried out the attack, then they would be prey for vengeance after the Americans left. He'd tried to explain this to the colonel, who said that to refuse to help the Americans was to side against them. It was better for Aziz just to pretend he'd talked to the villagers and they didn't know anything. All they wanted was to be left in peace by both sides.

Parveen wondered if he was saying this for the benefit of the village men, some of whom were passing within feet of them, ostensibly coming to drink from the river or to wash their hands but really, she suspected, to gawk at the two of them in conversation. To sit and talk like this was not something men and women here regularly did, and it was even more exotic to see an American and a military interpreter do so. That sense of possibility she'd had just moments before quickly constricted as it had on her first foray from Waheed's house. There were almost no private spaces where she and Aziz could talk, certainly not without opening herself to the same possibly dangerous judgment she'd feared for Shokoh. She didn't know whether it was her own reputation or Waheed's she was worried about or if, since she was his guest, the two could even be separated.

"So you'll lie to Trotter," she said a touch combatively, as if to put verbal, if not physical, distance between her and Aziz.

Aziz reached into the pack for another cigarette, then said, "Sometimes *not* lying puts people in danger."

This was her opening to ask about his fabrications regarding Commander Amanullah, yet she held back. The weight on him, the decisions he had to make, seemed heavier than anything she'd ever contended with and so rendered her moralizing frivolous, even impertinent. She would lead him to talking about Crane, she promised herself. But first she asked for his story, how he'd come to work for the Americans at all. She wanted to know more about his intractable life—not just the constraints on him but how he had flexed against them. This resistance, she was coming to see, was one of the things that made living a creative act.

He gave a sardonic smile. The first time he'd met Dr. Gideon, he said, he'd also had to give his story. Americans collected and offered them like they were business cards.

Parveen was embarrassed at having conformed so completely to this observation but pressed gruffly ahead anyway. "So what is it? What's the story?"

No story had a single beginning, he said, but he would start a decade earlier, when the Taliban had been three years in power. In Kabul, as in all Afghan cities, the Taliban imposed many dictates. They were trying to force urban Afghans back into rural conservatism, as one might lead a tall man into a room with ceilings so low he had to bend. While a few of these rules were sound, most of them were arbitrary, theologically or otherwise. And they were all cruelly enforced. Shops were supposed to close during Friday prayers, but one Friday, when Aziz's smallest sister was very sick, his father ran to the pharmacy to buy medicine for her, and although prayers were just starting, the pharmacist kept his shop open a few extra minutes to help Aziz's father. The Taliban arrested them both. Aziz's family had to borrow money from relatives to bribe officials for his father's release, which took several days. In that time in prison he was beaten, mocked, and who knew what else. He came home an old man. He didn't talk much, just smiled. It was as if his captors, his torturers, had opened him up and swept him out. He didn't want to leave the house. Although previously a teacher, he never worked again. It fell to Aziz, at twenty the oldest of six hungry children, to leave his studies at the university and support the family. At the time this didn't seem a great loss, as under the Taliban the school was barely functioning anyway.

"Kabul University?" Parveen interrupted, feeling an unexpected pang. That was where her father had once taught poetry. She had visited during her time in Kabul, looking for clues about who her father used to be. There weren't many; his department had been eviscerated during the Soviet invasion and most of his colleagues from the 1980s had died or dispersed. Strange to think that if life had been different, her father could have taught Aziz. She wasn't sure the interpreter had a poet's soul, but perhaps her father would have divined it.

Aziz only nodded in answer to her question. At the time, he repeated, it hadn't seemed a great loss, but later it did. Hearing her talk to Trotter about her studies had reminded him of this.

"I thought you were bored when I was talking," Parveen said. She turned to him as she said this, but he kept his eyes on the water.

Not bored, he said. Angry. It seemed unfair that she'd had a chance to learn so much, to think about how people live, while he was just trying to survive life, to help his family survive. Upon leaving school he'd gone to work for an international organization that trained him as a deminer. Telling Parveen this, he trailed a finger in the dirt, making figure eights. Mines were easy to plant, he said—almost anyone could do it—but they were dangerous to unearth. You had to move very slowly, either sweeping your detector over the ground or crawling across it, creeping, creeping, poking very gently every few inches. Aziz got on his knees, grimacing a bit at some old pain, to demonstrate. You were looking for hard metal, he said. Listening for its sound, its ping. He sat back on his haunches. You couldn't stop paying attention, he said, not for a moment. He'd done this for eight hours a day. The way truck brakes burn out on mountain roads? That was what happened to his knees. And even though he wore protection on his face, the dust coated his skin, all of it, his eyelashes, inside his nostrils, inside his throat, inside his lungs. He hadn't stopped coughing since, although he admitted that starting to smoke hadn't helped. He'd begun to walk bent over, because he was bent over all day. It started to hurt so much to stand up straight that he became convinced that his muscles had re-formed and hardened around his curved spine. He wouldn't even turn thirty until later this year, he said, but his body was already that of an old man.

"We should walk," he said. "I get stiff if I sit too long. It might be better for you too."

This was an oblique reference to their growing audience, the men squatting nearby or on the opposite bank. Suddenly Parveen was back in high school, or maybe the *Freaks and Geeks* version of high school, and she wished she could watch the show with Aziz and explain it to him.

They stood up and Aziz shouldered his Kevlar vest, kept his helmet in his hand. She suggested they do a loop along the fields, through the orchards, then back to the bazaar. As they began to walk he squinted up at the sky and said, "There was the sun too. It made my head hurt, made spots swim in front of my eyes. Doing that work, death becomes your shadow. It's as if you see the lid of your own coffin, and all that remains is to open it. It requires so much alertness that sometimes it seems easier to give in. I wonder if the soldiers who patrol in dangerous areas ever feel this way. I've never asked them. Only the thought of my brothers and sisters kept me going—who would feed them if I was gone?" They were like fledglings, he said, waiting for him to pluck worms from the dirt. Then his talk veered to a different topic. "Why'd you come back?" he burst out. "You had the good luck to leave. Why are you back?"

It's still my country, she nearly said, but it wasn't. And yet after the attacks, America hadn't felt entirely like her country either. She tried to explain what it had been like to be a Muslim then, and as she spoke, she reached some new understanding: perhaps that feeling, almost an internal exile, had also driven her back toward her origins. If so, Gideon Crane's book, which she'd thought had propelled her here, had merely been a spark for material ready to catch.

September 11 had changed a great deal for him too, Aziz said. Until then, for all his family's struggles, he'd considered them fortunate. His father was free. Aziz was working. They had food. But what you're grateful for one day, he said, can seem like too little the next. That was what happened when the Americans came and the Taliban left. Everything changed for everyone, it seemed, but him. All the young men he knew, even some women, were getting jobs with the Americans or the British, jobs that paid a lot. They were interpreters or drivers or computer technicians. He didn't know how to do any of those things. But he wanted something that would lift him up from the dirt.

He found English classes he could take at night, he said, which allowed him to work during the day. The Sunshine American English School, it was called. To get to it he climbed a flight of stairs over a copy shop, from which he could sometimes smell the ink of the machines. There were two teachers, Louisa and Caleb. Louisa was older—she had a long gray braid. Caleb had a weak beard and a belly like a small hill. He wore light blue button-down shirts. He spoke some Dari; Louisa, none. They were the first Americans he'd met—others he had only passed by in the street. These two were always cheerful.

He would finish his work, wash and eat dinner at home, then go to class. But after crouching all day in the sun, he mostly slept during the lessons, and phrases from the teachers—*Aziz is going to the bazaar; Khalil is happy*—floated across his dreams. But he kept going to the school, which seemed his only hope for a better life.

As they passed alongside the wheat fields, Aziz's story was interrupted at regular intervals by the greetings of villagers, some of whom stopped for extended salutations. They treated him a little bit like they treated her, she thought, welcome but foreign, as if Kabul and America were equally distinct from the village.

One day Caleb and Louisa asked him to stay after class. They'd noticed him sleeping. Was he okay? they asked. Americans could be so…sympathetic. He used some Dari and a little English but mostly pantomime to explain his job to the teachers, getting on his hands and knees for them just like he had for Parveen. But when he did it for them, he started to cry. When he stood up, Caleb and Louisa held his hands, which embarrassed him, because compared to their soft hands, his were cracked and hard from all the dust. And now he noticed how alike their faces were—the same blue eyes, the same full cheeks, even the same clean smell. They were mother and son, it turned out. They'd tried to explain this in the first lesson but he hadn't understood. Louisa offered him her handkerchief, which was embroidered, and this made him cry more, because it reminded him of his mother, who also did embroidery.

"I don't know why I'm telling you this," he said to Parveen. He gave her a furtive look, as if to ascertain whether she could be trusted with his disclosures. Whenever he turned toward her, she would get a whiff of his smoker's breath. Each time it bothered her less.

"Sometimes," she said, "when I have a heavy bag, I say to a friend, 'Pick this up, feel how heavy it is.' I don't want her to carry it. I just want her—want someone—to *know*. Maybe it's like that."

"Or maybe I've become like an American." He laughed at this. "Maybe more than English, this is what Caleb and Louisa taught me." They'd asked him questions about his history, he said, on that night and many nights thereafter. They wanted to know what it had been like living through the wars, all of them. Aziz didn't have the English to explain, and within a few sentences he'd had to switch to Dari. He'd never told his story to anyone before, had never even thought of it as a story. For him it was life. No more, no less. And no different than the lives of most other Afghans.

"They gave me my story," Aziz said, using the Dari word *dorogh*, which could also be translated as either "narration" or "lies." They'd even taught him the words to tell it. "So that was after the rockets landed in your neighborhood? I can't imagine your terror," they'd said. His English vocabulary grew: *Terror. Depression. Trauma. Post-traumatic stress. Anxiety. Loss. Fear.*

Parveen was amused at his careful pronunciation of these

words, imagining the long practice that must have gone into learning how to say *post-traumatic stress*, but then, chastened, she remembered the scarring experiences they connected to.

"I don't think they understood everything," Aziz said. There were things he didn't try to explain—for example, that his family thought his uncle had told the Taliban when his father went to buy the medicine because of a dispute the two men were having over a tiny piece of property in their ancestral home. "My uncle has that property now," he said.

They had arrived at the orchards. The trees were laden with peaches, apricots, and apples, and they wandered through, plucking the occasional fruit.

Not long after, Aziz said, Caleb and Louisa told him they'd found him a new job. He was surprised; he wasn't the best student in the class, perhaps barely in the middle. And he wasn't the only student with a sad history. Nearly every Afghan had one by then. But Caleb and Louisa wanted to help him. Besides, all of the best students were saving themselves, like rich or pretty would-be brides, for the American newspapers or the military or the United Nations, the jobs with real money. Aziz would never get one of those jobs—his English wasn't good enough at the time—which was why, when Dr. Gideon came looking for an interpreter to travel outside Kabul, Aziz's teachers suggested him.

Caleb and Louisa told Aziz that when Crane interviewed him, he should tell Crane, in English, the story of his life. Nervous, he practiced over and over with his brothers and sisters as audience. They knew no English, he said, but that didn't prevent their opinions: *Stop swinging your arms so much! Now you're too stiff, like a wooden soldier. Your mouth looks funny when you make those words.*

Then came the day for him to meet Dr. Gideon. Aziz was impressed by his height, he said, by his very long arms. Dr. Gideon kept using his hands to flatten back his hair, the color of ripe wheat, which rose up again as soon as he took his hands away.

Aziz, unable to read his eyes, simply told Dr. Gideon his story, using all the words that Caleb and Louisa had given him. To his relief, Dr. Gideon asked no questions. Instead, he told Aziz his own story. How he was an eye doctor and had cheated the government and gotten in trouble for it, which surprised Aziz, since he'd never known anyone in Afghanistan to get in trouble for cheating the government. But Dr. Gideon had "cut a deal," he said—Aziz had no idea what this meant—to do community service in Kabul instead of serving time in prison. He'd gotten lucky and "won the lottery," and now he'd "done his time" and was ready to "get out of Dodge," more phrases that meant nothing to Aziz. This was Aziz's introduction to the strangeness of English, its impossible idioms. Caleb and Louisa, he said, had been so careful to lead their students step by step, never using a word or phrase that couldn't be found in a dictionary or a grammar book, that wasn't building on something they'd already taught. Being careful wasn't of concern to Crane.

Dr. Gideon kept telling Aziz he wanted to go "off the grid," another mystery expression. He wanted to see the real Afghanistan, he said. The villages, the mountains, the Minaret of Jam, the hollows where the giant Buddhas of Bamiyan had been before the Taliban destroyed them, the yaks in the Wakhan. He planned to travel for two weeks, maybe more. It was adventure he was after, he kept repeating, adventure and penance, for he hadn't just cheated the government, he had cheated on his wife. He'd committed adultery.

"I hiccuped when he told me this," Aziz said, "I was so surprised." He stopped to do a full Crane imitation, first extending his arms, then running his hands through his hair as he said, "'I slept with two black nurses at the hospital, Aziz. Don't know what I was thinking. I mean, I do, but I'm not proud of those thoughts.'"

The imitation was almost too perfect; she wondered whom, over the years, he'd performed it for and felt somewhat chastened by her worship of Crane. Aziz clearly had a more jaundiced, or more balanced, view of him. She had been so...*devoted*, that was the word. To Aziz, Crane was only human.

They were nearing the khan's orchard, where she'd read to the women. She'd planned to show it to Aziz, to tell him about her project. Instead, unable to articulate to herself exactly why, she steered him away and suggested they head back toward the bazaar.

"Do you know what I asked him?" Aziz smiled in embarrassment. "I asked him, 'Why black?'" No one had ever confessed adultery to him before, he said. He didn't know what questions were proper. He didn't even understand what Dr. Gideon meant when he called the women "black."

"What was his answer?"

"He said, 'Why not?'"

This made Parveen laugh.

Aziz had concluded that it was through private stories like these that Americans made friends. He'd even adopted the habit himself; look at how much he was telling Parveen!

On the surface it seemed this way with Americans, she conceded. But what was it, really, that Crane had disclosed to him? Revelation could be a performance; it could be rehearsed. Didn't it seem like this processing and presentation of memories changed them, or at least discharged their emotion? Sometimes, even as you said what you'd felt, you no longer felt it. She told him about a junior-high science class in which she'd had to poke at a pellet regurgitated by an owl in order to deduce from the tiny bones the nature of its prey. It wasn't necessarily obvious but it was no longer mysterious, the way the hidden contents of a stomach are. It was probably the same, she felt, with these scraps of disclosure.

Aziz considered this for a moment, then said, "Maybe this is why, when Dr. Gideon finished his confession, I didn't really have anything to say."

As it turned out, he hadn't needed to say anything. Dr. Gideon decided they were a good fit, and that meant Aziz was hired. He didn't tell Dr. Gideon that for a tour guide he was poorly traveled. He'd been nowhere outside Kabul except his relatives' village, which was not far. He had never traveled merely to *see* something, as Dr. Gideon seemed to want to do. But his duties would be simple: arrange transport and food, help plan the journey, act as an interpreter, and get the American safely home. And the pay, while not large, was more than a deminer earned, and with much less danger. He could fake his way through their travels, he decided. "For all Dr. Gideon knew, I could call a pile of rocks the Minaret of Jam."

"So that's where it started," Parveen said abruptly. "That's when you began to make things up. Like when you told Crane that the commander here was Taliban." She hadn't meant to be so blunt, but she was relieved that at last it was out.

Aziz looked baffled. "Why would I say that? Everyone knows there were no Taliban here then. That commander fought against them."

Parveen paused, uncertain. Was Aziz sure he'd never said anything like that to Crane?

Of course, Aziz said. It was a horrible accusation to make if untrue. It could ruin a life.

Had Aziz been with Crane when he was kidnapped by the commander? she asked.

Kidnapped? Crane had never been kidnapped, Aziz said. At least, not while they were together.

How could he so blithely contradict part of the tale that Crane had told to millions? she wondered, though she quickly realized that her frustration wasn't with Aziz but with Crane. She could no longer pretend he hadn't invented the story about being kidnapped by a Taliban commander. Perhaps he thought the tale would never get back to Amanullah. Or perhaps he didn't realize what smearing a man's reputation meant in this part of the world. Either way, it burned her. "Did you even read Dr. Gideon's book?" she asked Aziz.

He hadn't, he said, dropping his head. His English wasn't good enough to read a whole book like that. He'd opened it, looked for his name, discovered that he was A., and closed it. When Colonel Trotter asked him questions about his time in the village, he said that whatever Dr. Gideon had written was what happened, and he couldn't remember anything more. He didn't want to admit to Trotter that he couldn't read the book, because it might make Trotter question his English skills. "But I told Colonel Trotter I read it, so please—"

"Like you told him the villagers had agreed to the road when they hadn't." Her tone was cutting because she was angry—angry at him for refusing to take responsibility for the lies about the commander. She could no longer deny that Crane alone was responsible, and this she found almost impossible to bear.

Aziz's eyes began to dart. "I didn't know then that you could understand everything."

This was hardly an acceptable excuse. But again she felt compassion for him, recalling her own recent transgression, which she described to him, reminding him of the day Trotter had mentioned to Dr. Yasmeen the woman who'd died of eclampsia. "I shouldn't have been talking to him about that—the doctor is, rightly, protective of her patients' privacy—so I didn't translate what he said. It was like I had this strange power, where only I could know everything that was happening." She wasn't sure whether to admit that she found it intoxicating, as if the fruit of the Tree of Knowledge were hers to distribute. "You have that power too."

It wasn't a power he wanted, Aziz said. The consequences felt too much for him.

They'd reached the bazaar, and Aziz was thirsty. Parveen suggested they go to the *chai khana*, a stall that intermittently served as a teahouse. Parveen never went there on her own—it was too clearly a space for the men—but today she confidently followed Aziz into its dark recesses. Because it was so small, everything could be overheard by the few other men there, and as if by instinct, Aziz began weaving much more English into his Dari, speaking in a code that only Parveen could crack.

In the beginning of his work with the Americans, he'd tried to translate every word, he said, but it was impossible. He sounded morose at his failure. Americans talked too fast, as fast as bullets. He couldn't keep up, and he worried that if he kept asking them to repeat what they'd said, he'd lose his job, because part of that job was to convey authority to the elders or whomever else the Americans were meeting with. He couldn't show his ignorance. At night, unable to sleep, he would replay over and over in his head what he'd missed, wondering if some catastrophe might happen as a result. But then he began to see that it didn't matter what he missed, because life—events—just formed around what he'd left out. It was like there was a place where a road split, and one fork followed the complete and accurate translation and the other the translation he was capable of, and he was directing them onto that second fork, which they would take to wherever it led.

As he spoke, Parveen could sense his wariness giving way to relief. "I've never been able to...never had anyone to talk to about this," he said. He continued: The other problem was that the Americans—especially the soldiers and most of all Colonel Trotter—were very efficient and often in a hurry. They didn't really want every word; they wanted the direct route in every-thing. Afghans, of course, often told stories to explain what they meant. "We love history—you know this," Aziz said. "We're very polite. An elder doesn't want to insult anyone, even an enemy, and sometimes being too direct can be an insult or sound like one." That roundabout way of talking frustrated the Americans, though, so Aziz felt he had to get to the point. But it seemed to him that the more each side talked, the less the other side under-stood. Or the unhappier each side became at what the other side was saying. So he began to make…choices. Changes in the translation that he thought would help avoid confusion, avoid conflict, and please each side. With time, his editing became habitual. "Sometimes I can't believe I'm the only way they have of understanding each other," he said.

"But if they don't agree," Parveen said, "isn't it better if they know that now?"

"If they *think* they agree, maybe they'll move forward in harmony." But ultimately, he admitted, his reasons weren't that lofty. "The most important thing for me is to keep the colonel happy. I need this job."

The words seemed to remind him of Trotter, and Aziz suddenly rose, ducking his head beneath the low ceiling of the stall. For her this only served to dramatize the puzzling dynamic in which the employer had the financial power and the interpreter the linguistic power. While she was sure most interpreters were honest—that even Aziz was, most of the time—it seemed a fragile basis for an occupation.

"I'd like to talk more," Aziz said as they walked through the bazaar toward the M-ATVs.

She wanted that too. In the *chai khana*, for the first time, they'd spoken face to face rather than side by side, and she'd felt him studying her features when he thought he was unobserved. Her body at that moment had begun to heat, and only then did she realize how profoundly her sexual hunger had diminished in the village, for lack of an object. Yet she had no idea what might come next. At college, she would have known exactly where this was going to lead, or where she wanted to lead it. But here? Aziz, though older, was less experienced, she intuited, but the real problem was practical, the impossibility for talking privately, to say nothing of touching, in this village. She felt a new kinship with Shokoh, longing for Naseer.

In Dari now, because they were approaching the Americans, she asked what Trotter would do if the attacks continued.

Aziz sighed and said he didn't know. "The colonel's frustrated. Doing this road was supposed to be easy. The war wasn't supposed to come here."

"I guess wars don't obey orders."

"Life doesn't obey," he said.

CHAPTER SEVENTEEN

ELVIS

As Trotter had predicted, Dr. Yasmeen was being brought in by helicopter now. On Wednesday mornings, she and Naseer would drive to the American base and then fly from there. The village was so quiet that you could hear the helicopter coming— the *rat-a-tat* of its rotors battering the air—well before you saw it. The sound suggested speed, but whenever Parveen saw a helicopter emerge from the gap between mountains, it moved slower than she expected. She always thrilled, secretly, to its arrival. The drama of its touchdown in the khan's field never lessened. Naseer loved these flights—his country was even more beautiful from above, he said. His mother, by contrast, looked green when she disembarked.

A couple of weeks after Trotter had interrogated the shura about the attack on the road, Dr. Yasmeen told Parveen that at the base that morning, the colonel had asked her to talk to the women about who might be planting the IEDs. This request, which came via his interpreter, had made her uncomfortable, and she'd told the colonel so. She couldn't ask her patients to report on others in the village, she said, nor could she repeat to Trotter anything her patients told her when she was examining them. "I'm a doctor," she said. "Not an intelligence service."

Parveen agreed that the request was untoward, though she also found it revealing. If the Americans were asking Dr. Yasmeen for information, they had to be pretty desperate. She speculated aloud that there must have been more attacks on the road.

Yes, Dr. Yasmeen said, that was what Colonel Trotter's interpreter had told Naseer. IEDs were being placed in culverts and construction barrels. There had been severe injuries—hands lost, legs maimed—to two laborers. Others were refusing to work because of the danger. Dr. Yasmeen thought she and Naseer were being flown in not because of work on the road but because the colonel didn't think it was safe to drive.

The colonel was looking for help wherever he could find it, Parveen soon learned. He wanted not just information but levers that would move the village to the American side. He was perceptive enough to have figured out that asking for help or information in front of the shura wasn't going to get him anywhere. "I need a mayor," he kept telling Aziz, who kept telling him that even unofficially, there wasn't one. These villages didn't work that way. There were people with more power, like the khan and commander, and those with less, but decision making was collective, consensual.

Trotter already knew this, since he'd devoured all the ethnography and anthropology and political science about Afghanistan he could find, questing for that elusive key to the villagers' "hearts and minds." But he decided that a private audience with the khan was worth trying, since the khan was profiting so richly from the Americans' rental of his field. Parveen went along on the walk to the khan's in the hope of talking more with Aziz, but it was Trotter who monopolized most of her attention. The model for what he was hoping to achieve, he told her, was the Sunni awakening in Iraq the previous year, during which sheikhs had rallied their tribes against al-Qaeda. Trotter hoped to inspire the villagers to rise up and protect their road.

Parveen, even knowing little about Iraq, thought this a fool's errand. The khan didn't have the power of a sheikh, and he wouldn't be able to keep any promises he might make about the village's cooperation. She had no intention of going inside the house to be prey for his lewd thoughts and, in keeping with her recurrent fantasy of threatening the khan with the Americans' retribution, even considered telling Trotter about his behavior. But she knew such retribution was no more likely than the awakening Trotter wanted. They were both without recourse.

At the house, the khan insisted it would be rude for Parveen to refuse his hospitality and tried to lure her inside.

"But I had so much of your hospitality in the orchard already," she said.

Aziz, who knew how impolite it was to refuse an invitation and could no doubt discern the archness of her Dari, looked with interest from her to the khan before following Trotter and two soldiers into the khan's compound.

The remaining eight stood guard outside. Several paced off in different directions, out into the sunlight, while a few others sheltered beneath the ancient trees shading the compound. They checked their weapons and talked quietly until Parveen joined them, at which point all conversation stopped. She cast around for a way to restart it—the weather? Their hometowns?—but every possibility felt wrong and none of the soldiers broke the lengthening silence. Trotter was easier for her to talk to, although it embarrassed her to think of how their earnest discussion about the Ship of Theseus must have sounded to these soldiers. In age, at least, they and not the colonel were her peers.

"Look at this wall, not a mark on it," said one of the soldiers at last, gesturing at the pristine compound exterior. He was tall and gangly with unusually pale skin and pale eyes, made more so by his colorless lashes. "If this were a base porta-potty, there'd be pictures of dicks from top to bottom."

"Dick wallpaper," said another soldier. He wore large glasses that made his head look tiny.

"Wallpaper's for pussies."

"My mama's got wallpaper," said a third soldier in an accent that was faintly Southern.

"Like I said."

The Southerner took a menacing step forward, then broke off laughing.

"I bet her mom's got a lot of wallpaper." The tall pale one, who appeared to be barely out of high school, jerked his head toward Parveen, and she concluded that he hadn't advanced beyond needling girls to get their attention.

"My mom's dead," she said.

There were a few low whistles at how badly she'd burned him; they seemed to expect her to follow up with *Just kidding!* When she didn't, there were murmurs of apology.

"You've got to excuse Boone, he doesn't know how to talk to women," said another of the soldiers. He was compact and sturdy with skin nearly as dark as Parveen's.

Boone nodded, dropped his head sheepishly, then grinned. "Shit, Kirby's mom is dead to his family."

The other soldiers shifted a bit, glancing nervously at each other. Kirby, whose head seemed so tiny, she now realized, because of the grotesquely muscled frame it sat atop, gave Boone a blood-curdling stare. At least, it curdled Parveen's blood.

"Shut your fuckin' flytrap, Boone," warned the Southerner. "Reyes," he said, addressing the darker-skinned one, "make him shut up."

Instead, in an apparent effort to defuse the tension, Reyes asked Parveen where she was from.

Union City, she told him.

"So how come Colonel Trotter calls you Berkeley?" he asked.

"You know he calls you that, right?" He imitated Trotter: "'Berkeley says the phenomenally phenomenological views of the women must be taken into account...'"

She laughed even though the imitation mocked her as much as it did Trotter and said Berkeley was where she'd graduated from, but Union City was where she'd grown up.

"We thought you were from this shithole," Reyes said, then caught himself. "Sorry, didn't mean it that way. It's a beautiful country, actually. Just a shitty one to be at war in."

She nodded as if in agreement or understanding, then told them that, even though Kabul was her birthplace, Afghanistan was almost as foreign to her as it was to them.

"Respect," Boone said, "but that's bullshit. You speak the language. We need Elvis to speak for us."

"Elvis?"

"That's what some of us, the dumb ones"—and Reyes cut his eyes at Boone—"call your boyfriend. It's easier."

"He's not my boyfriend," Parveen said curtly.

"Relax," Reyes said. "I'm just fucking with you."

"Fucking *with* women is as close as we get to them here," Kirby said. "How come we never see any? Not one other than you. God, I'm tired of hairy faces."

"That's sure going to be unwelcome news to your girlfriend," Boone cracked.

Again the fervid stare from Kirby.

"Ignore Kirby here," Reyes told Parveen. "He's only human when he's working out."

"Aziz told me he likes it when we call him Elvis," Boone said. "It's better than having the people whose doors we're busting down hear his real name."

"Shhh, she doesn't know about the doors—we haven't done that here," said the Southerner, whose name she hadn't caught.

"Yet," Kirby said. "Give us time."

She had an image of how terrifying it would be to have people with so much physical power, not even counting the weapons they would bring, burst into your compound at night. Kirby's words seemed to sour the air, reminding the soldiers that, despite the gorgeous valley of which the khan's house afforded such spectacular views, the road was dangerous, the locals unreliable, and their enemies nearby.

"So I have a question, Parvenu," the Southerner said.

Parveen, she reminded him, then hastened to add that even spell-check autocorrected her name to Parvenu. "Which is kind of funny for an immigrant."

At his blank stare, Reyes chimed in. "Vance doesn't know what a parvenu is. He didn't finish high school. They're so desperate for bodies to feed this machine, they keep lowering the requirements."

"Well, if I ever get home, I'll look it up," Vance said. "And last I checked, college douche, you were shitting in the same out-house I was. At least I didn't waste my time. Anyway, Par*veen*, can you explain to us why we're getting our asses shot at here when we're just trying to help? It doesn't feel so great."

"Vancey's feelings are hurt," Boone said.

"Shut up," Reyes said. "Let her answer."

All eyes were on Parveen, who didn't have a response. Ever since Trotter had come to discuss the trouble along the road, she'd been trying to ask Waheed a version of the same question. Not *who* was shooting, necessarily—he wouldn't tell her even if he knew—but why.

"They're trying to defeat a superpower," he'd finally said one night. "The road's just another battlefield to them."

To the soldiers, she said only "I don't know any more than you do."

"One more reason to get the fuck out of here," Boone said, sighing. "Just ninety-three more days."

"Don't count," Reyes said. "It makes the time pass slower."

"Is that physics, dickhead?"

"Count, don't count," Kirby said. "Either way you'll get home, hopefully not zipped into an HRP, and after about four days of boredom and hating on civilians, you'll want to reenlist." He ought to know, he said. He was on his third tour.

"Watch out or the same thing will happen to you," Reyes told Parveen. "Stay here too long and you won't be fit for anywhere else. You'll just keep looping back."

PARVEEN WAS SO ENGROSSED in talking to the soldiers that she felt mild regret when Trotter and Aziz emerged from the khan's. But within minutes, as they retraced their steps to the M-ATVs, she was back listening to Trotter, and the soldiers, spread out around them, were back looking ready to kill.

The colonel told Parveen that the khan had promised to use his influence to get more cooperation from the villagers, and in return, Trotter had promised to have an engineer draw up plans to improve the village irrigation system (akin to the false promise Aziz had made in the very first shura meeting, Parveen remembered). She surmised that this project would somehow benefit the khan, who controlled the water rights, and Aziz said as much to her later. The khan, he was sure, would profit from this bargain much more than Colonel Trotter.

"Did you actually translate Trotter's promise?" Parveen asked. She was speaking Dari, newly conscious that the soldiers might be listening.

Yes, he'd translated it, Aziz said, partly because he'd thought hard about what Parveen had said, that it was better for the Afghans and the Americans to know where they stood with each other. He was no longer going to try to control this small corner of the war.

Parveen was pleased but took pains not to show it. The soldiers' teasing had worked on her as a form of policing, she realized, and she was more circumspect with Aziz now.

"What's the history between you and the khan?" he asked.

She was right, then, that he'd noticed her discomfort. The khan had accosted her and tried to kiss her in the orchard, she said. Ever since, she'd avoided him.

Aziz weighed this and said, "I might have tried the same thing. Afghan men don't really know how to behave around women, especially women from the West. And there are a lot of stories about you."

He didn't mean her specifically, she knew; he meant Western women. Her cousin Fawad had explained as much in Kabul; they were presumed to be loose, available. She had tried to educate him and now found herself doing the same with Aziz.

"So you'll show me what's allowed," he said, and she suppressed a smile.

CHAPTER EIGHTEEN

THE BALD MAN

IT CONCERNED THE DOCTOR THAT, WHETHER DUE TO DANGER or construction, the road was largely impassable now. A village woman who was deathly ill would have no way to leave, even if she agreed to. Dr. Yasmeen wanted Parveen to be prepared for an emergency in her absence. They were going to start with Latifa, that reluctant progenitor of girls. She looked sickly, with protruding collarbones and yellow-gray skin everywhere except beneath her eyes, where violet pooled. She had delivered early last time, the doctor said, luckily only by four weeks, but it meant there was a high chance of preterm labor this time as well. She was roughly twenty-four weeks pregnant now, but her cervical length was short, barely more than two centimeters, and this was often, although of course not always, a predictor of early labor.

She should be spending the end of her pregnancy in a hospital, Dr. Yasmeen said, but instead she would stay here and cook and care for her family until her contractions began and her life was at risk. The doctor had offered, many times, to teach the dai what to do when there was postpartum bleeding or when the placenta wouldn't come out, but the woman refused, insisting she had more experience than the doctor. "She'll say it's in God's hands," Dr. Yasmeen said. "Better a woman dies than for her to admit she has something to learn." But the dai would not allow the doctor to train any other village women either. This was why, although Parveen had no medical training, Dr. Yasmeen wanted to teach her what to do. As an outsider, Parveen could stand up to the dai.

During Latifa's exam, over Parveen's protests, Dr. Yasmeen began to instruct her. If Latifa delivered and was still bleeding, she should take misoprostol, a single pill that did not require refrigeration. But if she didn't take the medication or it didn't work, Parveen should try to stop the bleeding manually. She was to put one hand up the birth canal and into the lower uterus and with the other hand press down on Latifa's abdomen.

The thought made Parveen woozy. "I can't put my hand in there. It's—too small."

"Have you never been examined by a gynecologist?" the doctor said, clearly amused. "Believe me, the hand goes up." She asked Latifa if Parveen could examine her, and when Latifa said yes, Dr. Yasmeen told Parveen to put on a sterile glove.

"I don't have your training, your experience," Parveen said.

"You're an educated girl. You can learn. You must," she said with an unmistakable edge.

Parveen had met few people with such persistent good nature—it was almost suspicious, especially when she learned how much the doctor had suffered under the Taliban—so it was perversely pleasing to hear dissatisfaction in her voice, even if it was aimed at Parveen. "What I want to learn, what I'm here to learn," Parveen said, "is why so many women in Afghanistan are dying in childbirth. Without understanding the structural reasons"—she didn't even know how to translate this into Dari, so she said it in English—"without tackling the power dynamics that prevent women from having a voice, let alone proper health care, nothing will change."

She was feeling proud of this declamation, and the doctor nodded as if she were agreeing, then said, "At the end of a labor, Parveen, a woman lives, or she dies. That is all that concerns me. Now try it."

Latifa was watching them, and she looked awful. Parveen imagined her being forced to take her chances in labor with a dai too stubborn to learn anything that might help. Could Parveen say she was any different right now, with her high-minded excuses? It came down to what her conscience could or couldn't bear. She wasn't the least bit confident that even with the doctor's instruction she would be able to save anyone, but she had to try. Maybe this was why Crane's book had come into her life—because, as a woman, she could provide the help he hadn't been allowed to give. Whatever the flaws in his book, this held true.

Parveen put on a sterile glove and wormed her fingers in.

"Move delicately, very delicately," the doctor instructed her. "There's a fetus inside."

Fuck, Parveen thought. As if she weren't nervous enough already.

Latifa's lower body hiccuped as Parveen's fingers squelched up her canal until they touched the cervix, the opening of the uterus, slimy but firm, like a wet rubber ball. Parveen grew giddy, high on the euphoria of doing something she hadn't thought possible, and she grinned ridiculously at Latifa, who responded with a dismayed look. Parveen's hand was still inside her.

"Now you know you can do it," Dr. Yasmeen said. "Let's hope you'll never need to."

"Was that all right? Did I hurt you?" Parveen asked Latifa nervously once she was dressed.

Her color seemed even more alarming now, her face sidewalk gray. "It hurt," she said, "but it was all right."

"If Dr. Yasmeen can't be here, I'll take care of you," Parveen said with what she hoped was reassurance.

Latifa replied, with a faint smile, "As the doctor said, let's hope you'll never need to."

THAT A LIFE MIGHT depend on her was not something Parveen carried lightly, and it gave her new empathy for Crane, who, seeing a woman in danger, hadn't been allowed to help. What would that feel like? Even worse was imagining how Fereshta must have felt to see him barred from coming to her aid.

Parveen asked Bina if she knew how her sister had died.

Giving birth, Bina said.

Yes, but did she know exactly what had happened?

Giving birth was all she'd been told, Bina said. Women died that way all the time. Even though Fereshta was her sister, she hadn't asked for more.

To be female here was to grasp at scraps of information and sew them into the shape you imagined reality to be. Into fictions, patterned on distortions and inventions. The women needed an accurate understanding of the peril in which they lived—and the reasons for it. Parveen spread the word that they would return to the orchard. She would share with them the chapter about Fereshta's death.

Was it possible that she also wanted to test the heart of Crane's book to see how it held up? Only later did she wonder whether this was why she set it all out before the women like meat to be sniffed for rancidity.

It was late summer now. The grass had browned and the trees' leaves drooped. The earth had been storing warmth for months, and convective waves of it rose from the ground. The women fanned themselves and one another. A few babies, cranky in the heat, cried out. The dai, entering the orchard with a regal hobble, paused over them, as if they were subjects she had knighted into life. Then, holding tightly to a wooden cane, she executed a series of dramatic bends to settle her arthritic figure. Wherever Parveen turned, she appeared, like a floater in her eye.

Parveen said that she was going to share the chapter about Fereshta's death with them. The name felt odd in her mouth today, as if even to speak it in this company was an appropriation or a presumptuous intimacy. If Parveen was being honest, had Fereshta ever been anything more than a name to her? A story borne on a donkey? A puppet she was making dance? Parveen had read in one of her anthropology classes about herders who would sacrifice an injured cow or sheep to piranhas so that the rest of a herd could safely cross the river. Was this the role Fereshta had been destined to play or the one she'd been shoved into? Her death had made so much possible.

The women were solemn, respectful, which was unnerving. She began partway into chapter ten.

Fereshta told me that her previous six births had gone easily enough, and she had no reason to expect that this time would be any different. She, like all the villagers, did not know her age, but I placed her in her late twenties. She had been bearing children every two years or less since she married Waheed.

When she went into labor, I was taking a walk. One of Fereshta's children came to find me. "My mother needs help," he said. I hurried back to the house with him. Inside, the midwife emerged from Fereshta's room. She was an ignorant crone with no medical training whatsoever.

With the dai present, Parveen skipped over this last line.

The midwife's face was grave. The baby was stuck, she told me. "Her condition is very dangerous, Dr. Gideon. You must see her. She's bleeding. She needs your help. There's nothing I can do for her—"

"No, no," the dai interrupted. "I was never allowed into where Fereshta was."

"Okay."

"I didn't see her. We couldn't agree—"

"You've brought enough children into the world to fill four villages," Parveen said, trying to placate the dai and so quiet her. "Surely you can't remember the details of each birth."

"Each birth wasn't attended by an American!" The dai's rheumy eyes seemed to glow; her voice hoarsened. "Of course I remember what happened with Fereshta. It was the American's fault. The sum he was willing to pay me was a pittance."

"I'm sorry, what? You and Dr. Gideon argued about *money*?"

The women were still, their eyes watchful.

"Because I'm a woman and not a doctor," the dai said, "he didn't want to pay." It had been six years since Crane had first come to the village, and her bitterness, rising all that time, was spilling over its banks. "I had five children to feed," she said, almost muttering to herself, rehearsing the condensed auto-biography she'd told Parveen and every woman here so many times before. Still, they listened with polite attention. "When my husband went, there was no one."

Parveen knew now that her children were mostly grown, her sons supporting her rather than the other way around, but hoarding sympathy had become a compulsion for her, the way bees store nectar or survivalists stockpile guns. Parveen wondered if the dai had tried to gouge Crane, to get him to pay some exorbitant fee because he was American, and if so, whether this had triggered some primal instinct in him, the traveler's fear of being exploited or tricked, which could lead to fighting over small amounts of money you wouldn't worry about wasting back home. It was about pride, the humiliation of being fleeced— Parveen had experienced similar flares of resentment after the khan told her how high her rent to Waheed was. But from the sound of it, Crane and the dai had haggled over the worth of a woman's life as one might over the price of a trinket in the bazaar.

The dai was defending herself to the other women as much as to Parveen. Back then, she said, Waheed had nothing. He was one of the poorest men in the village. He could barely feed his own children. For Fereshta's other births he hadn't even called her because he couldn't pay. He called her in this case because Fereshta was in trouble or maybe because the American told him to get help. "You know our saying," she said. "'If the bald man were really a doctor, he would have cured his own head.'"

Parveen had heard her call Crane "the bald man" more than once. The first time or two, Parveen had corrected her—"He's not bald!"—and the dai had cackled. After that Parveen had let it go, thinking the dai must be a little touched. Now dread dropped into her as she realized the dai had had her reasons all along.

"I wanted to help," she went on. "I'm not a cruel woman, but I was a widow with five children to feed and I simply wanted to know who would pay my fee. So my own children could eat. Dr. Gideon said he would, and that's when our argument began. He asked what the fee would be."

A widow with five children, just as Crane's own mother had been. Surely he wouldn't have tried to stint on paying her? Parveen looked around at the other women and asked what the truth was. She was sweating, rivulets trickling down her back and forehead. She wiped her face with the back of her arm. Her eyes stung.

"How would they know?" the dai asked, amused. "They weren't there. Only Dr. Gideon and I were."

So it was her word against Crane's, one story against another. The women evinced no angst about this. Life, history, memory— all were capacious enough to contain competing stories. As in their crowded homes, there was always room for one more; you just shifted a little to make space.

"Aziz, the interpreter," Parveen said. "Was he there?"

"Of course—how could we talk without him? The American couldn't find his own cock without Aziz. And I cannot ask for my own cunt in English."

Some of the women, perhaps relieved to have the tension broken, laughed. Not Bina, Parveen noticed. She looked uneasy, and partly because of that, Parveen snapped, "It's not funny!"

"No," the dai agreed. "No. But you see, it was because of Aziz that I knew Dr. Gideon had money and was trying to cheat me. He was paying Aziz thirty American dollars a day—Aziz had told us." She dropped her head, awaiting her crown of sympathy.

"But you left, right? You abandoned Fereshta?"

"I left," she said. "What more could I do?" A little later Jamshid came to ask her to return to Waheed's, she continued, but without challenge in her voice. Jamshid told her that his mother needed help, that Dr. Gideon was asking her to come back.

The dai stopped speaking.

Had she had gone with Jamshid? Parveen asked.

She hadn't, the dai replied, defiant once more. She'd still been angry with Crane; she felt he deserved to suffer. About Fereshta's suffering, she said nothing, although she looked at Bina and whispered, "It was God's will."

Bina kept her gaze on her own hands, which she stroked, roughly. The dai seemed nonplussed; Parveen could see her swallow even in the loose skin of her throat. It was almost a relief when her usual combativeness returned. "Dr. Gideon was rich, I was poor, what could I do?"

No one answered. Parveen had the same feeling of unsteadiness, of waking-falling, that she'd had all those months ago in Berkeley when she'd been panicking about her future. Now she was in that future, and it looked nothing like she'd imagined. With a sense of doom, she'd resumed the story.

I immediately began to prepare, ordering water boiled for sterilization. But before I could go inside to Fereshta, Waheed insisted the mullah had to approve. I assumed, wrongly, that this was a mere formality. The mullah was brought. He stroked his chin and consulted his Quran—with every minute that passed putting Fereshta's life at greater risk—then gave his ruling: It was not right for me, a male and an infidel, to treat Fereshta. All of the other village men backed him up. If they allowed it, they insisted, they couldn't safeguard their own souls or Fereshta's for the day of judgment.

"But she'll die!" I said.

"That's in God's hands," the mullah said. "Her virtue, her family's honor, matter more than her life."

"You'll have blood on your hands!" I shouted, but it was in vain. I wouldn't be permitted to help. Not by the mullah and so not by Waheed. I begged him to make up his own mind. But he wouldn't defy the mullah. Waheed said that whether Fereshta lived or died would be God's will.

Next I tried appealing to the commander, who had allowed me to treat his own wife's eyes. He insisted that the mullah had to be obeyed, that Fereshta should go to a hospital where there was a female doctor.

But there was no hospital anywhere nearby. Between us and the district center stretched that abysmal road. And we had no way to travel it; there was no car or truck in the village, not even a bicycle. The wheel—it's a stage of civilization, one the village hadn't yet reached.

"Someone must have a car," I kept saying to Waheed. No one did. There was only one way out, which was the way we had come in: by donkey. There were two of them. We put Fereshta on one and took turns leading it. These were the most agonizing hours of my life but far worse for Fereshta. She was barely conscious for most of the ride, although I tried to keep her talking. I told her stories of my mother, of brave and noble Americans—Paul Revere, Rosa Parks. I talked about my own daughter and Fereshta's children and my hope that one day they could meet. Waheed, by contrast, kept saying to no one in particular that it

was God's will whether she lived or died. His fatalism infuriated me. I felt he'd already made his peace with the failure to save her—and with his own failure to act more boldly.

At last we reached the hospital, where the doctors rushed her inside. Again, as a foreign man, I was barred. I paced around the outside of the small hospital as goats nibbled from trash heaps threaded with medical waste. Her screams came out the windows, tore me apart. I stretched myself on the ground, spread my arms wide, and asked God to take me instead. As I prayed, the screams ceased abruptly. I thanked God; the baby had been safely born. Then a bay, a single extended unearthly note that still echoes in my ears, broke the silence.

I rushed into the hospital and raced down the hall until I saw, through an open door, Waheed bent over his wife's lifeless body. I turned away to give him time with her and so that I could weep. My heart was ragged until it was inflamed by Waheed's first words to me: "It was God's will." No, I wanted to scream, it was the will—or the want of will—of men. But you can't scream at a man in mourning. I rented a cart to return Fereshta's body to the village. It was pulled by the donkey she had ridden, alive, to the hospital.

"But my sister never went on a donkey!" Bina said when Parveen paused. "She died in Waheed's house. In the room where we eat, the room where we sleep." She spoke with uncharacteristic intensity.

Parveen looked at her. "Who told you this?"

"Waheed. Jamshid. Everyone. It's what happened. I don't know much else, but this I know."

The other women nodded as Bina spoke. Having been in the village at the time of Fereshta's death, they knew what Bina said was true. Now Parveen waited, resigned, for the next blow, which was delivered by the dai.

"None of the part you've just told us is correct," she said. No one had stopped Dr. Gideon from trying to help Fereshta. "He tried, but he wasn't capable. He couldn't help. The bald man."

She sighed in what sounded like pity for his ineptitude. "When Jamshid came to me, it was to say that the baby was stuck and Dr. Gideon needed help getting it out. And then he crushed the baby's skull trying to get it out on his own, and after that Fereshta bled to death."

Vomit rose up in Parveen; her vision wobbled and wavered. She gripped a tree branch, scaly and psoriatic beneath her hand. She wanted not to believe the dai. She wanted the other women to rise up and deny, denounce, condemn the dai's words, to say that this was not how Fereshta had died. But no one did. The dai spoke the truth, and Gideon Crane was a liar. It seemed so unsurprising now; the clues had been everywhere. But the mind prefers order, it prefers logic, and it will do what is necessary to make sense of events. You could gaslight yourself trying to keep someone else's story intact. Parveen saw that now, but only now.

For the village women, the revelation of Crane's deceptions was less shattering. They'd never seen him as any kind of witness to truth. He was a storyteller, one whose tales occasionally intersected with events they'd experienced. Yet the gruesome particulars narrated by the dai had distressed them, Parveen saw. Absorbed by her own reactions, she'd failed to notice Bina's face, which looked like it was melting. Her mouth had softly collapsed; her eyes leaked tears. Parveen had never seen her cry, had secretly thought her incapable of it, and now rued that she herself had brought this about. Bina's friends hovered in a protective knot around her. Even Shokoh leaned in awkwardly, on her knees, to caress Bina's back. Parveen walked over, knelt down, and apologized to Bina, then hugged her, and feeling the tiny frame of Fereshta's sister shake with grief in her arms, she wondered whom it had served to exhume this truth.

* * *

LATER THAT AFTERNOON PARVEEN sat in the main room of the house and looked around at the walls, at the floor. Her mind inched toward practicalities: How had they cleaned it of blood? Of odor? How soon before they resumed eating here, or sleeping? There was nowhere else to sleep.

Waheed came home to find the atmosphere in the house unsettled. When Bina and Shokoh began to tell him about the orchard, he looked at Parveen, troubled. But over dinner, he agreed to answer her questions.

Fereshta had never gone to the district hospital, he confirmed. "She wouldn't have made it three stone's throws. Even here, she was already dying. Bilal, Jamshid—go check the cows," he said gruffly.

Though at this hour the cows were certainly fine, Bilal obeyed. Jamshid, however, stayed where he was. His words that day in the meadow—*I was there when she died. I heard it*—came to Parveen. Rather than believe him, she'd refashioned his experience to fit Crane's fantasia.

She asked Waheed if Crane and the dai had fought over money. When he nodded, Jamshid, startled, pressed him to explain. Waheed's account largely matched the dai's, but it differed in one respect. He said that when Dr. Gideon left, after Fereshta was dead, he'd had Aziz give Waheed money. It was much more than the dai would have cost. "But it was too late," Waheed said.

Jamshid rubbed his eyes, nearly scrubbed them, as Waheed spoke. He was trying not to cry, Parveen knew. She wished he could. Where did grief go in men? She imagined it packed like gunpowder, waiting for a fuse, a release, an explosion that might never come.

"My mother's life," he said bitterly. "Not worth a few more dollars to Dr. Gideon. What's money to an American?"

"Most Americans wouldn't behave that way," she said gently. "My question"—she turned toward Waheed—"my next question is whether anyone stopped Dr. Gideon from trying to help . . . your wife." After months of bandying about Fereshta's name, Parveen found herself unable to say it. "Did anyone tell Dr. Gideon that because he was a man and a foreigner, he shouldn't help her? The mullah? Anyone?"

"Why would they stop him?" Waheed said. "He was the hope." *He was the hope.*

"We thought God had sent him to save her," Waheed continued. "For the first time in my life, I felt lucky."

Parveen was dizzy, but she kept on. So—what then? What went wrong? To demand someone else's memories could be an act of aggression rather than empathy, she knew. But she needed the full truth.

"Dr. Gideon tried to save her but he couldn't," Waheed said, his voice rising slightly. "He didn't know what to do. She died, the baby died." He paused to collect himself. "It was God's will."

Crane, in his book, had quoted Waheed saying these very words, making them a reason to reprimand Waheed for his passivity. But now Parveen understood that they were an exoneration—Waheed's exoneration of Crane for failing to save his wife. Waheed, whom she'd judged harshly all these months, had done everything he could.

She held her breath for a few moments, then exhaled.

"I owe you an apology," she told Waheed. "All this time, I believed Crane's story. I thought she'd died because no one would let him help and you agreed—"

Confusion clouded his face and she stopped. It wasn't only that he'd never read *Mother Afghanistan*, she realized, it was that he'd never even heard the story it contained. He didn't know how Crane had described Fereshta's death. It fell to Parveen to explain it to him. As she did so, he slumped against the wall, blinking his amber eyes, and Parveen grasped the magnitude of Crane's deceit, or rather the intimacy of it. Waheed had been made unrecognizable to himself, transformed into the kind of man who, in the name of his religion, would allow his wife to die.

"This story, it is the one every American has read?" he asked. "It is the one Colonel Trotter has read?"

Parveen nodded, curious at the invocation of Trotter. It made sense, she supposed. He wore America's uniform. And he was powerful.

"So now this is what they think Islam is," he said slowly. "This is who they think Afghans are. That we are all like the Taliban."

Waheed's concern was not Crane's slander of him but his slander of his religion, which was also Parveen's, and of his country. Crane, by claiming to be the friend of the Afghans, by speaking about love, had crafted a beautiful vial for his poison. It wasn't as if some men here didn't mistreat their wives or claim that Islam sanctioned doing so. But Crane had deliberately distorted the truth. That so many Americans would believe the worst of Afghans after the 9/11 attacks didn't necessarily surprise Parveen. What stunned her was how readily she'd believed Crane's tale herself. Her adolescent alienation in that fall of 2001, when for a time she had denied her very identity, had embedded much deeper than she'd thought. The body dysmorphia that made the anorexic looking in the mirror believe herself fat—wasn't this a kind of equivalent?

Waheed heaved himself up, crossed the room to the aluminum trunk, and retrieved the family copy of *Mother Afghanistan*, the hardback of which they'd been so proud. "Here," he said, handing it to Parveen. He was done with it.

THE NEXT TIME HE and Parveen were alone, Waheed said, "You asked me if I remembered the first time I saw the face of Jamshid's mother, on the day we married. What I wanted to tell you, but not in front of my son, is that I watched my wife die, and after that every picture I had of her in my mind from before was gone." It was like when a snake swallowed a mouse, he said. For a while you could still discern the shape of the mouse, but you couldn't truly see it, you would never see it again. Then even the shape disappeared, and all that was left was the snake.

Chapter Nineteen

Kismet

Parveen walked a lot in the following days, as if steps could be expiation. Up and down the village lanes, through the fields, into the mountains, until skin began to flake from her feet. It felt like rightful punishment. She was crashing inside. Whatever part of her selfhood had been lashed to Crane had been loosed to fall and shatter.

And yet she wanted to know more. She wanted as many details about the truth of Fereshta's death as had embroidered Crane's fictions. She didn't know yet what she would do with the information. She vacillated between believing she had a moral obligation to expose his fraud and burning for vengeance. But all she had was the dai's dark sketch, which Waheed had confirmed, but he hadn't volunteered more details, and Parveen hadn't asked. It felt unseemly to demand more from him or Jamshid. She had little choice but to wait for the return to the village of Aziz, the only other witness.

When she spoke to him, he told her he didn't want to talk about what had happened between Dr. Gideon and Fereshta. He didn't like to think about it. He wished he couldn't remember it.

When he finally relented and told Parveen what had occurred, his eyes grew wide and still, like black glass.

Aziz and Dr. Gideon had been in the village only two days, sleeping at the mosque (Aziz confirmed they'd never stayed with Waheed and Fereshta), when a boy came running to say his mother needed a doctor. He'd led them to Waheed's. The dai was there, and Dr. Gideon insisted that, as a woman with experience in childbirth, she should be the one helping Fereshta, not him. Dr. Gideon said he would pay her fee, but they began to argue over the amount. She was greedy, having been told he was an American, and Dr. Gideon was stingy. Aziz couldn't get them to agree on a sum, a failure that still haunted him. The dai left in anger, and Dr. Gideon reluctantly went into the room. Waheed joined him, which was unusual—fathers didn't typically attend the births of their children—but for honor's sake, Waheed couldn't leave Dr. Gideon alone with his wife. That was the mullah's sole injunction.

"Wait," Parveen said. "The mullah said it was fine?"

Aziz nodded. "As long as Waheed was there." Waheed was to stay in the room with his wife and Crane, the mullah had said, and Aziz was to stay outside it. He stood just beyond the doorway, translating from there, unable to see but unfortunately able to hear, both Dr. Gideon's muttering and cursing and Fereshta's crying and screaming. Then Dr. Gideon yelled to Aziz that he needed forceps. Aziz didn't know what he meant—he didn't know the English word. "I was scared to tell him I didn't understand," Aziz said. "But I had to and then he started cursing at me: 'Jesus fuck! Something to pull out the baby! The goddamn baby is stuck.' Like what you use to pull out a tooth, but bigger, he said. But where did he think I would find such a thing in a village?"

Aziz explained what he needed to Waheed, who told him to try the blacksmith or the baker, to see what tools they had. Aziz ran to the bazaar, and from the blacksmith he borrowed forceps, large and heavy, and from the baker, tongs, the long ones used to pull bread from the oven. When he returned, Dr. Gideon called him into the room and instructed him to put the instruments in the fire several times to sterilize them. As Aziz did so, he stared only at the flames, determined not to look at Fereshta. Dr. Gideon kept telling him to hurry, but the instruments had to cool. When they had done so, he handed the tools to Dr. Gideon and returned to his post outside the door. Dr. Gideon asked him to tell Waheed that he didn't know whether the baby was alive, that its head was stuck in the birth canal. It might be too big to come out. He would have to try to pull it out to save both the baby and Fereshta.

Aziz told Waheed this but got no response. He could only assume Waheed nodded, because then came the awful noise: "Crane cursing, telling her to push, Fereshta screaming so loud that I couldn't think. It sounded like she wanted to tear open the sky."

Parveen asked whether Crane had given Fereshta anything for the pain. Anesthesia, for example—what a surgeon uses to put a patient to sleep.

"Where would Dr. Gideon get anesthesia in a place like this?" Then, as if struggling to recall, he said he did remember now that it wasn't just money that Dr. Gideon and the dai were fighting over; before that, they'd argued over whether to give Fereshta opium, which was used sometimes by the villagers in childbirth for the pain. Dr. Gideon was opposed because of some mistaken idea that she might become addicted. Then he fought with the dai over the money, too, and she left. It certainly didn't *sound* like Dr. Gideon had given Fereshta anything for the pain, Aziz said. The screams kept getting louder for what felt like forever, until they stopped, and he heard crying, though whose it was he never learned, not even whether it was a man or woman. Then Dr. Gideon came out.

"He looked terrible," Aziz said. "His face—awful. Gray.

Like people look when they're being shelled. His hair sticking up."

Dr. Gideon placed a tiny bundle wrapped in a dirty cloth in Aziz's arms and told him not to open it and to make sure Fereshta never saw it. His eyes avoided Aziz, avoided the bundle too. Then he went back into the room.

"I had it in my arms," Aziz said, bending his arms around air to show Parveen. He guessed it was the baby, and he thought, or maybe hoped, that it was still alive, although the way Dr. Gideon had wrapped it, covering it completely, suggested it was not. Aziz was afraid to open it, and he tried to stroke it through the cloth instead. Where he thought the head was, he felt pieces that moved beneath his hand, like a broken bowl. The cloth there was moist, as if whatever had been in the bowl had leaked out. He'd seen many horrible injuries from combat in the years since then, he said, and he'd learned more about medicine, and he now believed this must have been fluid from the brain. But he'd sensed it even then. "We're not strangers to death," he said, "we Afghans. But a dead baby in my arms?" He didn't want to hold it anymore, yet he couldn't put it down.

For a while there was no sound, then Aziz heard words tumbling from Fereshta's mouth—the names of her children, the names of God, bits of prayers. Waheed tried to quiet her, and Dr. Gideon called to Aziz to bring back the dai because Fereshta was bleeding. But Aziz didn't know where to find the dai and doubted she would even return, given the quarrel with Crane. He told Jamshid, who he realized only then had been crouched near the door, listening to everything, to run and fetch her.

Then time seemed to lag, to slow. Death in war often happened very quickly, Aziz had learned since, but not in childbirth. It took its time. Fereshta still talked, but less, and more dreamily, as Aziz's young siblings did when falling asleep. Aziz couldn't make out what she was saying anymore. There were moments he heard nothing at all, like when a radio loses its signal. Sometimes she'd moan, he said, not a moan of pain but one of sadness. Of a mother who knew she was leaving her children. Then quieter, quieter.

Aziz stopped talking. Parveen waited for him to continue, but he didn't. Quieter, quieter; between them, too, there was silence now.

"What happened next?" Parveen asked at last.

"There was no next," Aziz said. "She was dead." Dr. Gideon emerged from the room looking even worse. His shirt was striped with blood, and his eyes were so red they looked bloodied as well. He'd lost Fereshta too, he told Aziz. Then he washed himself and said they should go and leave the family to mourn. Aziz tried to hand him the bundle—the baby. But Dr. Gideon shook his head and moved away. He'd thought if he let the baby die, he could save Fereshta, he said, then he told Aziz to take the baby to Waheed and that while he was in there, he should re-trieve Dr. Gideon's medical bag and give Waheed any money he found in the inside pocket for the burial. Aziz did as Dr. Gideon instructed, keeping aside only a few afghanis for the journey back to Kabul. He didn't know how much he was leaving Waheed, but his hands shook as he put the money down. Waheed sat with his head slumped, as if he were sleeping, and didn't lift it even when he thanked Aziz. Blood was everywhere.

Jamshid was waiting outside to say that the dai wouldn't come. Dr. Gideon reached out his arm, that long arm, to put a hand on his head, but Jamshid ducked away. Maybe he was frightened by Dr. Gideon's appearance, by the blood on his clothes. It was left to Aziz to inform Jamshid that his mother was dead and to in-struct him to tell his brother and sisters and fetch women to wash and wrap the body. The boy started to cry, then fiercely wiped the tears from his face. Aziz had thought of him, of that gesture in particular, often in the years since. He'd seen soldiers, grown men, permit themselves more crying at the death of a friend, although usually they, too, tried to tamp down their grief.

By the time Fereshta was buried, Aziz and Dr. Gideon were gone. They barely spoke the whole way to Kabul. They'd ridden their donkeys back along the road—that part was true, although Aziz, not Dr. Gideon, had found the animals for them to ride to the village—then sold the donkeys for almost nothing to the first farmer they found and hitchhiked the rest of the way. When they reached the city, Dr. Gideon said he didn't have enough cash to pay Aziz because of the money they'd left with Waheed. He told Aziz to meet him the next day in the lobby of the Inter-Continental Hotel.

Parveen had visited the hotel during her stay in Kabul. It had been built forty years earlier, its cornerstone laid by the then king. It sat atop a hill in the western part of the city, overlooking Kabul University, and had a swimming pool. To reach it, you drove up a long, curving driveway, passing through several security checks.

Aziz, not having a car, had walked up. As he did, he was thinking that he didn't want Gideon Crane's money. He believed that he'd failed, that maybe it was a fault in his interpretation that had led to Fereshta's death. He felt shame every time he thought of the moment when he hadn't understood what Dr. Gideon was asking. Those words—*forceps, tongs*. But his family needed the money; he couldn't refuse it. Perhaps, he thought, he could seek the assistance of Louisa and Caleb, his old teachers who'd helped him get the job, yet he was reluctant, for they would ask how the trip had been, and if he told them what had happened in the village, they might judge him or, worse, give him sympathy.

Dr. Gideon arrived late to meet him, Aziz said, and right away he began making excuses. He said that the bank hadn't been able to provide him all the money he owed Aziz and that Aziz had given too much of his cash to Waheed, so he didn't have enough left over. It enraged Aziz that Dr. Gideon was blaming him when he'd only done exactly what Dr. Gideon had asked. As he recalled Dr. Gideon quarreling with the dai over money, his anger grew. The American, he saw, was treating him the same way he'd treated the dai, as if Afghans didn't deserve to be fairly paid. "I wasn't the one who left so many children without a mother," Aziz said pointedly.

And now Parveen knew why Crane hadn't used his interpreter's full name in the book. It wasn't Aziz he was protecting but himself. Aziz knew English, and Aziz knew the truth. Crane didn't want anyone to go looking for him.

Aziz told Dr. Gideon that Waheed, with six children, needed all the money the doctor could give. Dr. Gideon looked surprised, as if he hadn't paid attention to how many children Waheed and Fereshta had, and now he seemed terrified that he might be financially responsible for all of them. He asked Aziz a lot of questions about how the courts in Afghanistan worked. There was insurance for mistakes he might make at the eye hospital in Kabul, but he wasn't sure that covered any freelance doctoring in the countryside. It was important that Aziz not talk to anyone about what had happened with Fereshta, Dr. Gideon said, but he relaxed when Aziz told him he had nothing to fear from Afghanistan's courts, which barely worked for those with influence, let alone for a poor man like Waheed. There was no chance they could squeeze money from the pocket of an American.

The question of Aziz's pay still hadn't been resolved (it never was, Aziz added as an aside; even today, Dr. Gideon owed him money), but before he could begin to argue, Dr. Gideon pulled out a letter of recommendation and handed it to him. It described his translation abilities very generously—more generously than they deserved, given how new he was to English. Dr. Gideon said that he had given a copy to an American contractor he knew, and not long afterward, after a very brief interview, Aziz was hired as a linguist for the military.

So it was Crane's overly effusive letter of recommendation, Parveen thought—no more credible than anything else he'd written—that had launched Aziz's career as a military interpreter.

Aziz was assigned to units in the south, even though Pashto wasn't his first language. Then, some years later, he was assigned to Colonel Trotter. Neither the contractor who'd placed him with the colonel nor the colonel himself knew that Aziz was A. from Crane's fabled book, and Aziz hadn't known the colonel would be building a road to this village. It was the colonel who'd put the pieces together, Aziz said, and realized he'd been to the village before.

Kismet, Colonel Trotter had called it. "It's a word we also use in Afghanistan," Aziz said. "For us it means our destiny—what God has written for us." But while they both agreed that fate had brought Aziz back to the village, the colonel considered it a happy outcome, whereas Aziz did not.

The day he'd met Parveen was the first time he'd returned to the village since he and Crane had left six years earlier. As soon as they turned off the highway onto the road, he'd begun to feel uneasy. On their way into the village they passed the clinic. Aziz knew about it from what Colonel Trotter and others had said about *Mother Afghanistan*. Upon seeing it, he was impressed: Dr. Gideon had made something good from sorrow.

As he walked through the bazaar that day with Colonel Trotter and his men, he smelled bread baking and then the baker gave them fresh bread, straight from the tandoor. "I felt ill and had to turn away," Aziz said. "In my mind I couldn't stop seeing the bread being pulled from the oven with the baker's tongs, couldn't stop remembering those tongs..." He paused, unable to finish the sentence. "I walked off a bit to smoke," he continued. "To cut the smell of the bread. But then I heard the blacksmith banging and hammering and thought of his forceps, probably the same ones Dr. Gideon tried in Fereshta. Tools like that would never be thrown out. They can last through generations. Again I felt that broken bowl—the baby's skull—the cloth damp beneath. I couldn't stop my mind from building roads between the past and now. I wanted to smoke and smoke; it was the only thing that helped. Colonel Trotter doesn't like me smoking. He says it'll kill me too young, which for an Afghan is kind of a joke. But he means well."

Aziz hadn't known if Waheed would recognize him, he said. They hadn't spent time together until Fereshta went into labor, and for most of Fereshta's struggle, Aziz was outside the room, while Waheed was inside with Crane. Plus Aziz was in uniform now. But Waheed knew him. He thanked Aziz for having left the money and told him that his children had a mother now. He asked what it was like working for the Americans and why they'd come. It was Jamshid who'd looked at Aziz as if he were the messenger of death.

The rest, he said, Parveen knew. They'd walked to the grave-yard that day to see Fereshta's gravestone, with Aziz passing the colonel's questions to Waheed and Waheed's answers back to the colonel. And they'd gone to the clinic.

He'd seen many people die, both before and after Fereshta, Aziz said. He'd lived through violence in Kabul and then, as an interpreter, had been at war. It never became routine, he said, because every death was singular, each teaching you something new. He wished there were a way to unknow all the things he'd learned; the distances the parts of a body can fly, for instance, or how to lie to a dying man and tell him he will live, or that a bomb can make a person disappear, or that a leg can remain attached to a body by a string of flesh as thin as embroidery thread.

But while there were deaths fresher than Fereshta's, that first day back in the village it was only hers, her final hours, that he could think of. "It was like someone had hung pictures in my head without my knowledge," he said. "And now lights were turned on over them, and I realized they'd been there all this time. They still are. When I sit in my head, that strange sleepiness from when I was demining comes back, and I'm not sure whether it's better to fight against death or give in." So far in his life, he said, he hadn't seen a person die peacefully. Maybe Fereshta's death haunted him because she was a woman, or maybe it was because of the baby. "It should have been easy. That's what Dr. Gideon said to me when I told him about all her children: 'If it was her seventh delivery, it should've been easy.'"

How wrong she'd been to imagine Aziz inventing stories when the excruciating facts were etched in his memory, these bits of death lodged in him for good. He still grieved all these years later. Almost miraculously, it seemed to Parveen, suffering—enduring it, witnessing it—hadn't made him hard.

On behalf of Fereshta and Waheed and, most of all, Jamshid—the nine-year-old boy who'd heard his mother's screams of agony, who'd cowered beneath the ghoulish American's giant hand—she felt horror. Toward Crane, she felt revulsion, yet also an unexpected spasm of pity. No amount of good works or fame or adulation could compensate for a memory like that. She wondered if he'd lied because he was ashamed.

At the clinic the following Wednesday, Parveen told Dr. Yasmeen the story of Fereshta's death. The doctor wasn't surprised. She'd heard long ago that the death had been excruciating, though she hadn't known the details. Obstructed labor was common, and if you didn't have the right tools, it was almost impossible to save the mother or the baby. She interrupted herself then, held up a finger, left the room, then returned with a bizarre contraption. It consisted of a glass jar with a pressure valve atop it, a pump, and a mushroom-shaped metal cup that was attached to a tube. A vacuum extractor, the doctor explained, meant to assist in obstructed labor. Perhaps Gideon Crane had asked that it be placed in the clinic.

Please, please, don't make me learn how to use that thing, Parveen thought, but of course that was what Dr. Yasmeen intended. It would be preferable to demonstrate during a live birth, she said, but for now, the back of Parveen's fist would stand in for a head. As the doctor applied the metal cup, she said Parveen would have to be very careful with it so as not to injure the fetal scalp, and stabs of terror coursed down Parveen's spine.

She wanted to keep the focus on Crane. If his failure was understandable, she asked, why didn't he just write the truth?

"Maybe he didn't like the truth," the doctor said.

But wouldn't it be better, Parveen argued, if people knew how women were actually dying in the villages?

Yes, of course, that would be much better, Dr. Yasmeen agreed. She was pressing the pump now, and the cup lightly suctioned Parveen's hand. There were so many simple things that could be done, the doctor said. As she had advocated many times, village women and girls should be trained to be midwives. This, in her estimation, would save the most women. One day she would find time to do this...

But Parveen was barely hearing her, and the doctor knew it. She stopped, set down the equipment, and said, "I, too, have seen lives slip out of my hold, just as Gideon Crane did." Now she had Parveen's attention. Remember, she said, her story about the woman with convulsions, with eclampsia, whom the mullah had tried to choke? She had told Parveen that the woman died in her car. That was true. What she hadn't said was that she'd often questioned whether she should have put the woman in the car at all, whether it wouldn't have been better to keep her in the village and try to induce her labor or give her magnesium sulfate intravenously to control the seizures instead of putting her on that horrible road to get her to a hospital. Dr. Yasmeen did think the woman needed to be in a hospital, that she might need a C-section, that her baby should be delivered as soon as possible. But she was also furious at the mullah, and she'd wanted to get the woman away from his spells, his violence. "Decisions made in anger are usually mistakes," she said. "Perhaps that was one."

These words brought Parveen to the edge of tears. Had she

believed Dr. Yasmeen infallible or had she simply needed her to be? "But you didn't make up a story," Parveen burst out. "You didn't say the mullah or someone stood in front of your car to keep you from driving out and so she died. You didn't lie. You didn't lie to the *world*."

"No, I didn't, but then, the world has never asked me for my story. If it did, who knows what I would say?" Then, perhaps seeing the frustration, the childish petulance, in Parveen's face, she said, "I understand your disappointment. At your age I'm sure I also believed that people are better than they are. But my experiences make it hard to get too angry at what's written in a book or at the untruths people tell. Remember your fiancé?"

Parveen ignored this. She was on the edge of understanding something fundamental and also painful, which was that to be an adult was to have to make decisions and take actions that might be wrong. That might cause harm. To live was to bruise, the doctor seemed to be saying; there was no other way. Unlike Professor Banerjee or Gideon Crane, Dr. Yasmeen projected no certainty about which path was the right one to take, the one that would avoid error and hurt; indeed, she seemed skeptical there was such a path.

What made her angry, the doctor was saying now, was not that Dr. Gideon had lied about how Fereshta died but that he'd built this clinic without thinking to staff it. "Parveen, are you listening?" she asked, sensing that the girl had again drifted. "Or are you still thinking about that book?"

CHAPTER TWENTY

NEURATH'S BOAT

IT WAS A BLOODY SEASON IN AFGHANISTAN. THE COUNTRY HAD held an election, and the incumbent president, as anticipated, had been reelected, in part due to widespread fraud. Although the village itself had been peaceful, violence had flared across the country and the chaos, fear, and mistrust had traveled via radio into Waheed's house. So, two weeks later, had the descriptions of another catastrophic American air strike, this one killing perhaps ninety civilians in a northern province where the Taliban was newly active. And along the road to the village, the attacks were intensifying.

An IED, remotely detonated from somewhere in the mountains above the road, had tossed an M-ATV into the air. The driver, a father of four, and the nineteen-year-old soldier riding shotgun had both been killed, and the three other soldiers in the vehicle had been wounded. Parveen, offering Trotter her condolences, was relieved to hear that none of the soldiers she'd met were among the casualties.

Two of the injured, Trotter told Parveen, had no visible wounds; it was their brains that were stunned. He would give them a week of rest and hope they returned to normal. The explosion had left an enormous crater in the section of road they'd just paved, he admitted, but he mocked the insurgents for missing with the rocket-propelled grenades they'd fired after the attack.

Parveen wasn't fooled by his bravado. The Americans had arrived in the village with manned gun turrets attached to the tops of their M-ATVs and massive rollers, designed to preemptively detonate IEDs, attached to the front. The soldiers, edgy and more heavily armored, too, in their helmets and vests, their side plates and deltoid shields and groin protectors, seemed to be thickening before Parveen's eyes.

By contrast, the village men, in their flimsy clothing and plastic flip-flops, appeared nearly weightless. Exposed. At the Americans' request, they were gathering by the clinic. Males as old as time and as young as fifteen and every age in between were to come. Waheed arrived with Jamshid. It didn't need to be phrased as an order to be one, Parveen thought. To resist would be to provoke suspicion; what were you hiding? You asserted your innocence by complying.

Aziz was there, but other than a quick nod, he barely acknowledged Parveen. She couldn't be hurt; he seemed overwhelmed trying to get the men to stand next to the clinic wall, although there were so many of them their line stretched well beyond it. Usually Aziz spoke to the villagers with respect—it was one of the things Parveen liked about him—but today he sounded peevish, as if he was overtired or, more likely, out of cigarettes. The beefy captain who was in charge kept pointing out men who'd gotten out of line or were too slow to get in it, and Aziz hastened back and forth to tell them to follow directions. Then the captain handed Aziz a loudspeaker. He looked at it queasily, then spoke through it, informing the men that the soldiers would go down the line photographing their faces, getting digital scans of their eyes, and taking their fingerprints. It was strange for Parveen to see him in this role, as not just the interpreter for but the factotum of her country's army. As the Americans became more assertive, even more bellicose, he had no choice but to do the same, for he was required to convey not just their words but their tone.

The men stood unmoving as an American soldier with a boxy device moved down the line photographing their faces and scanning their eyes. Their irises, to be more precise, which showed up magnified on the device's display. "Wide, wide," Aziz instructed them, and the men made staring eyes. Each man's fingerprints were taken using a pad on top of the device, and his name, tribe, and occupation were input, upon Aziz's translation, into a laptop.

The captain was running the operation, but Trotter stood some distance off overseeing it. The technology, he explained to Parveen when she sought him out, was called HIIDE—*H-I-I-D-E;* he spelled it out—which stood for Handheld Interagency Identity Detection Equipment. It was being used all over the country, with the hope of capturing the biometric data of as many Afghans as possible, all of which would be stored in a huge database back in Virginia. The digitized faces, fingerprints, and irises of men who'd never left these mountains would live perpetually in a DC suburb. Eternal life of another kind.

The iris was taken, he told Parveen, because the pattern of every human iris is mathematically complex and also unique, different even in identical twins, different even in someone's left and right eye. The pattern is fixed by the time a baby is six months old and never changes. Humans were better at recognizing faces than computers were, this was true, but we could never match computers in recognizing the patterns of irises. It wasn't that fingerprints weren't helpful; those left on IEDs had been used to identify insurgents hiding in the population. But as an identifier, the iris was even more reliable than fingerprints, especially in a country like Afghanistan, where the pads of the fingers could be worn away by a lifetime of labor and many men were missing limbs or digits anyway. A computer could match any iris to a database of scans, thereby making it possible to identify enemy combatants or anyone else. Even the iris of a corpse could be scanned, as long as it was done within twelve hours of death, which allowed for everything from identifying suicide bombers, assuming the eye survived intact, to mapping Taliban networks.

"But the villagers aren't Taliban," Parveen said.

Then the HIIDE procedure would help U.S. forces establish that, Trotter said. They could separate the enemy from the civilian population. "It's a way for us to own ground."

The villagers were impassive. Parveen wondered if they knew why this was being done; Aziz had said what would happen but not the reason. Would they speculate about it or, as it appeared, quietly submit? They were to the Americans as the village women were to them: powerless. They acquiesced without protest to the soldiers' harvesting of their biological signatures. Yet they did so without exhibiting subservience. Afghan men never did in the presence of Westerners, Parveen had observed. Perhaps this was because they'd never been colonized by Europeans. They always managed to hold some piece of themselves in abeyance, to retain their independence.

As Trotter was talking, Parveen had been weighing what to tell him about *Mother Afghanistan.* Her initial instinct had been not to tell him at all. The village still needed the road, even if the story that had inspired its paving was untrue. And yet, watching the HIIDE operation, hearing about the deaths along the road, she had begun to question her own decision. Crane's myths had led the Americans down this particular fork, and the war had followed them to the village, devouring limbs and lives. This wasn't going to end simply with a smooth, drivable road; she could sense that now. Each side had its teeth in this stretch of dirt; neither would let go. And so the Americans veered from friendliness to force, one day asking permission to build a road, the next demanding that the men line up by the mosque. The soldiers' weapons were a reminder that they'd never really needed permission to do anything. What, Parveen wondered, did it mean to offer help to people you didn't trust?

"Tell him to open his eyes more," Parveen heard a soldier say to Aziz. "I'm having trouble getting the picture."

She was half listening while still talking to Trotter.

"This is as far as they open."

It was Jamshid's voice. Parveen glanced over. He looked sleepy, his eyes half lidded, which was not their usual state. He was deliberately narrowing them.

"Try harder," Aziz urged, not acknowledging that he knew Jamshid.

Jamshid began to blink lazily, as if experimenting with what his eyes could do. Watching, the friend next to him smiled and began to do the same. "Cooperate, or there will be trouble," Aziz growled.

But there already was. "Colonel," the soldier called, but Trotter, in midsentence, didn't hear him.

"Open your eyes," Waheed barked at Jamshid as if calling his son back from the adulthood he'd just leaped into, and Jamshid, as if waking from a dream, did.

"Proceed, it's fine," Aziz told the soldier, who recorded Jamshid's irises with the rest. With more questions, Parveen tried to distract Trotter, feeling some instinct to protect Jamshid and his friends, fearing the consequences for them otherwise. She remembered the first shura—hearing Trotter debrief his soldiers afterward about the body language they'd observed, what it said about the resistance they might encounter—and worried that, despite Waheed's intervention, this moment would redound on them unhappily.

This was now a combat zone, Trotter was saying. There was no point in laying more pavement until they eliminated those who were getting in the way of the mission. They had to get the intelligence right. Was it the insurgency flaring up here? Tribal rivalry? A criminal enterprise? A shakedown? Commander Amanullah kept suggesting they use his militia to guard the road, Trotter said, suspicion in his voice.

Parveen doubted that Amanullah had a militia. He sat in the bazaar all day doing nothing but gabbing. She guessed that, if the Americans hired him, he would just pay a bunch of village men with rusty Kalashnikovs and call them a militia.

"The commander knows how to play all sides," Trotter said. "We can't just ignore his history."

"What history?"

But they were finished with the HIIDE, and as the village men dispersed, Trotter jogged off to huddle with Aziz and a few of his soldiers. After a while Aziz broke away and walked toward the bazaar, again ignoring Parveen, who started to follow him. When he caught her eye, he gave a quick shake of his head, and she stopped where she was. He seemed as jittery as the first time they'd met, his eyes doing their wild flit. Perhaps ten minutes later, he returned with a pack of cigarettes in hand and Amanullah, who'd gone to the bazaar after the HIIDE, in tow.

The commander called out to Parveen: "The Americans are waking up at last! For weeks I've been telling Aziz-jan to tell them to hire my militia—we could stop this nonsense on the road." He climbed into the M-ATV that would take him to the American base, where he believed he would drink tea with Colonel Trotter and then negotiate the terms under which his militia would be employed to guard the road. Parveen heard him joke to Aziz that for all the Soviet tanks he'd helped to destroy, he'd never been inside an armored vehicle.

"I hope you come home soon," Aziz told the commander. His voice sounded odd to her. Strangled.

But the commander didn't return that day or the next. One of his sons traveled along the road to the American base to ask about his father. No American would come out to speak to him, but he learned from a sympathetic Afghan guard that Amanullah was being interrogated. He waited at the base another day, continuing to politely ask to speak to someone, until Aziz was delegated to tell him that the Americans believed his father was a Taliban commander and that he would be released as soon as he could prove that he wasn't. It was better for the son to wait in the village, Aziz whispered, lest the Americans decide that he, too, merited questioning.

It was an insult to call his father Taliban, the son insisted, when he'd fought so bravely against them. This had to be slander from an Afghan rival, an enemy.

No, Aziz said, it was worse; the American, Dr. Gideon, had written it in his book, which meant there was no way the U.S. forces weren't going to believe it.

In her mind, Parveen rewound and replayed the night she'd seen Gideon Crane speak at the college; she was considering everything anew. His lateness now struck her as nothing more than selfish disregard for the time of students like herself and for the university that had paid him. She wondered if his audience, rather than he, had supplied the emotion she heard in his tale, injecting his words with feeling, and now she attributed his evasion of questions after his talk to fear of exposure. She thought about all the statistics he'd rattled off: days on the road that year, number of talks given, number of books sold, amount of money raised for maternal mortality. That night, the data had added to her awe of him. When he had listed the celebrities and dignitaries he'd met and assured his audience that none of those luminaries had touched him as much as speaking to this gathering of students did, she'd seen humility. Now she saw it for the catalog of boasts it had been. How could her original perception have been so susceptible to priming, her recall of a night so subject to revision? That experience could be so contingent, memory so malleable, frightened her. Could she trust her own mind? She wondered if by lying, Crane had hoped to change not just how the audience saw him but how he saw himself, for it was inevitable, she knew, that over time, our lies become as true, or truer, than the facts they displace. Neurath's boat—swapping lie for truth, you could construct a whole new self, board by board, while keeping the ship afloat.

But these were speculations, even evasions, of the real conundrum, which was this: If a con man ignited your idealism, if he told you to go out into the world and do good, was it automatically a con? If one American dragooned a whole village into his fable, damn the consequences, did that mean everyone else should stay home? At the heart of Crane's tale was a mystery, but Parveen wasn't sure it was about him.

Chapter Twenty-One

Law and Order

After word of Amanullah's fate spread, Parveen went to his house. His wife, Amina, wept without cease and yanked at her own hair. The room was packed with children and with the other women of the village, the air so thick with body heat and humors that it was hard to breathe.

As Parveen pawed her way through, one of the women hissed: "This is your fault. You shouldn't have gone around telling stories about him being Taliban."

"I never said anything like that to the Americans, I promise. They read it in Dr. Gideon's book."

"Then tell Dr. Gideon to get him back!" she snapped.

Amina threw herself at Parveen's feet and wailed, then sat up, wiped her eyes and nose, and said, with unsettling calm, that she didn't believe what the others were saying, which was that Parveen had known her husband was going to be taken or that she had asked for him to be taken. But, she said, turning her head away slightly, perhaps to lessen the harshness of her words, Parveen *had* told those stories about him. There was a new strength to her—*empowered* was the word that came to Parveen, and she wondered guiltily if having the commander away for a while might be good for his wife's confidence. But of course, as Parveen quickly reminded herself, in every other way it was a disaster.

"I'm not ready to be a widow," Amina said. "And my family needs my husband's pension." Now her eyes met Parveen's again. "We all know you talk to the general."

Parveen was confused, then realized Amina was referring to Trotter.

"The Americans will listen to you," Amina said. "Bring him home."

Parveen didn't know how to convey her own impotence. What could she do—borrow Waheed's donkey and ride to the American base? She promised Amina she would write letters to "the general" and to Dr. Gideon, even though she wasn't sure it would do any good.

Talking to Waheed that night, Parveen mentioned the commander's pension. With his wry smile he explained that "pension" was a euphemism for a small tax on the villagers to keep the commander in food. When he'd returned from his last battle against the Taliban, he'd attempted to annex some of the khan's land for his remaining sons. The wily khan had convinced him that the villagers should pay their hero a pension instead. They'd been paying for close to a decade now. "I told you we'd forgiven him a lot," Waheed said.

That was what Waheed had meant? A tax? How clueless she'd been. Worse than clueless; thanks to Crane, she'd believed she knew all. There were so many basic questions she hadn't asked.

But Amanullah's sins, Waheed said, didn't lessen the villagers' anger at his abduction by the Americans. It was unfair, and humiliating, to have him accused, tricked, and spirited away. The commander was their bravest citizen, if not always their favorite.

*   *   *

A FEW DAYS LATER, a shepherd arrived in the village without any sheep. He wore a bedraggled blanket as a shawl and a *pakol* hat pulled low on his forehead.

It was Issa, in disguise. He had sneaked over the mountain passes. "I used to be a smuggler," he reminded Parveen with a roguish grin.

He claimed he'd come to check on the clinic's supplies, but Parveen half suspected he'd made the trek just to see if he could. She asked for his help in reaching Crane. Crane talked to generals, advised them, Parveen said. Surely he could get Amanullah back.

Issa laughed. "Gideon Crane won't tell the Americans how to fight their war." Amanullah's children had better go to work, he said. It would be a long time before their father came home. "Besides," he added, "even if the commander didn't do what they're saying, I'm sure he did something else he should be punished for."

Parveen winced at this, remembering the bruise on Amina's face. But the Americans hadn't taken Amanullah because he beat his wife or shook down his neighbors. The real commander was having to answer for invented sins. It was unjust, Parveen told Issa.

"The world is unjust," he replied. "You've had a fortunate life if you're only learning this now."

They ate together that evening—she, Issa, Waheed, and Jamshid—back in the reception room where they'd gathered on her first night in the village. Same cushions, same hairy walls. Issa, famished from his journey, scooped up food like water from a stream, stranding bits of rice in his mustache.

From him, too, Parveen sought information. Her hunger to expose Crane's lies felt bottomless. It wasn't much of a surprise when Issa said they hadn't met on the road to the village, as Crane had written, but at the Kabul guesthouse where Crane was staying. Issa went there regularly to peddle artifacts pillaged from archaeological sites. He had a knack for languages and a love of crime procedurals. It was mostly by watching pirated episodes of *Law and Order*, in fact, that he'd picked up enough English to talk, banter, and barter with the foreigners who stocked the guesthouse. One day, he said, he struck up a conversation with Dr. Gideon, who told him about his plan to build a clinic in a village. Issa was surprised that he would be doing it on his own, since most foreigners worked in organizations. But when he asked Dr. Gideon if he had the money for it, he said that he did. Although Issa had never attempted anything of the kind, he told Dr. Gideon that he could get his clinic built, which seemed to greatly relieve the American.

"He put all his trust in me," Issa said. "As a child might." He asked Dr. Gideon if the clinic could be in any village. This would make his job much easier, and after all, there were few villages in Afghanistan that *couldn't* use a clinic. Yes, any village would be fine, Dr. Gideon said.

"Wait," Parveen said. "You're saying he didn't care where the clinic was?"

"He didn't care," Issa confirmed.

Issa took him to a village only an hour from Kabul. There Dr. Gideon hired labor and bought materials. But a few days later he changed his mind. He said the clinic had to be built in a certain village and told a complicated story about a woman dying while giving birth there. Crane wanted to write a book about it. While there was no bringing the dead woman back to life, a picture of her husband, maybe her children too, in front of a new clinic would do. Americans needed hope, he said.

"It bothers you Americans that the world is the way it is, doesn't it?" Issa asked Parveen.

Issa was a scoundrel of many stripes, Parveen thought, but he hadn't yet proved to be a liar. His recounting was a freshet of truth biting at a riverbank of disingenuousness. He seemed to revel in the truth, actually. It was Crane's cynicism that made her quiver, partly in shame. Even then, he had been calculating, knowing that readers like Parveen would demand an ending that was, if not happy, at least redemptive, which made her one among millions of unwitting accomplices to his fraud. He told his readers what they wanted to hear. The clinic had been built to serve not patients but a book's narrative arc. No wonder Crane had given so little thought to how it would operate.

A Potemkin clinic, then. The story, which Parveen had learned in college, had fascinated her: Potemkin, Catherine the Great's aide and lover, was said to have built fake and portable settlements in postwar Crimea so as to deceive the empress with the illusion of reconstruction. But Parveen was equally intrigued by the lesser known theory that the story itself was an invention, a slander against Potemkin by a rival for Catherine's esteem. A false story about a false village, the fakery of fakery, truth as a floor that kept falling away.

Issa wasn't done. Crane didn't know how to find the specific village, but he said the translator who'd been with him would be able to provide directions. He and Issa went to the Sunshine American English School, where Crane had first found Aziz. The mother-and-son pair who ran it were very excited by Crane's project and eager to help. There was talk of Jesus and good works, and Issa guessed immediately that Caleb and Louisa were missionaries. He did a wicked impression of them now, their wide eyes and fluttering hands and pious ecstasy at Crane's plan. Do-gooders seemed to amuse him. He had thought that perhaps Crane, too, was a missionary, if a more discreet one. But once the two men began working together, his impression changed: Crane was as much an exploiter of opportunities as Issa himself was. The only time he mentioned Jesus was when he was cursing.

They reached Aziz, who'd kept in touch with Caleb and

Louisa, by telephone; he was by then interpreting for the military in southern Afghanistan. From him Issa got instructions on how to get to the village. He tried to persuade Aziz to come, but Aziz had no interest. "It's quite funny that he ended up back here anyway," Issa said, laughing. "I suppose it took the whole U.S. Army to make it happen."

His jest annoyed Parveen, since of course it wasn't funny to Aziz.

They made it to the village, Issa said, and located Waheed. Crane was anxious about seeing him again. He instructed Issa to convey immediately that they were building a clinic in honor of Fereshta.

"I thanked him for this," Waheed said. "I never expected to see him again. I thought he would forget my wife as soon as he left the village."

Jamshid, listening to all this but not speaking, was mashing his fist into his hand as a mortar grinds into a pestle.

"Did you see Crane then?" Parveen asked him quietly.

Issa answered for him. Crane had said that he thought it better not to see the boy, lest he upset him.

Parveen turned to Jamshid. "So you never spoke to him on his trips back to the village?"

Jamshid shook his head. But he'd found spots to watch Dr. Gideon from, he said. To study him. Sometimes he was sure that Dr. Gideon saw him too. He wanted Dr. Gideon to see him. But they never spoke.

"Now I know why he was in such a hurry to get the clinic built," Issa said, only half joking. There were a lot of headaches— he'd told Parveen of some, like the khan.

"And Dr. Gideon helped?"

Issa looked at her like she was crazy. No, he said, Dr. Gideon spent his time sitting in the shade with pen and paper, writing. Waheed confirmed this.

So the men had never learned the cowboy song, Parveen

thought. Such a minor detail, yet it still seemed important to tell the women.

Crane would pester Issa, who had his hands full, for help with translating his questions for Waheed or conjuring up characters and nuggets to add to the story. The book needed Taliban, Dr. Gideon insisted one day, or Americans wouldn't be interested. He explained to Issa that a book about Afghanistan without Taliban would be like a *Law and Order* episode without a criminal. Who would want to watch it?

"Then you have a problem," Issa had told him, "because there are no Taliban here. You're in the wrong part of the country."

But soon they encountered Amanullah. His petty extortion had annoyed Issa, but Dr. Gideon was delighted by him; Amanullah, he said, looked like a Taliban. So many of them, from what he'd read, were missing eyes or hands. And so, just like that, Amanullah had become Crane's villain, and, as Parveen noted to herself, Crane had found a publisher.

The absurdities continued to pile up. The logs being floated from Kabul, for example. She'd sat by the river countless times, so knew that it flowed toward Kabul, not away from it. Crane could never have shipped logs to the village via water, let alone ridden them to transcendence. When she mentioned this part of the story to Issa and Waheed, they laughed uproariously.

Why hadn't this inaccuracy, and many others, occurred to her before now? And why hadn't a single person of the millions who'd read the memoir consulted a map to see if the events it described were possible? When Parveen herself had first read *Mother Afghanistan*, she hadn't thought to question how one man could have so many dramatic adventures and close calls. Now, as one deception after another was made plain, the abundance of wild episodes was telling. Here was the overactive imagination of a man who'd read too many boys' adventure stories, a man for whom the mild topography of ordinary existence was not enough, who craved, in the landscape of his life story, mountains as impressive, as breathtaking, as those of Afghanistan. Who'd never abandoned his habit of exaggerating his exploits to his father.

"Your wife's *mantus* are almost as good as my mother's," Issa told Waheed.

How could Issa have tasted his mother's cooking when she'd died giving birth to him? Parveen knew the answer even before she asked, in a voice so small it embarrassed her, "Your mother's alive?"

Issa, his mouth full of beef dumpling, nodded, and when Parveen told him that Crane had written that his mother was dead, Issa nearly spit out his food. "If that's so, God is even greater than we imagine, because Dr. Gideon has eaten her cooking. Dr. Gideon wrote many things, you know. Some are even true."

PARVEEN DASHED OUT A hasty, scorching letter to Professor Banerjee that night, using all the details she'd amassed. She wanted to give it to Issa before he left. During the past months, as many of Parveen's cherished abstractions had disintegrated, her professor's hold over her had diminished. Yet there was no one else whose advice she could think to seek. If she told her father about the violence along the road, he'd only worry that she was in danger.

So it was to Professor Banerjee that she wrote about Crane's lies, about how the Americans had been lured to the village under false pretenses, as had Parveen herself. She complained that she'd been manipulated and compared her situation to the American citizenry being misled about the reasons for the Iraq War. The consequences of Crane's deceptions, she wrote, had been almost as ruinous: the commander's detention, the insurgency's arrival in the village, the deaths along the road. She described Waheed's pain when he learned how Crane had portrayed the Afghans. She wanted to know what to do with this information, how to think about it.

Then she tried to write to Crane, filling pages with her rage. But every draft seemed wrong, and she tore them all up. After an hour of this she was spent and had no letter to show for it. In the end, "Fuck you" was all she really wanted to say.

Chapter Twenty-Two

Young Deer

It took two weeks for Parveen's letter to reach Berkeley but only two hours for Professor Banerjee to type it up and send it to the *Huffington Post*, the *Journal of Medical Anthropology*, and her critical-anthropology listserv, from where it spread like flame through old growth. Since no one could reach Parveen, she was described only as a "recent college graduate who has gone to Afghanistan to attempt anthropological work." Professor Banerjee did not edit the letter at all. Parveen's pondering and floundering, her confusion, were in full view.

But Parveen was still ignorant of her newly public existence when Trotter brought Commander Amanullah back to the village. The copter landed, and as word spread that the commander had emerged from it, Parveen hurried with Waheed, Jamshid, and the rest of the village men to the bazaar. It took a long time for Amanullah to walk from the khan's field, and when he drew near, Parveen saw why. His gait was unsteady, his beard grayed, his girth shrunken; where he had been bulky, he was baggy. He blinked a lot, as one does when emerging from the dark, and peered around with a perpetual question on his face. Parveen thought of Aziz's father, hollowed out by the Taliban, never the same again. Aziz, who was holding the commander's elbow, had to be thinking of him too.

Trotter was there, although looking like he didn't want to be. "Tell him he's free," he said curtly to Aziz. "He's free to go."

Instead, Aziz led Amanullah toward the villagers, who were watching from the end of the bazaar, where its central path curved down to the fields. An elaborate dance ensued in which Aziz relinquished the commander before reaching the knot of men, who then waited for Aziz to retreat before advancing to encircle Amanullah. As a group they escorted the commander toward home.

He found his voice, although it too was diminished, nothing like the basso profundo in which he'd once bellowed at Parveen. "The same questions, over and over," she heard him say. "Taliban this, Taliban that. Nonsense." He still seemed to believe it was all part of the "security clearance" to get his militia hired, but even if the Americans wanted his militia, he said, he'd have nothing more to do with them.

None of the village men had spoken to Aziz. A penumbra of resentment or hostility seemed to extend from them over him. Even when he bought a pack of cigarettes at the sundry stall, there was none of the customary banter or gossip. In the villagers' eyes, he was a traitor who'd led the commander into detention. "Trotter's dog," she'd heard Jamshid and his friends call Aziz a few times. Determined to defy his ostracism, she walked right up to him and asked how he was.

He offered her a cigarette, even though he knew she didn't smoke, and said, "Sometimes I think demining wasn't such a bad job after all."

"Why'd they finally bring back the commander?" she asked in a whisper.

"Colonel Trotter will explain that to you," he said. He was speaking English, which surprised her.

"You make it sound like I'm in trouble," she said, half joking.

"I think we both are. So stop talking to me and go to him. You know what they say: if two thirsty men get together, they'll both die."

What kind of trouble? she was about to ask, but Aziz motioned with his head toward the M-ATVs, where Trotter awaited her, and, stung, she backed away. As she neared the colonel, she apprehended how much he'd changed. When they'd first met, only a few months ago, his vigor had seemed inextinguishable. Now his face was rumpled with lack of sleep, his eyes puffy, his hair, she thought, grayer. He was clean-shaven, as always, yet the faintest shadow seemed to adhere to his jaw.

Without speaking, he handed her a sheaf of papers.

She began to read, and her hands began to shake. Her mouth went dry. The words on the page were hers, the same words she'd written in her last letter to Professor Banerjee. "She *published* my letter?" Her first thought was that she would rather the world had seen a picture of her naked.

"You sound surprised," Trotter said.

"I'm shocked! I was just writing to her for advice."

"I guess she gave it, then: just put it all out there, regardless of the consequences. Those are yours to keep, by the way."

She scanned the interviews he'd printed out in which Professor Banerjee explained her decision to betray Parveen's confidence. Her kind of anthropology allowed for no loyalty to student or friend, to family or country, Professor Banerjee said. Not to anyone but the powerless. It was the largest airing for this view she'd ever had.

Learning that the powerful must always be held to account was a necessary part of Parveen's education, Professor Banerjee said. She attributed Parveen's solipsism, notably her comparison of her own situation to the Iraq invasion, to ingenuousness. The true cost of Crane's deceit, she insisted, wasn't Parveen's betrayed idealism but rather the lives that had been lost and the bodies maimed during the roadwork, the laborers and soldiers who'd shed their blood in a place they had no business being. In her telling, the road was an allegory for Afghanistan, a land where America didn't belong. If Crane had told the truth—that this woman's death was the result of his own bumbling—would the military be sending men to that corner of the country to die? As for the millions who'd bought and believed his memoir or contributed to his foundation, they should have known better.

Trotter was watching her read. "No loyalty, huh?" she heard him say. "Every soldier here lives or dies by it."

He spoke as if his mouth were full of ash, and at that moment Parveen shared his disgust for her and people like her, those whose loyalty was only to themselves, to their own desires. She wondered what it would feel like to be within a circle like the military rather than perpetually standing outside and judging it. She regretted not having told Trotter about Crane's lies herself. She felt, somehow, that she'd owed him this. It couldn't have been easy to have news from up the road boomerang from half-way around the globe.

And yet she also felt relief that her professor had done what she herself didn't have the courage to do, which was expose the truth, because Parveen agreed that, as her professor put it, only total transparency gave people a hope of making a just world and understanding their place in it. Or was she simply flattered when Professor Banerjee called her letter an "important document" that, without its author's meaning to (a qualification that reduced the flattery), had provided "the most complete and damning portrait of the folly of this war." That her professor had first argued against Parveen going to the village was conveniently omitted from her assessment.

"Let me tell you the cost of no loyalty," Trotter said.

Parveen looked up from her sheaf of papers to meet Trotter's eyes, which were severe, like the gray rocks fixed beneath the clear water of the river.

By exposing the resistance his battalion was encountering

along the road, he said, Parveen was undermining public support for the war back home. This would hurt his soldiers' morale, but worse, it would further endanger them, further endanger all pro-government forces across Afghanistan, by emboldening the insurgents. "Roads ain't roads," the army's counterinsurgency guru liked to say. They were symbols. Until her letter was published, this road had symbolized all the good America could do and the success it could have in Afghanistan. Thanks to Parveen, now it symbolized how the war was going wrong.

But the war *was* going wrong, she said. Here and, from what the BBC reported, not just here. Shouldn't Americans know that?

"Any single snapshot of the war gives a false picture," he said. War was about controlling the story as much as the territory. That made information—its release and sometimes, if necessary, its withholding—a weapon.

Parveen was flummoxed. Did that mean Trotter thought it was fine, even defensible, to lie? she wondered. There was something condescending in this lesson about war, a province from which women were mostly barred only to be damned for their ignorance of it.

"'A herd of dumb deer,'" Trotter said, quoting her. "Couldn't have been any clearer how you see us."

He saw condescension in her words too, she realized. More than revealing the folly of the war, her letter illuminated for him the gap between the tiny number who served and the civilians who judged them. "'Young deer,'" she corrected him. "That's what I said. '*Young* deer.'" Though even this was somewhat disingenuous. Her exact words had been *They seem to me like a herd of young deer, separated from their mothers, crashing through the forest wide-eyed and dumb with targets on their sides.* "And I didn't mean you."

"Just my grunts."

What she'd meant, she clarified, was that Trotter and his men were victims of Crane too, that they'd all been played. The colonel's mouth twisted in disapproval. Men, Parveen had noticed, didn't like to be called victims, even when they were. Women were used to it.

"To be honest," Trotter said, "I couldn't care less whether *Mother Afghanistan* is twenty or eighty percent true." He hadn't read the book for truth, he said. He'd read it for guidance on how to fight and win this war. He'd read it for lessons, the same way he always read: in extraction mode. What knowledge could he take away from this piece of material? For him, it was more like a counterinsurgency manual. *Here's how you can win this thing. Get the population on your side.* Commonsense stuff. His wife was more into the story, he said. Was it sexist to say maybe that was more of a woman thing?

Yes, Parveen replied.

Well, fine, he said, call him sexist, but it was irrelevant to him exactly how Fereshta had died. Or maybe he should say that how she'd died didn't surprise him. That fundamentalists would rather let her die than be treated by a *kafir* man pretty much confirmed everything he'd read.

But that wasn't what happened, Parveen pointed out.

"But it *has* happened, Parveen. If not in this case, then in many, many others. Maybe Crane didn't tell the truth about some things, but he sure nailed *a* truth about this place." Its women had been oppressed for too long.

"But the truth matters!" she cried like some desperate prophetess. "*The* truth. Not *a* truth. Talk to Waheed about it, the damage those lies have done. He cares what you think. Crane owes him an apology."

"Then Crane should give him one," Trotter said curtly. Would Parveen honestly say an easier way out of the village wasn't needed? he asked. Because of Crane, the U.S. military was here helping people who'd been forgotten. Because of Crane, Parveen was here helping—or whatever it was she was doing. Tearing down heroes was easy, Trotter said, but all that did was leave people without hope, and who wanted that? Even if some details in Crane's book were off, it was still a useful story, and that over there was a useful clinic. A fact on the ground.

"But it's not useful because—"

He cut her off to say that Americans didn't expect Crane to be perfect because they knew he was trying to do good. Which is why when Parveen returned to the States, she was probably going to find a lot of people angry not at him but at her. She must have looked unsettled at this, because he seemed to soften a bit. "Look, it's not that I'm blind to certain things that are— that could be working better in our effort," he said, choosing his words carefully. The coalition was constantly revising its approach. But you couldn't fight a war by getting bogged down in your mistakes. Afterward was for lessons learned. "We're still processing the lessons of Vietnam," he said.

It was less that Trotter wasn't bothered by Crane's inventions, Parveen thought, than that he couldn't afford to be. The projection of certainty required that there be no despair or anger confessed, no doubt acknowledged, at least not publicly. The only indication that he accepted that Crane's book was wrong was the commander's return.

Without knowing what answer she wanted, Parveen asked Trotter if he was going to stop work on the road.

A slight twitch, like a tiny beating heart, took up at the corner of his right eye. They couldn't stop, he finally said, although the long pause suggested that he'd given it some thought. The problem was that the enemy didn't know the Americans had come because of Crane's book, and if Trotter and his men left, they wouldn't know that was why they were leaving. They would think they'd driven the Americans out. "The optics," Trotter said, as if it were self-explanatory. Not to mention that at this point the investment was too big. He had men who'd paid the highest price. He couldn't just walk away.

*   *   *

THERE WAS A STORY Aziz had told Parveen. The previous year he'd bought a plot of land in the desert outside Kabul. Thanks to the influx of foreign aid and opium cash, real estate in the city proper had inflated to punishing levels, and this parcel was all he could afford. There was nothing in the desert, as yet, but officials had promised to install electricity and water, developers would build houses, and eventually Kabul and the place where Aziz had bought land would meet. When construction was finished, he and his family, who were currently living in a rented house with a leaking roof, would move there.

On one of his weekends home, he decided to check on the progress of construction. Although he'd dutifully made his monthly payments, it had been many months since he'd visited the site. He borrowed his brother's car and drove out. It was a smoggy day, the air the color of a cigarette filter. The landscape was flat except for, in the distance, a wall of chocolate-brown mountains with the faintest purple tinge. The sign for the development was still there, but it was surrounded by nothing—no houses, no holes, no plots marked off, no foundations, no construction machinery, no poles, no pipes. Nothing. Just dust, which the wind blew into his eyes.

He got back into the car and drove to the developers' office. It took an hour and a half; Kabul's traffic, as Parveen had learned in her two weeks in the city, was that bad. It was hard to sustain a rage for so long, and by the time Aziz reached the office, he already felt defeated. Inside were all the slick maps and renderings that had first seduced him. They were probably printed, now that he thought about it, not in one of Kabul's crappy shops but by professional outfits in Dubai. These top-quality materials boasted detail down to the tree level. As if a single sapling could live out there.

The broker who'd sold him the plot and promised progress every time Aziz came calling was Karim, a man who wore a suit and carried two, sometimes three, cell phones that rang all the time; who used English terms like *cul-de-sac* and *investment potential;* who wore, when they'd first visited the desert together, giant blue-tinted sunglasses that looked like they'd been carved from one of the blue-glass buildings all over Kabul; who'd waved his arm over the empty land before them and spoke with practiced reverence about solar-powered streetlights and hot-water tanks and garages of dimensions greater than Aziz's current house, then told Aziz to "act fast" because so many government officials were trying to buy into the development that he was lucky he'd even learned about it (Aziz remembered only too late that he'd learned about the development from the glossy billboards shading his family's muddy home) and added that there weren't many plots left, they were about to raise the prices to capitalize on demand, so if Aziz was going to buy, he should buy now, and Aziz had.

But this Karim had been let go, the slightly older version of him (more sober shoes, grayer hair) who was now manning the office informed Aziz. They'd had to let him go for making false promises to people about the schedule.

So there was a schedule? Aziz asked hopefully.

No, that was just the problem, the man said. Karim had claimed, wrongly, that there was.

But what was the plan? Aziz asked. When would they put in the water pipes? The electric lines?

For this they were dependent upon the municipality of Kabul, the man said. Once they put in the infrastructure, then they could begin to build the houses. Until then, they could do nothing.

"Nothing except collect my money," Aziz said sourly to Parveen. He'd almost told the man that he worked for the Americans and would report them for fraud, an instinct she recognized from her own fantasies about the khan. But he couldn't tell anyone whom he worked for, and the Americans wouldn't have done anything anyway. They talked and talked about the rule of law, he said, but they didn't enforce it, which was the reason he'd had to go to the desert in the first place. The people with power in Kabul just took the land they wanted in the city limits, with no consequences.

But the man at the developers' office was older than Aziz and so, unlike Karim, deserving of respect. Politely, Aziz asked him why they kept taking his family's money if they couldn't build.

They had to be ready for the day they *could* build, the man said. It was up to Aziz if he wanted to forfeit his deposit. The man could only tell him that one day the desert would become a city, that Kabul would grow out there, just like the pictures showed, because Kabul was bursting, overflowing; people were running out of hills to live on, and the city had to go somewhere, so it would grow. Aziz had to have patience, the man counseled, and remember that everywhere there was a palace now there had once been nothing.

"And everywhere there are ruins," Aziz told Parveen, "there was once a palace." He didn't believe in the vision the man tried to make him see. Yet he would keep paying, even though it wasn't likely to lead anywhere but disappointment, because he'd already paid so much.

PART THREE

Chapter Twenty-Three

Clear Sight

Each afternoon now, the trees' shadows stretched farther into long elegant lines. Red and yellow seeped across leaves, plant stalks browned, the donkey's coat thickened. In the hills the villagers gathered dry vegetation to store as fodder, and in the fields they sowed wheat with haphazard flings of the seeds. It was late October. The mountain winter, with its feet of snow and months of hardship, would soon come, which meant that it was time for Parveen to go.

This, at least, was what Dr. Yasmeen kept telling her. If Parveen waited too long, the doctor warned, snow and floods might cut the road off for months, and the weather would become too treacherous for helicopters to land. The village in winter was no place to be, the doctor said, and she worried, too, about Parveen's health. During her nearly five months in the village, she'd lost perhaps twenty-five pounds. She had never acquired a taste for Bina's food, which was both monotonous and excessively oily, and she'd had not infrequent bouts of gastroenteritis. The publication of her letter had only increased her physical attrition, as the stress killed what was left of her appetite. Bina was constantly taking in her dresses, and Shokoh joked that she was gaining the weight Parveen had lost. She felt desiccated, her skin coarse and dry and beset by occasional blooms of rash, and she was having regular yeast infections. But she dismissed the doctor's concern; compared to the ailments of so many villagers, hers were minor.

For if winter scared Parveen, so did the prospect of going home. Even her father, not exactly a *Huffington Post* reader, was aware of the furor her letter had caused; he had written, via Dr. Yasmeen, to implore her to leave. It was the violence along the road, which she'd detailed in her letter to Professor Banerjee, that concerned him. At his request her cousin Fawad had tried to travel to the village to retrieve her, but the Americans wouldn't let him onto the road. They claimed the ongoing construction made it impassable; the locals he asked for information said it was too dangerous. He'd returned to Kabul.

Parveen's father, as an educator himself, was deeply distressed by Professor Banerjee's violation of his daughter's trust. *Not being Muslim*, he'd written, *perhaps she didn't understand that, for you, the blowback was always going to be more extreme.* There'd been a certain amount of "agitation" in the wake of her disclosures, he explained. Some of Gideon Crane's legions of fans, no doubt angry at themselves for their naive credulity, had redirected that anger at Parveen for bringing down their hero. (In this respect, she realized Trotter had been prescient, and perhaps Crane had been too. Was this why he hadn't worried that Parveen would learn the truth in the village and then expose him? Because he sensed that, even if she did, many of his readers wouldn't care? He understood how essential, how indispensable, was the myth that he had created.) A small number of those were blaming her Afghan roots, accusing her of disloyalty, as if questioning Crane was akin to questioning America itself. And some faulted her for putting U.S. troops in danger, neglecting to consider the fact that she herself had never intended her letter to be published. Her father's position was that if military leaders had truly approved and persisted with this enterprise on the slender basis of a memoir, then they bore the blame: *I told the reporters who called that you had merely toppled a statue that should never have been erected in the first place.*

At this last line, Parveen's whole body tensed. Reporters contacting her father? She didn't know whether to believe him when he said not to worry, that Americans had short attention spans and this would pass. Meanwhile, he wrote, President Obama was even now trying to decide whether the war was folly or necessity, whether to bring troops home or send more there, and Parveen's letter had become ammunition for both sides. To some, if such a simple gesture of goodwill was being met with resistance, it proved that America's involvement in Afghanistan wasn't as welcome and successful as military leaders claimed. To others, it showed why the nation's involvement was essential: to support decent Afghans, and Afghan women especially, in the fight against terror. Her father admitted that he didn't know the right answer. All he knew was that he wanted her home.

Almost every hour Parveen would remember, with the same stomach jolt each time, that she—or the cartoon version of herself floating around the internet—was being discussed and, in some quarters, reviled, though she also carried the faint hope that Obama had been among her readers. She'd written an angry, anguished letter to Professor Banerjee but she hadn't sent it because she didn't trust her not to publish it. She waited in vain for an apology or explanation from her professor, or at least an acknowledgment of what she'd done. It was as if Professor Banerjee had forgotten that there was a real person at the other end of her correspondence or as if she'd wrung what she needed out of her former student and discarded her. Parveen believed this only at her most bitter moments. More often she focused on those maternal flashes from her professor—the Indian food she'd brought her in her office—although she wondered if, in grieving her own mother, she'd given these small gestures too much weight. Perhaps Professor Banerjee cared more for what was good for the world than what was good for Parveen.

The village had become a safe limbo she didn't want to leave. Her imagination sputtered out, like the generator at night, when she tried to think about what she would do back in California and who she would be. Her past, all she'd done and learned before coming here, seemed to have little bearing on her future. What Shokoh had said about her own life—about the parts being so unconnected that only one of them could be real—fit Parveen too.

She'd been dwelling on the absence, from the village, of Aziz. Their last encounter had been upon Commander Amanullah's return, when Aziz had told her they were both in trouble. Parveen knew why Trotter was angry with her, but what Aziz's infraction had been was still a mystery, and she worried that something in her letter had turned Trotter against him. If the colonel dismissed Aziz and he returned to Kabul—which, for all she knew, might already have happened—she would never see him again. Even if he was still with Trotter, what was she supposed to do upon leaving the village, stand at the gate of the base and ask for him? This would make her feel pathetic and exposed; she couldn't forget the soldiers' teasing. And yet if she went back to America without seeing Aziz, a question she couldn't even phrase would stay forever curled in her.

She read and reread the articles Trotter had brought until, nauseated, she could look at them no more. Many of them contained interviews in which Crane defended himself. Memory wasn't a machine, he said when questioned. It was fallible. "I call it the 'fog of life.'" He had done his best, even if a few details were off. Perhaps the fault lay with his interpreter, on whom he had depended for information, or perhaps it lay with his wife, Gloria, who had helped assemble the book from the notes and jottings he'd brought back from Afghanistan. ("They were in a Marshalls bag," she told one interviewer.) Or perhaps it lay with the publishers, who believed memoirs should work as predictably as the human eye. But no matter: The important work would carry on. The focus should stay on the women.

Besides, he told one sympathetic interlocutor, fiction disguised as nonfiction in the service of justice had a long and noble history. Abolitionists had invented or amplified escaped slaves' narratives to dramatize their cause. Benjamin Franklin had written the first-person account of a made-up woman named Polly Baker, supposedly prosecuted for bearing illegitimate children, and passed it off as true to show the unfairness of the law toward women. Americans hadn't faulted him for this—they'd *celebrated* him. Not that Crane was comparing himself to Benjamin Franklin, of course. And not that he'd written a fiction. He insisted he hadn't. Moreover, there was nothing fake about what his readers had felt.

Issa, who came to the village a couple of weeks after Trotter had returned Amanullah, provided a less lofty picture of Crane's mental state. Once the scandal broke in the States, Issa said, he'd begun receiving calls from Dr. Gideon at all hours. Perhaps forgetting that his own foundation had facilitated Parveen's journey to the village, Dr. Gideon raged about her, insisting that rival nonprofits or antiwar activists had put her up to her disclosures. Sometimes he even cried to Issa, who in describing this sounded less amused than annoyed. Dr. Gideon cried because his funding was drying up and members of his board were resigning. Or he cried because he had the taint of a baby's grisly death on him now. He was not only seeking a sympathetic ear (though the ear he reached could hardly have been less so), but also warning Issa that the two of them were, as Dr. Gideon put it, "in for it." No doubt reporters would begin digging into their record keeping, their staffing, their finances, and their operations.

They will question everything, Dr. Gideon had told Issa, and this proved true. The same journalists who'd celebrated Dr. Gideon were now investigating him, like a swarm of bees suddenly shifting direction. They'd discovered what Issa had long ago learned from *Law and Order*, that the villain was rarely whom you expected and often the person who seemed too good to be true. The reporters pestered Issa with questions and scurried to the foundation's work sites. Only the American soldiers' insistence that the road couldn't be traveled right now kept the journalists from coming to this village; otherwise, Issa said, there would be hordes. It was as if Parveen's letter had been sent through a wormhole that had since collapsed.

Crane had told stories of elders from other villages begging for clinics of their own, but no one, least of all Issa, knew who these men were. Most Afghans had never heard of Crane or his book. As Parveen knew, it hadn't ever been translated into Pashto or Dari. Nor would these men have known where to find Crane. For help, for hope—for clinics or schools or peace— ordinary Afghans sat in the waiting rooms and courtyards of war-lords, provincial officials, and minor personages like the khan. And most of the time, they went home empty-handed. The foundation had built some other clinics, Issa said, most nearly as nice as this one, in villages that were easy to reach. But they'd come at the foundation's directive, not that of the villagers, and their numbers were far fewer than Crane or the foundation's publications had said. And most of them, like Fereshta's, were closed except for when journalists or VIPs planned a visit.

This was adding to the credibility problems of the foundation. Everything was falling apart, Issa said. He was going to return to smuggling soon; it had fewer headaches. He'd come to tell Waheed and Parveen not to talk if there was an investigation. He wanted to bury all the diesel cans in the mountains. Parveen he rebuked for quashing Waheed's hope for a better life—what ingratitude she'd shown toward the family that had hosted her. Issa was grateful that she hadn't mentioned him and Waheed in the letter, but he warned her against making any further disclosures. He'd lived on the wrong side of the law for a long time without going to jail and he wasn't about to go now.

This was the man whom Crane had chosen to work with in Afghanistan, a mercenary whose devoted character had been another of Crane's inventions. He seemed devoted only to himself, although when he said, in the guest room, "I'll miss this place. I'll even miss you, Waheed," Parveen had an inkling of why Issa had remained a bachelor, and she guessed that his life would be lonely.

To reach the village this time, Issa had bribed a subcontractor working on the road to hire him as a laborer so he could travel along it. There was no reason other than his love of subterfuge for him to have done this, Parveen thought, given how easily he'd come over the mountains before.

Issa showed off his laminated ID and said that, with such poor security, it didn't surprise him the Americans were getting beaten up. Insurgents could infiltrate the work crews as easily as he had. Issa himself had moved along the road entirely unmolested with no one remarking on a new face. "Even one as ugly as mine," he said, beating Waheed to their habitual joke.

Parveen hadn't been on the road since her arrival more than four months ago, and it gave her a small shock to realize how completely she'd succumbed to the cloister of the village. From what Issa said, she wouldn't recognize the twenty-five kilometers she'd jolted along back then. It was wider, of course, and flatter, and the blasting had exposed rich stripes of geologic color in the mountainside, which to Issa looked newly fragile. Everywhere the landscape was populated by men in neon-orange vests and helmets and their equipment: steamrollers, graders, pavers, asphalt mixers. And meanwhile, Issa said, you couldn't turn around without having a gun pointed in your direction, whether by the American soldiers or by all the private security the contractors had hired. The construction activity felt frantic, for they were in a race against the snow, which would completely degrade an unsealed surface. Issa thought they had no chance of finishing in time, in part because the tarmac was being sabotaged almost as soon as it was done. Dozens of explosives had been discovered and removed, laborers told him. Even so, Issa said, he'd still counted half a dozen craters bowled out by IEDs. The winter might halt the saboteurs' drive to undo the Americans' work, but only because during that time, the weather would do it for them. In the spring, Issa said, their efforts would resume.

TROTTER WAS SUPPOSED TO leave Afghanistan in December, Parveen remembered him saying, and she wondered how he'd react to ending his deployment with the road unfinished. The road had become a symbol each side wanted for its story of the war, but it was also a measure, *the* measure, she suspected, of Trotter's own war. His area of command was much larger than this valley, but this was the project with resonance for him, for Americans, and for his superiors. Mixed in with his rectitude and idealism, she was sure, was ambition. You didn't get to be a lieutenant colonel without thinking about your career.

In moments of clarity she understood that the village was a backdrop against which Americans played out their fantasies of benevolence or self-transformation or, more recently, control. She was as guilty of this as Trotter or Crane. She'd come to play at being an anthropologist, and play was all it had been, because at some point, without much thought, she'd set all her anthropological work aside. In nearly five months in the village, she'd done little more than interview a handful of women about their childbirth experiences and make some notes about the clinic's minimal effect on the local population. What had she done with all her time? There'd been the daily walks, and the hours at the clinic and in the fields. She'd taught Jamshid and read to the women in the orchard; she'd played with the children and helped in the house when she could; and she'd written, both letters and journal entries. But mostly it seemed there'd been an unconscionable number of hours spent daydreaming. Was she any less of a poser than Crane?

Yet she felt no regret over abandoning her ostensible anthropology project. Professor Banerjee's path wasn't going to be hers, not after she'd learned what, and who, her professor was willing to sacrifice for her principles. Parveen didn't possess that ruthlessness. Dr. Yasmeen seemed to urge, by both example and philosophy, a less dogmatic but more concrete course of action, and while Parveen knew she didn't have the constitution to be a doctor herself, she'd begun to consider a life in public health. The doctor was right—of all Crane's failings, his greatest wasn't Fereshta's death or his book of lies but the fact that his clinic wasn't set up to truly help the village women.

Perhaps, then, she would return home and apply to grad school in this newly chosen field, but she still couldn't see how to end her story in the village. Thanksgiving, which she'd promised her father she'd be home for, was just weeks away. Yet her reluctance to go was unabated, and it felt both arbitrary and anticlimactic to simply pick a date and fly out with the doctor. That wasn't the final image she wanted the villagers to have of her. She'd never been particularly good at finding the right time to leave a party, always fearing that she'd miss out on something or be talked about or, worst of all, have her absence go unmarked. The same worries flickered now, maybe because she guessed that the family and the villagers wouldn't pine for her the way she would for them.

Thinking that departing would be easier if she could obtain some proof of sentiment, she probed various family members in turn, telling them that the doctor thought she should leave soon, before winter.

"That's good," Waheed said. "The goats and chickens will want their room back. The donkey too." Soon it would be too cold for them outside, he said. It didn't sound like he was joking.

Disappointed, she suggested that maybe she would return to the village in the spring.

"You could build a school," he said.

She was crushed to think that to Waheed, she was just another Crane. Americans he expected to come, go, return to build something. Which she hadn't even thought to do, so she was also embarrassed. She'd been content with imagining the joyful reception on her return, a fantasy that blunted the awkwardness of leaving.

"And maybe you'll bring a husband," Waheed said. As they spoke, he was chopping wood in the yard; either he or Jamshid was always chopping wood these days, like all the other village men, in preparation for winter.

The statement was so unexpected that at first she thought he meant Aziz, a leap that told her something about where her mind was. But no, she realized, Waheed meant her fictional American fiancé, although she hadn't mentioned him in so long that she wondered if anyone in the family still believed in him. The permanent crinkling around Waheed's eyes made it hard to tell when there was mirth there. But his words implied that she wasn't valuable enough on her own, which was hurtful. He seemed as excited by the prospect of meeting her mythical husband as he was about seeing her again.

Next she tried Bina, who commented only that in winter the snow would be as tall outside the windows as she was. This made Bina recall Shokoh's arrival the previous winter, and she grew subdued and seemed to completely forget Parveen's impending departure. Parveen was left still searching for evidence that she'd made an impression on this family at all.

Only Shokoh displayed any true emotion. "You can't go!" she implored Parveen, holding her hands and treating her to a velvet gaze. They would have so much fun with the baby, she insisted. But first she had to get through the delivery, and she couldn't do that without Parveen or Dr. Yasmeen. "What does the silly dai know?"

"What do I know?" Parveen asked honestly.

Her entire tenure in the village struck her, newly, as ridiculous: an American hanging around, not doing much of anything at all, as the rhythms of this family and the march of the seasons continued undisturbed. Even Amina's weeping gratitude for Parveen's help in facilitating Amanullah's return was undeserved, since the help had been accidental. Nor had the appreciation lasted long, given the commander's diminished condition. He was still doddering, and Amina, who seemed to spend more time at the river complaining about this than actually being with him, broadly blamed "Americans," a sweeping judgment in which Parveen had the sense she was included.

Amanullah's detention was over but it would not be forgotten. Jamshid and his friends continued to call Aziz "Trotter's dog." They seemed to savor the phrase, to look for excuses to say it, and Parveen cringed every time. But she left it to Waheed, who was also disturbed by this talk, to take it up with his son.

As upset as Waheed had been by the commander's detention, he made it clear that he didn't blame the interpreter. Aziz might not have known the Americans' true plans when he was told to fetch Amanullah from the bazaar, Waheed told Jamshid one evening after dinner. Besides, if he was working for them, he had to do their bidding. What choice did he have? He was supporting a large family. "When you're doing that too, you can judge him," Waheed said. "Not before."

"There are many ways to support a family other than drinking from an American's teat," Jamshid snapped.

Waheed's eyes narrowed at the implication of Jamshid's rejoinder. "Should I have kept trying to suckle from a stone, like most poor people do?" His voice was low. "At least milk comes from the Americans."

"The Americans aren't my mother."

"And your new friends aren't your father. I am, and I'm telling you, take care. You can be lured into danger too."

Parveen was back in the half comprehension of her first night, but it wasn't a question of language. Who were Jamshid's new friends? she asked. When neither father nor son answered, she sought to explain—to defend—Aziz, saying, "It's hard to be caught between the two sides."

Jamshid turned toward her, his eyes bright, and said, "Don't see clearly for others and be blind for yourself."

A common proverb, yet it chilled her. When someone changed in front of you, it could be hard to discern; she'd thought this once about Waheed's failure to recognize how age had softened Commander Amanullah. Now she wondered if Jamshid had been undergoing a transformation without her realizing it. She kept trying to shift her focus, to get some distance, in order to study him. To see him clearly. Without doubt he was surlier than he'd been even a month or two earlier. He was inattentive to his siblings and uninterested in her lessons, as if his hunger to be taught by her had passed. Then again, he was a teenager, and she remembered how moody she herself had been in those years, sullen one minute, tempestuous the next. Whether in America or Afghanistan, it was a time of natural separation from parents, from adults.

When she told Jamshid she'd be leaving before winter, he said brusquely, "Yes, you should go." When she suggested that maybe she could return in spring, he said, "It will be a dangerous season for Americans," then again shut down.

The insurgents, while invisible to Parveen, were an increasing presence to everyone else, seeping into the village like dye into water. At the river the women whispered to Parveen about men who came down from the mountains at night to demand food and a place to sleep. Ghosts, they called these visitors. Shadows. The villagers gave what was asked and hid their resentments. There were rumors of warnings against cooperation with the U.S. forces, although it seemed to Parveen that if there was a house to be warned, it would be Waheed's, where an American slept, and unless he was keeping it from her, no warning had come. But at night sometimes she bolted awake, picturing these insurgent ghosts bedded down in guest rooms throughout the village.

One morning word spread that the insurgents had brutally beaten a villager—a man whose bout with meningitis had left him with diminished mental capacity—because he'd denied them shelter. Parveen went to see him and was shocked; one side of his head had been pulped by a rifle butt. His eyes were swollen shut, his lips clownish. They wanted to make an example of him, the villagers said. From now on, no one would dare to refuse.

When Dr. Yasmeen came next, Parveen asked her and Naseer to visit the man. The doctor administered various salves, left a supply of over-the-counter pain medications, and said time would heal him. When they left the house, she turned to Parveen and said, "Now. You must go now, my dear. Not later. Do you think these men in the hills don't know you're an American? They're just waiting for the time they can make use of you."

Parveen shivered at the doctor's words, but she argued anyway. She was a guest and therefore protected, she insisted. Just as she was a "third sex"—not governed by the usual rules of gender— she was a "third nation" too, neither American nor Afghan exactly. No harm would come to her here.

All the way back to the clinic, Dr. Yasmeen tried to convince her otherwise, even as Parveen offered reasons why she should prolong her stay. As politely as possible, she asserted that by now she knew the village better than the doctor. "I'm part of it," she said.

And here the doctor rebuked her. "Parveen, I understand your heart. I know you want to help. But don't forget you grew up in America. You're deluding yourself if you believe this is your home, and to think you understand everything happening here is to wager your own safety. Please don't."

They hugged as usual when the doctor left that day, but it was an awkward parting, and beneath Parveen's confidence ticked unease. In truth she didn't know all of the villagers by sight, and unfamiliar faces now became objects of fear. Had they been here all along or were they new? Other times she would pass men with their faces wrapped and wonder if it was to ward off the cold or to camouflage their identities. She no longer roamed freely, and not only because of the weather.

It was a cliché of this war to describe Afghans as being squeezed between the Americans and the Taliban, but Parveen was coming to see that didn't make it less true. As wary as the village men might be of the insurgents, they were equally afraid that the Americans might swoop in and take them as they'd taken Commander Amanullah. When the military helicopter brought the doctor each week, Parveen noticed, the bazaar and lanes emptied. No one attempted to travel the road anymore, not even to buy seeds or needed medicines. The khan hadn't been seen in the village in weeks; he felt safer, it was said, in the provincial capital.

Returning to her room one day Parveen found dried flowers, flat and powdery, on the floor. They were the ones Bilal had collected that day in the meadow and that she'd compressed in the pages of *Mother Afghanistan*. The flowers were all that remained. Both her copy of the book and the one Waheed had given her in disgust were gone.

Chapter Twenty-Four

Eye of Nothing

IT DIDN'T SURPRISE PARVEEN THAT THE INSURGENTS WOULD BE seeking shelter. The nights now were brisk, sometimes bitter cold. The family often ate dinner around a *sandali*, a small, low table covering a pit of warm charcoal, which they used to warm their feet. Parveen slept beneath layers of blankets, and she was grateful when Aakila and Adeila, and sometimes Zahab and Bilal too, smuggled themselves onto her bedroll. She might find them there when she went to sleep; other times they sneaked downstairs in the dark. They didn't ask and Parveen didn't object, even when there were as many as four crowded in with her, farting, snoring, kicking, squirming, planting their feet in her face, tucking their heads in the hollows beneath her arms. They moved in waves and sleep-spoke in tongues and often spilled off the bedroll onto the floor, where they slept soundly. Parveen's palm would settle on a sleeping child's chest, the heartbeat pulsing in her ears, or on the soft belly beneath the ribs, which she'd feel rising and falling with metronomic regularity, the comfort of this flooding her with endorphins and also distracting her from worrying about who was in the dark beyond the walls.

On one such night, an especially cold one, Parveen woke to

shouts and merciless banging on the compound door. She sat up, breathless with alarm. They'd come for her. The children huddled into her in fright, and she braced herself; there was nowhere in the room to hide. Waheed was descending the steps, calling out to see who was there, and she froze, waiting to see whether he would open the door, whether he would surrender her.

Now he was shouting for her. "Parveen, come! Parveen!"

Even knowing that the story of Crane's kidnapping was false, that was all she could think of: a black bag over her head, the terror that she would die this way, so far from her family. It was as if Crane had cued her responses, her imaginings, and she couldn't divert them onto another track. She put on her coat, hugged the children, and walked slowly out her door even as Waheed urged her to hurry.

Then her head cleared enough for her to understand what he was saying. The man at the door was brother-in-law to Latifa, whom Dr. Yasmeen had instructed Parveen how to help. Still stunned at this reprieve from her kidnapping and execution, Parveen nearly smiled, but she sobered as Waheed spoke. Although Latifa, who was six weeks from her due date, had been fine at her last checkup with Dr. Yasmeen, earlier in the evening she'd gone into labor and quickly delivered. Now the complications had begun.

Parveen returned to her room to grab the small kit, containing, among other items, surgical gloves, razor blades, cotton, and soap, that Dr. Yasmeen had prepared for this eventuality. She took a kerosene lantern from Waheed and followed the brother-in-law through the dark lanes, sucking lungfuls of clean cold air. As they walked hurriedly, she recollected the night she'd arrived here, when she had trailed Issa blindly. It was all so familiar now. She knew the turns the paths took, she knew who lived behind which door, she even knew the wood the doors were made from and where those trees grew. The noises of the animals no longer startled her, and their smells, even their dung, no longer repelled her. The map of this place had settled inside her. She was, in a fashion, home, a sentiment that was heightened by her relief at not being under threat tonight. She wasn't sure why she'd doubted Waheed. He wouldn't have surrendered her.

Inside the main room of the house, a fire burned orange in a corner, and shadows flickered against soot-stained walls. Latifa lay alone on a mound of dirt shrouded with blankets and rags. Parveen held up her lantern and gasped—the cloth beneath, around, and over her legs was crimson, a skirt of blood. The blood itself didn't surprise Parveen; the doctor had warned her. But she wasn't prepared for the force, the horror, of there being so much of it, and her childhood wooziness at the sight of her own blood briefly returned, made worse by the noxious, briny mixture of odors—blood, urine, feces, straw, and dirt—that hit her next. Alien cries and whimpers emanated from Latifa. Her skin was colorless, her eyes wildly lit.

From the shadows, hunched over a tiny bundle, the dai emerged to say, almost triumphantly, that it was she who had delivered the baby. Casting an eye to Parveen, she tossed a small object, the size of a pinkie, into the fire. A sound like popping corn erupted; then smoke, its scent foreign and herbaceous, boiled up. She chanted something about the evil eye—"eye of nothing, eye of relatives, eye of enemies"—and then said, "Whoever is bad should burn in this glowing fire."

Did she mean Parveen? The smoke, the smell, the words entranced and disoriented her. But she centered herself and studied the soaked cloth, trying to estimate how much blood Latifa had lost. Enough to soak a sheet, and still more was leaking from her into a dark pool. Parveen had a passing wish to capture it in a cup or container, although she knew that blood, decanted this way, had no value. She was watching a life drain, which meant that every moment she wasted weakened Latifa further. The perineum had to be cleaned. (It calmed Parveen to attach the medical terms the doctor had given her to what she saw, since the language connected her to countless practitioners more experienced than she was who, through time, across the world, had confronted the same sight. It wasn't a mound of clotted blood and pubic hair and skin and sliminess with the scent of salty wet seaweed. It was the perineum.) Using gloves and sterilizing wipes from the small kit Dr. Yasmeen had prepared, she cleaned the area, only to see it covered by blood again almost instantly.

The dai claimed to have delivered the placenta too but Parveen wondered if pieces had been left behind, which could cause bleeding. She asked Latifa if she'd taken the pill, misoprostol, that the doctor had provided her with. It would make the uterus contract enough to empty it of any leftover fragments, the doctor had said.

The dai answered: Latifa couldn't remember where she'd put the pill.

Parveen bit back her frustration, regretting that the family hadn't fetched her sooner. Bring the placenta, she told the dai, so that she could check for missing pieces.

The dai made no haste to comply, though she ultimately did so. In the dai's mind, Parveen knew, the placenta was meant to be buried, not studied.

To Parveen it looked like a bloody, dark piece of raw meat. Its edge was jagged. Again she cleaned the perineum, then put on a surgical glove and, ignoring Latifa's moan, pushed her hand all the way up to the uterus, shoving away the memory of helping her mother clear gizzards and organs from raw chickens. She found and extracted stray pieces of spongy, gelatinous placenta and puzzled them into place. The blood kept coming. *Postpartum hemorrhage*, she thought. The uterus needed to contract.

Remembering that Dr. Yasmeen had said breastfeeding could help, Parveen pulled off her bloody gloves and commanded the dai to give her the baby. Grudgingly, she did.

The infant girl felt ethereal, dandelion-light, like a precarious halo of seeds a mere breath from dispersal. She seemed, beneath her swaddling, hardly bigger than Parveen's palm, the features in her pinched face so delicate they could have been squeezed out of a dropper. Clumsily, Parveen brought the infant to Latifa's nipple as the dai hissed from behind: "It's dirty."

The colostrum, she meant. Like many Afghan villagers, she believed the thick, sticky early milk was unclean, probably because of its yellow-orange color. In a newborn's first days, mothers in the villages often gave sugar water or sometimes cow's milk instead, with predictably disastrous results. Dr. Yasmeen had tried to disabuse every pregnant woman she saw of this notion, explaining the nutritional riches the colostrum contained.

In this case, it didn't matter; the baby, too small, too weak, couldn't latch on, not even when Parveen overcame her pride and asked the dai to help. Parveen's hands began to tremble. There was a malevolent presence in the room, and she understood that it was death, could almost see him sitting with his legs crossed on an imaginary chair in the corner, cleaning his fingernails while he whistled a tune. *No rush*, his posture seemed to say. He could wait for both the mother and her child. But once the time came, there would be no appeal. Dashing through the darkened lanes on the way to this house, Parveen had watched the clouds swallow the moon. A life could vanish as fast.

She handed the baby back to the dai, yanked on a new pair of surgical gloves, and laid her left hand on Latifa's skin where she determined the top of her uterus to be, just as Dr. Yasmeen had taught her. The odor of blood was so overpowering Parveen could taste it. "Here we go," she said brightly, and with her right hand she pushed back into Latifa, disregarding her cry of pain and surprise, up through the wet, ragged, stretched tissues of the birth canal, until her fist found the uterus. Whereas in her lesson at the clinic it had been firm, now it was flabby and slack. To make it contract, which would slow the bleeding, she kneaded her fist against it while pressing down with her left hand from the outside on the upper uterus. *Push, press, push, press.* She did this for a while, then checked the bleeding; it continued, and so she resumed. *Push, press, push, press.* The focus required cleared her head. Until then, despite the tenuousness of Latifa's life, the ghastly pallor of her face, and the blood, the relentless blood, Parveen had been thinking about herself—how she would perform, how *she* would be judged, the repercussions for her. Now she set all that aside. At stake were two lives, the one ebbing under her hand and the fragile new one struggling to survive.

Dr. Yasmeen had said to put the newborn in the incubator if she came more than a few weeks early. She was six weeks premature, so her lungs might not be fully developed, especially with the poor nutrition on which her mother had been subsisting. Naseer had shown Parveen how to use the machine, giving what seemed at the time hilariously detailed explanations for every step, wanting to discuss each possible complication. She wished she'd paid more attention. No one but her knew how to operate the incubator. She needed to take the infant herself, and soon, but she couldn't leave Latifa. It felt as if time itself were kneeing her in the back. *Push, press, push, press.* At last, with her left hand on Latifa's abdomen, she sensed a change in the uterus: it was beginning to harden. Once she was sure, she pulled out her right hand to check the bleeding. It slowed. Then it stopped.

Parveen allowed herself one sob of relief before hurrying to tell Latifa's husband, who was waiting just outside the door, to bring clean blankets to warm his wife. He was also to send word to Waheed to get the clinic ready and the generator running. The newborn needed to be put in a special machine that would keep her warm—"Like being inside her mother," Parveen explained—and help her grow more. They would bring Latifa to the clinic too when she was strong enough to be moved.

Parveen went over to the dai, who stood against a wall, and held out her arms. The dai squinted up at her. At last she passed the bundle, and their hands briefly touched beneath the infant, whose eyes were closed. In terror Parveen fingered open the wrapping to confirm the child's breathing. Yes, it was there, though rapid and shallow. She slid her hand inside the blanket and smoothed her fingers over the head to verify that it was intact. "Don't worry," she told Latifa, who appeared distressingly listless. "We'll take care of her."

"I'm not so worried," she whispered, faintly enough that Parveen had to bend her ear to her mouth. "She'll live, or she won't."

Parveen couldn't tell whether Latifa was fatalistic or, having borne her fourth girl, indifferent to yet another daughter's fate. Her husband, too, seemed concerned mostly for his wife, which redoubled Parveen's dedication to the child. The husband followed Parveen, thanking her with profuse courtesy and un-concealed anxiety, as she went down the stairs and into the courtyard. How much would her help and this machine in the clinic cost? he was asking. He would pay what he could, but he didn't have much.

He didn't need to pay her anything, Parveen said, and nothing for the clinic either. It was for circumstances like this that it had been built. What she wanted was to make him agree that Latifa could have an IUD implanted. Another delivery would likely kill her, and her husband was probably desperate enough at this moment to consent. But to extract such a promise now would be every bit as paternalistic as the village men themselves were, and he would likely break it anyway.

"I must be paid," the dai caviled from behind, reminding them that she'd delivered the child.

And nearly let the mother die, Parveen thought. Was her fury at the dai's grasping what Crane had felt? "Go inside and care for Latifa," she ordered. Instead, the dai trailed her to the compound door, at which point Parveen chased her off with a pledge to bring her money the next day. "But leave the family be," she warned. "Let them use what money they have to buy meat for Latifa so she can feed her baby."

"If the girl lives it will be because of God," the dai said, "not because of you."

Parveen hurried through the cold, dark lanes with her bundle. Ahead of her, the clinic blazed with light, looking exactly as she'd imagined it would before her arrival in the village. This buoyed her, as did finding Waheed waiting inside. Her head scarf had come off at Latifa's, and he stared at the dried blood crusted on her clothes, her face, her hair. She told him how to scrub his hands, and once he'd done so she gave him the baby to hold so she could clean herself. He bore the infant up tentatively, like a piece of hot bread. Parveen swiftly washed her hands, then took the child upstairs and switched on the incubator, which blinked to life. As she waited for the interior temperature to rise, she unwrapped the infant and placed her inside her own clothing, on her skin, to warm the tiny body. The newborn's sleepy eyes blinked open, and she nuzzled into Parveen, gaping, gaping, searching by some atavistic instinct for a breast. Not finding one, she squalled, her first sound in the world a hollow cry. When the incubator was ready Parveen placed the baby inside and watched her miniature limbs flail and coil beneath the bright light. What a shock birth was, less a passage than an ejection. An eviction.

The baby slept. While she did, Parveen opened a can of formula and mixed it with water that had been boiled, then cooled. She'd observed Dr. Yasmeen cup-feed a newborn, but she was nervous. When the baby woke, Parveen lifted her out of the incubator and held her close. Then ever so gently she placed the rim of the cup against the edge of the tiny lips and waited until her tiny pink tongue began to lap.

When the baby was back in the incubator, Parveen stayed fixed to her side. She'd latched onto this rickety existence: the purity of her smell, the pinkness of her mouth, her jerky movements; her fuzzy head, her fleshy tonsure; her curling fingers and the delicate shells of her fingernails; her responsiveness to being held, the way her waving arms would suddenly compose; her kitten-like way of eating. As dawn approached, Parveen spoke aloud, casting stories, facts, poems, even songs into the incubator as if to hook the child more firmly to life. By degrees the infant's color improved ever so slightly, or so Parveen told herself. She was desperate for signs the baby would live.

In the morning, the village women began to come in such large numbers that Parveen had to force most of them to wait downstairs, taking up only a few at a time. Some of them tapped on the glass of the incubator until Parveen cried, "Stop!" Any noise was magnified inside, Naseer had warned—those taps would be as jarring as a ringing phone. Others reached through the portholes to touch the baby until Parveen explained the risk of infection. Surrounded by these faces, the infant seemed less human than a specimen under glass. Again and again Parveen explained the machine's functions, which were to provide warmth so the baby could fatten, quiet so she could rest, and a barrier to protect her from germs. Americans had once been as suspicious of incubators as the village women were, Parveen assured them. One of her professors, in fact, had once shown a slide of babies lined up in incubators on the Atlantic City boardwalk, where they'd been put to convince the public of the merits of the machine.

Around midday Latifa's husband carried her to the clinic and up the stairs to the maternity ward. Her complexion was pallid, her speech still weak, but seeing her settled on a hospital bed, the other women eyed her enviously. With assistance from Bina, Parveen gave her a sponge bath, then helped her beneath the blankets. Latifa looked around in a daze; it was the first real bed she'd slept on. Parveen drew the curtains closed on windows that framed a view of the mountains and then chased the women from the room.

She was eager to have Dr. Yasmeen come so she could share every detail of the previous night with her, receive her accolades as well as her guidance. But Wednesday was five days off. She tried to channel the doctor, to think of what else she should do. Food, she realized; Latifa needed to eat, and eat well. She ran to Waheed's to fetch the money hidden in her room, then gave it to Bina to buy large quantities of meat, vegetables, and bread, asking her to organize the women to cook it. Perhaps, she hoped, she could get a few good meals into other undernourished women too. By the second day after the delivery, color was returning to Latifa's cheeks and she could sit up a bit. Parveen showed her how to raise her head or feet by manipulating the bed's handheld control. The other women—Bina, Saba, Ghazal—stared open-mouthed at this thing moving of its own accord, then they climbed on top and clutched the sides as if it were a bucking bronco.

"Off! Off! Watch out for Latifa!" Parveen shouted over their hysterical laughter. Then she unplugged the bed and promised that when Latifa was better, they could all have rides of their own.

Shokoh, whose pregnancy was now in its third trimester, reclined on another bed in the ward, trying to make clear to the other women that, as a city girl, she knew how it was done. She wanted to give birth at the clinic, she told Parveen, and she would put her baby in the incubator too.

Parveen explained that it would be better if this wasn't necessary.

"Or maybe I'll just stay here until the baby comes," Shokoh told Bina, who cut her with a look.

Latifa's milk had come in, but the baby was still too weak to suckle, and Bina warned that if the child didn't get started, the milk would dry up. Parveen knew little about breastfeeding other than what she'd observed in the village and at the clinic with Dr. Yasmeen. She vaguely remembered her sister struggling at first with the latch, a word that at the time had amused her. Now, though, she regretted that callousness. Here, as in many matters, Bina and the other women became her tutors. Bina suggested that Latifa nurse her sister-in-law's twins to keep the milk coming until her own child could feed. After that, every couple of hours, one of the babies would be brought to the clinic to nurse from her.

They were crowdsourcing this baby's survival, Parveen would think as her adrenaline surged. Then she'd crash, teary and spent from lack of sleep, and want nothing so much as to collapse. She tried to measure the baby's heart rate but didn't really know what she was looking for.

It seemed Wednesday would never arrive, but at long last, the day was at hand. Soon Dr. Yasmeen would spell Parveen from her duties and shower her with praise.

But that week, for the first time since Parveen's arrival, the doctor didn't come.

Chapter Twenty-Five

Tears from Blind Eyes

It was a day both glorious and melancholy, the sky a blue of almost vexing purity, the fields stubbled and gray. Women crowded into the clinic, asking about the doctor.

Maybe the Americans didn't have a helicopter available, Parveen suggested. Or perhaps Dr. Yasmeen was sick. Or her husband. Or maybe Naseer had an important exam.

The doctor wouldn't miss them for such a trivial thing, the women admonished her. As much as her treatment and advice, the doctor's willingness to make the journey and her consistency mattered to them. The eyes of a few—those more knowing or less trusting—betrayed the fear that she had decided they were no longer worth the bother.

"Only if she is dead would she not come," said Saba, who was promptly reprimanded by the others.

To appease them, Parveen made a list of every patient who wanted to see the doctor and, after conferences in the exam room, what their ailments were so that when Dr. Yasmeen did come, she could move quickly. By now they trusted Parveen enough to talk about their bodies, to relate their pains, to describe their discharge, even their beatings. Or at least they trusted her as a conduit to the doctor. But by late afternoon, when the single tree's shadow pointed like a finger across the courtyard, it was clear the doctor wouldn't be coming.

They waited again the next day, and the one after that, listening, in vain, for the sound of the helicopter that would bring her. Her absence unsettled Parveen. She scanned the mountains, the snow creeping down their flanks. Was winter closer than she'd thought? Perhaps the doctor had decided to wait until spring to return. But surely she would have sent word with the Americans if that was the case. Parveen felt a peevish sense of abandonment. In the wake of her success with Latifa, she was hungry to learn more, to try more.

At night the family listened, as usual, to the BBC. One brief report caught their ears because it referenced the district they were in and because it was unusual: coalition forces had killed two suspected insurgents, one of them female. In this war, there were no female insurgents, at least none that Parveen had heard of.

"It's the new Malalai!" Bina joked, a reference to the fearsome female warrior who was said to have rallied Afghan fighters against the British at the Battle of Maiwand in 1880. Even uneducated Bina knew about her.

Jamshid scoffed. It wasn't the new Malalai, he said, probably not even an insurgent. "They've killed an innocent woman, I'm guessing. You can call a dead body anything you want."

Mornings in the valley often began now with a thick fog, a ground cloud, into which family members disappeared as they went about their work in the yard. Like anyone who'd lived in the Bay Area, Parveen knew fog, but here it was denser and colder, a thief of light and heat. Each day, until it lifted, it felt as if they might swim in it forever.

Parveen had spent the night in the clinic, in a bed next to

Latifa's, as she had done for the past week and a half, since the birth. Latifa, still recovering, was mostly quiet, but Parveen enjoyed sharing the room with her. It was like being back with her sister, whom she'd missed terribly when Taara first married and moved away. In theory, being at the clinic should have felt like a hotel stay—to sleep in an actual bed!—except that the building had no central heating system, just a few space heaters, and it was poorly insulated. The baby, thankfully, was warmed by the incubator, and at night Parveen piled blankets atop Latifa, then layered long underwear, a sweater, and a coat on herself, her warmest clothes already not warm enough. If it was this cold in early November, Dr. Yasmeen was right that she wouldn't be able to manage the winter.

In the mornings Parveen made tea for herself and Latifa, and together they waited for the delivery of warm bread, eggs, and yogurt that the women took turns bringing. On this foggy morning, three days after the doctor's failure to come, the Americans came instead. Parveen was surprised they'd made the drive, because the lack of visibility as they twisted along the canyon would have turned the road treacherous even if it were in good shape. At first she heard the M-ATVs but couldn't see them out the room's window for the fog. Then, like a latent image becoming visible, they emerged. The convoy entered the village as slowly as a cortege and parked by the clinic.

Parveen told Latifa that she would go see if the Americans knew anything about Dr. Yasmeen. She walked outside, hugging herself. The sun nudged through the fog, and after days of fretting, first about Latifa, then about the doctor's absence, that hint of light made Parveen hopeful. It was possible that the Americans had brought Dr. Yasmeen and Naseer, and Aziz would have to be with them too, and she could tell all of them about saving Latifa's life.

But from the moment she approached the three M-ATVs, something seemed off. She waved at the driver and front-seat passenger in the lead vehicle, and they raised their hands in return, but no one emerged. She waited for a strange minute until, at last, the doors opened and soldiers climbed out. Trotter was among them, and Aziz too. She felt such relief at seeing him that she gave an embarrassingly broad grin, then cringed at the memory of her last, charged interaction with Trotter, when he'd brought the news about her letter. Neither the colonel nor Aziz returned her smile. They both looked as if the drive had made them queasy.

Trotter took her elbow, guided her toward the clinic, and said, to her surprise, that he needed her help. Did she know anything, could she tell him anything, about Naseer, the doctor's son? Was he a member of any militant groups? Did he have a relationship with Commander Amanullah? Meetings with anyone in the village?

"Why? Have you detained *him* now?" Parveen asked, stopping short. That would explain why neither he nor his mother had come to the village. Dr. Yasmeen would be frantic—and furious.

No, Trotter said uneasily. No, they hadn't detained him. His men were running a checkpoint on the highway near the base when a car came at them. Its driver was Naseer.

"Naseer tried to run them over?" Parveen asked. This was preposterous, and she laughed. She and Trotter were facing each other. She sensed the other soldiers and Aziz watching from a few feet back. "You're joking, right? Why would he do that?"

"We don't know. I don't know. Did you ever hear him express support for the insurgency? Or mention any anti-American or anti-government sentiments?"

"Give me a break—he wants to go study in America more than anything."

Trotter was quiet. The pulse beneath his eye was back.

"So you *have* detained him," she said, suspicious now. "If you're saying he threatened your—"

"My men had to defend themselves. There were multiple commands to stop. He didn't stop, Parveen."

Trotter's words seemed to tumble slowly toward Parveen, coming apart before they arrived. There was some essential point she was missing, a connection she couldn't make.

"His mother, Dr. Yasmeen, was she with him? They were probably just talking about her cases and not paying attention—"

She was in the car, Trotter said. The pulse beat faster, and she stared at it, briefly mesmerized. Her staring only seemed to speed it up, and she remembered her ninth-grade math teacher halving each of his steps as he walked across the room and explaining that if you were able to do that indefinitely, cutting your steps in half each time, that's what infinity was, and if the pulses beneath Trotter's eye got closer and closer in time beyond what was physically possible, was it the same, was that infinity? Her mind was circling away like a plane refused permission to land, except in her case it didn't want to land; it wanted to rise into the clouds and disappear.

"They haven't come here," she said finally. "It's the first week they've missed since I got here."

"Because they're deceased," Trotter said. "Both of them. Dr. Yasmeen and Naseer—they're deceased."

The word, with its peculiar passivity, made it sound as if they'd just fallen over, Parveen thought. "You mean they were...killed," she said, hesitating in spite of herself, because to say that was to accuse.

"My men had no choice but to engage the vehicle—"

"Engage."

"Fire on it. In a situation like that, you see a car coming toward you, a split second of morality can mean you end up dead. They acted appropriately."

"They killed them."

"Verbal commands, hand gestures, shouts, you name it, they tried everything, but the car kept coming. If someone doesn't recognize our authority, we have to assume they're opposed to it."

"You killed—" she started, but then, woozy, was down on the ground in an instant, her fall broken just in time by Trotter, who'd reached out when she wobbled. She bent her head over her knees and heard a woman tell her, in English, to take deep breaths. This woman was offering water, a PowerBar, all of it surely an aural hallucination. But no, it was real, for when Parveen looked up, there beneath a helmet was the face of an American woman, with freckles splashed across her nose and blue eyes wide with concern.

"This is Charlie, she's a medic," Trotter said. "We brought two for the women here—"

"Because you killed their doctor," Parveen said stonily. "You brought female medics because you killed the female doctor." Rage—grief—burst in her, and regret at her last strained meeting with the doctor, who'd been so worried for Parveen even as her own life and that of her son were days from ending. Parveen began to shout "Fuck you! Fuck you!" and then to cry, sending out great yawps of sadness. She wanted to make Trotter's ears hurt. The medic's hand was rubbing her back, as a mother might, as her own mother once had, and unable to stop crying, she remembered the day her mother died, when, after months of tears during her illness, Parveen had been unable to cry at all. She'd felt numb, depleted. Some of their relatives, her sister told her later, found this odd. How strange, then, to be so uninhibited here, among strangers, for the loss of a woman who wasn't blood. Not blood, and yet she saw how, like Professor Banerjee, Dr. Yasmeen had come to seem a maternal substitute, and she wondered if the lesson forevermore would be never to get attached to anyone. It seemed like a sign when she looked around for Aziz and couldn't see him.

When Trotter suggested they go into the clinic courtyard so that she could sit down there, Parveen knew it was because the village men were staring. Through tear-blurred vision, she saw Jamshid standing maybe fifty feet away with a knot of his friends, watching her, watching Trotter. She hadn't seen them come, and Jamshid's expression, cold but not curious, surprised her. This was no longer the boy who'd accosted her in the yard and begged her to teach him.

With the two medics supporting her, one on each side, Parveen walked haltingly into the clinic courtyard, then sat down with her back against the wall. The cold in the ground began oozing into her, immobilizing her.

Trotter, fully armored, paced as he spoke, stopping occasionally to plant himself directly in front of her, to loom over her, only to resume pacing. He could tell her more about what had happened, he said, but he needed to know whether she planned to write to her professor, or anyone, about it. If the news of Dr. Yasmeen's death was broadcast widely, he said, it could stir up a lot of resentment among Afghans and put American soldiers in danger. Surely she wouldn't want that.

"You want me to lie for you?" Parveen asked. "Help you cover it up?"

"We're not trying to cover up anything," he said and stopped abruptly in front of her—she'd insulted his dignity now. "It's about the strategic release of information."

She thought for a moment. "The female insurgent—we heard that on the radio. That was Dr. Yasmeen. That's what you mean by 'strategic'?"

Trotter scrunched up his nose, an almost comical pantomime of regret, then folded his arms and gazed off into the distance. "That went out too quickly. There was a lot of confusion—there always is in these situations." It would be corrected, he said, but the mistake at least had bought them time to think about how to put this out there.

"You want to control the story."

He nodded gratefully, believing he had her agreement. Did he imagine her as his student, dutifully imbibing his rules of war? She would capitalize on his imaginings to learn what she wanted, then write to whomever she chose.

"I guess you're in luck," she said, trying to make her tone friendly. "Dr. Yasmeen was the one who sent my letters for me."

He grimaced, then bowed his head in a way that recalled his visit to Fereshta's grave. Yet he must have been secretly relieved, or at least put at ease, for he began to talk. Four of his soldiers had been staffing the checkpoint, he said, two of them new to country. There was intelligence about possible suicide attacks, and his men had been briefed on these threats. No doubt it had put them on edge. As Parveen knew, the doctor had for weeks now been driving onto the base so that she could be brought to the village by helicopter. But the soldiers, maybe because they were new, or maybe because they were stationed some distance down the highway, didn't recognize her car. It came fast and it wouldn't stop. They assumed—had to assume, based on the intelligence—that the car itself was an IED or that the driver planned to run them over. Trotter hoped Parveen could see that under those conditions, they had no choice but to engage. His soldiers were still sorting out who among them had fired first, Trotter continued. They couldn't rule out that they'd been fired upon.

The way he related all of this, it was almost as if he expected Parveen to sympathize with him for the burden of having to reconcile such a crosshatch of conflicting testimonies. But sympathy was far from what she delivered. Naseer would never have done anything to endanger his mother, she told Trotter vehemently. That was all the colonel needed to know about him. He'd put out lunch for Dr. Yasmeen every week! "You met him," she said. "You flew on a helicopter with him. He wanted to talk to you about photovoltaic technology or whatever it was. He wasn't a terrorist; he was a nerd. He was a teenager."

In a theater of war, Trotter said, one where boys started fighting before their balls dropped, there were no teenagers, only military-age males. The enemy embedded itself in the population, took advantage of the population. You never knew where the next attack was coming from or how it was going to look. An old man could be just an old man, or he could be the enemy's newest recruit. Trotter spoke as though his words were bricks building a defensible wall, and he seemed surprised that he had to explain all of this to Parveen. Given the strain his men were under, he felt they'd shown remarkable impulse control. Some of them wanted to be driving down the road shooting anything that moved. How were they supposed to respect people who were trying to kill them? He was asking—ordering—his boys to suppress the completely natural response to fight back. More than natural; they'd been trained for it, trained to kill. It's what they'd signed up for. And now in this war they were having the rules of engagement changed on them every single day, sometimes more than once a day. "He should've obeyed the commands," he finished.

Parveen wished she could stretch up her arm and scratch Trotter's face, the only breach in his carapace. A balloon of sorrow and rage had swelled so thickly in her throat that it was blocking her breath. Maybe violence could free it. Wanting, at least, to be closer to his level, she struggled to her feet, her limbs stiff with cold, and leaned against the wall for support.

Perhaps because of her movement, he began to talk about the day they'd met. It might have turned out differently if it had happened today, he said. She'd taken her time disclosing who she was, he reminded her. She hadn't spoken all the way to the graveyard and back. He'd thought she was Waheed's wife. Then, after the shura, she'd walked toward him with a directness so out of character for an Afghan woman that he'd thought, just for a moment, she might be weaponized. If his men were less disciplined, they might have shot her. Instead, she came up to him, opened her mouth, and started speaking perfect English, which was the last thing he was expecting. He mustered an unconvincing smile at the memory. He and his men were jittery now, he said. They'd been made that way. Today, in that same situation, with Parveen walking toward him, there would be one second to think, and what he would inevitably think was *It's either her or me*.

Then he quoted Clausewitz to her—"'War is the realm of uncertainty'"—and added, "The fog of war, it's real, Parveen. At any single moment in any given combat situation, it's hard to see or know exactly what's going on."

"But this wasn't a combat situation. They were just driving along a highway."

"We *thought* it was a combat situation, and we had to react accordingly."

They could snipe at each other all day, Parveen thought. It wouldn't change a thing. The doctor and her son would still be dead. Just outside this clinic wall, at Parveen's suggestion, Dr. Yasmeen had stood in front of her battered car to testify that the road badly needed improving. Would that video still serve as propaganda for this mission, Parveen wondered, even though the car was full of bullet holes and the woman who'd been interviewed was dead? For eternity, perhaps, in an obscure corner of YouTube, Dr. Yasmeen would be praising the American initiative that had killed her. But determined to preserve the illusion of a truce with Trotter, Parveen spoke none of this aloud.

Trotter said that he was working on finding a replacement for Dr. Yasmeen, but given the scarcity of female doctors in the province, it might take some time. He asked, his tone nearly plaintive, "What can we do? For the village, I mean. How can we make things right? I'm not unaware of how damaging this is. We're here to help, and then...if you have any thoughts..." He trailed off.

She had no thoughts, and her silence made this clear. His willingness to ask her advice wouldn't make her agree to whitewash his mistake.

Could she at least provide guidance and interpretation for his medics? he asked, and when she agreed, he left the clinic court-yard so they could get to work.

In her head, Parveen ran through the chronicle of the women's complaints and needs that she'd made on Wednesday, when the doctor hadn't arrived. Mira had preeclampsia; should Parveen check her blood pressure? Storai's ankles had swollen again, elephant-big; was that normal? Anisa was complaining of pain during sex. Reshawna burned worse than ever when the urine came. Nadia had run out of her iodine tablets, and the mullah, fearful that the Americans might take him as they had the com-mander, was refusing to travel for more. Fatima had missed her period and was in tears at the prospect of another child so soon. Mashal had told Parveen of a lump in her breast; her husband, hardly observant, had noticed, so it must be large. What could you do for *that*?

The medics, the first American females she'd seen since coming to the village, were disorienting. Their helmets were off, and from their hair—Charlie's blond and butch; Mandy's long and copper, catching the light—came a whiff of familiar, nearly forgotten American smells: baby shampoo, coconut, laundry detergent. For some reason, this made Parveen cry again.

"I'd give you a hug but it probably wouldn't feel that great," Charlie said, knocking on her Kevlar-shielded chest.

Although the joke was a lame one, it softened Parveen a bit. "I just don't understand," she blubbered. "Do you agree with Colonel Trotter? That they had no choice?"

"We always agree with him," Mandy said with a raised eye-brow. "He outranks us."

"Just like the private will agree with the sergeant who says the car was speeding," Charlie added, "even if the private thought it was crawling. Honestly, once the shooting starts, it's a shit-show trying to make sense of something like this."

Parveen asked if either medic had treated Yasmeen or Naseer, if they'd tried to save them. Charlie said she'd been sent to the scene as soon as they realized there was a woman in the car.

"They wouldn't let a male medic treat her?" Parveen asked in disbelief.

"They're trying to respect cultural sensitivities," Charlie said. Sometimes, unfortunately, these different priorities tripped over each other. And the truth was that no one had been allowed to treat either of them at first. The unit had to scan the car and the bodies with robots to make sure nothing was booby-trapped. That was SOP. But she could see how upset Parveen was getting, and she hastened to add that she was pretty sure both the doctor and her son had died instantly. There'd been a lot of soft-tissue injuries, a lot of organ damage, she said, as if she were merely speaking to another medic. But when Parveen, unable to form words, simply stood there, rigid, Charlie said, "I know this doesn't make anything better, but the soldiers—I think they felt terrible."

IF THEY WERE GOING to examine any women, Charlie and Mandy said, they should probably get started because Trotter wasn't going to want to linger.

Parveen looked around. The dai was watching them from her habitual spot beneath the tree. Should she tell her that the doctor, her erstwhile rival, was gone? Other than the dai, there wasn't a village woman in sight. As usual when the Americans came, they'd stayed home. And she suspected that the women wouldn't want to be treated by medics who, in their uniforms and body armor, were bigger than many of their husbands. Only children were in the courtyard. They kept daring one another to run over and touch Mandy's red hair.

Latifa, of course, was in the clinic, along with her baby. Parveen knew she should take the medics in to check both mother and child, but she couldn't bear to go in there yet, knowing the doctor was dead.

Mandy and Charlie stood awkwardly, then announced that they'd brought some pens and stuffed animals for the children. "Hearts and minds," Mandy joked. "At least the little ones." While they walked to their M-ATVs to get the swag, Parveen clapped her hands and called together the children. "Line up quietly," she told them, "and you'll be given something."

Mandy and Charlie and a few soldiers entered the courtyard carrying boxes, which they set down. The men exited, Mandy and Charlie opened the boxes, and the line of children exploded. Boys and girls barnacled themselves onto the two Americans, who, unable to move, began tossing pens and small stuffed cats and dogs to any outstretched hands they could reach. To Parveen, the toy animals, with their synthetic fur and big plastic eyes, looked garish and cheap, their hot pinks and electric blues artificially bright next to the natural palette of the village. But the children wanted them badly. Fights sprang up, tears ran, the strong stole from the weak. Children who lived cheek to flank with real animals, who could cuddle live calves and lambs anytime, were crying and screaming because they couldn't get hold of plush ones. In no time the medics had been stripped of even the pens in their pockets. They stood frozen amid the mayhem.

Soon after that the village teenagers—Jamshid and his friends—began to call their younger siblings home, virtually chasing them out of the courtyard, sometimes pulling them by the ears. Parveen, remembering the day of the HIIDE, wondered if this, too, was about asserting some kind of resistance to the Americans, or at least rejecting their efforts to buy the children's goodwill.

"Parveen-jan, you should go home too," the dai called, then she herself left.

But Parveen wasn't going back to Waheed's. She needed to find Aziz for both information and consolation. He was outside the clinic wall, smoking, of course, and the way he angled his head in sympathy when he saw her red, swollen eyes nearly made her cry again. Even as she stood stiffly a couple of feet from him, an imagined self, ungoverned by convention or propriety or fear, moved toward him, and the real Parveen watched with envy.

Once Aziz began to talk, he didn't stop. Because news of the shooting had come when Colonel Trotter was away at meetings in Kabul, Aziz had accompanied a captain to the checkpoint. He recognized the car right away. Naseer and his mother were inside. "Don't make me describe it," he begged Parveen. It was better if she didn't have the pictures in her head; they were worse than she could imagine. Aziz had had no choice but to see. He lit one cigarette after another.

When he informed the soldiers who the passengers were, they grew panicky, defensive. The incident had happened so fast they hadn't had time to recognize the car, they said. The driver, whoever he was, had been bent on their murder, they insisted. Aziz listened to their stories evolve. Their arguments over who'd yelled or signaled which commands to the driver, the distance the car had been from them when they'd opened fire, and which soldier had shot first slowly cohered into a single version, defensible as a fortress. Although each of them had experienced the moments differently, with time, all of them would describe them the same way.

From the Afghan laborers, Aziz secured different accounts. As was often the case in Afghanistan, it was hard to separate the directly observed from the secondhand. Some said the car had braked, others that it had continued driving slowly despite commands to stop. Had those commands been given in Dari as well as in English? Were there commands at all? One worker claimed the soldiers had been playing cards and the approaching white car had caught them by surprise. This possibility, with its suggestion of dereliction, Aziz had chosen not to relay to Trotter.

The soldiers kept looking for ways to prove they'd been

in the right. But a search of the car turned up no weapons, no explosives. Naseer's iris and fingerprints matched no known insurgent's. It was clear, at least to Aziz, and he suspected to some of the soldiers as well, that they had killed two completely innocent people. Of course, in the Americans' eyes, these two weren't innocent, because they hadn't obeyed orders. So it was a terrible mistake, yet not a mistake, a contradiction that Aziz was finding hard to bear. Whose country was this?

At dusk, he said, a full eight hours after the shooting, the soldiers returned to the base with both the bodies and the bloodied car. Aziz couldn't sleep, thinking about Dr. Yasmeen's husband, who had to be wondering where his wife and son were. And according to the Muslim tradition, they needed to be buried as soon as possible, ideally within twenty-four hours of death.

The next morning, as soon as Colonel Trotter came back, Aziz went to tell him that he thought the doctor's husband should be notified immediately and the bodies returned. It was a painful, awkward conversation, he said, for the colonel still seemed to be scouting for—or maybe just hoping for—evidence that might put his soldiers in the clear.

"Even with me, he was doing that," Parveen said.

Aziz nodded. There were the obvious reasons—how bad it looked and the revenge attacks it might spawn—but Aziz also had the sense that Colonel Trotter didn't want his men, two of whom were only weeks into their deployment, to have this on their conscience. Part of being their leader was finding a way to make it clean. Who could blame him for wanting the dead to be insurgents? It was hard to justify his soldiers having shot a doctor, a female doctor, one of the few in the whole province, and her son.

But Aziz kept insisting that there was no way to change the facts of what had happened or who Dr. Yasmeen and Naseer were. "You know Naseer wasn't an insurgent, you know she wasn't, you have to tell the family and let them be buried properly." It was by far the most confrontational he'd ever been with Colonel Trotter, and he could see in the American's face how unwelcome it was. But Aziz reminded the colonel that he'd always asked Aziz to interpret not just language but the culture. To bring the bodies to the doctor's husband with an acknowledgment of the wrong that had been done wouldn't make the situation better, but it might save it from becoming worse.

Colonel Trotter balked at first, then did the right thing; he had Aziz call the husband. For Aziz the long silence over the phone line was like a punch beneath the ribs. Dr. Yasmeen's husband came to collect the bodies of his wife and son. Aziz told him what he knew. Her husband was, as Parveen would have expected, an educated and dignified man. He seemed in complete shock, not least when Lieutenant Colonel Francis Trotter, on behalf of the United States of America, apologized to him.

The next day, Aziz said, on the advice of the provincial governor, Colonel Trotter decided to provide the doctor's family with compensation: twenty-seven thousand dollars and three sheep. Aziz was sent to buy the sheep, which rankled him. He was from Kabul and knew nothing of livestock. The colonel was the one who'd grown up on a farm.

Two soldiers escorted Aziz to the bazaar. On the way, the trio passed a shepherd grazing his herd. Aziz stopped to ask whether there would be sheep at the district bazaar today and also what he should look for when buying them.

When the shepherd saw the soldiers, his eyes brightened— he imagined supplying a whole battalion with mutton and lamb. Upon learning that only three sheep were needed, he slumped a bit, then quickly revived and said that Aziz should take his.

"The best ones," Aziz replied.

"For the best price," the shepherd said. They both knew it would be exorbitant.

Aziz told the soldiers that this man was the seller of the best sheep in the province and that by buying the sheep now rather than at the bazaar, they would get a better price, even though he knew the soldiers didn't care about the price. They cared about finishing as quickly as possible. A month earlier and this might have been fun for them, larking about in the countryside, cracking sheep jokes. But the attacks on the road and at the checkpoint, where many of the soldiers believed they'd faced mortal danger, had played on their nerves. They wanted to get back on base. Although the shepherd's attire—his ragged clothes, his plastic slip-on shoes, his dirty *pakol*, the old blanket slung over his shoulder—was what most Afghan men wore, the soldiers eyed him with suspicion. But they agreed nonetheless.

Aziz inspected the small flock, shoving his hands into their dirt-brown fleeces to feel the muscle and fat beneath, peering into their ears, commanding the shepherd to show the teeth and lift the legs so he could look at the hooves. He realized he was performing for the soldiers, but he couldn't say why. They seemed amused by all this and by the haggling that commenced once he'd selected the three sheep.

When he finally told the soldiers the price, an amount that would feed the shepherd's family for three months, they laughed. They'd spent more on their Oakley sunglasses. The sheep were loaded into the M-ATV. They stank, as sheep do; one of them shat, which made the soldiers curse wildly.

That afternoon the sheep, along with the money and a more formal apology, were presented to the doctor's bereft family. Colonel Trotter didn't take Aziz along. Until then, he'd taken his interpreter everywhere.

Chapter Twenty-Six

Washing Blood with Blood

As she and Aziz spoke, Parveen glanced occasionally at Trotter, who was in a heated conversation with a captain and his intelligence officer next to the M-ATVs. His eyes roamed in agitation over the mountains and back toward the clinic, then he swiveled his head to study the bazaar and, presumably, the cropland and valley in the distance. His stare landed everywhere but on her, which only seemed to confirm the guilt she thought he should feel. It puzzled her, angered her, that even after having compensated the doctor's family, he was still seeking a way to clear his men.

"Elvis, where the fuck is everyone?" an approaching soldier called out. "Where are the villagers?"

It was Boone, the one who'd made the mistake of teasing her about her mother's wallpaper that day outside the khan's house. And with him was Reyes, the one who'd warned her—presciently, she saw now—that it would be hard to leave.

Her stomach plummeting, Parveen realized that not a single villager remained in the area. There was no one but her, Aziz, and the Americans.

Aziz noticed it too. "They've all gone home," he said with urgency. "Why are we still here? What are we waiting for?"

"To get the shit kicked out of us," Boone said.

His eyes, like Trotter's, were on the move, and now Parveen understood that it hadn't been evasion but vigilance that she'd observed in the colonel.

They were all stuck for the time being, Reyes explained. There'd been an attack at the turnoff from the highway, and they had to wait until it was cleared.

"We should've fucking flown," Boone said.

"The fog," Reyes reminded him.

"Fog, my ass," Boone said. "They want to show we still own the road. That we're the boss. All they're showing is that we're stupid."

"Doesn't take much to do that," Reyes said, and he suggested they go tell the captain that Elvis thought they were fucked. The two soldiers drifted back toward the M-ATVs, with Reyes softly rapping: "'N-now, th-that that don't kill me can only make me stronger.'" Boone came in louder, as if to scare off any threats: "'There's vomit on his sweater already, Mom's spaghetti. He's nervous, but on the surface he looks calm and ready...'"

"Mom's spaghetti" was still in Parveen's head when the first shots sounded. Although she'd grown used to seeing guns, she'd never heard actual gunfire and was slow to react. She was saved only by virtue of being next to the courtyard wall, which shielded her, and by Aziz slamming her to the ground, his body, armor and all, atop hers. She had the faint thought that he'd broken her ribs. They lay against the wall as the soldiers scrambled to figure out where their attackers were, then began to return fire, sending hundreds of rounds toward the clinic. It was from its roof, perhaps the one place Trotter might not have expected, that the ambush had been launched.

Latifa, Parveen thought in horror as bullets clattered against the building's walls and its windows shattered. Her newborn. She hoped that if they survived this initial onslaught, Latifa would have sense enough to get her baby and hide under the bed.

"We've got to move!" Aziz shouted in her ear. Bullets skipped through the dust near them and plinked off the wall above. "Follow me!"

He scrambled away on his belly but Parveen didn't. Couldn't. Instead, she stretched her body out against the wall, her face to it, and prayed that no bullet would find her. Her senses were charged but her muscles paralyzed. Then a cloud of yellow smoke obscured everything, and someone was tugging her by the back of her coat as though she were a sandbag. She closed her eyes and surrendered to being dragged, nearly serene except for the grit abrading her face and, despite her clothes, stripping her skin. When she opened her eyes, she was behind one of the M-ATVs. Aziz had pulled her to safety.

As if in the heightened colors and slowed time of a dream, Parveen saw that she was in a makeshift hospital, the patients laid out in the dust. To her left Charlie was tending to a soldier whose blood soaked his uniform and the ground beneath, resurrecting the specter of Latifa's skirt of blood as she'd hemorrhaged.

"I'm bleeding out, I'm dying, I'm dying," he cried. "Oh, fuck, I'm bleeding out."

"Shhh, stay calm, you'll be fine," Charlie said.

From her right Parveen heard "Morphine, morphine." Nausea buckled her knees when she turned toward the moaning to see a soldier missing a chunk of his face. "Morphine," he said again, as if trying to hold to life with the word. Parveen couldn't believe that he was still breathing, let alone speaking. She stared at him, at the pale eyes flapping open and closed like wings pumping in slow flight. It was Boone.

"The morphine's in, it'll kick in in a sec, squeeze my hand," Mandy urged him. "You're not going anywhere. Squeeze, damn it, squeeze!"

Inwardly, Parveen urged the same.

There was a scuffle of dust as another soldier scooted toward them. It was Reyes, clutching his bleeding arm. Mandy shouted that someone, anyone, should put a pressure dressing on the wound. But when another soldier tried, Reyes shouldered him off. "Boone, listen, it's me!" he said. "Listen, you've only got sixteen days on your fucking countdown, man. Sixteen days! Don't give up now. I should've told you the real reason not to count: it's bad luck, it's bad luck. Shit like this always happens near the end. But you're almost home—" Reyes was crying now, though, because he'd seen what Mandy had, which was the private's eyes rolling back in what remained of his face. "Fight, Boone, fight it," he said through gritted teeth, but Mandy, after putting a stethoscope on his chest and hearing nothing, was calling for a body bag, and now Reyes wept shamelessly. Mandy put a hand on his back and then, without him noticing, applied the pressure dressing to his arm.

Parveen was shaking. She'd witnessed her mother's death. She'd been holding her hand when it happened, but even though her breath had rattled a bit, that had been peaceful compared to this; it was as if her mother had walked across the line over which Boone had just been hurled.

Then, with a searing boom, an M-ATV not forty feet away burst into flames, the heat so strong it singed her eyebrows. There were screams; inside, a driver was burning alive. Around her, men shouted terms she couldn't understand—*Fucking indirect! Where the fuck is close air?*—as they tried to figure out the direction the RPG had come from. Gunners in the other M-ATVs launched grenades toward the hills as Trotter emerged suddenly from the smoke and pointed.

In the passing seconds, Parveen's thoughts slowed with painful clarity and remorse. Her every mistake loomed up before her, none more than ignoring her father's letter pleading with her to come home. Why hadn't she listened? She pictured him and Taara receiving news of her death, only a few years after her mother's. For that reason alone, she decided that she had to survive—she couldn't make them endure another loss. She wouldn't be passive anymore; she wouldn't yield.

Trotter was blitzing out instructions: "Make smoke! Head to the mosque!"

"Careful, careful" from Charlie to Mandy as they and two other soldiers prepared to ferry away the dead and the wounded.

Then again the billow of yellow smoke: another grenade. No longer able to see, Parveen stopped. Gunfire popped and voices sounded all around her. Someone was shouting her name.

"Aziz?" she called in reply.

"Which way is the mosque?" he said with a note of panic. "I'm turned around."

"Follow my voice," she told him, suddenly confident. She knew the terrain between the clinic and the mosque better than anyone around her. Faint images emerged through the smoke— other soldiers, but also the trunks of trees she recognized. Little by little, scraping along on their hands and knees, they made their way to the mosque.

In its courtyard she fought to catch her breath, her lungs burning in the thin mountain air. Perhaps afraid of offending, none of the soldiers went into the mosque itself. Instead, at least a dozen of them, including the medics with their dead and two wounded men, sheltered along with Parveen and Aziz in the small courtyard beneath the paltry wall. Parveen moved close to Aziz, having settled on him as her protector. Around her, smoke-reddened eyes peered out from grimy faces. Two soldiers on their bellies pointed their weapons out the courtyard open-ing, ready to blast anyone who approached. Others aimed over the low wall or tried to force holes into its chinks, the mosque now a makeshift fort. Speech compressed to murmured orders and curses.

Then, in the distance, rotor blades beat the air, and the soldiers gave half smiles and quiet fist pumps. Soon two helicopters— smaller, darker, meaner than the kind that used to ferry the doctor and her son to the village—swung into view.

"Hellfire that fucking clinic," a soldier muttered.

Remembering Latifa, Parveen shouted, "No!" and crawled a short distance to Trotter, who was crouched in a corner next to the radio operator. She told him a woman and her newborn were in the clinic. "If you hit the clinic, you'll kill them," she said. "You can't just keep killing innocent—"

Trotter cut her off with a glare as if he wished the Apaches could take her out instead. It seemed as if he thought forever, though it couldn't have been more than a few seconds. "No clinic," he said to his radio operator, who, after a pause, transmitted the order, and a chorus of *Fucks* broke out around them.

Then gunshots burst from the mosque right behind them and everyone dropped back to the ground and Trotter's men unleashed a torrent of bullets on the structure. Aziz again grabbed Parveen's hand, and on their bellies they shimmied across the dust of the courtyard; after reaching the gate, they ran hunched over to the bazaar, twenty yards away, where they hid in the first stall they came to, the tailor's. Gunfire crackled like burning wood, the rare pauses sodden with tension. Parveen, high on having survived the fiercest part of the danger, unexpectedly laughed, and Aziz silenced her with a look.

Then a skinny young insurgent with an unkempt beard who was bearing an AK-47 dashed into the blacksmith's stall. Aziz, in his uniform, had no weapon. The two men stared at each other in surprise.

"The Apaches, they'll come here," Aziz said in Dari. "We need to run."

And in almost slapstick fashion, the three of them took off all at once, the insurgent going in one direction, Aziz and Parveen in another. They sprinted down the path to the fields, then crawled across them, raked by thistles, harrowed by insects. Brittle stalks crunched beneath their weight and stabbed at their legs. Dirt and dried wheat tickled Parveen's nose until she sneezed.

At last they reached a row of poplar trees, their remaining leaves blazing yellow, and took shelter. They sat next to each other, their backs against a thin trunk, legs stretched out. Parveen, drenched in sweat, began to shiver in the cold. Her ankle, which she'd twisted, was throbbing. Her ribs ached. Her throat burned with smoke. She stared at the silver-white tree trunk next to her, its markings like watchful eyes.

In the distance, back up the path, the Apaches hovered above the village. One of them fired into the bazaar again and again, blast after blast, smoke rising in answer. The noise rang down the valley, shattering its stillness. The other helicopter chased insurgents trying to flee. Aziz and Parveen clutched each other's hands, not speaking, as the men gunned down in the fields toppled and fell. Soon there was no more movement on the ground.

Parveen cleared her throat, trying to see if she still had a voice.

"You're okay?" he asked.

"Scared."

"Me too."

For a long time they sat without talking.

"This is okay?" Aziz said, then squeezed her hand, which was still clasped in his.

"It's okay," she said.

Parveen didn't know how much time was passing. The only units of measure were events, which came irregularly. The Apaches, after circling for a while and firing a few more shots into the bazaar, flew off, though they remained tattooed in her mind's eye.

They began to speak in broken streams, pausing often to listen for footsteps or voices, though they heard nothing.

"I always felt sorry for Boone," Aziz said. "He seemed to forever be saying the wrong thing. But he was so young—maybe he would've outgrown it." Given Boone's mouth, Reyes was constantly having to keep him out of trouble, to save him from himself. And from Kirby! Anyway, Aziz said, Reyes was like a big brother to Boone, always looking out for him, so Boone's death would hit him like a brother's. Reyes would feel responsible for failing to protect his friend. "I've seen this a lot," Aziz said. "The ones who survive feel like they should've been killed instead."

Parveen thought about the letter Trotter would write to Boone's family. No doubt it would play up his heroism, the sacrifice he'd made for his country. But in its own way, it would be as fictive as anything Gideon Crane had written. Absent would be Boone's goofiness and crude jokes; absent would be the absurdity of his death, struck down as he loped along exchanging raps with his friend. The letter wouldn't say that Boone had been scared just before he died, that he'd sensed something was coming. The truth about a death in a faraway war was both sacred and secret, Parveen thought. So many witnesses—commanders, fellow soldiers, innumerable Afghans—carried this kind of knowledge, yet they kept it to themselves. As, most likely, would Parveen.

"What'd they die for?" she asked Aziz. Regardless of what Trotter might tell the men's families, she said, it was hard to see the through line from dying in this village to protecting America. So had they died to protect Afghanistan?

Aziz made a sound of understanding and said, "That's the question, isn't it. I know I wouldn't want to die for someone else's country. If I'm honest I don't even want to die for mine. I'm not brave." And yet, until the Americans showed up here, there had been nothing to defend. Aziz knew this as well as anyone else. "Will you leave this place now?" he asked.

The question surprised her. She wouldn't, she told him.

"That's because you can," he said, and he withdrew his hand from hers to scratch his face. Her own hand felt naked now.

She didn't understand and told him so.

"You don't think about leaving because you know you can go whenever you want. I have no way to go, and so I think about leaving—this job, my country—all the time!" He said it lightly, as if it were an amusing paradox, but his face in profile was grave.

Parveen swallowed. Why couldn't he go? she said.

There was no way out, he said. It wasn't easy for an Afghan to get a visa to anywhere, not even to America, despite working, as he had for so many years, for the Americans. There were now "special immigrant" visas for those who were in danger from their employment with the Americans, but only fifteen hundred a year were issued, and you needed your superior to testify to your "faithful and valuable service" to the U.S. government. He wasn't sure Colonel Trotter would do this. The colonel had been angry that Aziz had let him think everything in Crane's book was true—Amanullah's dastardly history, even the story of Fereshta's death—and Aziz had been forced to confess that he hadn't read it. This had diminished the colonel's trust in him. This, then, was the trouble Aziz had been in.

Then, more recently, he'd challenged Colonel Trotter about the doctor's death and how he was handling it. It was the first time he hadn't told the colonel what he wanted to hear. So in his way Aziz *had* been brave, Parveen thought; he'd stood up to Trotter even knowing what it might cost him.

Aziz asked if she'd heard on the radio about the air strike in Kunduz. She had. And had she also heard about the reporter who had gone to investigate and been kidnapped by the Taliban?

Yes, she said, but the news was that the reporter had been rescued.

He was rescued, Aziz confirmed, by the British army, because he had a British passport. But the interpreter with him, a man who was said to have the purest character but who also had only an Afghan passport, was shot and killed during the rescue, then his body left behind, as if he wasn't deserving of, wasn't in need of, a proper burial. Local villagers had recovered the corpse and made sure it was returned to the family.

It was partly because of this story, Aziz said, that he'd argued so fiercely with Colonel Trotter after the doctor's death. At that point, of course, nothing could be done to save Dr. Yasmeen and

Naseer, but even in death they deserved to be treated as humans, no less than any American. During the firefight in the village, it was this interpreter Aziz had thought of—that and whether Parveen was safe.

She reached for his hand again and muscled her fingers through his. Adrift, they needed to hold tight.

If you asked Colonel Trotter, Aziz continued, he wouldn't say he valued an Afghan life any less than an American one. But of course he had to value American lives more, just as the soldiers believed they were justified in shooting at Dr. Yasmeen's car to save themselves. It was the nature of war. Of nations. Of an occupation. "If I was shot, would anyone remember me?" he said. "Or would they leave me behind?" That was his fear: that when things became difficult, even though there were soldiers in this battalion who'd called him their brother, his life would matter less than theirs.

"But Trotter said the day I met you that you'd done more deployments than any of his soldiers. That you should have combat stripes. He appreciates what you've done."

"You're American, they'd save you" was all Aziz said, and Parveen could think of no reply. She didn't want the passport she held to make her worthier of living.

AFTER A TIME ANOTHER helicopter made landfall far off, in the khan's field.

"Medevac," Aziz said.

They rose from their tree and moved toward the helicopter. American soldiers had debarked and were running with stretchers toward the bazaar and the mosque. They returned with the wounded and also two body bags, black and anonymous, the purgatory preceding the flag-draped coffins in which Boone and the dead M-ATV driver would return home. The bags had handles for carrying, and Parveen couldn't get past the thoughtfulness, as she acidly phrased it to herself, of the design, couldn't get past the objects themselves, because it allowed her to avoid thinking about what they contained. War's signal achievement, it struck her, was to strip the significance from individual deaths, to make them just numbers. These soldiers, like the doctor and her son, were motes of dust that would vanish when the light shifted.

Except in the eyes of their intimates. Dr. Yasmeen and Naseer would never disappear from their family's consciousness or Boone from that of his friends. Weak from loss of blood, the bullet still in his bandaged arm, Reyes nonetheless insisted on walking next to Boone's body. Kirby and Vance were there with him, impromptu pallbearers all, yet with nothing to carry. Their eyes were vacant with grief, and Parveen grasped how much affection their roughness with one another had camouflaged.

The copter was loaded with its human cargo, living and dead, and after a few shouts, unintelligible beneath the rotor's noise, it lifted off. Charlie was on board with the wounded, who included Reyes, and also the soldier who'd believed himself to be bleeding out, to be dying. He was, almost unfathomably to Parveen, alive. The medics so far had saved him.

Mandy stayed behind to help any villagers who might have been hurt, although everyone knew there were none. Noticing Parveen's limp, she offered to take a look at her ankle, and, after pressing and twisting it enough to make Parveen wince in pain, she said it was only a sprain and that she should elevate and ice it. Parveen, while appreciative, also wanted to punch her; where did Mandy imagine that she would get ice?

Trotter had already given orders to construct a combat outpost in the village. The war had come to stay. Even now, Parveen could picture his first, jolly approach across the fields, waving hello to Waheed. His optimism, his faith in his own intentions, had run up so quickly against the elders' resistance. She wondered if they'd seen this coming—if when they said they didn't want the road paved, they'd meant they didn't want the war, knowing it would follow the Americans here. Waheed had said once, when Parveen asked how the village had changed since Crane, "Before any Americans came here, we were nothing. This village mattered to no one."

Within the hour, a Chinook landed in the khan's field, and a batch of fresh soldiers, charged with adrenaline, boiled out the back. The grim survivors of battle filed in. They'd been victorious, yet they dragged with defeat. What was winning when two of their brothers had been lost and all the obliteration a superpower could summon would never resurrect them? The bravado with which the firefight would likely be described didn't match the ashen, beleaguered faces of the soldiers who'd fought it.

Trotter's face was caked with black soot and white dust except for where runnels of sweat exposed red skin. He was more like Waheed than she'd realized—responsible, like a father, for keeping all his charges alive. In war, as in poverty, the odds were long. As the medevac took off, mourning contorted Trotter's face. But within moments that expression had been replaced by something more chiseled. He still had a war to fight, and the mortal losses seemed to have redoubled his determination to win it.

"I'm sorry," Parveen said. "I'd talked with Boone—he seemed like a great kid." That word sounded funny; he couldn't have been more than a couple of years younger than she was. "Person," she amended.

"He was," Trotter said. "Nicholson too. Fine boys, both." He paused, then said, "We drove right into their trap." Without looking at her, he asked, "Would you still say the people here haven't chosen a side?" He already had his answer. Even with the battle over, not a single villager was in sight.

"They've chosen survival," she said, a lump in her throat, but he was walking away, marching along the fields toward the bazaar with Aziz and newly arrived soldiers, skittish and green, at his side.

When the colonel was called to the dead bodies in the fields, Parveen limped behind. The insurgents' remains were gruesome, pulverized by the Apaches' giant bullets and caked with blood. At Trotter's instruction, their eyelids were closed.

Parveen gagged and wondered whether the young man who'd come into the stall was tailor's in the ranks of the corpses. She caught Aziz's eye, and as if reading her thoughts, he gave a subtle shake. No, that one wasn't here. Aziz, in seeking to drive him out, had likely saved him.

They walked up from the fields to the bazaar. Holes as big as heads perforated the walls and roofs of any stalls still standing. The rest were in cindery chunks, amid which she spotted a few more bodies draped at odd angles. The world she'd come to know, the one she'd imagined to be mapped within her, was gone. Only rubble remained.

"The shops," she said, distressed.

They'll rebuild, Trotter replied. Afghans were resilient, and it wasn't exactly complex architecture. Maybe it would serve as a reminder that there was nothing to be gained from sheltering the enemy. Sometimes you had to attempt progress to find out who was in opposition to it. "We didn't ask for this fight," he said. "We came to build a road. And we didn't fire the first shot, but you can be sure we'll fire the last."

Platitudes had a certain altitude, Parveen thought, which could be seductive when things got bad. Kevlar talk, she would come to call this—language that sounded as though it had been issued just like the uniforms and body armor had, language that protected you against the existential questions. Against doubt. Even Trotter the philosopher, Trotter the classics expert, was not immune to it.

The clinic—that white glowing building—had always looked, in this earth-toned landscape, like a pill slipped from God's pocket. Now bullet holes pocked the walls broken windows gaped, and the courtyard glittered with shattered glass. Trotter said they would get the engineers in to look at starting repairs, and it angered Parveen that he would think Crane's white elephant worthier of fixing than the villagers' shops.

After telling the colonel that she wanted to check on Latifa, Parveen picked her way across the shards. She went inside and upstairs to Latifa's bed. Which was empty. Parveen stared and stared. Of course—she was hiding, Parveen thought. She would've been terrified when the firing started from the roof. Parveen looked under the beds, in closets and corners, in every room. No Latifa. Worse, the incubator was empty too. Both gone. How? Had the insurgents dragged her off? Had she run?

Parveen couldn't think clearly, and when she went outside she told Trotter that Latifa was fine. Shaken, but fine. She lied by instinct, nothing more, a sense that she should find Latifa herself and that Trotter's help would only complicate things.

"Well, that's good news, isn't it?" he asked, and she realized that her tone had suggested otherwise, and also that Trotter expected gratitude for exercising the restraint she'd demanded. "It's great," she said. "Thank you."

The colonel asked if Latifa had seen the insurgents or knew anything about how or when they'd gotten up to the roof.

"She was asleep when it started. She didn't see anything."

Trotter seemed to accept this. But Parveen couldn't stop puzzling over where Latifa might be. She was so preoccupied that she didn't hear Trotter telling her she should go pack up until he repeated it. "You've got a spot on the next helicopter out of here," he said.

"But I'm not leaving," she said. "I can't."

She couldn't leave without finding Latifa. But also, here was Trotter confirming exactly what Aziz had said and what she was sure the villagers thought, which was that as an American, with an American's privileges, she could end her sojourn and call for rescue whenever danger threatened. Part of her wanted to be rescued, wanted to fly with Aziz away from the danger and chaos of the village into a hazy romantic future. But the paradox was that doing so would prove him right, and he would think less of her. And part of her disdained the idea of rescue altogether; she was stubborn that way. She wasn't some damsel in distress who needed Trotter to ride in on his M-ATV to save her. Besides, the doctor's death had made Parveen newly essential. She couldn't abandon the women to the hands of the dai; Dr. Yasmeen wouldn't want that.

It was true that during the battle she'd been determined to get home to her father, her sister, her nephew. But surviving had given her a sense of immortality, accompanied by an adrenaline rush that, as it wore off, had her craving more. This was what the soldiers she'd talked to that day outside the khan's—one of whom was now dead and another wounded—had been trying to tell her. That she would miss this. That there was no rush to get to whatever life awaited her in California.

She wasn't leaving, she told Trotter again. The villagers needed her.

His mouth thinned to a grim line. He couldn't make her go, he said, but he could see where her staying would lead. She'd get in a jam and they'd have to come back for her at a high cost to taxpayers and at great risk to his troops. "You're going to put lives in danger if you stay, Parveen. You think you're doing good, but this is selfish."

His words cut deep enough to make her reconsider, but she held firm. "The women here don't have a doctor anymore," she said, trying to inflict pain on him in return. "I'm all they've got."

She accompanied Trotter and Aziz back to the khan's field, where they would get on the waiting Chinook.

"Last chance," Trotter said.

She shook her head. Her ankle throbbed.

Before he boarded, he told her that if she needed him, she should get the word *Berkeley* to his men. Say it, write it, sing it, whatever she had to do, and his men would get it to him.

Parveen knew he was just doing his job; he was nothing if not professional. But she was grateful nonetheless.

Then he turned his attention elsewhere, which gave her a few furtive moments with Aziz. "Come with us," he whispered in Dari. "You're not safe here."

His words nearly convinced her. But pride, stupid pride—imagining Trotter's satisfaction when she climbed on board—held her back.

Aziz hastily touched her fingers, urged her to be careful, and said that he would pray for her.

PARVEEN LIMPED TO WAHEED's, then collapsed in her room as soon as she reached it. The children crowded in, both relieved and delighted to see her. "We thought you were dead," Hamdiya said. The force of their hugs affirmed her decision to stay.

They fetched Bina, who examined Parveen's bulbous ankle with the same combination of gentleness and detachment she used on her beloved cows. The queen of remedies had one for Parveen too—she left and returned with a chopped onion contained in a soft cloth, which she placed on Parveen's ankle.

Parveen asked, as Bina adjusted the poultice, if she knew that the doctor was dead.

Yes, Bina said, showing little emotion. Death was not a novelty for her. She merely posed a few factual questions that Parveen couldn't answer: Who had washed the body for burial? Where was the car?

"There's something else," Parveen said, and she told Bina that Latifa was not in the clinic.

"Yes," Bina answered without surprise. Her eyes, when she lifted them to Parveen's, were calm.

How was that possible? Parveen asked.

"We have been good to you, yes, Parveen-jan?" Bina whispered. "Very good."

"Then be good to us."

"I—of course." Parveen waited for more.

"Jamshid is his father's eldest. Help keep him safe."

"What would make him unsafe?"

Bina took the poultice off the ankle, opened it, shook up the onions, rewrapped them, and placed the poultice exactly as it had been.

"His new friends," Parveen guessed.

The barest flicker of a nod.

"He helped them get onto the clinic roof."

Silence.

"Did he take Latifa out?"

"He protected her," Bina said. "She is home, she and the baby both."

Parveen instinctively removed her ankle from Bina's touch. Her face burned, and her ears buzzed. Jamshid had saved Latifa, but he hadn't tried to protect Parveen, with whom he'd shared a house all these months, by whom he'd been taught. Nor had the other villagers. They'd called their children from the clinic courtyard and left Parveen out there exposed. Of all people, only the dai had suggested that she go home.

"So Jamshid knew it was going to happen," she said finally. "Did you, Bina?"

When there was no answer, for the first time Parveen thought to be as afraid as Trotter wanted her to be. They didn't see her as one of them. She wasn't one of them. If they'd told her, she would have warned Trotter—what other choice would there be? She couldn't have allowed anyone to walk into an ambush. But if she confirmed the colonel's suspicion that the villagers had known the attack was coming and that perhaps some had facilitated it, he would come down on them all indiscriminately.

CHAPTER TWENTY-SEVEN

BETWEEN THE FAR SKY
AND HARD EARTH

IT WAS THE IMAGE OF JAMSHID AND HIS FRIENDS WATCHING EX-
pressionless as she wept over the doctor's killing that Parveen
couldn't shake. The lack of surprise on his face. He'd already
known that Dr. Yasmeen and Naseer were dead. She hazarded
that he'd found out about the killing a day or two before the rest
of the family, the news traveling faster in whispered messages
over mountain passes among the insurgents than it did along
the road. As she and Bina and the others speculated about the
doctor's whereabouts, as they joked about the BBC report and
the warrior Malalai, he must have been seething inside.

When word came that the Americans were on their way to the
village, the insurgents, aware that Waheed controlled the clinic,
sought access to it through his oldest child. From its roof, they
would hold the high ground. They knew the fog as sailors knew
tides; they knew how much time it gave them, how much cover.
Jamshid provided the keys and asked the women to evacuate
Latifa. When Parveen went out to talk with Trotter, mother and
baby were hurried out, probably through the back entrance.

But this was just a theory, one she didn't know how to test with
Jamshid. He wanted to talk only about the Americans, to hear

how they explained the deaths of Dr. Yasmeen and Naseer. He was so insistent that she saw no choice but to share what she'd learned. Waheed, within earshot, said little, but he didn't object to his son's questions.

"So any of us could be killed," Jamshid said hotly, "if we don't follow the Americans' orders. If we drive too fast or too slow. If we don't hear them or we hear them and choose not to listen. If we're in the wrong place." For any of these things, he repeated, they could be killed. But it was their land. How could there be such a thing as a wrong place? If there could be, then they had no freedom in their own country.

In that statement was a history every Afghan knew—a history of imperial armies that had attempted to conquer and subdue Afghanistan. The British. The Soviets. And now the Americans. As Jamshid saw it, the elders and his father had been right to oppose the road: "The Americans came here saying they could solve our problems," he said, "but they only grow them."

The same could be said of the insurgents, Parveen thought, but not in Jamshid's mind. He had chosen a side, and she wasn't sure whether to blame him. She supposed she couldn't even say definitively that he'd chosen; it was possible he'd been coerced. Threatened. Yet somehow, she didn't think so.

Young people, it occurred to her, were like foreigners in their own culture: they could see clearly what the natives—the adults—no longer did. Jamshid understood that there was no such thing as a benevolent occupation. In other contexts, Parveen had known this too. She'd been raised, for instance, to sympathize with Palestinian kids throwing stones at the Israeli defense forces. How else were they to resist? Against power, there was only canniness, deception, or symbolism—the fly razzing the beast, maybe even driving it mad. Unlike adults, young people didn't build hedges out of reasons *not* to act. Not so very long ago Parveen had been consumed by that same passion, that same impulsiveness. It had brought her here.

She was as angry about the doctor's death as Jamshid was, yet she felt obliged to temper his wrath, to push him to see the other side. The Americans were acting this way because they were frightened, she said. Because they were being attacked just for trying to build a road. They'd made an awful mistake.

Then, unable to help herself, when Waheed went to the outhouse she asked Jamshid directly if he'd let the insurgents into the clinic.

"'If the mullah invites himself to dinner, you must accept,'" he replied.

SHE HAD TO LEAVE, this much was clear now, but she'd turned down Trotter's offer. And she was stuck not just in the village but in the house, where Waheed, for her safety, insisted that she remain. This precluded her from visiting Latifa and learning who'd smuggled her and the baby out of the clinic.

Mother and child were fine, Waheed would say whenever she expressed concern. She'd refrained, for reasons she didn't entirely understand, from telling him what she knew, what she suspected, about Jamshid. It seemed better, safer, to leave it unspoken.

In a way her confinement was a relief. Paralysis had set in, leaving her uncertain what course to take. She understood now that there was no such thing as an innocuous interaction with the villagers; there were always repercussions, always collateral damage, for others. The freedom in being an American that she'd boasted of early on—carnage could come from it too.

The only mention of the battle on the BBC was a report that two American soldiers had been killed and two wounded in a firefight in the district—nothing about the circumstances surrounding the casualties, nothing about the clinic's destruction. Nothing that would tell anyone that this battle had taken place in Fereshta's village. The world knew whatever the Americans decided should be known.

Waheed left the compound only when necessary. He took to fetching water himself, not wanting his wives or his children to walk down to the river. Every other man did the same. The bazaar was closed, as was the mosque, which had also been strafed by the Apaches. The village was eerily empty, while the skies, through which American planes, helicopters, and drones regularly crossed, were full. In the distance the occasional explosion sounded. One day Jamshid reported, flatly, that the meadow was gone. Via one of their drones or planes, the Americans had seen a group of men there—goatherds, insurgents, who could ever say?—and dropped a bomb.

Days, then a week, passed this way. Sometimes, in the very early morning, Parveen would climb to the roof to survey the valley. Condensation hung above the river, as if the water had reconstituted itself more ethereally. The last blazes of yellow and orange had dampened, leaving a palette of rust and lead, and in the diminishing sunlight, the snow on the mountain peaks glittered. The first frost was close.

The Americans had set up their combat outpost high above where the road came into the village. They chopped down trees that obscured their sight lines; they dug up earth to fill their sandbags. In metal barrels brought specially for the purpose, they burned their waste. The COP, as it was known, was named for Private Boone, while the road would be named for the dead driver whose last act had been to navigate it, just as roads, radio stations, and bases all over the country had been named for dead Americans, their history superimposed on the Afghans'.

During the days, the soldiers patrolled the village and the mountains overhead, keeping a vigilant watch for any sign of insurgents. At the COP they worked out with pulleys and weights. Parveen thought, sometimes, about walking up to the outpost and asking to be taken home. But she remembered the doctor and Trotter's description of his troops' heightened state of anxiety. It was safer to stay away.

When dark came—incrementally earlier each day—the family crept to bed. Waheed hadn't turned the generator on since the battle. He was running low on fuel, and as Issa had made clear, no more would come. Besides, light would only draw unwanted attention—from the insurgents hiding in the hills or from the Americans overhead or from rivals like the mullah and the khan, who might use the conflict to expunge the source of their envy. It was not a good time to think yourself better than, or to be better off than, anyone else in the village. Waheed was sinking back to the position he'd occupied before Crane entered his life. He had as much control over this as he did over the passing clouds. Even so, his equanimity in the face of his diminishing status was striking; it was almost as if he'd always known he was merely on vacation in the guise of an important man, and now the trip was over.

SHOKOH HAD BEGUN TO sob, as a child might, when she learned that Dr. Yasmeen and Naseer were dead, and for several days she barely stopped. Her eyes swelled shut, her voice grew hoarse. The family went about its business until Bina made clear she would tolerate no more. Then Shokoh grew sullen and dull, devoting her free time to dozing or lying next to the woodstove and staring blankly into space. The flush of energy, of hopefulness, that had bloomed with her pregnancy was gone. She no longer talked of the road and where it might take her. Her devastation began to seem out of all proportion to her relationship to the dead; it was as if she had been the doctor's own daughter or Naseer's betrothed. Parveen's efforts to talk to her about it were fruitless. Shokoh couldn't explain it, Parveen suspected, even to herself. When she spoke, it was to complain—her head hurt, she couldn't see well, she couldn't pee, she was nauseated. It was as if having no doctor to treat her had made her aware of all the ways a body could fail. When Parveen tried to get her to write about her grief, Shokoh turned on her. "You just want poems to put in a book."

But Shokoh's lack of luster didn't exempt her from her domestic duties. Bina told Parveen several times that she herself had worked up until and even after her labors began. She expected the same of Shokoh. Parveen once would have said this was cruel, but her sympathies kept tilting back and forth, never finding the perfect place to rest. In Parveen's time in the village, Bina had never gotten sick or even pretended to be sick, which Parveen would have done in her shoes, just to get a few hours off. Seen through Bina's eyes, Shokoh was lazy and entitled, someone who wrapped herself in drama as armor against obligation. But then, as Shokoh groaned to her swollen feet—the same feet and ankles that had once been so delicate—and eased herself down the stairs to milk the cows, Parveen would repent of her own assessment. She wasn't the only one who noticed Shokoh's discomfort. More than once, Jamshid emerged from the house just in time to relieve her of the milk bucket and carry it to the kitchen.

One late afternoon, Zahab ran upstairs shouting that something was wrong with Shokoh. Parveen found her outside, bent over, collared by golden light, shaking and foaming at the mouth. A cow with innocent eyes and impatient legs stood a few feet away. The bucket lay nearby on its side, the milk soaking the dirt. Rather than tend to the girl, Bina picked up the bucket. Was this simply an instinct for survival so muscled that it looked like callousness? Or did Bina think Shokoh was shirking?

Then Shokoh collapsed to the ground, her breathing rapid, her eyes closed. Parveen and Bina both knelt over her, calling her name, pressing her hands, lifting her eyelids. After a minute or so she came to and asked if the cow had kicked her. They didn't know. They helped her into Parveen's room to rest. She slept fitfully until dinnertime.

That night Parveen begged Bina to let her assume all of Shokoh's chores. "We both know I can milk as well as she can."

Bina laughed, knowing this was more of a dig at Shokoh than a boast by Parveen, who had, it was true, tried milking a few times over the summer. She found she enjoyed it, enjoyed connecting to the world through not just her brain but her hands—the soft hide, the rubbery udders, the spurt of warm milk. She couldn't say she was adept, and Bina definitely wouldn't say that, but she agreed that Parveen wouldn't be any more useless than Shokoh, especially in Shokoh's current state.

As they worked together the following morning—baking, milking—Bina talked. She told stories of the animals her family had kept in her childhood, of the games she'd played with her siblings and friends. She described Fereshta's wedding to Waheed, remembering how the impish expression of the young boy who'd played the harmonium in the women's area had made all of them laugh, and the girl cousin with whom Bina had climbed a tree to spy on the men, who were dancing and playing cards. Fereshta had cried when she left home with Waheed, just as Bina herself would cry many years later. Some of her own tears, Bina admitted shyly, had been because she had always believed she would marry a cousin with whom she'd played those same childhood games. Instead, just like she'd always been given her elder sisters' old dresses, she'd been given her sister's old husband too.

Her journey to Waheed's, on the back of a borrowed donkey, was the first time she'd left her village. They climbed high in the mountains. At the top of the pass, before descending to the next valley, she turned back to look at what she was leaving behind. "I saw it whole," she said, then cupped her hands. "I saw it small."

The journey took two days, and that whole time there was little conversation between the two other than Waheed asking if she was thirsty or hungry. Her first days in his house were trying—so much to learn, to do. She'd inherited six children, but as the youngest in her own family, she'd had very little experience caring for any child, let alone six at once! When she kept mixing up the twins, they told her their mother had never done that. Only God had given her the strength to go on, Bina insisted, although Parveen urged her to give herself more credit. The first time Bina lay with Waheed, which was the first time she had lain with anyone, she cried. She didn't want her sister to be forgotten, and yet she also worried that Waheed was thinking about Fereshta rather than her. The sex itself was painful too, and for her this never changed. In that sense Shokoh's arrival had been a relief but in no other, for Bina had come to care for Waheed and believed he cared for her too, which was why his marrying Shokoh had so destroyed her. But what could she do? she said. Where could she go? This was her life. She had to make peace with it. And now she met Parveen's eyes directly. "This is my home," she said. "This is my family. I will do everything I can to protect them."

Which was when Parveen realized that Bina's sudden openness with her had a point, all of this meandering talk a destination: it was her way of warning Parveen that her presence here was endangering what Bina had inherited, what she had made.

"Waheed will never ask you to leave," she said. Parveen was his guest; his honor demanded that he protect her. His hospitality would hold. The question was whether Parveen, in choosing to stay, was abusing it.

THE THREAT CAME A couple of nights later, when Bilal found a letter near the door of the compound. *American, go home or the family will pay*, it said in Dari. And yet, reading it, Parveen felt strangely calm. She fingered the paper, its size and lines clearly matching her own notebook from which, she deduced, it had been torn. She traced the handwriting, which she also recognized, because it was she who'd taught Jamshid to write some of these very words: *American, home, family*.

Had she become the enemy to him? Or was this an act of protection? Perhaps he was trying to warn her, as Bina had, telling her that she was putting the family in danger or that she herself was in danger. A foreboding squeezed her lungs. Jamshid was no longer under Waheed's control. Parveen didn't know what he would do if the insurgents demanded that the family turn her over to them. Perhaps they were already making this demand.

If Waheed knew that Jamshid had written the letter, he didn't say. He did say that, for Parveen's safety, she should start sleeping with the children upstairs. Where once she'd disdained the idea of sharing that crowded room, now there was nowhere else that she wanted to be. But she didn't sleep much. By the single lantern left burning, she tried to memorize faces that looked like masks in the glow, the funky smell of so many bodies pressed together, the soundtrack of their sleeping—sighs, snores, the occasional sharp cry. The warmth.

For his part, Jamshid seemed almost monk-like, alone with his thoughts in the bustle of the house. He ate little and dropped weight, his cheekbones protruding, his eye sockets deepening. Parveen wondered if he was squirreling food away for the insurgents or preparing to go into the mountains himself. Then again, the whole family was eating less. Winter was essentially at hand, the temperatures in the thirties. And Waheed, not immune from the insurgents' demands himself, had turned over a goat, he told Parveen after the fact.

One night as they ate chicken—an old rooster that Bina had killed and cooked only because if they waited any longer he'd be too tough to eat—Jamshid emerged from his brooding to hold up a bone and ask Parveen if she knew what Mullah Omar, the founder of the Taliban, had said about Osama bin Laden.

"Jamshid," Waheed said firmly.

Parveen waited without reply.

Jamshid, undeterred, continued. "Mullah Omar said, 'He's

like a bone stuck in my throat. I can't swallow it, nor can I spit it out.'"

He was talking about her, Parveen knew. "I guess the Americans got him out," she whispered. "They got the bone out." For although the military hadn't yet caught bin Laden, they'd driven him from Afghanistan.

"They removed the throat as well," Waheed observed, because Mullah Omar, too, had been forced out of the country.

Jamshid put the bone in his mouth and coughed, pretending to choke.

SHOKOH HAD A SECOND seizure early one morning. Parveen, called by Waheed, found her foaming at the mouth as her muscles convulsed. It lasted less than a minute, yet it felt like forever. When Shokoh came to, she had no memory of what had transpired. Sitting at Shokoh's side as she shifted futilely in search of comfort, Parveen feared the girl might die. She racked her brain for the possible cause of Shokoh's fits. Her best guess, based on the informal tutelage of Dr. Yasmeen, was eclampsia. It would explain the symptoms whose danger Parveen had overlooked: the bloating, the difficulty urinating, the headaches, all of which could be caused by excessively high blood pressure. Parveen squeezed her eyes shut and tried to conjure the doctor, her full, smiling face, her smooth skin, and for a few moments it was as if she heard the doctor talking to her about the woman the mullah had choked because of her seizures—seizures caused by eclampsia. She remembered Dr. Yasmeen saying that maybe she should've given the woman magnesium sulfate or tried to induce labor.

Parveen asked Waheed to take her to the clinic to look for magnesium sulfate. They walked slowly so as not to alarm the Americans in their nearby COP. Parveen didn't know any of the soldiers, who were new, and she called out to them that she was just looking for medicine.

In the clinic, her feet crunched over bullets and shards of glass. She found magnesium sulfate but put it back when she realized it had to be given intravenously; she wasn't about to try sticking a needle in Shokoh. Nor did she have a way to make a baby come if it wasn't ready. Maybe the dai had a potion—an herb culled from the hills, a root yanked from a mountain crevice— that could draw a baby out of a girl, but Parveen doubted it. And even if she did, then what? Parveen remembered Shokoh's slim figure in the examining room and the doctor's words about the risks that delivery posed for a girl whose pelvis wasn't yet fully formed. She'd been lucky enough to save Latifa. She didn't think she'd be able, on her own, to save Shokoh too.

The next day, when Bina rose at dawn to start her day's work, Parveen followed her to the kitchen. Bina lit the oven and began to make the bread. She nodded, as if she'd been expecting Parveen, and silently passed her some dough to knead.

"Shokoh has to leave the village," Parveen said. "She needs a doctor."

"It will pass, she'll be fine," Bina said, her old sharpness back.

"But if it doesn't? It'll be too late to get help."

"So? What choice do we have?" The veins popped on the back of her hands as she kneaded the dough. She had the strongest hands of any woman Parveen had ever known.

"I want to take her out of the village."

The hands froze. "And how would you do that?"

"I'll ask the Americans to take us." Parveen paused. "Both of us." The idea had come to her in the night; there was a way to save Shokoh that, as it happened, could also save Parveen. Shokoh would be Parveen's donkey, and Parveen hers. "I'll say she needs to be rescued. That if she isn't, she might die."

"Both of you," Bina repeated.

"I couldn't send her alone."

The truth, of course, was that Trotter wouldn't come for Shokoh alone. But as Aziz had reminded Parveen, as Trotter himself had reminded her, if an American needed help, the colonel would send it. When he did, Parveen would insist that they take both her and Shokoh. She was trying to avoid admitting, even to herself, that Trotter had been right in his final speech to her.

The hands unfroze and began to knead again, forcefully now, as if punishing the dough. Parveen would always carry with her the image of Bina poring over the photographs in Crane's book, her finger on each one as if to pin it in place. These glimpses of a world she would never see or know.

"You think I can't take care of her," Bina said. "Or that I won't."

"No!" Parveen was taken aback. "No, that's not it at all. She needs a hospital—she's in real danger. And you need to take care of Latifa." Parveen had a flash of insight just then, and of regret. It was Bina, not Parveen, whom Dr. Yasmeen should've been training. Was there still time? Before Parveen left, she would teach Bina what she could. How she'd stopped Latifa's bleeding. How to use the suction cups. When to challenge the dai and when to help her. It would place yet another burden on Bina, but Parveen understood her better now. For Bina, being of use gave meaning to a life in which she otherwise had little say.

Bina asked if Waheed knew what Parveen was planning to do. Not yet, Parveen said; she'd wanted to tell Bina first. For this, she got a quarter-smile.

SHE'D EXPECTED WAHEED TO protest. Instead, when she told him that she wanted to contact the Americans for help, he asked if they would bring a doctor or take Shokoh to a hospital, and if they took her, whether Parveen would escort her. Parveen assured him that she would. He thought for a moment, nodded, then said that she should summon them. No emotion accompanied this directive. His motives were inscrutable.

She wrote out a message—*Col. Trotter: I need to go / Berkeley.*

Waheed thought it a bad idea for her to be seen talking to the soldiers at the COP, and she wondered if it was safe for her even to approach them. More and more, she had this awareness of belonging to neither side, of being distrusted by everyone. But despite the tensions in the village, the soldiers remained friendly to the children, and so the note was entrusted to Bilal to deliver. Parveen still worried on his behalf, less concerned about the soldiers than the insurgents, who might label him a spy for carrying a message to the Americans. She was on edge the whole time he was gone, and when he returned after successfully handing over the note, she held him tightly.

She gave Bina what lessons she could, then prepared to wait. Trotter would come, she knew; he was a man of his word, and she realized now that she'd implicitly counted on that conscientiousness when she'd insisted on staying in the village. To distract herself she went to check on Shokoh, who was in her usual spot next to the woodstove. Parveen patted the girl's hand absently until Shokoh asked where Bilal had gone. Chagrin pricked Parveen; she hadn't thought to get Shokoh's consent to leave the village any more than Waheed had.

When Parveen relayed the plan, Shokoh grew alarmed. Had Waheed agreed to this, to her leaving? she asked.

He had, Parveen said.

Would he come?

How could he? Parveen said. He had to stay with the family, with the house.

Shokoh withdrew her hand from Parveen's and placed it on her swollen belly. In her bloated face, her eyes, still beautiful, were troubled. "I'm afraid," she whispered.

"There's nothing to fear," Parveen lied.

Chapter Twenty-Eight

Distance

ALL DAY BRUTISH CLOUDS HAD BEEN HUDDLING, AND SOON AFTER Bilal's return, they bullied the weak sun into hiding and began firing icy raindrops at the earth. Inside, everyone circled around the *sandali*, trying not to dwell on whatever noises the storm might be obscuring. Then the drama passed, leaving behind an ordinary rain that was almost pleasant, the water light-footed overhead. When it stopped, Parveen walked outside. Pleats of sun fell through stone-gray clouds. She climbed the ladder to the roof. The valley was still. Only the light moved, playing fleetly on the mountains.

Parveen went to her room and sat alone for a while. She'd never actually dispensed any of the gifts she'd brought the family, never needed to, because what was hers had long ago become theirs. Still, she earmarked a few books for specific people. Louis Dupree's *Afghanistan* would go to Jamshid, she decided. He cared for his country. She thought of that long-ago conversation they'd had about what, other than a farmer, he might be, and she didn't know whether he was finding or losing himself.

In the hope that the book might allow them to reconnect, she went in search of him. He wasn't upstairs or in the yard or in the kitchen. The outhouse, she decided, seeing that it was occupied. But it was Zahab who emerged. She didn't know where Jamshid was, Zahab said, before hurrying up the stairs.

Dread slid through Parveen. Perhaps Jamshid had gone to tell the insurgents that the Americans might come, perhaps even now they were readying another ambush. She was contemplating sending Bilal back to the outpost with another message, this one to abort, when he shouted from the roof. Parveen ran outside, saw nothing, but then heard, as he must have, the distant sound of rotor blades. Knowing the Americans wouldn't linger, she dashed upstairs.

The plan was for her and Waheed to take Shokoh to the field. Bina handed over the packet of food she'd prepared along with a neatly tied bundle of clothing for Shokoh. They all helped her to stand and make her way down the stairs. At the compound door, Bina whispered in Shokoh's ear, kissed her three times on the cheeks, then drew, with an almost mournful tenderness, a chadri over the girl's head. Time bent before Parveen, and she saw an image of Bina wrapping Shokoh in white for burial. Then the image flew off. Instead, together they wrapped Shokoh in brown blankets for warmth.

"Friendship cannot be broken by distance," Bina said to Parveen, who hugged her and then each of the children in turn.

As they stood at the compound entrance, Jamshid materialized, as if he'd been teleported there. She weighed whether to offer him her hand, then decided against it for fear that he might refuse. Yet she still had the instinct to reclaim some bond with him. Maybe, she suggested, he should accompany her and Waheed to the field, in case Shokoh faltered.

Alarm crossed Waheed's face, but it was Bina who spoke. "Our son should stay here," she said, "with the family. I'm asking you this." She took Parveen's hands in hers, their rough texture jolting Parveen back to her first night, and her eyes sought Parveen's.

They thought she wanted to turn him over to the Americans, Parveen realized. It had never crossed her mind to do so, but now she wondered if she should. Jamshid hadn't killed Boone and the other soldier himself, but she believed he'd made it easier for the insurgents to do so. What did she owe Trotter, who had come to her aid? She understood what Professor Banerjee hadn't, which was that having no loyalties was easy. It was having too many that was hard.

"We need to go," she said, as much to herself as to the family, although she didn't move. "If the insurgents attack the Americans again, there will be nothing left of this village."

"Yes, we should go," Waheed said, "but there won't be an attack." He spoke calmly, moving nearer to Jamshid as he did so. "We promise you."

Again Parveen had a sense of how little she knew, of how much, as Dr. Yasmeen had tried to tell her, she didn't understand. It wasn't a promise Waheed would make lightly; he, like Trotter, was a man of his word. But she also knew he wouldn't tell her how he could make this guarantee. Perhaps in order for Shokoh to depart unharmed, the elders of the village had negotiated a temporary peace with the insurgents, the price to be paid later. Or maybe Jamshid himself had persuaded them to forgo another ambush so that she and Shokoh could safely pass. All Waheed wanted in return was that his son be allowed to remain at home.

"*Khodahafez*," Jamshid said—it meant "Go with God"—and she repeated it back to him. Bina and the children murmured it too, "*Khodahafez, khodahafez*," their final shared word.

Then she and Waheed each took one of Shokoh's elbows, left the house without Jamshid, and began to walk. Yellow leaves, slick from the storm, cobblestoned the lanes. They moved slowly, with caution, their breath puffing from their mouths. The fields, when they reached them, were boggy, and Waheed picked Shokoh up and carried her as Parveen squelched alongside. The dormant Chinook, guarded by tense soldiers, waited in the khan's fallow field, which the Americans' continuing usage had made more lucrative than any crop ever could. At the trio's approach, the engine started and its rotors spun to life. The noise drowned out all talk. All thought.

Waheed set Shokoh down, and when Trotter emerged from the Chinook with ear protection for Parveen, she put an arm around Shokoh's waist to guide her toward him. The colonel, in full body armor, pointed at Shokoh and shook his head. Parveen couldn't hear it, but his mouth formed the word *no*. Except he wasn't saying no to Shokoh; he was saying no to a sack of green fabric draped in brown blankets, which was all he could see. She could have been anyone. Anything.

The soldiers, not knowing who or what was beneath the chadri, raised their weapons, and Parveen's heart beat so hard it hurt. Trotter's remarks about his soldiers' jitteriness pinballed in her head and she put her hands in the air. With each second she had the most heightened consciousness of being alive, of *continuing* to be alive. In any moment of life there were so many things not happening that could be happening, but it was rare to consider all the possibilities that were evaded. Parveen wasn't just alive. She was Not Dead. Not Shot.

But she was, again, naive—and her plan, she realized, had been ill-considered. Trotter had no idea what she was trying to do, and she had no way to tell him; the roar of the helicopter canceled out all but the most gestural human exchange. He was yelling and pointing at her, that was all she knew, and she was pointing back at Shokoh and trying to explain. Then he disappeared back into the copter and within moments the engine cut off. The startling quiet demanded recalibration.

Trotter reemerged, removed his earmuffs and earplugs, and walked right up to them. "What's happening here," he said flatly, then nodded at Waheed.

"We need to take her," Parveen said. "She's pregnant, she has eclampsia—"

"This isn't a medevac."

"It's Waheed's wife, and if you don't take her, she'll die. Another wife of Waheed's will die. What kind of story will that make back home?"

"I'm authorized to take Americans."

"Aren't you in Afghanistan to save women? Isn't that why you're paving the road? Right here is a woman who needs saving."

All of their encounters, Parveen thought, all of their talks had led to this moment of decision. Now Trotter would have to reveal whether he cared about Afghanistan's women as anything more than an abstract cause or a justification for war. Would he leave an Afghan in danger behind, as Aziz maintained? She willed Aziz to be in the helicopter, because believing him to be there strengthened her resolve to test Trotter, who was saying he would do only what he had authorization to do, which was evacuate Parveen.

"You don't take her, I don't go." Her own words surprised her. Terrified her. If Trotter called her bluff, if he refused to take Shokoh, she would have trapped herself in the village. And yet she meant them.

"Goddamn, Parveen." Trotter checked his watch, then glanced at the sky, these gestures of his by now familiar to her. "I need to see her," he said.

Parveen thought to ask Waheed's permission even as she was appalled at the instinct. In the end she didn't ask; she announced in Dari loud enough for both Waheed, who stood some distance away, and Shokoh to hear that she was going to lift the chadri, then translated her words for Trotter.

Waheed said nothing but he pivoted in the direction of his house. It wasn't the first time he'd had a wife exposed to an American man, and he'd never seemed especially insistent on the chadri. But for all the brutal, fatal intimacy between Crane and Fereshta, when every curtain of privacy had been torn, this unveiling, at an American's insistence, was different. It shoved Waheed's impotence in his face.

Parveen caught the hem of the garment and pulled it up. Shokoh trembled and the air around her seemed to tremble too.

"Jesus—his wife?" Trotter said at the sight of her young face.

Shokoh stared straight ahead, her cheeks flushed, the crushed fabric crowning her forehead, as queenly in appearance as she was powerless in fact.

Time paused, as if at the crest of a hill, then rolled on. Trotter gave the pilot a thumbs-up, then again protected his ears. A soldier handed Parveen two sets of gear. She put hers on—first the plugs, then the earmuffs over them—and then did Shokoh's. The Chinook's engine started. Trotter motioned that they should bend when they went beneath the rotors, and they did. Boarding the copter, Shokoh, who was in front, halted and turned, trying to see Waheed. But he was gone.

FETTERED BY SEAT BELTS, their backs against the copter's side, Parveen and Shokoh clutched hands as the Chinook lifted off. Its back was open so the soldiers could keep their weapons trained on potential hostiles below, and the cold rain from earlier in the day tamped down the dust that the blades usually churned up. Nothing obscured Parveen's view; nothing dampened her exhilaration. She could sense already how hard it would be to adjust to the lack of such highs, to a tepid daily life back home.

She spotted Waheed on the far edge of the khan's field, walking away, shrinking. Shokoh gave no indication whether she saw him too. Their connection to him was spinning out, stretching thinner, and soon would snap. Parveen wondered if she would ever find out what became of him or of Bina, Jamshid, and the other children. She didn't think so. She'd always considered herself a cosmopolitan, a believer in the mixing of people, of cultures. Her parents had believed in this too. But her greatest wish for Waheed, for his family, for his neighbors, was for them never to have another foreigner come. Another American. In trying to help the village, they—Trotter and his men, Crane and Parveen—had destroyed it. To live was to bruise, Dr. Yasmeen had said, but this was wreckage of a different order. Among their sins was leaving the women worse off, with even less care, than Parveen had found them.

She could only hope that what she'd stirred up wasn't all to the bad, that maybe when each of their times came, Waheed's four girls—Hamdiya, Zahab, and the twins, Adeila and Aakila— would tell their father they weren't ready to marry yet, that they wanted to travel as that American woman who'd lived in their house had, and perhaps Waheed would agree. She hadn't properly said goodbye to him, she realized; she hadn't even said thank you. Was she still pretending she would return? She'd taken nothing with her; she had not a single picture of these people, this place.

This place—the fields beneath them stretched into ribbon, the peaks dissolved into sky. The beauty worked on her no less this last day than it had her first. She feared the loneliness of trying to translate it to those back home, of having to shelter it from their conceits and imaginings. In her head lived swatches of color: young wheat, fall sky, the blood of the living, the blood of the dead. Of all the things she'd seen and learned, the most powerful couldn't be conveyed. This view was the same one Dr. Yasmeen would have seen, the same one Naseer thrilled to, when they were brought to and from the village. It was silly, but she regretted that she'd never translated Yasmeen's words of anxiety about flying to Trotter. It was a small thing; it would have changed nothing. But Parveen felt that she'd robbed the doctor of her voice.

Light entered the helicopter only through the open back and the porthole windows. In the dim interior, Parveen couldn't see Trotter and she was glad for that. But now, partway down the row of perhaps twenty soldiers seated opposite her and Shokoh, she made out Aziz's profile, his familiar nose. He turned his head toward her and gave her a neutral nod that made her wonder if he judged her harshly, either for ignoring the warnings she'd been given or for availing herself of the rescue that being an American guaranteed her. She pointed to Shokoh as if to say, *She's the only reason I called for help* and also *See, he would take you, he would save you.* But Aziz wouldn't understand until they landed, and she mentally urged the helicopter on. At the possibility of freer exchange with him, if not at the base, then perhaps later, in Kabul, she felt unsteady, in a pleasurable way, but also uncertain. The fact that nothing was possible in the village had made everything desirable. In the light of relative freedom, how would he appear?

The clinic, battered but intact, came into view. *Fereshta's clinic.* It had been a long time since Parveen or anyone else had called it that. What, then, was Fereshta's legacy? She hadn't written a word to leave behind; no image of her was preserved, other than Crane's invented one, which in its falsities threatened to extinguish her. But Fereshta's family members hadn't read Crane's book, and when it came to their memories of her, this was their salvation. She wasn't special. She wasn't beautiful. They cared for her—they loved her—just the same.

Shokoh was still gripping Parveen's hand, which was damp with sweat. When Parveen tried to free herself, Shokoh grasped harder. Her fingers were so small, their nails so gnawed. What had Parveen done? This helicopter ride gambled with Shokoh's life almost as much as her staying in the village would have. *We will live, or we won't.* At the base, she'd be in good hands— American medics had sewn blown-off limbs to soldiers' backs for proper reattachment later, they could safely get a baby out of a girl. But then what? Parveen hadn't imagined that far ahead, caught up as she was with the excitement of extracting both of them. While it was true that she was trying to save Shokoh's life, it was equally true that she'd used Shokoh for her own purposes, to give herself an excuse to leave. With chagrin she imagined Professor Banerjee's reaction to her so-called rescue. Even now Parveen couldn't shake her former mentor's voice in her head, and she knew Professor Banerjee would condemn, in the baldest terms, her coercing Trotter into taking Shokoh. In her professor's eyes, Parveen would be no different than the missionaries trying to save Muslim souls or the American soldiers using their concern for Muslim women as a pretext for killing or occupation. No different than Crane, who had made an Afghan woman's life his bestseller material. Professor Banerjee would disdain the very act of asking the Americans to save a woman.

The urge to intervene, a high of its own, was a hard habit to break. The salvation of others could become an addiction too. For months, Parveen realized, the fantasy of rescuing Shokoh had percolated in her head. Only now did the magnitude of its consequences begin to sink in. The rescue was ephemeral, the responsibility it yielded eternal. Shokoh couldn't simply be taken from home, then left, along with her newborn, to her own devices. If Shokoh was going to return to the village, Parveen would have to find a way to get her back there. But she wasn't even sure Waheed wanted Shokoh back. He'd relinquished her so easily, without so much as asking when or how his treasured young wife would return. Was it as simple as him choosing Shokoh's health, her life, over his own needs, his own honor? More likely he'd sacrificed her because he wanted Parveen gone. It was a woman's fate to be as expendable as she was desirable.

And what if Shokoh herself didn't want to return? This was Parveen's hope and also, now, her fear. Shokoh would then go back to her family—far from a simple matter. There was the question of her father's health, which Parveen had never told Shokoh was failing, and of the family's finances. If they wouldn't allow her back or couldn't afford to keep her, Shokoh and her child would be Parveen's burdens to carry.

A very long time ago, it seemed, she had imagined promoting Shokoh as a poet in America. Now, one step closer to that possibility, it struck her as unrealistic, even ridiculous. There was no money in poetry. How would she even get Shokoh to the States; how would she support her there? The girl spoke no English, had no marketable skills. She would be a teenage mother. Against the backdrop of the village, Shokoh seemed remarkable, but in America she would be just another refugee struggling to survive. She was intelligent, yes, but also petulant, prone to depression, and traumatized by the circumstances of her marriage. She would need—demand—considerable help, and Parveen didn't have a plan for earning a living herself. She imagined Shokoh sleeping in the bed that had once belonged to Taara, then remembered that bed, that room, and that apartment were no longer her family's. Would the two of them—three, with Shokoh's baby—crowd in with her little nephew in San Jose? Her love for Ansar by now felt more like a memory of love. Their bond would be restored, she knew. But that didn't mean she wanted to share his room for more than a few days.

At the end of a labor, a woman lives, or she dies. That is all that concerns me. The words had formed Dr. Yasmeen's mantra, and by that standard, evacuating Shokoh was the right choice, which didn't make it a good one. But then Dr. Yasmeen had also taught that sometimes there was no good choice. Parveen tried again to imagine how Shokoh might subsist in America. Her story, truth be told, was the most commodifiable thing about her. Perhaps she could publish a memoir that Parveen would help her write. Would this please Professor Banerjee? Shokoh's story as told, mostly, by Shokoh...

There were so many people in Parveen's head, all trying to direct her. So much mental noise that it was impossible for her to hear. The only person she hadn't consulted, she realized, was the one right next to her, the one most affected by her whims and plans. She turned to Shokoh and shouted, "What do you want?"

Shokoh, unable to hear, shook her head with a look of

consternation. Parveen patted her hand in reassurance. She would ask again when they landed or once the baby had come. *What do you want?* It was the question no one had thought to put to Shokoh or to any of the women in the village about the road, the war, or anything else in their lives. *What do you want?* Those shura gatherings were absent of women, yet Trotter had never objected. Had he even noticed?

Shokoh, not Parveen, needed to choose whether to return to Waheed, go back to her family in the provincial capital, or try to get to America. It was the choosing that mattered. And as for her story, it would be hers, not Parveen's, to tell.

They were over Trotter's road now, the one he'd promised that Parveen would drive out on. Instead, they were tracing its path through the air, and it was still less than half paved. Craters filled with water reflected the pewter sky and, in miniature, the helicopter flying beneath it. Piles of gravel glistened from the rain. The equipment was mostly covered by blue tarps, and a few men, their bright orange vests glowing in the gray landscape, milled about.

Would the paving ever be finished? For now, she was sure, the Americans would persist, Trotter would persist, because to abandon the road would suggest that the American soldiers who'd died for it had died for nothing. You wouldn't try to cut your losses; you'd try to redeem them, even if that meant sending an arm after a leg, one death after another. The war would continue to be fought because it hadn't yet been won. Lambs to slaughter. Sheep for dead doctors. Her nightmares would collide.

One day, Parveen guessed, they would abandon it all—cancel the road project, close the combat outpost, leave the lives lost unredeemed—and the road would become one more loose thread in a war shaggy with them. Perhaps they would blame the ingratitude of the villagers. Perhaps no reason would be given at all. The same, she suspected, would be true of the war— years more of wastage and death, then an end that America's leaders would pretend made sense of what had come before. The dragon's tail of 9/11 swept back and forth, back and forth, devastating everything in its path.

Yet even though this project had never been a good use of resources, financial or human, Parveen felt a keen sadness at the prospect of its end. She remembered how elated she'd been, sure that improving the road would change so much for the women. And how invigorated Jamshid had been, imagining the arrival of a new life: a bride, a job, a way out. It pained her that he'd defected to the side of those intent on sabotaging it. The insurgents made no pretense of trying to help; they cared nothing for the village except as a platform to strike at the Americans. Her glimpse of their cruelty made her fear for Afghanistan's women once the Americans left. She wished Jamshid could see this, but maybe it was she who needed to see that for him there was no other way to become a man, an Afghan, than to refuse the empire trying to extend its reach.

Aziz, by contrast, had become, for lack of a better job, a servant of that faltering empire. His whole life had been lived in war, and his future—how long he would stay with Trotter, how long the Americans would stay in Afghanistan—was as uncertain as it had ever been. He too was a loose thread, as were all Afghans who had tied their fates to the Americans' doomed enterprise. It wouldn't be easy to weave them back into the fabric of their country. Her heart contracted. Perhaps it was only pity she felt for him. But if so, why did her body, her blood, stir whenever his eyes turned her way?

She would help him get a visa, she decided, as the Chinook veered away from the road to fly over the river. She had to try. Even as she guarded against another fantasy of rescue, she knew her own parents had once been every bit as much in need. Entanglement was the natural order of things.

Entanglement even with the lies of others. Gideon Crane's map had been full of distortions, but Parveen couldn't say she regretted where it had taken her, or what she had learned there. Realizing this, she relaxed for the first time since coming on board. She was going to enjoy the ride, because there would never be another like it. She wanted to register everything: the storm-fattened water, the dark pelt of cloud, and the mountains that hemmed her in like village walls.

ACKNOWLEDGMENTS

I am indebted to many books for information or inspiration, including these: *No Good Men Among the Living*, by Anand Gopal; *Little America*, by Rajiv Chandrasekaran; *Veil of Tears*, by IRIN News; *Three Cups of Deceit*, by Jon Krakaeur; *Afghan Post*, by Adrian Bonenberger; *Zarbul Masalha*, compiled by Captain Edward Zellem; *The Unforgiving Minute*, by Craig M. Mullaney; *When Bamboo Bloom*, by Patricia A. Omidian; *Death Without Weeping*, by Nancy Scheper-Hughes; *Snapshots*, edited by Tamim Ansary and Yalda Asmatey; *Soldier's Heart*, by Elizabeth D. Samet; *Pink Mist*, by Owen Sheers; *Zinky Boys*, by Svetlana Alexievich; *Points of Departure*, by James Cameron; *A Fortunate Man*, by John Berger; and *Memorial*, by Alice Oswald.

Also the documentary *Motherland Afghanistan*, by Sedika Mojadidi, with reporting by Mujib Mashal, Azam Ahmed, Carlotta Gall, Pamela Constable, C. J. Chivers, Thomas Gibbons-Neff, Elizabeth Rubin, Sebastian Junger, and other journalists who have documented eighteen years of war; and the Instagram accounts of Andrew Quilty, Morteza Herati, Everyday Afghanistan, and others that illuminate the beauty of Afghanistan and the gravity of the stakes there.

Profound thanks to the following:

The staff of the *New York Times* Kabul bureau from 2001 through

2005, including Abdul Waheed Wafa, Ruhullah Khapalwak, Abdul Samad Jamshid, and the late but never forgotten Sultan M. Munadi, all of whom provided both friendship and an education.

My literary agent, Bill Clegg, for more than a decade of guidance, editorial acuity, and support; my editor, Ben George, for his intelligence, patience, doggedness, and good humor; my publisher, Reagan Arthur, for her enthusiasm; Pamela Marshall, production editor, for professional grace and great tolerance; Tracy Roe, who in being a physician as well as a copy editor saved me from both medical and grammatical errors in the text; Sabrina Callahan; Alyssa Persons; and all others at Little, Brown who helped publish this book.

For reading early (and sometimes late) drafts and making this book better in so many ways: Stefan Forbes, Nell Freudenberger, Eliza Griswold, Juliette Kayyem, and George Packer.

The MacDowell Colony, for three invaluable weeks in 2018; and the Ucross Foundation, for nine days in Wyoming early on.

And: Katherine Boo; Courtney Hodell; Scott Rudin and Eli Bush; Carlos Sirah; D. W. Gibson; my monthly women writers' group; and Katherine Wolkoff.

My parents, Don and Marilyn Waldman; the Waldman, Ephraim, and Star families, especially Brenda Star; and Nola Hanson, who's like family.

My husband, Alex Star, for reasons that could fill a book of their own, which he would no doubt brilliantly edit while also cooking, cleaning, caring for our children, and keeping me (relatively) sane. My children, Oliver and Theodora, aka Ollie and Theo, whose love of reading keeps me writing; for putting up with my disappearances, both mental and literal, to work; for suggestions about plot turns and cover designs (and to Theo for asking the crucial question: "What do the women want?"; and to Ollie, for catching, in the final hour, a word repetition that had eluded the closest readers and his mother). To all three for their curiosity, hilarity, music, goodness, and love.

ABOUT THE AUTHOR

Amy Waldman's first novel, *The Submission*, was a national bestseller, a PEN/Hemingway Award finalist, and the #1 Book of the Year for *Entertainment Weekly* and *Esquire*. She has received fellowships from the American Academy in Berlin, Ledig House for International Writers, the MacDowell Colony, and the Radcliffe Institute for Advanced Study. She was previously a reporter for the *New York Times*, where, as a bureau chief for South Asia, she covered Afghanistan. She lives in Brooklyn.